Available in August 2010
from Mills & Boon® Blaze®

BLAZE 2-IN-1

Amorous Liaisons
by Sarah Mayberry
&
Naked Ambition
by Jule McBride

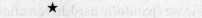

Storm Watch
by Jill Shalvis

Endless Summer
by Julie Kenner, Karen Anders
& Jill Monroe

AMOROUS LIAISONS

There was a gorgeous, almost naked woman in his bed.

Max woke to find himself curled around Maddy, her rear nestled into the cradle formed by his hips and thighs. One of his arms was wrapped around her torso. Her hair was everywhere, streaming across the pillow, across his shoulder and arm.

He was painfully hard, his erection pressed against the roundness of her backside. His hand somehow crept beneath her T-shirt to rest just below the lower curve of her breasts.

God, she felt good. Small and sleek and feminine.

He wanted to flex his hips and grind himself against her so badly it hurt. His whole body tensed as he imagined sliding his hand up a few vital inches and cupping her breast. He could almost feel the softness of it beneath his hand.

He closed his eyes. He had to back off. Now.

Then Maddy stirred, her body flexing in his embrace, her backside snuggling closer to his hips.

He'd never been so close to losing control in his life.

NAKED AMBITION

She was dreaming again...

"Miss me, Susannah?"

"No, I don't," she said, but her arms snaked around JD's neck and tugged him closer. He felt so good and hard, a lean male with sculpted, taut thighs that fell between hers, not to mention knees that pressed insistently, telling her what he wanted. Then a delightful graze of warm, smooth lips – but the kiss burned.

"C'mon, say you still love me."

But she didn't. It was over between them. Yet he was breaking her resistance and, each time his lips touched hers, she felt more languid and insubstantial.

Susannah muttered, "I hate you, JD."

"I can tell."

She'd become attuned to him, learning the idiosyncrasies of his body as well as those of her own, committing them to memory, just so she could drive him crazy with lust...

Suddenly she startled awake and her eyes blinked open. She'd been dreaming.

And just as before, her sensual fantasies seemed impossibly real...

First published in Great Britain 2010
Harlequin Mills & Boon Limited,
Eton House, 18-24 Paradise Road, Richmond, Surrey TW9 1SR

Amorous Liaisons © Small Cow Productions PTY Ltd. 2008
Naked Ambition © Julianne Randolph Moore 2009

ISBN: 978 0 263 88139 4

14-0810

Harlequin Mills & Boon policy is to use papers that are natural, renewable and recyclable products and made from wood grown in sustainable forests. The logging and manufacturing processes conform to the legal environmental regulations of the country of origin.

Printed and bound in Spain
by Litografía Rosés S.A., Barcelona

AMOROUS LIAISONS

BY

SARAH MAYBERRY

NAKED AMBITION

BY

JULE McBRIDE

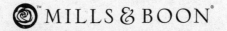

MILLS & BOON

AMOROUS LIAISONS

BY
SARAH MAYBERRY

Sarah Mayberry has moved eight times in the past five years and is currently living in New Zealand – although that may change at the drop of a hat. When she's not moving house or writing, she loves to read, go to the movies, buy shoes and travel (mostly to find more shoe shops). She has been happily partnered to her man for over fifteen years and plans to make it many more.

Bless you, Chris, for your enormous sympathy and patience with me as I grieved, anguished and swore over this book. I love you very much.

To Wanda, for being so calm and supportive and damned smart as always – every time you make me lift my game and this time you had your work cut out for you.

And to my friends and family who all made sympathetic noises and passed the chocolate at the right times. Where would I be without you?

1

MADDY GREEN was finding it hard to breathe. She lengthened her stride, eager to reach the rehearsal studio. She could almost feel the familiar smoothness of the barre beneath her hand and almost see the glint of bright lights in the mirrors and hear the regular scuff and thump of other dancers leaping and landing and twisting and turning around her.

She needed the comfort of the familiar very badly right now.

The double doors to the Sydney Dance Company's rehearsal studio A came up on her left. She pushed through them and the scent of warm bodies, clean sweat and a dozen different deodorants and perfumes and aftershaves wrapped itself around her.

Home. She was home.

"Maddy! How did your doctor's appointment go?" Kendra asked the moment she spotted Maddy.

The other dancers turned toward her, faces expectant. Maddy forced herself to smile and shrug casually.

"It's all good," she said. "No problems."

She couldn't bring herself to say the other thing. Saying it out loud would make it real. And for just a few more minutes, she wanted to lose herself in the world that had held her enthralled since, at the age of four, she first saw a picture of a ballerina.

Kendra flew across the room to give her a hug, her slender arms strong around Maddy's back.

"Fantastic. Great news. The best," she said.

The other woman's gauzy rehearsal skirt flared around her legs as she returned to her place in the center of the room. Kendra was only twenty-two. She had her whole career ahead of her. She was a beautiful dancer—powerful, delicate, emotional, intense. She would soar.

Maddy felt someone watching her and lifted her gaze to find Stephen Jones, the choreographer, eyeing her closely.

She turned her shoulder, breaking the contact. Stephen had been watching her a lot lately, checking her range of movement, testing the capabilities of her injured knee. Had he known, or guessed, what she'd been told today? Had everyone known except her that she was over? That she would never dance again?

Her heart pounded against her ribs and again she couldn't quite catch her breath.

She threw her bag into the corner and slid off her street shoes, bending to tug on a pair of slippers with shaking hands. The ribbons whispered through her fingers as she wrapped them around her ankles and tied them neatly. She shed her skirt to reveal tights and leotard and took a place at the barre to begin warming up.

Pliés first, then some *rond de jambes,* keeping her head high and her arms relaxed. Every time she rose up *en pointe,* she felt the seamless, fluid glide of her body responding to her will, saw her reflection in the floor-to-ceiling mirror, posture perfect, form ideal.

Her heartbeat slowed. She was a dancer. Always had been, always would be.

"Maddy."

She tore her eyes from her own reflection to find Andrew McIntyre, the company director, standing behind her. He, too, had been studying her perfect form in the mirror.

"Why don't you come to my office?" he said. His voice was gentle, as was the light in his eyes.

He knew.

He'd spoken to Dr. Hanson. Of course he had. Hanson was the company's doctor, after all. When she'd come on board four years ago she'd signed a contract agreeing that the company could access all health matters pertaining to her career.

"After rehearsal," she said. "I'm warm now. And the rest of them are waiting for me."

"I think we should do this now, don't you?" he said.

He was frowning, as though what she'd said pained him in some way. He moved closer, reached out a hand to touch her.

She took a step backward. Rising *en pointe* on her bad leg, she lifted her right leg in *grand battement* to the side then up, up, up, until her toe was pointing toward the ceiling, her thigh straight beside her ear.

She held the position in a blatant display of skill and strength, her eyes daring Andrew in the mirror.

He held her gaze, never once looking away. And when her muscles began to scream and shake from the pain of holding such a demanding, strenuous position, he stepped forward and rested his hand on her shoulder.

"Enough, Maddy. Come to my office."

She let her leg drop and relaxed onto her flat feet. Her knee throbbed, as it always did these days when she demanded too much of it. She hung her head and stared blindly at the polished floorboards.

She felt Andrew slide his arm around her shoulders. Then he led her toward the door. The other dancers stopped mid-rehearsal to watch her. She could feel their silent stares as she and Andrew stepped into the corridor. Andrew didn't let her go until they were in his office.

"Sit," he said.

He crossed to the wooden built-ins that spanned one wall of his office and opened a door. She heard the clink of glass on glass as he poured something.

"Drink this."

Brandy fumes caught her nose as he lifted a glass to her lips.

"No," she said, turning her head away.

Andrew held the glass there, waiting. Finally she took a token mouthful.

"And again," he said.

She took a bigger mouthful this time. The brandy burned all the way down her throat to her belly. She shook her head firmly when he offered a third time.

He took her at her word and placed the glass on the coffee table in front of her. Then he sat in the armchair opposite her.

In his late fifties, he was a former dancer, his body slim and whippet-strong even after years away from the stage. His tanned skin was stretched tightly across high cheekbones, and thin lines surrounded his mouth from smoking. His eyes were kind as he studied her, a rarity from a man who was known throughout the dance world as a perfectionist first and a human being second.

"We will look after you, Maddy. Please know that. Retirement pay, any teaching work you want—you name it, you can have it. You've been one of our greatest dancers, and we won't forget you."

Maddy could feel the sweat cooling on her body in the air-conditioned chill.

"I want to keep dancing," she said. "That's what I want."

Andrew shook his head decisively. "You can't. Not for us. Not professionally. Your spirit might be willing, but your body is not. Dr. Hanson was very clear about that. We always knew that complete recovery from such a significant tear to your cruciate ligament was going to be a long shot. It's time to hang up your slippers, Maddy."

She stared at him, a storm of words closing her throat.

Anger, grief, resentment, denial—she didn't know what to say, how to react.

"I want to keep dancing," she said again. "Give me more time. I'll show you I can do it. I'll do more rehab work, more Pilates. Whatever it takes."

Andrew's face went slack for a moment, and he leaned back and closed his eyes, rubbing the bridge of his nose with his hand. He looked defeated, sad.

"Maddy. I know how hard it is to give it up. Believe me. It nearly killed me. But I made a second chance for myself." He paused a moment to let his words sink in. "You're a beautiful, smart, resourceful woman. There's another life out there waiting for you. You just have to find it."

I don't want to find it.

She almost said it out loud, but some of the numbness and shock were leaving her as the brandy burned its way into her system.

The doctor had handed down his decision, and Andrew had made his, too. She was broken, old. They had no use for her anymore.

"We'll throw you a party. A real send-off. And we'll help you any way we can. Retraining, or, as I said earlier, if you want to teach…?"

The thought of a party, of standing in front of her peers while people made toasts to her former talent made bile rise up the back of her throat.

"No. No party," she said.

Suddenly she didn't want to be here anymore. When the doctor had given her the news an hour ago, the company had felt like home, like the safe place to be. But now she knew it would never be her home again.

"People will want to say their goodbyes, pay their due respects," he said.

"I'm not dead," she said, standing abruptly.

She strode to the door. She hesitated for a beat outside the rehearsal studio, then braced herself to duck in and collect her bag. Head down, she did just that, not responding when Kendra asked if she was okay.

They would hear soon enough. Another dancer would be promoted into her role in the latest production. Maybe Kendra. Maybe one of the other soloists. Life would go on.

Outside in the warm summer air, she took deep breaths and fought tears.

She had never been more alone and scared in her life. Her entire world had crumbled around her—the discipline and passion that had formed the boundaries of her days and nights had dissolved into nothingness. She had no future, and her past was irrelevant. She was the owner of a broken body and broken dreams and precious little else.

She found her car keys in her handbag, but she had nowhere to go. No current lover to offer his shoulder, and no former lovers to call on, because her affairs never ended well. Her mother was miles away in America, enjoying the fruits of her third marriage. Maddy had never known her father. All her friends were dancers, and the thought of their ready sympathy had the bile rising in her throat again.

Where to go?

Where to go?

Out of the depths of her subconscious, a face rose up. Clear gray eyes, dark hair, a smile that offered mischief and fun and comfort and understanding in equal measure.

Max.

Yes. She needed Max. Even though it had been years. Even though their friendship had been reduced to occasional e-mails and Christmas cards.

He would understand. He always had. He'd hold her in his big, solid arms, and she'd feel safe, the way she always had with him.

And then maybe she could think. Imagine a world without dance. Construct a way forward.

Max.

MAX SHUT THE FLAP on the box and held it down with his forearm. He reached for the packing tape and used his thumbnail to find the leading edge.

"I'm all done in here. How about you?" a voice asked from the doorway.

He glanced up at his sister, Charlotte, taking in her smug expression and the way she'd planted her hands on her hips.

"Don't even think it," he said, tearing off a piece of tape and sticking the flap down.

"My room's finished. Technically, that means my work here is done," Charlotte said.

Max tossed her the spare roll of packing tape. So far, he'd only managed to pack away half of the books in his late father's extensive collection.

"The sooner you start helping, the sooner we can both get out of here," he said.

Charlotte propped herself against the door frame.

"Should have picked an easier room, Max," she teased.

"I was being gallant. Giving you the kitchen and taking on this Herculean task to save you hours of hard labor. In case you hadn't noticed."

Charlotte's smile faded a little as she straightened.

"Where do you want me to start?" she asked.

Max glanced at the solid wall of books that remained unpacked.

"Pick a shelf. Any shelf," he said.

Charlotte busied herself assembling a box as he started stacking books into another carton.

Dust hung in the air, dancing in the weak winter sunlight filtering through the dirty windows of his father's apartment.

It felt strange to be back here, and yet he'd only been gone two months. The whole world had shifted in that time.

His father was dead.

He still couldn't quite believe it. Ten weeks ago, Alain Laurent had succumbed to a bout of pneumonia, a constant hazard for quadriplegics. After a week-long battle, he'd died quietly in his sleep. Max had been out of the room, taking a phone call at the time. After eight years of constant care and devotion, after being there for so many of the major crises of his father's illness, Max had missed the most important moment of all.

Had his father known that he was alone? Or, as his sister contended, had his father chosen that moment to slip away for good, sparing his son the anguish of witnessing his final moments?

"Stop giving yourself a hard time," Charlotte said from across the room.

He frowned. "What?"

"You heard me. Don't pretend you weren't sitting there, thinking about Dad again. You did everything you could. We both did," Charlotte said firmly.

He made a dismissive gesture and packed more books.

"It's true, you know. What you just said. You are gallant. Which is charming on one level, but bloody infuriating on another."

He smiled at his sister's choice of words. They were half-Australian, half-French, but he always thought of Charlotte as being essentially European, with her dark hair and elegant fashion sense. Then, out of the blue, she'd toss out a bit of Aussie slang and remind him that they'd spent their teen years in Sydney, Australia, swimming and surfing and swatting flies away from backyard barbecues.

"I'm serious, Max," she said. "You're always riding to the

rescue, thinking of everyone else except yourself. You need to learn to be selfish."

He made a rude noise and continued to work.

"The day you think of yourself first, I'll give it a go."

Charlotte pushed her hair behind her ear, frowning. "That's different. I have a family. I gave up the right to be selfish when I became a parent."

Max dropped the book he was holding and pressed a hand to his heart. Moving with a quarter of his former grace and skill, he half staggered, half danced to the side wall, playing self-sacrifice and martyrdom for all he was worth.

"Very funny," his sister said.

He dodged the small book she flung his way.

He tossed the book back and she shook her head at him. They packed in silence for a few beats, busy with their own thoughts.

He wondered who was looking after Eloise and Marcel today, Charlotte's children with her merchant banker husband, Richard. He knew Charlotte was between babysitters at the moment. It was hard finding people competent to deal with Eloise's special needs, but having them here hadn't really been possible. Any disruption to Eloise's routine inevitably led to distress.

"I never really thanked you, did I?" Charlotte said into the silence.

He pushed the flaps shut on another full box of books. The secondhand dealer was going to have a field day with their father's collection. Everything from 1960s dime-store novels to Proust and Dante.

"That's because there's nothing to thank me for."

"Do you miss it? Dancing?" Charlotte asked quietly.

He started assembling another box.

"Sometimes. Not so much anymore. It's a long time ago now."

"Only eight years. Perhaps you could—"

"No," he said, more sharply than he'd intended. "Eight years is a lifetime in dance, Charlie. I'm too old now. Lost my flexibility, my edge."

And he'd moved on, too. When the call had come through eight years ago that his father had been in a car accident, Max had flown straight from Sydney to Paris in the hope that he'd be able to say goodbye before nature took its course. As it turned out, he'd had eight years to say his goodbyes.

As soon as it became apparent that their father would survive his injuries but be confined to a wheelchair, Max had made the changes necessary to ensure his father's comfort. He'd resigned from the avant-garde Danceworks company where he'd been earning himself a name in Australia and arranged to have his belongings shipped to Paris. Then he had moved into his father's apartment in the genteel, refined arrondissement of St. Germain and started the renovations that had made it possible for him to care for his father at home.

It hadn't been an easy decision and there had been moments—especially at the very beginning when he and his father had been acclimating to their new roles—when Max had bitterly regretted his choices. He'd left so much behind. His career, his dreams, his friends. The woman he loved.

But Alain Laurent had been a generous and affectionate parent. When their mother had died when Max was ten years old and Charlotte just eight, Alain had done everything in his power to ensure they never felt the lack of a mother's love. He had been a man in a million, and for Max there had never been any doubt that he and Charlotte would do whatever was necessary to make the remainder of his life as rewarding as possible.

"You could have left it to me. Thousands of men would have," Charlotte said.

"On behalf of my gender, I thank you for your high opinion of us," he said drily.

"You know what I mean."

He stopped and faced his sister.

"Let's put this to bed, once and for all. I did what I wanted to do, okay? He was my father, too. I loved him. I wanted to care for him. I couldn't have lived with it being any other way. Just as you couldn't have lived with having to choose between Richard and your children and Dad. End of story."

Charlotte opened her mouth then shut it again without saying anything.

"Good. Can we move on now?"

Charlotte shrugged. Then, slowly, she smiled. "I'd forgotten how bossy you can be. It's been a while since you read me the riot act."

"Admit it, you miss it," he said, glad she'd dropped the whole gratitude thing.

Of course, willingly supporting his father didn't stop the what-ifs from leaking out of his subconscious in the unguarded moments before falling asleep at night.

What if he'd been able to follow his dream and dance in London, New York, Moscow, Paris? Would he have made it, achieved soloist status and seen his name in lights?

And what would have happened with Maddy? Would he ever have told her how he felt? How much he loved her—and not just as her reliable friend and sometime dancing partner?

As always when he thought of Maddy, he pictured her on stage, standing in a circle of light, her small, elegant body arched into a perfect arabesque. Then came the memories of her as a woman, laughing with him on the ratty couch in the dump of a house they'd shared with two other dancers, or lounging on the back porch in the hot evening air.

False memories, he knew. Gilded by time and distance. Maddy couldn't possibly be as funny, as warm and beautiful and sensual as he remembered her. He'd turned her into a symbol of everything he'd given up.

"So, what are you going to do now?" Charlotte asked as she slid a box across the worn parquetry floor to join the others he'd stacked against the wall.

He deliberately misunderstood her.

"Finish packing these boxes, then find someplace warm to have a cold demi of beer," he said.

She rolled her eyes. "I mean next. What are you going to do now that you've got your life back?"

He shrugged, even as his thoughts flew to the apartment he'd rented in the Marais district across the river. His sister hadn't seen it yet. It had been hell holding her off, and he would have to tell her his plans soon, but he wasn't ready for her disapproval yet. He was still coming to terms with his own audacity himself.

"I haven't really thought about it," he lied.

Charlotte dusted her hands on her butt. "Well, you should. You could use Dad's money to go to university, get a degree. Or put a deposit on a place of your own. Start making a life for yourself. Hell, you could even get a girlfriend. Really shake things up."

It was Max's turn to roll his eyes. "Why is it that married people always think that everyone else would be happier in a relationship?"

"Because it's true. And you're made to be a husband, Max. If any man should have children, it's you. They'd be gorgeous, for starters. And talented. And smart and kind."

"Why does it sound like you're writing copy for a personals ad?"

"Relax. I haven't stooped that low. Yet. But I do have some wonderful friends I'd love you to meet."

"No."

"Why not? Give me one good reason why you don't want to meet an attractive, available woman?"

"I'll find my own woman when I'm ready." The truth was,

the next twelve months were going to be challenging enough without adding a new relationship into the mix.

"For God's sake. Surely you must want the sex, at the very least? How many years can a man survive on hand relief alone, anyway?" Charlotte asked.

He nearly choked on his own tongue. Half amused, half surprised, he stared at his sister. She was many things, but comfortable with earthy talk was not one of them.

"*Hand relief?* Are you serious?"

"What's a better word for it? Happy ending? Spanking the monkey? Choking the chicken?"

He laughed because he couldn't help himself. "Are you done yet?"

"Max, I'm serious," Charlotte said.

He saw with surprise that there were tears in her eyes. "Look, your concern for my…um…monkey is sweet. I think. But I'm not going to discuss my sex life with my sister."

"That's because you don't have one. And it's such a waste, Max. I know women who would crawl over broken glass to get to you. Let me hook you up with one of them."

He held up a hand. "Spare me the broken-glass crawlers. Please. And take my word for it that I have a sex life."

He thought of Marie-Helen and Jordan, women he'd slept with on a casual basis over the years. He liked them both, he enjoyed the sex, but he was not compelled by either woman. That lack of engagement had been important in his former life, when all his energy had been focused on his father's well-being.

"Well. I hope that's true." Charlotte studied his face. "I want you to have all the things you've missed out on."

"I get that. Thank you," he said. "Now, can we talk about something else? Anything else, in fact. Global warming? The extortionate price of tropical fruit?"

Charlotte let the subject go. They spent another two hours

boxing up the library. By the time they exited the apartment, they were both dusty and weary.

"What time are you letting the dealer in tomorrow?" he asked.

"Around ten."

They both stood on the threshold, glancing around the apartment that had been their father's home, hospital and prison.

"Will you miss it?" she asked.

The apartment had been in their family for two generations. He could remember his grandmother serving Sunday meals in the dining room, the family gathered around. But he could remember more clearly his father's pain and suffering.

"No. You?"

She shook her head. "Too many sad memories."

He locked up for the last time and handed the key to his sister. They parted ways in the street and he walked two blocks to the Metro. After changing lines twice, he climbed the stairs of the St. Paul station and emerged into the weak afternoon sunlight.

It was early February, and he could see his breath in the air. He stopped to buy a bottle of wine and some fresh-baked bread on his way home. Then he let himself into the former shop that he'd leased on a cobblestoned side street of Le Marais.

His footsteps echoed as he made his way across a wide expanse of floorboards to the kitchen.

Normally a place the size of his loft would cost a mint to rent, but he'd managed to discover the last shitty, unrenovated hole in the upwardly mobile third arrondissement. What it lacked in ambience, hygiene and plumbing it gained in space. More than enough to accommodate his bed, a couch, an armchair, a kitchen table and all his workshop materials and leave him with plenty of room to fill with his art.

His art.

He studied the handful of small sculptures and the one full-size figure in bronze that stood next to his workbench.

For a long time he'd fooled himself into thinking that his sketches and small-scale sculptures were a hobby, mindless doodling to chew up the time between tending to his father's needs and fill the hole that losing dancing had left. He'd always drawn and experimented with clay, ever since he was a kid. It was harmless, he'd figured, pointless.

But as his skill had increased, so had his drive to capture more and more of his ideas in clay, plaster, bronze—each time bigger and better than the time before. He'd pushed away the urge as it became more insistent, but when his father's health had deteriorated a few months ago, he'd found himself thinking about what would happen after his father had found his peace. Max's hands had itched as he imagined what he could do with his art if he had more time, more space, more energy.

The past eight years had taught him that life was never predictable, often cruel, and even more often capricious. Men plan and God laughs—he'd often thought the quote should be men *dream* and God laughs.

But he'd had a gutful of what-ifs. He'd had eight years of being on hold, in limbo, living for someone else.

He and Charlotte had inherited a small sum of money from their father's estate. There would be a little more when the apartment sale was finalized—but not much since they'd taken out a mortgage to fund their father's care—and Max had decided to recklessly, perhaps foolishly, use his share to give himself a year to prove himself. The rent paid, food supplied, his materials purchased. And if he had nothing to show for it at the end of it all, so be it. At least he would have followed one of his dreams through to its conclusion.

His hands and face felt grubby from the hours amongst dusty books. He stripped and took a quick shower. His hair damp, clad in a pair of faded jeans and a cashmere sweater that had seen better days, he slit the seal on the merlot he'd bought and placed a single glass on the counter.

The sound of his doorbell echoed around the loft. He eyed the distant front door cautiously.

He wouldn't put it past Charlotte to pay a sneak visit after the conversation they'd had today, trying to catch him in the act of having a sex life so she could truly rest easy.

He ran his hands through his hair. His sister was going to find out her brother was chasing a rainbow sometime. Might as well be today.

His bare feet were silent as he made his way to the white-painted glass front door. He could see a small silhouette on the other side of the glass and he frowned. Too short for Charlotte. And too slight for either Jordan or Marie-Helen.

He twisted the lock and pulled the door open.

And froze when he saw who was standing on his doorstep.

"Maddy."

"Max," she said.

Then she threw herself into his arms.

2

MADDY PUSHED HERSELF away from Max's embrace and brushed the tears from the corners of her eyes. He appeared utterly blown away to see her. She suddenly realized how stupid she must seem, arriving on his doorstep unannounced and crying all over him.

She was feeling kind of blown-away herself. It had been eight years since she'd last seen his face, and she was surprised at how much older and grown-up he seemed. He was thirty-one now, of course. No longer a young man. She hadn't expected him to remain untouched by time, but the reality of him was astonishing. He almost looked like a stranger, with new lines around his mouth and eyes. His formerly long, tousled hair was cut short in a utilitarian buzz cut. His body was different, too. As a dancer, he'd been all lean muscle and fluid grace, but the man standing before her seemed bigger, wider, taller than the friend she remembered.

She laughed self-consciously as she realized they were both simply staring at each other.

"Always knew how to make an entrance, didn't I?" she said.

"It's great to see you," he said. "I didn't realize you were in town. Where are you dancing? Or perhaps I should ask who's trying to steal the great Maddy Green away from the SDC?"

She opened her mouth to tell him her news, but nothing came out. Instead, a sob rose up from deep inside and she felt her face crumple.

"Hey," Max said. He moved closer, one hand reaching out to catch her elbow. "What's going on? Who's got you so upset?"

She pressed her face into the palms of her hands. She couldn't look at him when she said it. God, she could barely make herself say the words.

"They retired me. I had a knee reconstruction in July after I tore my anterior cruciate ligament. It's been coming along well, getting stronger, but the company's surgeon won't clear me to dance. So it's all over," she said, the words slipping between her fingers.

"Maddy. I'm so sorry," Max said.

She dropped her hands. "I didn't know what to do, where to go. And then I thought of you. And I caught the first plane to Paris. Didn't even bother to pack," she said. She tried to laugh at her own crazy impulsiveness, but the only sound that came out was an odd little hiccup.

Max's eyebrows arched upward and his gaze flicked to her dance bag, lying on the ground at her feet where she'd dropped it when he opened the door.

She understood his surprise. What kind of person took off around the world on the spur of the moment and lobbed on the doorstep of a man she hadn't seen in over eight years?

"Guess I wasn't really thinking straight," she said.

An icy breeze raced down the alley, rattling windows and cutting through the thin wool of her sweater. She shivered and Max shook his head.

"You're freezing." He tugged her through the doorway as he spoke, reaching to grab her bag at the same time.

"*Merde.* This thing is still as heavy as I remember," he said as he hefted the black suede bag.

The ghost of a smile curved her lips. Max used to give her a lot of grief about all the rubbish she hauled around. He always wondered how someone as small as she needed so much stuff.

One time he'd even tipped the entire contents onto the coffee table and made her justify every piece of detritus. They'd been laughing so hard by the time they got a third of the way through the pile that Maddy had begged him for mercy for fear her sides really would split.

"Girl's got to have her stuff," she said, the same response she'd given him all those years ago.

He smiled and kicked the door shut behind him.

"I was just opening a bottle of wine. That'll help warm you up," he said.

She glanced around as he led her across the large open space. Ancient beams supported the roof high overhead, and the walls were rough brick with the odd, haphazard patch of plaster smeared over them. A workbench lined one wall, filled with hand tools, and a row of sculptures sat side by side near a painted-over window.

She knew from the mass e-mail that Max had sent to his friends that he'd recently moved into a new apartment after the death of his father, but this was the last place she'd imagined him living. In the old days, he'd always been the one who complained the most about the moldy bathroom and crusty kitchen in their shared rentals. He'd even painted his bedroom himself because he couldn't stand the flaking, bright blue paint that had decorated his walls.

But maybe his appearance wasn't the only thing that had changed. Maybe the years had given him a different appreciation for what made a home.

"I was sorry to hear about your father," she said as he dumped her bag on a low modern leather couch. At least that conformed to her idea of the old Max's tastes—sleek, well-designed, high quality.

"Yeah. Thanks for the flowers, by the way. I can't remember if I sent a thank-you card or not," he said. "It's all a bit fuzzy, to be honest."

"You did."

They were both uncomfortable. She wondered if it was because she'd brought up his father, or because she'd miscalculated horribly in racing to him this way. She hadn't expected it to be awkward. She'd expected to walk through the door and feel the old connection with him. To feel safe and warm and protected.

Stupid. She could see that now. E-mails and Christmas cards and the occasional phone call were not enough to maintain the level of intimacy they'd once shared. She'd run halfway around the world chasing a phantom.

"Maybe I should come back tomorrow," she said, stopping in the space between his makeshift living zone and the counter, sink and oven in the back corner that constituted his kitchen. "You've probably got plans. I should have called before coming over. We can meet up whenever you're free."

Max put down the bottle of wine he'd been opening and walked over to stand in front of her. He reached out and rested his hands on her shoulders. The heavy, strange-but-familiar weight warmed her.

"Maddy. It's great to see you. Really. I wish it was for a happier reason, for your sake, but I'm honored you thought of me. Now, make yourself at home. I don't have a thing to do or a place to be. I'm all yours," he said.

More foolish tears filled her eyes. She blinked them away, then nodded. "Okay. All right."

He returned to the wine bottle, and she sat at one end of the couch. She was tired. Emotionally and physically. She felt as though she'd been holding her breath ever since Andrew had looked her in the eye and confirmed Dr. Hanson's pronouncement that her career was over.

"Here."

He slid a large wineglass into her hand. Red wine lapped close to the brim and she raised an eyebrow at him.

"Save me a trip back to the kitchen to get you another one," he said.

"I haven't been drunk in years," she said, staring down into the deep cherry liquid. "I guess if there was ever a time, this is it."

"Absolument," he said.

She drank a mouthful, then another.

"I was wondering what else was different about you," she said when she'd finished swallowing. "Apart from your hair and your face. It's your accent. It's much stronger now."

"That would come from speaking my native tongue for the past eight years," he said wryly. "These days, the only time I get to practice my English is when someone from the old days calls or visits."

"It's nice," she said. "The girls from the corps would love it. I remember they used to be all over you because of your accent."

"I think you're forgetting my stellar talent on stage and my legendary status as a lover," he said mock-seriously.

Her shoulders relaxed a notch as she recognized the familiar teasing light in his eyes. There was the old Max she knew and loved, the Max she'd craved when her world came crashing down around her.

"Right, sorry. I keep forgetting about that. What was that nickname you wanted us all to call you again?"

He snorted out a laugh and she watched, fascinated, as his face transformed.

He's been too serious for too long, she realized. *That's what's different about him, as well.*

She could only imagine what caring for his wheelchair-bound father must have been like. Terrifying, exhausting, frustrating and rewarding in equal measures, no doubt.

"The Magic Flute," he said. "I'd forgotten all about that. Never did catch on."

"We had our own names for you, don't worry," she said. She

toed off her shoes. As always, it was bliss to free her feet. If she could, she'd go barefoot all day.

"Yeah? You never told me that. What did you use to call me?"

He settled back on the couch. He filled the entire corner, his shoulders square and bulky with muscle.

"Not me, the corps. Wonder Butt was the most popular," she said. "Because of how you filled out your tights."

Another laugh from Max. The warm wine-glow in the pit of her stomach expanded. The more he laughed, the more the years slid away and the more she saw her old friend. Maybe it hadn't been so stupid coming here after all.

"Some of the girls called you Legs. Again, because of the way you filled out your tights."

"We'd better be getting to the Magic Flute part soon or I'm going to be crippled with size issues for weeks."

She felt her cheeks redden as she remembered the last nickname the other ballerinas had for Max. She shifted on the couch, not sure why she was suddenly self-conscious about a bit of silly trash talk. It had been a long time since she'd been coy or even vaguely self-conscious about anything sexual.

She cleared her throat.

"I believe they also used to call you Rex, too," she said.

He frowned, confused. She made a vague gesture with her hand. She couldn't believe he was forcing her to elaborate.

"You know. As in Tyrannosaurus Rex. Big and insatiable."

He threw back his head and roared with laughter. She found herself joining in.

"Maddy Green," he said when he'd finally stopped laughing. His light gray eyes were admiring as he looked at her. "It's damn good to see you. It's been too long."

A small silence fell as they both savored their wine.

"Do you want to talk about it?" he asked after a while. "Call people names, throw a tantrum? I'm happy to listen if you do."

She drew her legs up so that she was sitting cross-legged.

"I wasn't ready for it. I mean, they told me the surgery was a long shot, but I've always been a good healer. And the knee was getting better. If they'd just given me more time…"

She looked down and saw her left hand was clenched over her knee, while her right was strangling the glass.

"What did the doctor say?"

"A bunch of cautious gobbledygook about my body being tired and not being able to compensate anymore. I know my body better than any of them. I know what I'm capable of. I know I've got more in me. I can feel it here," she said, thumping a fist into her chest so vehemently that the bony thud of it echoed.

"Careful, there, tiger," he said.

She took a big, gulping sip.

"I still can't believe that Andrew took Hanson at face value like that. Like it was gospel."

"Hanson? I was wondering who treated you. He's supposed to be pretty good, right?"

She shrugged a shoulder dismissively. "Yes. The best, according to Andrew. Which is why they use him exclusively. But he's not the only doctor in the world. Remember Sasha? He was told he'd be crippled for life if he kept dancing, and he went on to score a place with the Joffrey Ballet. He's one of their lead soloists now."

He smiled. "Fantastic. Good for him. I've lost track of so many people, I've been out of it all for so long now. Is Peter still dancing? I tried to keep an eye out for him. Always thought he'd make it big."

"He got sick," she said quietly. "You know what he was like—never could say no."

Despite the well-known risk of AIDS, there were still plenty of beautiful, talented dancers who slept their way into an early grave. The travel, the physicality of the dance world, the camaraderie—passions always ran high, on and off the stage.

"What about Liza? I heard she'd gone to one of the European companies but then that was it."

Max and Liza had had a thing for a while, Maddy remembered. Was he thinking about making contact with her, now that he was free to make decisions for himself once again and Maddy had turned up on his doorstep, reminding him of the past?

"She's with the Nederlands Dans Theatre," she said. "I heard she'd gotten married, actually."

Max looked pleased rather than pissed. She decided he'd merely been curious about an old friend. For all she knew, he was involved with someone anyway. She'd seen no evidence that there was a woman in his life in his apartment, and he'd never mentioned a girlfriend in any of his e-mails, but that didn't mean a thing. He was a good-looking man. And there was that whole Rex thing. A man who enjoyed sex as much as Max apparently wouldn't go long without it.

She frowned. Since when had Max's sex life been of any concern to her? Their friendship had always been just that—a friendship. Warm, loving, caring and totally free of any and all sexual attraction on either side, despite the fact that they were both heterosexuals with healthy sex drives. Without ever actually having talked about it, they had chosen to sacrifice the transient buzz of physical interest for the more enduring bond of friendship. Which was why Max remained one of her most treasured friends—she hadn't screwed their relationship up by sleeping with him.

She lifted her glass to her lips and was surprised to find it was empty.

Maybe that was why she was wondering about things she didn't normally wonder about where Max was concerned—too much wine, mixed in with the unsettling realization that her old friend had changed while she'd been dancing her heart out around the world.

He pushed himself to his feet. "Let me fix that for you."

She watched him walk away, drawing her knees up to her chest and wrapping her arms around them. There was no hint of the lithe young dancer she'd once known in his sturdy man's walk. He still moved lightly, but his feet didn't automatically splay outward when he stopped in front of the counter, and there were no other indications that he'd once been one of the most promising, talented dancers she'd ever worked with.

Max had abandoned his career as a dancer to care for his father. Walked away just as his star was rising. At least she had had the chance to realize many of her dreams before Andrew and Dr. Hanson had written her off.

Her bleak thoughts must have been evident in her face when he returned because he shoved a plate of sliced, pâté-smeared baguette at her.

"Eat something, soak up that wine. I don't want you messy drunk too soon," he said.

"I'm off carbs," she said before she could think. "Need to drop weight."

How stupid was that? She didn't need to drop weight anymore. She could eat herself to the size of a house if she wanted to.

She looked at Max, desperately seeking some magic cure for the hollow feeling inside her.

"How did you do it?" she asked in a small voice. "How did you walk away? Didn't you miss it? Didn't you need it?"

He slid the plate onto the table. There was sympathy in his eyes, and old pain.

"I had lots of distractions. Worry over *Père,* practical things to sort out. I didn't have the time to think about it for a long while."

"And then?"

"It was hard. Nothing feels like dancing. Nothing."

She nodded, swallowing emotion. "It's my life. I've given it everything, every hour of every day."

"I know. It was one of the things I always admired about you. You were the most passionate dancer I knew."

Her jaw clenched.

"Sorry. I didn't mean to use past tense," he said.

God, he was so perceptive. Always had been.

"I can't believe it's over. It's too big, too much," she said.

A heavy silence fell. She could feel Max trying to find something to say, something that would make it all right. But there was nothing he or anyone could say or do. The decision had been made.

She shook her head and shoulders, deliberately shaking off the grim mood that had gripped her.

"Tell me about you. About your dad and…Charlotte, right? That's your sister's name, isn't it?"

They talked their way through the first bottle of wine and then the second. Maddy ate more than half of the bread and pâté and by ten was bleary-eyed with fatigue and alcohol.

"I need to go find a hotel," she said.

"Don't be ridiculous. You're staying here."

As soon as he said it, something inside her relaxed. She'd been hoping he would offer. She could still remember how she used to crawl into bed with him when it was cold and the heating wasn't up to the task of fending off the drafts from the many, many cracks and gaps in their house. The smell of Max all around her, the warmth of his body next to hers. He used to pull her close and she'd fall asleep with her head on his shoulder.

Just the thought of feeling that safe again made her chest ache.

"You can have my bed, I'll sack out on the couch," he said, standing to clear the dishes.

She stared up at him.

"I don't mind sharing with you. We used to sleep together all the time. Remember?" She hoped she didn't sound as desperate as she felt.

He hesitated a moment. "Sure. I'll try not to hog the quilt. It's been a while since I've shared with anyone."

She smiled up at him, relieved. "You know, I'm glad I came. It was a bit weird at first, but that was only because we hadn't seen each other for a while. And now it feels like the old days."

He looked away, his focus distant.

"The old days. Yeah."

"Do you mind if I have a shower first?" she asked.

"Of course not. I'll get you a towel."

He moved away, disappearing through a doorway to one side of the living area. Maddy began weaving her long hair into a braid to prevent it from getting wet.

She had no idea what tomorrow held. Even acknowledging that fact was a scary, scary thing for a dancer who had lived a life of strict self-discipline.

For a moment she got dizzy again and her heart began to pound. No rehearsal. No costume fittings. No classes. No gym or Pilates. What would she do with the time? God, what would she do with the *rest of her life?*

Max reappeared with a fluffy white towel and a fresh bar of soap.

"The bathroom's pretty primitive, but it gets the job done," he said.

The panic subsided as she looked into his clear gray eyes.

It would be all right. She was here with Max, and somehow she would find a way through this.

She stood and took the towel, then rested her hand on his forearm for a few seconds to feel the reassuring warmth of him.

Definitely she had done the right thing coming here, no matter how crazy it had seemed at first. Definitely.

MAX RAN A HAND ACROSS the bristle of his buzz cut as Maddy disappeared through the bathroom door.

Maddy Green. He couldn't quite believe that she was in his apartment after all these years.

The shock of seeing her on his doorstep continued to resonate within him. It was almost as though thinking of her today at his father's apartment had conjured her into his life.

She was still beautiful, with her long, rich brown hair and deep brown eyes. And being in the same room with her was still an experience in itself—her body vibrated with so much emotion and intensity, she was utterly compelling. It was one of the reasons she was such a joy to watch on stage—she had presence, star quality. She'd always drawn people to her.

He heard the shower come on and began collecting glasses and plates.

Her perfume hung in the air, something flowery and light. The same perfume she'd always worn.

Jesus. I still remember her perfume. How sappy is that?

A part of him was flattered that she'd thought of him in her hour of need. But he also wasn't sure how he felt about her barreling back into his life.

Once, she'd been the center of his world. He'd devoted half his twenties to loving her.

The wine bottles clinked together loudly as they hit the bottom of the recycle bin. Max wiped his hands on the thighs of his jeans.

His gut tightened as he thought of her news. Her career was over. Tough enough for someone like him to walk away from dancing. He'd only been in the early stages of his career. But Maddy had given her whole life to dance. She'd flown high—and the resulting fall was going to be long and painful.

He thought of her wounded look as she'd told him the doctor's verdict. Despite his ambivalence about seeing her again, he wished he could take away her pain. The old feelings still had that much of a hold on him. He didn't want to see her hurting.

He bounded up the stairs to the sleeping platform suspended above the kitchen zone. If she was staying in his bed, he needed to change the linen.

He was spreading a clean sheet across the mattress when she spoke from behind him.

"You didn't have to do that."

"Bachelor lifestyle." He turned, and something primitive thumped deep in the pit of his belly.

She wore one of his T-shirts. The hem hit her at midthigh and her hair was loose around her shoulders. He could see the soft outline of her nipples through the well-worn fabric. She'd always been small in the breast department, like most dancers, but she was nicely rounded and very perky. His gaze dropped to her bare, finely muscled thighs. Was she wearing any underwear?

Damn.

"I borrowed a T-shirt. Hope that was okay?"

He shifted his attention back to the sheet and concentrated on making the crispest hospital corners in the history of mankind.

"Sure."

"I've always wanted a loft," she said, wandering to the rail to look down over the rest of the apartment.

If he looked up, he knew he'd have a great view of her ass and the backs of her slim thighs. He kept his gaze fixed where it was.

Eight years had passed. How could he still want her so badly?

He glanced toward the stairs. It was one thing to want to comfort her, but it was another thing entirely to desire her. He'd been down that road before and he knew it went nowhere.

He unfolded the top sheet and flicked it hard to send it ballooning out over the bed.

You don't love her anymore. You stopped loving her years ago.

The thought sounded clear as a bell in his mind. Some of the tension left his shoulders. He was getting wound up about nothing. It was true—he'd gotten over Maddy long ago.

Stopped thinking about her, fantasizing, wondering. It had literally been years since he'd been a slave to his feelings for her.

Which was reassuring, but didn't quite explain the hard-on crowding his jeans.

She's a woman. A gorgeous, almost-naked woman. And you spent the better part of three years fantasizing about her. That kind of sexual attraction doesn't just die. But it doesn't mean anything except that you're horny, and she's hot.

He looked at Maddy.

She *was* a beautiful, sexy woman. That was undeniable. Probably any guy would feel something down south at the sight of her in his big T-shirt and precious little else.

Okay. Good. He'd rationalized his hard-on to death. Now he had to deal with the minor problem of their sleeping arrangements. The last thing he wanted was for Maddy to realize he was hot for her. She'd come to him seeking solace, not sex.

"You know, I think you'd be much more comfortable if I slept on the couch," he suggested casually. "I tend to toss and turn a lot. And you need to get over your jet lag."

She turned from studying his apartment, a frown on her face.

"I don't want to kick you out of your bed, Max. If you're worried about it, I'll sleep on the couch," she said.

"I'm not worried. I was just thinking of you."

A little too much, as it turns out.

"Well, if I get to choose, I'd rather sleep with you. I don't really want to be alone right now, you know?"

The lost look in her eyes sealed it for him.

"Fine. I'll just go brush my teeth," he said.

And try to find something to sleep in. Preferably something armor-plated.

By the time he'd brushed his teeth, discovered he had a choice of workout pants or boxer-briefs and opted—reluctantly—for the boxer-briefs since he could only imagine

Maddy's reaction if he rolled into bed wearing full sweats, ten minutes had passed. When he climbed to the sleeping platform, Maddy was curled up on one side of the bed, her eyes closed and her head pillowed on one hand.

She stirred as the mattress dipped under his weight.

"I thought you were never coming to bed."

"Had to put the dog out and check on the kids," he said.

She smiled faintly, her big eyes drowsy. Up close, he could see how fine and clear her skin was, as well as note the few endearing freckles that peppered her nose. She'd always hated them, calling them her bane and covering them every chance she got.

He smiled.

"What?" she asked.

"I'd forgotten about your bane."

She pulled a face.

"Trust you to notice them."

"They're cute."

"On a ten-year-old. Not on a prima ballerina. I bet Anna Pavlova didn't have freckles."

He saw the exact moment that she remembered, again, that she was no longer a prima ballerina. The light in her eyes dimmed and her full lips pressed together as though she was trying to contain something.

"Come here."

He held out an arm and she shifted across the mattress until she was lying against his side, his arm around her shoulders, her head on his chest.

If he kept concentrating on the lost, bewildered look in her eyes, he figured he had a fair to middling chance of pulling this off without embarrassing either of them. She needed him. That was enough to push all other thoughts into the background.

"It's going to be all right, Maddy," he said. "You'll see."

"I should have been ready for this. All ballet dancers have

to retire, I know that." Her words were a whisper. "Is it so wrong and greedy to want a little more? Another year? Two?"

Max tightened his embrace. He could feel how tense she was, could feel the grief and confusion in her.

"It'll be all right," he repeated, smoothing a circle on her back with the palm of his hand.

He felt the tension leave her body after a few minutes as the wine and jet lag and emotion caught up with her. He lay staring at the ceiling, listening to her breathing.

Knowing Maddy, she would probably be off home again tomorrow, her mad, impulsive trip having served the purpose of helping her express her grief and confusion. She had friends in Australia, a home. A life. She'd want to go back to the familiar as she tried to work out what happened next in the Maddy Green story.

She shifted in her sleep. As her perfume washed over him, a memory hit him. When they'd lived together, she'd left a scarf in his car after they'd gone to the movies one night. Rather than give it back to her, he'd hung on to it because it smelled of her perfume. A secret memento of Maddy.

Talk about besotted. He'd been so far gone it was a wonder the words hadn't appeared over his head and followed him around: *I am in love with Maddy Green.*

Another memory: the night he'd decided to tell Maddy how he felt. It had taken months to screw up his courage enough to risk their friendship. He'd arranged candles and red roses and bought a bottle of French champagne. The kitchen of their crappy rental had looked like a bordello by the time he'd finished decking it out—a kid's idea of a romantic scene, he recognized now. Then Maddy had come home, jumping out of her skin because she'd just been invited to join the Royal Ballet in London. He'd watched her unalloyed joy, untouched by regret for what she would be leaving behind. When she'd ducked off to call her mom, he'd quietly snuffed the candles and hidden the champagne in the back of the fridge and left his declaration unmade.

Thinking about it now, he could only thank God she'd been so preoccupied with her own news that she'd never thought to ask why she'd walked into the best little whorehouse in Sydney. She'd saved them both a painful and awkward conversation.

Maddy murmured in her sleep, her head moving on his shoulder restlessly. She rolled away from him, sprawling across half the bed.

He rolled the other way and resolutely closed his eyes. He had his first session with the life model he'd hired tomorrow. He needed to sleep, despite his circling thoughts and how aware he was of Maddy lying just a few feet away. He wasn't a kid, held to ransom by his body and his emotions. If the past eight years had taught him anything, it was to grab sleep when he could find it.

HE WOKE TO FIND HIMSELF curled into Maddy's back, her butt nestled into the cradle formed by his hips and thighs. One of his arms was wrapped around her torso.

He was painfully hard, his erection pressed against the roundness of her backside. So much for the protection of his boxer-briefs. His hand had somehow crept beneath her T-shirt to rest beneath the lower curve of her breasts. He could feel her ribs expand and contract as she breathed in and out.

She felt good. Small and sleek and feminine.

He knew he should back off, roll away before she woke and realized where she was and who he was and what was happening in his underwear.

He didn't move. He wanted to flex his hips and press himself against her so badly it hurt. His whole body tensed as he imagined sliding his hand a few vital inches and cupping her breast. He could almost feel the softness of it in his palm.

Thanks to the notorious lack of privacy in dancers' changing rooms, he'd seen Maddy in various states of undress over the years. She had small, pink nipples, and when she was cold they puckered into tight little raspberries.

He imagined plucking them, rolling them between his fingers. Pulling them into his mouth and tasting his fill of her.

His hard-on throbbed.

Man, oh man.

He closed his eyes. He had to back off. Now.

Maddy stirred, her body flexing in his embrace, her backside snuggling into his hips.

He'd never been so close to losing control in his life. His hand lifted from her torso. But instead of sliding it up and over her bare breasts, he twisted away from her warmth.

He slid to the side of the bed and sat up, scrubbing his face with his hands.

Talk about close. Too close.

His underwear bulging, he made his way downstairs. The cold water of the shower hit him like an electric shock, but it took care of business below stairs very effectively.

He eyed himself in the mirror as he shaved. He wasn't going to give himself a hard time for waking with an erection. It was pretty much an everyday occurrence, with or without a hot woman in his bed. He wasn't even going to give himself grief for horning onto Maddy while she slept. He was only human, after all.

But those few moments of temptation...

They were a whole other ball game. His jaw tensed as he imagined Maddy's reaction if she'd discovered him feeling her up. She'd come to him seeking comfort and understanding and he'd almost jumped her when she was at her most vulnerable.

Just as well she'd probably be going home tomorrow. He clearly couldn't be trusted where she was concerned.

Dressed in faded jeans and a long-sleeved T-shirt, he headed into the kitchen to make coffee. He worked as quietly as possible to fill the stovetop espresso maker. While he was waiting for it to brew, he cleared away some of the debris on the kitchen table. Which was when he saw the envelope icon flashing on his cell phone, indicating he had messages.

He clicked it open with his thumb, frowning when he saw it was a message from Gabriella, his life model.

pls call ASAP.

He dialed her number, a bad feeling in his gut. The message was time-stamped early this morning, and Gabriella was due in an hour. It didn't take a brain surgeon to realize something was up. As her phone rang and rang, he hoped the news wasn't terrible.

It had taken him over a month to find the body type he'd wanted to act as model for his latest project. The works he planned had been inspired by his years in dance, and he'd been excited when a mutual friend had put Gabriella in contact with him. She was a dancer—nowhere near Maddy's level, but she had the refined, defined muscles and flexibility he required.

He tried to anticipate the reason for the last-minute contact. She might be sick. Her car might have broken down. Or— disaster—she might have broken a leg or something else equally debilitating.

The phone clicked as someone answered.

"Max. I'm so glad you got my message," Gabriella said. "I was worried you wouldn't see it in time."

"Hi, Gabriella. What's up?"

"I'm so sorry, Max, but I won't be able to make it today. I got a job."

"Right. Congratulations." He tried to sound genuine. He knew that Gabriella had been looking for dancing work for some time now without much luck.

"I know this ruins your plans, but I had to take it," she said apologetically. "I hope you understand."

"Of course. We'll just reschedule. What's your timetable like? Is it weekend work?"

"Oh, I didn't explain very well, did I? The job's not here in Paris. It's a touring show, a kids thing. I'll be on the road for the next three months."

Shit. Might as well have broken a leg.

He leaned against the kitchen table and rubbed the bridge of his nose.

"Right," he said.

"I can still sit for you when I get back, if you're happy to wait," she offered tentatively.

"Sure. Give me a call when you're back in town."

He'd need to find someone before that, of course, but there was no need for Gabriella to feel needlessly bad. She had to make a living, and what he could pay her as a life model wouldn't come even close to what she'd earn as a full-time dancer.

"Okay. I'm really sorry for the short notice, Max."

"Don't worry about it. I'll work something out."

After wishing her best of luck with her new job, he ended the call.

He fought the urge to kick something. It had been a long time since he'd wanted something wholly for himself. Was it too much to ask that even the simplest of his desires—that his chosen model be available to sit for him at a convenient time—be answered?

"What's up?"

He turned to find Maddy halfway down the stairs. She was rumpled and sleep-creased and warm-looking. He made an effort to keep his eyes above the hemline of the T-shirt.

"Nothing. Just a work thing," he said.

"Of course. You're back in the workforce now. What are you doing?"

He stared at her. There were a handful of people who knew about his artistic ambitions. None of them were close friends or family. Still, he had to start owning his desires sooner or later.

"A bit of stonework. Mostly working with bronze. Mostly figure-based stuff," he said.

God, he felt like a pretentious wanker saying the words out loud.

She frowned. She had no idea what he was talking about, of course.

I'm trying to be an artist.

That's what he should have said.

Her baffled gaze slid over his shoulder to where his earlier works marched along the wall beside his workbench.

"Oh! Those are yours?" she asked, incredulous.

As well she might be.

Her eyes were wide as she walked over to inspect them.

"God, Max, I thought you'd brought them over from your dad's place or something and didn't know where to put them in your new loft," she said.

He stayed where he was, his whole body tense as she circled his most recent piece, a full-size bronze figure of a woman balanced on one leg, her other leg bent at the knee and held at a right angle from her body, her pointed foot hitting her supporting leg above the knee. Her arms were lifted high, joining in a graceful arch over her head.

He'd been happy with the emotion he'd been able to capture in the piece, but it still needed work.

"This is great! Wow. Max, this is amazing. I can't believe someone I know made something this beautiful."

Something—relief?—expanded in his chest and he let himself move closer.

Maddy ran a hand over the curve of the woman's waist and hip, her face lit with admiration.

"I can almost feel her moving. How did you do that?" she said. Then she snatched her hand away. "I'm so sorry! Is it okay if I touch it?"

Her expression was so contrite he had to laugh.

"It's bronze. It could probably survive a nuclear holocaust," he said.

She looked at him, shaking her head.

"I can't believe you didn't mention this last night, or in any of your e-mails, for that matter. I remember you used to sketch, but this is…I don't have the words. What a dark horse. How long have you been doing this?"

He shrugged. "I've just been dabbling, really. But I'm about to get started on a new series I've been planning."

"Was that what the call was about?"

"Yeah. Gabriella, my life model, pulled out at the last minute. I'm going to have to find someone else."

He sounded pissed. Probably because he was.

She'd moved on to inspect his smaller, earlier works. He shuffled from foot to foot, then shoved his hands into his back pockets. They weren't as good as they could be. He'd been learning his craft when he made them, honing his skills. He should have destroyed them. Or put them in storage somewhere.

Maddy's eyes were warm when she looked at him again.

"Max. I don't know what to say. These are really, really good."

He was embarrassed by how much her praise meant to him. "Thanks."

She stroked the bronze figure again. "Losing this life model is a pretty big deal, yeah?"

"It's a setback. It took me a while to find her. The series is dance-based, and ordinary models aren't up to it."

"Dance-based." She looked at the bronze woman again. "Like this?"

"More dynamic. I want to capture that moment when dance

becomes more than just movement," he said. Then he stopped. Could he sound like any more of a tosser, crapping on about his work like some beret-wearing poseur?

She looked at him. There was a new light in her eye, as though she'd made an important decision.

"Use me," she said.

"Sorry?" He actually shook his head, convinced he hadn't heard right.

"You need a new life model, right? Someone to portray a dancer. Why not me?"

3
___

HE WAS GOING TO SAY NO. Maddy could tell by the way his eyes darkened and his jaw tensed.

She had no idea if she was the right model for what he wanted to do. But as soon as the idea popped into her head it had felt right. Especially given the realization she'd woken to this morning.

"Before you say no, hear me out," she said. "I decided something this morning. I'm not going to take this forced retirement lying down. I'm going to get a second opinion—hell, a fifth and sixth if I need it. I'm going to keep doing my rehab work and I'm going to find a way to dance." She said it like a challenge, daring him to disagree with her.

She'd given up too easily; the thought had been waiting for her, fully formed, when she opened her eyes and blinked at Max's ceiling half an hour ago. Dr. Hanson was one doctor, and she'd allowed his opinion to count for more than it should. She wasn't prepared to give up. Not yet. Not until she'd explored every avenue. Her future happiness depended on her efforts.

Only when Max nodded slowly did she release the breath she'd been holding. If he'd looked disbelieving—God, if he'd laughed—she wasn't sure what she would have done.

"I think that's a good idea," he said.

She smiled.

"Thank you. I needed to hear you say that. The thing is, most of the top dance medicine gurus are here in Paris. I couldn't be in a better place, even if I only came here because you were here. I'm going to call around today, try to get an appointment."

"That might take a while. Months, even."

"I know. I'm going to lean on some old colleagues to put in a word for me, see if I can't jump the waiting list."

"Stay here," he said. "It's no palace, but it's a roof."

She felt a rush of gratitude. The idea of staying with Max was infinitely preferable to twiddling her thumbs in a faceless hotel room for weeks while she gnawed her nails to the bone waiting for another specialist's pronouncement. But she couldn't mooch off him.

She said as much, and he made a rude noise.

"We're friends, Maddy. It's not mooching."

"Look, it's one thing to show up on your doorstep, drink your wine, eat your bread and crash in your bed for a night. But I can't foist myself on you for weeks at a time. Not unless you let me help you in return. That's why I offered to model for you. It would be a sort of barter—my body for your accommodation."

"You don't need to offer me a deal to stay here. You're welcome anytime."

"Thank you. But I can't live here and not offer anything in return. I know you well enough to know you won't accept money," she said. His instant frown was more than enough to prove her point on that score. "And, let's face it, my cooking skills aren't exactly great. Please let me do something for you in return for your helping me out."

"It's a sweet offer, but I don't think it's a good idea. If you really want to help out, I'm sure we can think of something else you can do."

She studied him, trying to understand his objection. He sounded so adamant, so immovable. Surely it would solve his problem as well as her own?

Or maybe he was just being polite. Maybe she was the last person he wanted to sketch.

"Is it because I don't have the right body type? It sounded like you were looking for a dancer's shape," she asked.

"It's not that." He rubbed a hand over the back of his neck, the picture of discomfort. "I don't think it'll work out, that's all."

He was over the conversation, she could tell, but she wanted to get to the bottom of this. She wanted to stay with him, but her pride wouldn't let her accept his hospitality without some kind of quid pro quo in place.

"Do you think I'll get fidgety, is that it? I promise I can stand still when I have to."

"It's not that."

She fiddled with the hem of the T-shirt, disappointed. "Okay. If that's the way you feel, I'll find a hotel this afternoon."

He looked annoyed. "Maddy. I said you could stay here, no strings. Don't be stubborn."

"I won't leech off you. I want to help. You're helping me, why can't I return the favor?"

"I would have thought that was pretty obvious. You've seen my stuff."

He gestured toward the row of statues. She glanced at them, then shook her head, baffled.

"Yeah. So?"

"My figures are all nudes, Maddy."

She blinked, then looked at the figures again.

Right. They were all naked forms. Huh.

"Well, that's no big deal, is it? It's not like you haven't seen me naked before. God, I think you know me better than my doctor after we did that season of *Wild Swans* together," she said.

Created by an avante-garde Australian choreographer, the ballet had been modern, intimate and daring. She and Max had worn thin body stockings and little else. By the end of the performance, they'd been so in tune with one another it had been hard to work out where his sweat finished and hers began.

"This is different," he said stubbornly.

She studied him closely and realized that color traced his cheekbones. He was embarrassed. Or self-conscious. Or maybe a bit of both.

"Max, you're blushing," she said. Mostly because she knew that nothing would get his back up faster. He might have changed, but not that much.

"No, I'm not."

"You're embarrassed at seeing me naked, aren't you?" She found the thought highly amusing. Had he really become so conservative?

"I was thinking about your comfort, not mine."

"Then there's nothing to worry about. Because I'm perfectly comfortable taking my clothes off in front of you. You're one of my oldest friends, for crying out loud. We used to live together, we've danced together. You even held my hair while I threw up after Peter's birthday party that time. We have no secrets, Max," she said.

He opened his mouth to object, but she waved a hand. "No. Not another word. You were planning to start this morning, yes?"

"Yes," he said grudgingly.

"Great. Then I'll have a shower and we'll get started."

She was still smiling when she closed the bathroom door on him.

Really, he was too cute. Worrying about her modesty. Totally wasted on her. Her body was the tool of her trade. She'd performed with dozens of male dancers throughout her career. Hands had caressed, gripped, slipped, pinched and God knows what else over the years. Standing naked in front of Max would be a piece of cake by comparison, and about as eventful for her as going to the supermarket was for other women.

It wasn't until she was standing in front of him, about to bare all that the first stab of self-consciousness hit.

She hadn't bothered dressing after her shower. She'd pulled on Max's oversize bathrobe, laced up the scuffed pair of ballet slippers she carried in her dance bag and stepped back into the main apartment.

He'd set up a stool for himself alongside a small table filled with charcoals, pencils and Conté crayons. A space heater had been turned on to ensure she wasn't too cold.

She took up position in front of him. Then she suddenly considered that maybe there *was* a difference between dancing intimately with someone while hundreds of people watched and standing completely naked in front of one man. Even if he was a friend.

Her fingers clenched around the tie on the bathrobe. Her stomach lurched with nerves.

She frowned, trying to work out why she was feeling…well, *shy* all of a sudden. She'd never been self-conscious about her body in her life. She knew she was in good shape, not an ounce of fat on her, her muscles lean and defined. Okay, she wasn't exactly a knockout in the rack department, but that had never bothered her before. Big breasts would only have gotten in the way when she danced, and that had always been the most important concern in her life.

But this morning she found herself wishing that instead of her half handfuls she had a little bit more action going on up top. Lord only knew how many women Max had slept with. She'd hate for him to look at her and find her lacking. Unfeminine, even.

She sneaked a glance at the bronze figure she'd admired earlier. Bronze Lady definitely had breasts. A good B cup, maybe even a C. Most of the time, Maddy didn't wear a bra at all. In fact, she had no idea what cup size she was these days. Which was something of a giveaway in and of itself.

Good grief, girl, get it together. Who cares if you have small breasts? Certainly not Max. You're a dancer, with a dancer's body. That's what he's looking for. Not tits and ass.

She forced her hands into action, unknotting the tie and almost throwing the robe open in her haste to get the moment of exposure over with.

She took a deep breath and made herself look up to make eye contact with Max. The sooner they normalized this situation, the better.

But he was busy with his supplies, selecting a pencil and sorting his charcoals into order.

Okay. Good. She had a few seconds to get her shit together without him watching her every move.

She slid the robe off her shoulders, letting it pool around her feet. The air was cool on her naked skin and she could feel her nipples tightening. She smoothed her hands down her hips and rolled her shoulders.

"Did you want my hair up or down?" she asked.

Max looked up at last. His gaze swept over her body. She couldn't read a single emotion on his face and she fought the instinct to cover herself with her hands.

"Up. I need the line of your neck and shoulders," he said. Then he returned his attention to his supplies.

She stared at him for a beat. Then she gathered the length of her hair and twisted it until it formed a loose knot on top of her head. She could feel her heart pounding in her chest, as though she was waiting in the wings, ready to run onstage and perform.

What had she expected him to say or do at first sight of her naked body? Break into applause? Go slack-jawed with admiration? Spout poetry?

She couldn't believe she was being so ridiculous. Juvenile, even.

When she focused on Max again, he was watching her, his expression still unreadable.

"How do you want me?" she asked.

He took a few seconds to answer.

"Let's start with first position, and move on from there."

She set her heels together and turned her feet out, joining her hands together in front of her and lifting them till they formed a gentle oval in front of her hips.

"Perfect," he said quietly.

She kept her eyes fixed on a point on the far wall. She could hear the soft rasp of pencil on paper as he began to sketch.

Five minutes passed, then ten. The room grew warmer. She let her gaze drift toward him. He was bent over his sketch pad, his hand moving quickly across the page as he split his attention between her and what he was creating. She wanted to talk, to ask him something to dispel the uncomfortable awareness she was feeling, but he was so inwardly focused she knew conversation wouldn't be welcome.

She forced herself to think of something else. Automatically her mind reverted to fretting over Andrew and her forced retirement from the company. There was no comfort to be found there, she knew. Instead, she started to make a mental list of her contacts in the various Paris-based ballets. She'd toured the country twice in her career and danced with several French soloists. Nadine, Jean-Pierre, Anna—they were just a few of the fellow dancers she could call on to ask for the favor of hooking her up with specialists. This afternoon, she would—

"Okay. Let's try some variations," Max said.

She blinked and let her body relax. "You're the boss."

"Third position this time," he said, eyeing her body assessingly. His regard was slow, steady. "*En pointe,* for as long as you can hold it."

"How long do you need?" she asked. She could hear the ego in her voice. He smiled.

"Not long," he said.

He started sketching, then stopped. "Can you look up for me?"

She lifted her chin. He frowned.

"Try angling your head a little more to the left."

She shifted. His frown deepened.

"It's not quite right...."

He stood and moved toward her. She stiffened, quelling the odd urge to retreat. Almost as though she was afraid of him, of his touch. Which was crazy. This was Max, after all. Her friend.

She could feel the heat from his body as he stood in front of her, studying the angle of her head. With her hands raised high above her, her weight supported on her toes, she was as tightly strung as a bow. And very exposed.

He reached out and nudged her chin up with his finger. A little higher. A little more to the left.

"That's good," he said.

His gaze swept the rest of her body and she felt a quiver of awareness deep in the pit of her belly. That odd instinct to retreat hit her again.

Then he was turning away, striding back to his sketch pad.

She took a deep breath, then another.

"You okay? Warm enough?" he asked as he took up his pencil.

She realized her breasts had puckered again, her nipples once more begging for attention. She fought a wave of self-consciousness.

"I'm fine," she said. "You just do your thing."

He took her at her word. She heard the scratch of pencil on paper and closed her eyes briefly. She felt rattled, off balance.

She forced her gaze to the back wall, concentrating on a crack in the plaster.

This is Max, she reminded herself. *Your* friend. *He held you while you slept last night. He's always been there for you.*

Slowly, by small degrees, she relaxed. There was no reason for her foolish awareness. Not with Max, of all people. He was like a brother to her. Always had been, always would be.

MAX TIGHTENED HIS GRIP on his pencil as he attempted to commit the curve of Maddy's hip to paper. His gaze kept sliding from the subtle arc of her waist down the flat planes of her belly to the curls at the juncture of her thighs. A neat little patch, waxed into submission, just enough curls there to hint at the secrets they concealed.

His hard-on throbbed. He still couldn't believe he'd let Maddy bulldoze him into this situation. But she'd been so determined to have her way. And he hadn't been strong enough to resist the temptation she'd offered. Back in the days when they'd lived together, he'd sketched her. Lying on the couch, asleep. Dancing, the expression on her face full of joy. Laughing, her eyes closed, her head thrown back.

But this was what he'd always wanted—Maddy gloriously, utterly naked, her body his to capture, if not to touch.

Heat flooded him as he remembered the temptation of standing close to her as he angled her head into position. He'd wanted to touch her so badly. To run his hands down her back to cup her pert, firm butt. To shape the small mounds of her breasts. To slide his fingers between her thighs and make her gasp with need for him.

Man.

He had to get his head together. He forced himself to concentrate on the paper in front of him, on the fine lines his pencil was shaping on the page. Slowly, Maddy's body emerged from the white. The taut readiness of her muscles. The discipline of her stance. The beauty of her features.

"Okay," he finally said.

She dropped down onto her flat feet.

"How's the knee?" he asked.

She frowned. "Fine. What next?"

She didn't like being reminded of her weakness.

"Arabesque *par terre,*" he said.

Her frown deepened. "That's not very dynamic. I can hold *à la hauteur,*" she said, referring to a pose where her back leg would be suspended in the air.

"I know. Show me an arabesque with your back leg on the ground first," he said.

She looked as though she was going to argue for a couple of beats. Then she gracefully moved into a sweeping arabesque, balancing on one leg while the other stretched out behind her, finally coming to a rest on the ground on her pointed toe. Her whole body arched into the pose, one hand extended behind her, the other in a straight line ahead. She looked as though she was about to take flight, the epitome of potential.

"Beautiful," he said involuntarily as he watched the play of muscles along her legs and torso.

Her breasts strained upward, and he could see her ribs expand and contract with every breath. Once again he was hopelessly torn between admiring her skill, wanting to capture her perfection on paper and needing to touch her so badly his groin was aching with it.

Start drawing, moron. It's going to be like this all morning. The sooner the session is over, the sooner you can have your sanity back.

His pencil held in a death grip, Max started to sketch.

An hour later, he'd captured a dozen poses and sustained a hard-on for longer than he'd thought was humanly possible. No matter what he told himself, or how many times he lost himself in the discipline of translating what his eye saw through his hand onto the page, his animal need for Maddy hummed constantly in the background.

By the time he put down his pencil and shut his sketch pad, he was literally shaking with desire.

He wanted to cross the space that separated them and get his hands on her so intensely that his mouth was dry and his belly contracted. It almost hurt to breathe, he was holding himself so tightly in check, in case his body sprang into action without his say-so.

"We're done?" Maddy said as she registered the slap of his sketchbook hitting the table.

"Yep."

Desperate to minimize the temptation, he strode forward and scooped up his bathrobe from where it lay pooled at her feet.

"Here," he said, holding the robe wide for her.

She turned her back and slid first one arm then the other into the sleeves. She reached up and tugged at the mass of hair knotted high on her head. Before he could pull away, it was tumbling down her back and over his hands. He stepped backward, but not before her scent surrounded him.

"I might grab a shower," he said abruptly.

They'd only been working for three hours and he'd hardly broken a sweat, but he had to get away from her. And he had to do something about the tent pole in his jeans before she saw that her good friend was packing wood.

Embarrassing? *Oui.* Big-time.

"Okay," she said. "I noticed a *boulangerie* on the corner yesterday. I could go get us some bread for lunch, maybe some quiche," she said.

"Great idea," he said, already heading for the bathroom. Her plan had the added advantage of getting her out of his apartment for five minutes. Long enough for him to get a grip on himself. He hoped.

The bathroom door safely closed behind him, Max shed his clothes and stared down at his straining boner. His body had a mind of its own where Maddy was concerned. No matter what he knew to be true—that it was never going to happen with her—his body had other ideas.

He twisted on the cold tap. Then he gritted his teeth and stepped beneath the spray.

Chill water hit him like a slap. He closed his eyes, willing his body into submission.

After a good minute, he glanced down at his resilient, determined hard-on, still standing proudly. Whoever heard of an erection so stubborn, so deeply committed to its cause that it could withstand the brutal effects of a cold shower?

His skin pebbled with gooseflesh, he finally gave up and twisted on the hot tap. There was more than one way to skin a cat, after all. Reaching for the soap, he lathered his palms until they were slippery and reached for his erection.

A few minutes, fast and furious, ought to take care of business—and hopefully keep his body under control for the rest of the day.

He closed his eyes and angled his face away from the spray. Hot water hit his chest and ran down his body in rivulets as he stroked his shaft.

Sensation washed through him and images filled his mind. The soft outline of Maddy's breasts against his T-shirt. The curve of her butt pressed against his hard-on this morning. The dark, mysterious shadow between her thighs as she posed for him. The puckered pinkness of her nipples, tight from the cold.

He tried to force his thoughts away from Maddy, but for the life of him he couldn't summon up an image of Marie-Helene or Jordan. Could barely remember their faces, let alone their bodies. He wanted Maddy. And, so help him, in the safe confines of the shower and his mind, he was going to have her.

He gave himself up to the fantasy. A dozen scenarios flitted across his imagination, but he settled on the one that best suited the moment.

He imagined Maddy entering the bathroom, wearing nothing but his robe. He could almost see her standing there, steam rising around her as she let the robe slide to the floor.

He groaned in the back of his throat as he imagined himself touching her at last, pulling her close, kissing her, plunging his tongue inside her mouth, his hands racing over her body.

Squeezing her breasts, teasing her nipples. Nudging a knee between her thighs. Sliding a hand into that tempting thatch of curls, then into her slick folds.

She'd be wet for him. So wet and ready that when he slicked a finger over her she'd twist and moan. He'd bend her over his arm and pull a nipple into his mouth, sucking and biting her. He'd keep stroking between her thighs, slicking over and over her until she begged him to give her what she needed.

Max's fist worked up and down his shaft, his eyes tightly closed as he lost himself in the rising tide of his own desire.

He'd push Maddy against the tiles, cup her butt in his hands and lift her till he could slide inside her. She'd be so tight and wet. She'd grip him with her inner muscles and he'd start to pound into her. Deep, hard, relentless. His hardness to her wet softness. Her need meeting his.

He frowned as desire built within him and guilt warred with need. He knew he shouldn't be eroticizing Maddy this way, that it would only make things more difficult, not less. But he was so close. Just this once, he promised himself. Just this once he'd indulge himself where Maddy was concerned.

His hand a blur, Max pushed himself toward the edge.

MADDY GRABBED HER PURSE and slung the strap over her shoulder. The bakery was just a few steps away on the corner, but she pulled on Max's coat for the short walk. When she'd arrived last night, she'd had a taste of how bitterly cold a Parisian winter could be, and she didn't need to learn the same lesson twice. She needed to shop for a coat of her own and a bunch of other stuff now that she'd decided to stay. The few tops and changes of underwear she'd thrown into her dance bag were barely good for a couple of days.

She was on her way out the door when the phone rang. She turned, eyeing it uncertainly for a beat, waiting for an unseen answering machine to pick it up. But the phone rang and rang. Finally she returned to the living space and picked up the receiver. If Max objected to her answering his phone, she'd find out soon enough.

"Max's apartment," she said.

There was a short, surprised silence before a woman spoke in accented English. "Is Max there? I need to speak to him."

"Um, he's in the shower. I can pass on a message," Maddy suggested. She hoped like hell this wasn't a girlfriend who would get the wrong idea about her and Max from the fact that she was in his apartment answering his phone.

"No. I need to speak to him now. Tell him it's his sister. Tell him it's about Eloise."

There was an urgency in Charlotte's voice that was undeniable.

"Give me a second, I'll get him for you."

Phone in hand, Maddy crossed to the bathroom door and tapped lightly.

"Max. It's your sister. It sounds urgent," she said through the door.

Nothing. She tapped on the door again.

"Max, I think your sister really needs you," she said more loudly this time.

Still nothing. She could hear the splash of water on the other side of the door. She knew from experience how noisy Max's stall could be with water pounding on the tiles and the plastic shower curtain.

She eased the door open, very aware of Charlotte waiting. Maddy hoped she wasn't about to embarrass herself and Max by barging in on him. There was a shower curtain, after all. And since the shower was still going, there was no chance she'd catch Max drying off. So this wasn't a total invasion of privacy.

She felt faintly stupid even worrying about catching him naked, given she'd just spent the past three hours posing in the buff for him. There was nothing he had that she hadn't seen before, after all.

"Max," she said as the door swung open.

The rest of what she'd been going to say got stuck somewhere between her lungs and her mouth as she saw that the shower curtain wasn't fully pulled across and that she had a perfect view of Max standing under the water, erection in hand, a look of pleasurable pain on his face as he stroked himself toward fulfillment.

He was totally oblivious to everything except the matter in hand and she literally didn't know what to do. Breathe. Retreat. Say something. Die on the spot.

She couldn't take her eyes off him. Golden skin, covered in fine dark hair. A muscular body, bunched and flexed slightly forward as he neared his climax. Strong thighs. And a powerful-looking erection that jutted arrogantly from his body.

He groaned, a low sound that snapped her into focus. Heat rushed up her body, sending prickling tendrils beneath her armpits and the back of her neck before filling her face with warmth. Eyes glued to Max, she took a step backward, her shaking hand reaching for the door handle as she pulled it shut behind her.

Oh, boy.

Her knees were weak. She felt hot, as though she'd been rehearsing for hours. She fanned herself, then suddenly remembered the phone call.

The receiver was still in her left hand. She lifted it to her face. "He won't be a minute." Her voice came out as a croak. "He's just getting out of the shower."

Then she counted to ten before knocking very, very loudly on the bathroom door. Opening it a crack, she hollered through the gap.

"Max, your sister is on the phone. It sounds important," she said.

She left the phone on the kitchen table where he would be sure to find it and hightailed it toward the door.

Once she was outside she walked up the street and around the corner before she felt safe enough to stop.

She was shell-shocked. There was no other word for it. She'd caught Max touching himself, on the brink of having an orgasm, and she was blown away.

She leaned against the wall of a building and closed her eyes. Instantly she was in the bathroom again with Max naked and aroused, his hand sweeping up and down his shaft, his head thrown back, his whole body tense with anticipation.

God, he'd looked amazing. So...masculine. She huffed out a small, humorless laugh at how woefully inadequate her vocabulary was. *Masculine* didn't even come close to describing how vital and overwhelmingly male he'd looked with his legs braced apart, his back against the wall, all that hardness in his hand.

No wonder they called him Rex.

The thought popped into her mind before she could censor it.

"Oh, God," she said, pressing her hands against her burning face.

She should not be thinking about his generous schlong. Definitely she shouldn't. It was wrong, wrong, wrong. He was her friend, her lovely, platonic friend who had danced with her, lived with her, laughed with her, cried with her.

And now she knew with absolute clarity how he looked naked. And not just *undressed* naked, either. She knew how he looked fully aroused, ready-to-go, big-and-proud naked. And she didn't know what to do with her new knowledge.

"Max is my friend," she said out loud.

An old man braving the cold to walk his dog gave her a curious glance as he passed by.

Great. She was a voyeur *and* a crazy, talking-to-herself-in-the-street person.

She pushed her frozen hands into her coat pockets and turned toward the *boulangerie.* Her French was rusty, but she managed to greet the woman behind the counter and buy half a dozen croissants and a baguette. The baguette was fresh from the oven and the paper bag it was wrapped in grew warm in her hand as she walked the short distance to Max's front door.

She had no idea what to say to him. Or how she would look at him without breaking into a sweat.

She should have knocked louder. And closed her eyes or looked the other way when she opened the door. Better yet, she should have let his answering machine take the call.

She was going to have to simply pretend it had never happened. There was no other alternative. She certainly wasn't about to tell Max what she'd seen—God forbid.

She knocked, then swallowed a lump of acute discomfort as she heard footsteps moving toward the door. Just like yesterday, except this time she wasn't imagining her old dancing buddy on the other side. No. Now she was imagining a naked, rampant man with a huge—

"Hey. I was wondering what was taking you so long," Max said as the door swung open.

He was fully dressed. Thank heaven for small mercies.

"There was a queue," she fibbed.

"I have to go to my sister's. She's had some problems with her latest babysitter. I'm going to go hold her hand for a while," he said. "I might be a while."

"Okay."

For some reason, she was having a lot of trouble keeping her attention fixed on Max's face. Her gaze kept wanting to slide down his chest to his crotch. Like a criminal returning to the scene of the crime.

"I've left a spare key for you on the kitchen table. Feel free to use the phone, the Internet, whatever. And don't wait for me if it gets to dinnertime and I'm not back."

"Sure. Don't worry about me. Your sister sounded really worried."

He sighed. "Yeah. She gets worked up sometimes. Her husband travels a lot and she struggles with the kids on her own. I couldn't help out as much as I wanted to when *Père* was still alive, but now it's better."

He was worried, distracted. She bet he was a great brother, despite his own assessment. She knew how great he'd been with her. No doubt he moved mountains for his sister. Which was why it was wrong, twisted, just plain freaky that she kept getting flashbacks to the shower scene as she looked at him. One second Max was standing decently clothed in front of her, her old friend looking platonically handsome and solid and reliable in faded denim and a chunky-knit sweater, and the next he was naked, gorgeous, hard as a rock and about to lose it.

"You'd better get going," she said.

Like, right now. Before my head explodes from all the illicit images bouncing around inside it.

She stepped aside to clear the way to the door.

"I've got my cell phone with me. Call if you need anything," he said.

He gave her a friendly pat on the shoulder as he passed. She found herself staring at his butt as he walked away, mesmerized by the perfection of his rounded, hard ass. A dancer's ass, even though he'd long since retired. Wonder Butt, indeed.

She registered what she was doing and made a frustrated noise in the back of her throat as she shut the door behind him.

One look. Ten seconds, maximum, and she felt as though nothing would ever be the same again. Which was crazy. She and Max had known each other for more than ten years. One moment of full exposure couldn't shift their friendship so profoundly.

Could it?

"No," she said out loud, just to hear the certainty in her own voice.

Barely twenty minutes had passed since she walked into the bathroom. Of course she was feeling antsy and uncomfortable still. The image of Max all hot and bothered was etched large in her memory. But it would fade. Soon, it would even be funny.

She frowned.

Okay, maybe not *soon*. But definitely what she had seen would be amusing one day, rather than disturbing and unsettling in ways that she simply wasn't prepared to examine.

She spent the rest of the day chasing up contact numbers for her dancing colleagues and making phone calls. Jean-Pierre and Anna both offered to contact their specialist, Dr. Rambeau. Apparently he was young but innovative and growing in reputation. She couldn't get through to Nadine and left a message, crossing her fingers that she wasn't out of town performing.

By midafternoon, Max still wasn't home. Maddy did some Pilates and worked her way through a series of stretches and strength-building exercises. Darkness came early, and at six she rummaged through the few groceries on Max's shelves and wound up having more pâté spread on bread for dinner. She switched on the TV afterward, but her French wasn't strong enough to make much sense of anything. By nine she was tucked in Max's bed, one ear cocked for the front door as she waited for him to come home.

She was wearing his T-shirt again, and his aftershave clung to the sheets. She shifted restlessly, feeling tense and edgy. No matter how hard she tried to distract herself, she kept thinking about what she'd seen.

She punched her pillow then rolled onto her back and glared at the ceiling. Why was seeing Max in such a revealing way so confronting for her? Yes, she'd walked in on an intensely personal, private moment, and if Max had seen her, they both would have been embarrassed. But he hadn't. So there was no reason for her to feel so…itchy and scratchy. No reason at all.

She swore and rolled onto her stomach, burying her face in the pillow.

The truth was, a long time ago she'd made a decision to ignore any attraction she felt for Max in order to keep him as a friend. He'd been startlingly attractive as a young man, and like a lot of the women in the Danceworks company, she'd taken one look at him and felt the tug of desire.

But at nineteen years old, Maddy had already learned the hard way that men and ballet didn't mix. No matter how much any man admired her skill, no matter how great the sex was, jealousy and resentment always drove a wedge between her and her lovers.

She'd been burning from the latest breakup with the most recent of her boyfriends when Max joined Danceworks, and as much as she was attracted to him, she'd seen the writing on the wall without even squinting. A few months of hot sex, fun and laughs. Then the demands would start. The sulking. The fights. The cold silences. Finally, the angry betrayal with another woman. Or—worse—the angry ultimatum. She'd been there, done that, and a few conversations with Max were enough to make her not want to go to the same ugly, sad place with him. He'd been so funny and smart and generous. She'd felt instantly comfortable with him, and she'd made a conscious decision not to let sex become a thing between them. He'd become her first and best male friend.

And now she'd caught a glimpse of the virile, sexual man behind her dear friend and she was afraid that she wouldn't be able to forget it.

Because the real, stark, unadorned truth was that seeing Max in such a blatantly sexual situation had been a huge turn-on. The unrestrained need in him, the intensity of his expression, the hard strength of his body—even now she felt a rush of damp heat between her thighs.

For the first time in over ten years of friendship, she was looking and thinking of Max as a potential lover and not as her friend.

And that scared the hell out of her.

4

IT WAS LATE when Max eased the front door open. He paused on the threshold, listening. The apartment was silent. Maddy had gone to bed.

Good.

He carried the foldaway camp bed his sister had loaned him inside and propped it against the wall. She'd raised an eyebrow when he'd asked if he could borrow it. His explanation that he had an old friend staying for a few days hadn't gone far toward satisfying her curiosity. She'd already been suspicious of his continuing presence in her apartment.

The crisis she'd called him over—a problem with the latest babysitter the agency had sent—had been resolved in the first hour. Charlotte had really only wanted a stand-in for her absent husband, a shoulder to cry on while she expressed her fury and disappointment that her little girl had once more been let down and misunderstood.

Her gratitude had slowly turned to inquisitiveness as the hours wore on and he'd stayed to help bathe Marcel and Eloise then cook dinner. By the time he'd settled beside her on the couch after dessert she'd been looking at him out of the corners of her eyes, clearly wondering why he was still hanging around.

He'd been avoiding going home, and they'd both known it. As soon as he mentioned the bed and the fact he had an old dancing friend staying over, he'd seen the cogs begin to turn in his sister's mind. Which was why he'd made his escape and finally come home. He wasn't up for twenty questions regarding his friendship with Maddy. Not that there was a lot to discuss; he just preferred not to have his sister jumping to conclusions.

He eased off his shoes and crossed to the stairs. He could make out the pale oval of Maddy's face on the pillow as he moved toward the chest where he kept his spare linen and blankets. He found a sheet by feel, then what he hoped was a pillowcase.

"Is everything okay at your sister's?"

Light washed over the bed as Maddy flicked on the lamp and propped herself up on one elbow.

"She was fine once she calmed down. Just a problem with an inexperienced babysitter. Sorry, I didn't mean to wake you."

"I wasn't really asleep, anyway." She frowned when she registered the linen in his arms. "Max, tell me you weren't about to sneak down to sleep on the couch," she said.

"I borrowed a camp bed from Charlotte. If you're going to stay for a while, I figured you might prefer a bit of privacy."

There was a moment of silence. He felt about as transparent as a teenager. It didn't help that the mere sight of her in his bed springboarded him into about a million different sexual fantasies.

She threw back the covers.

"I told you, I'm not stealing your bed. If anyone is sleeping on the camp bed, it's me," she said.

She stood and crossed the space between them, pulling the folded sheet from his hands.

"Wait a minute," he said, trying to grab it back.

She stepped away and shook her head. "No. You're already doing me the hugest favor, letting me crash here. Plus, I'm about half your size. There's no way you'll be more comfortable on a camp bed than me."

He started to protest again, but she held up a hand.

"Have you got a spare quilt?"

She turned and grabbed her pillow from his bed, tucking it under her arm. She looked immovable and determined. He yanked a thick duvet from the chest.

"Maddy, this is crazy. I've slept on the camp bed a million times, it's no big deal. We kept it for when *Père* was bad and needed constant care in his room."

"Not listening," she said as she started down the stairs.

He had no choice but to follow her. She was wearing his T-shirt again, and he was acutely aware of her bare legs beneath it and the way her pert backside swayed from side to side with each step.

"Help me set this thing up," she said, eyeing the bed frame.

"Maddy. This isn't what I brought it home for," he said.

"Stop being so damn noble." The bed frame protested with a rusty groan as she unfolded it flat. "I've slept in far worse places, believe me."

She tugged the duvet from his arms.

"Go to bed. You've spent the whole day thinking about everyone else. Get some sleep."

He stared at her. If only she knew that from the moment she'd arrived on his doorstep she'd dominated his thoughts, pushing almost everything and everyone else aside.

The realization made him turn away. Maddy was a friend in need. That was all. His days of obsessing over her were in the past.

"Fine, you win. I'll see you in the morning," he said over his shoulder.

"Night, Max."

Upstairs, he stripped to his boxer-briefs and slid into bed. The sheets were still warm from her body. He lay on his side, staring at the wall. He could hear her moving around downstairs, making the bed up. Then there was nothing but silence.

If he hadn't brought the bed home, she'd be beside him right now, the sound of her breathing soft in the darkness.

He rolled onto his belly and fisted his hand beneath the pillow.

Getting the camp bed had absolutely been the smart thing to do. He just wished like hell he didn't regret doing it quite so much.

FORGET ABOUT what you saw. Go out there, take your clothes off, start working. Max is waiting for you.

Maddy reached for the bathroom door handle for the third time that morning, and for the third time she hesitated.

She'd spoken to Max yesterday. Argued over the camp bed last night, in fact. So it wasn't as though this was their first meeting post-shower scene. There was absolutely no reason for her to be loitering in the bathroom. Hadn't she decided this wasn't going to be an issue between them, that she was going to push the memory of what she'd seen into the very darkest corner of her mind and ignore it?

"Idiot."

She pushed the door open and marched into the apartment. Her stomach dipped as she stopped in front of Max. He was sitting on his stool opening a new box of charcoals, his head bent over the task. She watched the muscles work in his forearms, the way his deft fingers teased the packaging open. Instantly she flashed to an image from yesterday: Max's arms rigid with tension, his biceps flexing as his fist slid up and down his erection.

He glanced up, a frown on his face. Almost as though he'd somehow guessed what she'd been thinking.

"I forgot to ask. How did you get on with the specialists yesterday?"

She blinked stupidly at how normal the question was. While she agonized over the illicit glimpse she'd inadvertently gotten into his sex life, it was business-as-usual for Max. He didn't know what she'd seen. He never would.

"Really well. I spoke to Anna yesterday and she texted me

first thing this morning. She got me an appointment next week with her specialist, Dr. Rambeau."

"That's great news."

"He hasn't got a huge reputation, but both Anna and Jean-Pierre swear by him. Now I just have to contact Dr. Hanson and get my records sent over." Frankly, she'd rather chew glass but it was something that had to be done.

"Not looking forward to it?" His gray eyes were sympathetic.

"Asking for a second opinion is a slap in the face, no matter how you look at it. He's not going to be gracious about it," she said. And, rational or not, she was angry with Dr. Hanson. Both he and Andrew had given up on her before she'd had a chance to prove herself. The last thing she wanted was talk to either one of them.

"Want me to do it for you?"

"Yeah. But I'm not going to let you. You know, Monsieur Laurent, I'm beginning to think you have a bit of a Sir Galahad complex. You're always primed to ride to my rescue at the drop of a hat."

He made a dismissive noise.

"What do you call trying to sleep on the camp bed last night?" He looked caught out.

"Exactly. You're too gallant for your own good."

"Humph."

"What?"

"My sister said something similar the other day."

"Well, then, it must be true."

He smiled, and she smiled back, and for a long moment they enjoyed the camaraderie.

See? This is normal. Just like old times, B.S.S. Before Shower Scene.

Then he looked at his watch.

"Guess we'd better get started, huh?" she said.

That quickly, she was nervous again.

"Guess so. Unless you need to do something else today?"

"No. Nothing else." Unfortunately.

She reached for the sash on the robe. This was her way of repaying Max for his hospitality. It was the least she could do for him.

She let the robe slide down her arms.

Like yesterday, he was busy organizing his pencils when she looked at him. She turned her feet out and pulled in her belly and squared her shoulders.

"Okay, I'm ready when you are," she said.

He barely glanced up. It struck her again how commonplace this must be for him. She was simply another model, another body. Which made it even more stupid and pointless to feel so self-conscious and uncertain.

"Let's start with fourth position, *en pointe,*" he said.

She moved smoothly into the pose, concentrating fiercely on achieving perfect form and posture. Anything to stop herself from thinking about the fact that she was standing naked in front of Max, and that yesterday he'd been so hard and—

Enough!

She gritted her teeth and arched her back a little more. He began to sketch. She kept her mind busy reviewing the choreography for the production of *Giselle* she'd been rehearsing before Dr. Hanson ended her career. After ten minutes, Max asked for a second pose, then a third, each of which she held for close to fifteen minutes as he worked. Nearly an hour later, he paused to flick through his sketch pad. She stretched out her calf muscles and surreptitiously massaged her bad knee.

"Do you feel up to something more dynamic?" he asked.

His gaze was on her knee. He'd caught her rubbing it. She turned her feet out and stood tall.

"Whatever you've got."

"I don't want to aggravate your injury."

"You won't. It's healing. Work is good for it," she said. "I have to start building my strength up again."

He looked doubtful. Self-consciousness forgotten, she rose up *en pointe* and began a series of battements, her feet flashing as she flicked one pointed foot in front of the other in a rapid, beating movement, her arms held in a graceful curve at midchest height.

"Okay, okay. Point taken," he said, shaking his head.

"What were you thinking of?"

"Do you remember the season of *La Sylphide* we did right before I left the company? There was that series of *fouetté rond de jambe tournants* toward the end of the last act."

She tried to recall the choreography he was referring to. It had been a long time ago and there had been many, many sequences since.

Max stood and took up position, rising up onto his toes in his bare feet. Despite the fact that it must be years since he danced professionally, his form was perfect as he began to spin on his left foot, his right leg raised and bent at the knee as he demonstrated a *fouetté*. His right leg whipped around his body again and again as he spun, powering his turns, while his arms were held extended at shoulder height.

"Yes! I remember now," she said. The sequence spilled into her mind in an unbroken chain. The *grand jeté,* followed by the increasingly frantic *fouettés,* then the despairing collapse and surrender at the end.

Max stopped, barely breathing hard from the exertion.

"Still got the old moves, Max," she said admiringly.

He'd been such a wonderful dancer. Watching him was like seeing a ghost from the past.

A shadow passed over his face. Yearning, regret, disappointment—she saw it all in his eyes for a few unguarded seconds before he picked up his sketch pad.

"A few more rotations and I probably would have spun into a wall or torn a muscle," he said dismissively.

She took a step toward him.

"Do you think you can hold the end position for me?" he asked without looking up.

She stilled. He didn't want to talk about it or acknowledge his reaction. For a long beat she considered how she would feel if their positions were reversed. Then she pivoted on her heel and walked to the farthest corner of his work space.

Some things were too painful and private to talk about.

When she turned to face him, he was once more armed with his charcoals.

I don't ever want to know what it feels like to not have dance in my life.

The thought came from her gut. Rationally, she knew she had to retire someday. No dancer could perform forever. But she wasn't ready to hang up her slippers yet. Not even close. The thought of losing the most important, fulfilling thing in her life was unthinkable. Unbearable.

"Do you have enough space?"

"Yes."

She pulled her focus into her body. She reviewed the choreography in her mind, then found her starting point. With an explosion of power she sprang into a *grand jeté*. Her muscles stretched and her body soared as she leaped across the space. Everything receded into the background. She landed and rotated fluidly into the first *fouetté*. Her support leg *en pointe,* she spun, her working leg whipping the turn to greater speed with each rotation.

As her speed increased, her moves become more desperate, more frantic. She allowed her spin to waver, let her arms drag her off balance. Finally, she fell out of the spin, collapsing onto the ground in an abandoned-yet-controlled sprawl, one leg bent beneath her, the other stretched forward, her body draped over it in a posture of absolute despair and defeat.

There was a moment of silence. She could hear her own breathing, feel her chest heaving against her extended leg.

"Beautiful, Maddy. Beautiful."

She heard him begin to draw. She kept her body alert despite the temptation to relax into the stretch. She knew without asking that Max wanted the dynamic tension of the position and the emotion of the dance, not simple anatomy.

After five minutes, her body began to stiffen. She concentrated on each protesting muscle in turn, tensing and releasing them without changing posture. After ten minutes, she heard the scrape of Max's stool on the floor.

"That was great. Absolutely what I was looking for," he said as he approached.

She allowed herself to sit upright at last. He extended a hand to help her to her feet. She started to rise, but the leg that had been bent beneath her buckled, refusing to hold her weight. She stumbled, but his arms were around her before she could fall, one big hand splaying beneath her rib cage, his fingers grazing the lower curve of her right breast, the other grabbing her hip. Instinctively she reached for him, too, one hand finding his shoulder, the other his back.

For a shocking moment she was pressed against him, breast to chest, hip to groin.

She froze.

The soft fabric of his T-shirt brushed against her breasts. She inhaled pure Max—soap and sandalwood. She could see each individual hair of his morning stubble, the whiskers black against his olive skin, and feel his warm breath on her cheek.

Her heart began to pound against her rib cage. If he moved his hand, he would be cupping her breast in his palm.

The thought made her tremble with sudden, hungry need. Her nipples tightened in anticipation.

"You okay now?"

She could feel his deep voice vibrating through her body.

"Yes," she said, even though it was a big fat lie.

His grip slackened and he stepped away from her.

The loss of his heat and hardness was a shock. She blinked and tried to pull herself together. She was afraid to look at him, afraid he would see only too readily the thoughts that had been racing through her mind. She ducked to collect her robe, painfully aware of her aroused nipples. Only when she'd tied the sash did she dare look at him again.

He was studying the drawing he'd completed, an expression of concentration on his face. He seemed utterly unaware of the fact that he'd just held her naked body pressed against him and that she was vibrating with the aftershock of the contact.

"I think we're done for the day," he said. "That last pose was great, Maddy. Thanks." He looked up, his face unreadable. "Sometimes I forget what it's like when you dance."

She stared at him for a long moment. How was it possible that she'd felt so much when he held her while he was completely unaffected?

You don't want him to be affected. He's your friend. Sex is the best way to destroy that. Remember how every relationship you've ever had has ended?

She tightened the sash on the robe again. For the second time in as many days, Max had reduced her to incoherent jelly. It confused the hell out of her, as well as being damned embarrassing. She could only imagine how he'd respond if he knew what was going on in her head. Since when did old friends suddenly want to jump each other?

She crossed to the camp bed and scooped up her clothes. In the bathroom, she dressed quickly, ignoring the sensitivity of her skin and the telltale heat between her thighs. She stared at her reflection in the bathroom mirror.

"What are you doing?" she asked herself, her voice low and serious.

She'd come to Max seeking sanctuary, not sex. She was on the verge of making a mistake she knew she would regret for the rest of her life.

He was at the kitchen table working on one of his sketches when she emerged.

"I'm going out," she said, hovering awkwardly at a distance. "I need to buy some things. A coat, another pair of shoes." *And get away from you for a few hours.*

"Sure. I should be around but take the spare key. I want to do some more work on these sketches."

"I'll bring something back for dinner. Maybe some chicken fillets," she said vaguely.

He surprised her by laughing.

"What's so funny about chicken fillets?"

"Have you had cooking lessons or bought a cookbook since we last lived together?" He was grinning at her, highly amused.

"I signed up for some classes, but I never got there," she admitted.

"So what were you planning on doing with the chicken?"

"Something."

He looked so damned familiar, sitting there with his eyes alight with laughter as he teased her. Her old Max, the friend she'd instinctively turned to in her most desperate hour. Which only made it even more confusing that five minutes ago she'd been ready to jump his bones.

"Tell you what. Why don't I take care of dinner? In the interests of it being edible," he said.

She stared at him, utterly bewildered. Why was she suddenly having these feelings for him, after all these years?

"Fine. I'll buy some wine," she said.

She grabbed her purse and headed for the door. Out in the street, she blinked and wrapped her arms around her body.

She had to get a grip. Stop thinking about Max in any terms other than as a friend, and start thinking like a normal person.

A normal, really, really cold person. She shivered and hugged herself tighter. It was damned frigid, and she was too used to the blue skies and searing heat of home.

A normal person would go buy herself a coat rather than stand freezing in the street. A coat, some shoes and maybe some jeans. And, while she was at it, some underwear and toiletries.

She kept herself occupied with a mental shopping list as she walked along the cobblestone street and out into the main thoroughfare. Traffic whizzed past as she looked left, then right. She shrugged. It didn't matter where she went. She was just getting away from Max. She knew Paris well enough to know that she would find good shopping no matter which direction she headed.

Within an hour she was bundled in a full-length black wool coat, a long, brightly striped scarf and a stylish scarlet wool cap that covered her ears and reflected some color onto her pale face. She found jeans, a pair of low-heeled black ankle boots she could wear with pants or a skirt, underwear and various other essentials at the huge BHV department store on Rue de Rivoli. Twice she forced herself to put down small items that caught her eye for Max. A scarf the exact color of his eyes. A pair of gloves made from the softest calfskin. Today was not a day to buy gifts for Max.

After she was satisfied that she had enough to survive a week or two, she rode the escalators to the top floor and sat in a corner of the vast cafeteria nursing a cup of watery, burned-tasting coffee.

She didn't want to go home yet. She stared out over Paris,

her mind zigzagging between worrying over her inappropriate attraction to Max and speculating about her appointment with Dr. Rambeau. He had to give her hope. He had to have a magic rabbit to pull out of his hat. If he didn't… She couldn't let herself go there.

She left the department store and struck out aimlessly into the winding streets of the third arrondissement. Her shopping bags banged her calves as she meandered blindly past colorful window displays.

She was about to seek refuge from the cold in a bistro when the passionate, hip-swinging beat of Latin music met her ears. She followed the music down a busy side street and beneath an archway into a cobbled courtyard. A tall, whitewashed building surrounded her on three sides, the ground floor of which was open to the world thanks to large floor-to-ceiling windows. She stared into a wooden-floored dance studio, filled with brightly clad women in various interpretations of Spanish flamenco costumes. Frills and lace and full skirts, petticoats, fishnet stockings—one woman even had a mantilla in her hair. A teacher stood in front of them, demonstrating a move.

Maddy watched with a smile as they all began to dance, feet stomping, fingers clicking and curling and gesticulating, skirts swirling as they spun. They weren't all good. Some were very bad, in fact. But that was beside the point. They felt the music. They were having fun.

She'd always loved Latin. When she'd first started out as a professional dancer, she and her friends would seek out the small Latin-American nightclubs in Sydney's inner city and spend the night dancing for fun instead of perfection and achievement. Max used to come with them, she remembered. She'd loved matching her moves to his to the demanding beat of a rumba or samba. She couldn't remember the last time she'd danced for fun, until she was sweaty and laughing and ex-

hausted. Too long. Even before her injury her life had become
so defined by her career and her position within the company
that her world had shrunk to rehearsal, performance and more
rehearsal.

A particularly bitter gust of wind reminded her that it was
too cold to be standing around. She returned to the street, but
the rhythm of the music stayed with her. For some reason, she
felt calmer, more settled. Ready to go face Max and put the cra-
ziness of the past few days behind her.

If she hadn't heard the music and seen the dancers, she
probably would have walked right past the dress. She wasn't
shopping for frivolities, after all. The vibrant red of roses on a
black silk background caught her eye first, then the style of the
dress, with its tiny spaghetti straps and buttoned bodice. It had
an old-fashioned full skirt, and she could imagine spinning in
it, the fabric floating around her. Even though she had nowhere
to wear it, she added it to her purchases. It would be a souvenir
of her time in Paris.

She stopped at a wine shop then ducked into the *fromagerie* to
buy some of the thick, oozing Camembert she knew Max adored.

She was feeling considerably lighter of heart by the time she
turned her key in the front door. Time away from Max had given
her the perspective she needed. This morning's confusion had
assumed its rightful place as a momentary aberration. She was
under stress. She'd had an unexpected, explicit glimpse into
another side of Max's life yesterday. Combined, the two things
had made her silly for a few hours. Nothing more.

He was lounging full-length along the couch reading the
newspaper when she entered.

"You're back. I was starting to think I'd have to send out a
Saint Bernard."

"I bought some things," she said, holding her bags high to
illustrate her point.

"Ah. Silly me. I thought five hours was far too long for any one person to spend looking at shoes."

"Hey! I only bought one pair. And I found a dance school." She dumped her bags beside the coffee table and sank into the armchair. "In this funny little courtyard. There was a flamenco class on. Remember when we used to go to Carmen's and The Latin Bar and dance all night?"

She eased off her shoes and wiggled her toes to relieve the ever-present ache in her feet.

"God, yes. What a pack of show-offs."

It was true. Wherever they went, they'd dominated the dance floor, reveling in their superior skill and flair. She laughed, remembering some of their worst moments.

"We were all so desperate to be onstage. But you're right, in hindsight we must have been pretty obnoxious."

"And the rest."

She reached into her shopping bags and slid the wine and cheese onto the coffee table.

"My contribution, humble as it is," she said.

Max leaned across to inspect the cheese.

"My favorite," he said.

"I know."

He looked surprised, then pleased. She told herself the warm pleasure she felt was just happiness at making him happy. Nothing more.

"I've made us coq au vin for dinner," he said, swinging his legs off the arm of the couch.

"Delicious. I'm starving."

Technically, she needed to be vigilant about what she ate. But it had been cold out, and it wasn't as though she was going to pig out on the cheese alongside Max.

He served the chicken with fresh green beans and baby carrots. She had two glasses of wine and was feeling mellow and sated by the time he pushed back his chair from the table and started to collect the plates.

It's going to be all right, she realized with relief. *This morning is history. We've moved on already.*

The invisible tension that had been banding her chest eased.

"I'll do that," she said, standing and tugging the plates from his hands. "The chef should never have to clean up."

"We'll do it together," he said. "Then you can help me eat this cheese."

"I don't think so," she said with a laugh. "The pâté yesterday was bad enough. No man will ever be able to lift me again if I keep packing it on."

He gave her a reproving look. "Maddy, there's not a spare ounce on you."

"Says the man who doesn't have to fling me around a stage."

They crossed to the kitchen together and he threw her a tea towel after she'd dumped the plates in the sink.

"I hate drying," he said unapologetically.

"Another thing I remember."

"And you hate to vacuum."

"And clean the bathroom. Don't forget that. But I'm great with laundry."

"Together, we almost make the perfect housemate," he agreed.

"Except for forgetting to take the garbage out," she said.

They both laughed.

"Remember the tantrum Jacob pulled that time when we missed the garbage collection two weeks in a row?" she said. Jacob had been one of several dancers who had lived with them.

"Definitely an eleven on the Richter scale."

"Nothing like a gay man for a really good, wall-shaking, knee-trembling tantrum."

He squirted detergent into the sink and reached for the taps.

"Did I ever tell you about the time he tried to seduce me?"

Maddy gave a shout of surprised laughter. "No way!"

"Way." Water shot out of the faucet with a hiss and spray ricocheted off the plates and up into his face.

"Merde!" he said, flicking off the taps and wiping water from his face with his hands. "The water pressure in this place is completely screwed. Half the time it's a trickle, then this happens."

"You see? Drying does have its good points," she said with a grin.

He shot her a wry look, then reached for the hem of his soaked T-shirt. Before she understood what he was doing, he'd whipped it over his head. She watched, mesmerized, as he used the balled-up T-shirt to dry his face and mop up any excess moisture on his broad chest. Then he threw the T-shirt to one side and reached for the taps again.

She could barely do more than blink and breathe as she stared at his chest and shoulders and belly. Dark hair curled across his defined pectoral muscles, narrowing down into a sexy trail as it moved south. His jeans rode low on his hips, revealing the hard planes of his abs and the beginning of the delicious, uniquely male groove where his belly muscles met his thighs.

All her hard-won comfort flew out the window. Her mouth was dry. She wanted to reach out and touch him so badly that her fingers clenched into the tea towel. He was beautiful. Perfect. And so damned sexy she wanted to rub herself against him like a cat in heat.

"It was after that party we had when Georgie went off to America. We were all wasted, since we had a long weekend to recover. Remember?"

He was watching her, waiting for her response. She lifted her eyes to his face but was unable to stop her gaze from dropping once more to his chest. He was so male and hot….

"Um. Yeah. That was the party where Georgie threw up in someone's shoe, right?"

He laughed. She stared, fascinated, as his head tilted back on his neck and his belly muscles flexed.

Oh. Boy.

She was in big trouble. Big, big, big trouble.

"I woke up at about four in the morning and Jacob was standing beside my bed, the corner of the sheet in his hand, about to slide in with me. I asked him what he thought he was doing and he said—and I shit you not—'my mother always told me it never hurts to ask.'"

He laughed again. And again his belly muscles did their compelling flex-and-contract thing. She was officially obsessed. And about to do something really, really stupid. She'd never been good at denying her sexual needs. She'd never had to be. She enjoyed sex, and she'd been lucky enough to live and work in a community where she'd never been judged for her appetites. There had been very few men who she'd desired in her life that she hadn't had. She drew the line only at married men—and Max.

But now... Standing so close to his half-naked body, it was difficult to see him as anything but a sexual prospect.

"I told him that if he got into bed with me, he was going to find out that his mom was wrong. Big-time. Then he actually tried to talk me into it. Like he was a car salesman, and all it would take was a bit of good sales patter to get me to change teams."

He shook his head, grinning at the memory. She took a deep breath, then another. She forced herself to take a step backward.

"Jacob always had a thing for you," she said. She could barely recognize her own voice, it sounded so tight and controlled.

"Yeah, it was called a penis."

He passed her the first clean plate, and she almost dropped it she was trying so hard to avoid making contact with his bare skin. One touch. That was all it would take to slip the leash off her self-control right now. He was way, way too sexy and masculine and desirable.

Somehow, they got through the dishes. If Max noticed that she barely lifted her gaze from the floor and that she kept a good few paces between them at all times, he didn't show it. She sighed with relief when he disappeared upstairs afterward and returned wearing another T-shirt.

But to her dismay, it didn't help any. Not enough, anyway. Now she had two images vying for attention in her subconscious—Max in the shower, horny and hard, and Max's chest and belly, up close and personal. Every time she so much as glanced at him both images danced across her mind. Heat fizzed along her veins. Her skin felt sensitized and she could hear her own heartbeat in her ears.

"There's a Godard movie on tonight," he said as he dropped onto the couch, propping his long legs on the coffee table in front of him and palming the remote control. He patted the couch next to him. "Come on. I'll translate for you and tempt you with cheese."

She stared at the couch. There was no way she could survive a whole evening sitting next to him without climbing aboard and taking him for a ride.

She closed her eyes as she imagined his reaction if she tried to enact any of the fantasies running riot in her mind right now. He'd be stunned. He might even laugh at her. Whatever he did, it would be the end of their friendship as she knew it, the comfort and ease between them a thing of the past.

"Let's go out," she suggested.

He frowned. "Out? It's too cold, Maddy. Below zero, in case you hadn't noticed."

Her glance skittered around the apartment, seeking inspiration, and finally landed on her shopping bags. She remembered the dress she'd bought and the flamenco class that had inspired her purchase.

"Let's go dancing," she said. As soon as she said it, she

knew it was right. Dancing was safe. She could churn up the dance floor, get sweaty and breathless in the safety of numbers.

Max was still frowning.

"There must be someplace nearby. Somewhere with Latin-American music?" she asked. God, she was almost begging. She needed some outlet for all the frustration and confused tension building inside her.

"There's The Gypsy Bar. They have dancing. I've been there a few times with a friend of mine," he said.

"Good. Great. Let's do that."

She grabbed the shopping bag with her new dress in it and retreated to the bathroom. She seemed to be spending a lot of her time doing that lately.

Get a grip, Maddy. Get over this. Don't screw up the one good, enduring relationship in your life.

Excellent advice. She just hoped she had the sense to take it.

THE GYPSY BAR was heaving with people and throbbing with loud music as Max pushed open the front door. Maddy bumped into him as he halted to let a couple of women pass by. He stood to one side to make room for her in the crowded foyer. He watched as she tackled the buttons on her coat, knowing already what was beneath it. He'd stared like a tragic schoolboy when she'd stepped out of the bathroom half an hour ago, her new dress swirling around her legs. Slim straps accentuated the delicate lines of her shoulders, while the tight bodice outlined her breasts. He'd known instantly that she wasn't wearing a bra. Her breasts moved with each step, and the gentle, pouting outline of her nipples was visible against the silk.

She was his own personal siren, sent by some higher power to tempt and taunt him. As if it wasn't tough enough to stare at her naked body half the day, wanting what he could never have. Hell, he could still remember the feel of her when he'd hauled her to him to stop her falling this morning. Soft yet strong, her skin warm and velvety, the curve of her breast just the slide of a hand away.

It was getting harder and harder to deny his body's desires. In that respect, her wish to go dancing tonight was a godsend. He needed to let off some steam, release the tension binding him tight.

On the other hand, there was that dress. And the way her hips were already moving in time with the music. It was highly probable that he'd simply traded one form of torture for another.

"Where's the dancing?" she asked, standing on her tiptoes to shout near his ear. The music was so loud the beat reverberated through his heels.

"Up front," he said.

She nodded and immediately began to push her way through the crowd. He followed more slowly and was just in time to watch as she found the edge of the dance floor, filled with gyrating bodies. She didn't hesitate, she simply slid in amongst them and started to move. She'd piled her hair high on her head, leaving wispy tendrils free to hang around her face and shoulders, and she lifted her hands high and shook her head and shoulders and hips in time with the music.

It didn't take long for a man to home in on her, a tall, dark-skinned guy with an appreciative gleam in his eyes. Max watched as they began to salsa together, their bodies locked in rhythm. The other man was smiling with delight at the way Maddy moved in his arms, limber and light and provocative.

Max turned away. He could watch her and go crazy, or he could find his own release in the steamy darkness of the club. He pushed his way to the bar and ordered a cognac. He downed it in one swallow and slid the glass back onto the bar. Then he turned back to the dance floor and let his eyes find her again.

She was spinning, her skirt a swirl of silk around her legs.

She stopped only when her partner reeled her in, her body slamming into his.

"Max. What are you doing here?" He felt a tug on his arm and turned to find a tall slim blonde standing beside him, a surprised smile on her face.

"Marie-Helene," he said. He leaned close to kiss both her cheeks and she caught his mouth in a third kiss before he could pull away. She tasted of wine, and he realized she was a little drunk.

"You haven't called me for an age," she said, cocking her head assessingly. "Have I done something wrong? Worse, have I been replaced?"

He forced a laugh. "I've been busy." He shrugged. They had no ties between them, after all. With Marie-Helene, it had always been about sex and nothing else.

"So you haven't settled down or anything disgustingly boring like that?" she asked, a suggestive smile curling her mouth.

"No."

"Then come dance with me, Max," she said.

She took his hand and led him onto the floor. Eyes holding his, she slid into his arms, their bodies touching from chest to hip. She began to move, and he quickly found the beat.

She was a good dancer, but nothing compared to Maddy. He pushed the comparison from his mind the moment he registered it. This was about forgetting Maddy, losing himself for a few hours.

His step sure, he spun Marie-Helene. She laughed with delight, quickly closing the distance between them so that their bodies were once more pressed together. Her full breasts flattened against his chest, and she ground her hips against his.

If he wanted to, he could go home with her tonight. The invitation was there in every move she made. He could close his eyes and pound into her and find release in her welcoming body.

She smiled, almost as though she could read his thoughts.

She was a generous lover, uninhibited, sensual. But she wasn't Maddy, and he didn't want her the way he wanted Maddy. He wasn't a saint, but the idea of using Marie-Helene as a human scratching post held little appeal.

He wouldn't be going home with her. More fool him, he suspected.

Marie-Helene leaned close to be heard.

"Stop scowling, Max. You look so serious," she said.

The music changed to a fast-moving rumba. He stepped up the pace, turning with Marie-Helene, his hips leading hers.

She laughed with pleasure and at last he felt the music begin to take over, his body following instinctively. This was what he'd wanted, what he'd needed. No thinking, no second-guessing. Just sweat and movement and mindlessness.

A reprieve only—but he'd take what he could get right now.

MADDY TRIED TO STOP herself from watching Max dance with the blond woman. They'd been together for over an hour. She told herself she didn't care what he did, that it was good that he was with another woman. The best thing, in fact. If he went home with her, he'd be well and truly out of bounds. But she couldn't stop herself from watching them.

The way Max splayed his hands over the other woman's hips. The way the blonde pressed her pelvis and her breasts against him. The way she laughed with him, her eyes flashing an unmistakable intimate invitation. There was something about the way they moved together, a certain sure knowledge in their touch that told her they'd been lovers before, that she'd already lain in Max's arms and felt him inside her.

Jealousy burned in Maddy's belly at the thought. Jealousy and envy. Standing on the edge of the dance floor, Maddy toyed with the straw in her drink and tried to make herself look away.

Sweat cooled on her skin now that she was no longer dancing, but her body still hummed with the exhilaration of losing herself—even for a short while—in movement. She'd lost her first partner when he'd suggested they go somewhere more private to dance, her second partner when he'd slid his hand down to cup her ass and she'd slid it back up onto her hip again.

A few years ago, she might have gone home with one of them after a few hours of foreplay on the dance floor. She might have let the excitement and rhythm of moving with a skilled partner spill over into the bedroom. But one-night stands had lost their appeal some time ago. She'd had a series of regular lovers for a while now—successive men who she'd kept at arm's length for as long as possible, then broken off with when it became clear they wanted more than she was willing or able to give.

Across the room, the blonde slid a hand behind Max's neck. Maddy knew what was coming, knew that she should look away, but she couldn't. She watched, her hands clutching around her glass, as the other woman pressed her lips against his. Maddy held her breath as she waited for Max to take up the invitation. After a few taut seconds, he pulled back. She saw the scowl on the other woman's face.

He isn't interested.

Maddy experienced a surge of bone-deep satisfaction. Which was so stupid, she didn't even have the words. But there it was.

She wanted Max for herself.

They were talking now, the woman gesturing toward the bar, signaling she wanted a drink. He nodded and followed her as she fought her way off the dance floor.

The music slid from one song to the next, this one a throbbing, driving salsa. She didn't stop to think. She pushed her way forward and intercepted Max before he disappeared into the crowd near the bar.

She met his eyes, smiled and hooked her finger through one of his. *Just one dance,* she promised herself as she led him back into the thick of things.

He pulled her into his arms the moment they found a spare inch of space. His hips started to move, and she matched his rhythm instantly, easily. One of his hands rested on her hip, the other held her hand, pulling her close. He moved effortlessly, confidently. A sharp, fierce joy hit her. She'd forgotten how good it felt to dance with him.

They danced a salsa, then segued into a rumba. The club was a whirl of lights as Max spun her in his arms. Then the music changed again, switching to a sultry, sexy tango. He pulled her closer again, his hips finding hers, his hand occupying the small of her back.

Locked hip to hip, they strutted across the dance floor. His shirt was damp beneath her hands, clinging to his back. Sweat dripped between her breasts and ran down the column of her spine. Once, twice, three times his thigh inserted itself between hers. Her hand slid from his shoulder to trace his back, then the taut muscles of his arm. His skimmed the top of her backside, his long fingers burning her through her dress. Her breasts tightened, the damp silk of her bodice rasping against her sensually as their bodies moved in unison.

She eyed the column of his throat, watching the pulse that throbbed there. She wanted to press her mouth to his skin. She wanted to taste the salt on his skin and feel the throb of his blood racing through his veins. She wanted to rub herself against him, measure him with her hands and discover if he really was as big and hot and hard as she imagined he would be.

Slowly she lifted her face to his. They locked eyes. Their steps slowed. She didn't stop to wonder if what she was about to do was smart or wise. And she certainly didn't think about tomorrow. She stood on her tiptoes, palmed the back of his neck. Then she kissed him, her tongue tracing the fullness of his bottom lip before sliding into his mouth.

He tasted of brandy and coffee and heat. His tongue met hers, danced with it, stroked it. He pulled her closer. She felt the unmistakable ridge of his erection pressing against her belly. A shiver of need raced through her as she rubbed herself against him.

Max said something in French and his hand swept from her shoulder down to her breast. She arched herself into his palm, her hands gliding over his back to find his butt.

The sudden jostle of another couple backing into them broke their kiss. For a long moment they stared at each other, breathless with need.

Maddy glanced over her shoulder, saw an exit sign. She stepped away from him, linking her fingers with his.

"Come with me," she said.

And she led him outside.

5

THEY EXITED into a small, cobblestone courtyard. A single light illuminated the far corner. She tugged Max into the shadows and pressed herself against him, desperate to finish what they'd started.

He didn't need to be asked twice. His hands cradled her head, his fingers delving into her hair. She heard the faint clatter of hairpins falling to the ground as he kissed her, his tongue sweeping into her mouth. Her hair fell over her shoulders, and he grabbed two fistfuls of it and used it to haul her head back and deepen their kiss.

He pressed closer and she could feel his hard-on throbbing against her stomach. Her whole body was shaking with need. She clutched at his shoulders, digging her fingers into the muscles of his back.

He released her head, one hand shifting to cover her breast, the other to cup her backside. She forgot to breathe as his thumb brushed over her nipple through her dress. She moaned, and he used his grip on her butt to hold her as he ground himself against her. Wet heat throbbed between her thighs, beating out a demanding tattoo.

"Maddy," he whispered, his French accent very pronounced.

He nudged one strap then the other off her shoulders. She felt the coolness of the night air on her bare breasts as he pushed her bodice down. And then he was touching her, cupping her, shaping her, his thumb brushing over and over first one nipple then the other.

She gasped, so turned on she could barely stand. She pulled Max's shirt from his jeans and fumbled for his belt. His hand swept under her skirt. She sucked hard on his bottom lip and slid his zipper down.

Her hand found the hot, hardened length of him just as his closed over the fullness of her butt cheek. He squeezed her once, then slid his hand lower, fingers delving between her legs. Her hand closed convulsively around his thick shaft as his fingers brushed the damp satin of her panties.

"So wet," he whispered roughly.

Then suddenly she was against the wall. Her heart leaped with excitement as Max fisted his hand in the elastic of her panties and pulled. They gave easily and he hitched one of her knees over his hip before both hands found her bare backside. He lifted her and she guided his hardness to her entrance with a shaking, desperate hand even as she locked her ankles together around his waist.

She gasped as he plunged inside her to the hilt. It was almost painful he was so big, but as soon as he began to move, pleasure vibrated through her body in overwhelming waves.

"So good," she murmured, throwing her head back. "So good."

He tightened his grip and began to pump into her in earnest. The slick length of him sliding in and out of her, the granite hardness of his body straining toward hers, the demanding passion of his kisses—she couldn't get enough of him. Then he lowered his head and sucked a nipple into his mouth. His tongue teased, taunted. She dug her fingers into his shoulders and offered him everything she had.

Tension spiraled tight inside her. Sensation rippled through her body. It was all so good. Any second now she would find what her body was chasing. Closing her eyes, she gave herself over to the madness.

SHE WAS INCREDIBLE. So tight and hot and wet. Each thrust into her body, each taste of her sweet nipples, each moan that eased from her throat pushed him nearer to the edge. She was everything he'd ever imagined and more. So soft, her skin so silken, the muscles beneath so sleek and strong.

He couldn't get enough. She felt so good, so right. He wanted to stay inside her forever, but he also wanted to lose himself, to make her lose herself.

He switched his attention from her left breast to her right. Her nipple was already sitting up, begging for his attention. She was the sexiest woman in the world.

He pulled her nipple into his mouth, sucked on it hard. She started to pant. He soothed his tongue over her, then bit her gently. She gasped and writhed. She was close. He could feel her tightening around him. He stepped up the pace, plunging in and out of her, holding on, holding on, no matter how tight and wet she felt, no matter how badly he wanted to find his own climax.

She started to shudder. Her head fell back on her neck. He switched focus to her other breast, sucked hard on her nipple, laving it all the while with his tongue. Her whole body tensed, her spine arching, her hips pushing toward him. Then she was pulsating around him, her inner muscles throbbing.

He gave up the fight to hang on. She was too much. Too hot, too slick and needy and tight. He groaned as his climax roared through him. He nestled his face into her neck, inhaling the scent of her as pleasure washed through his body.

Maddy. So beautiful. So sexy. His at last.

He wanted it to last forever, but his thighs and arms were burning with the effort of supporting both their weights. He withdrew from her reluctantly. She unlocked her ankles and he lowered her to the ground. The moment he stepped away from her, the coldness hit him.

He couldn't see her face clearly in the darkness. She pulled up the bodice of her dress. Then she ducked down and he realized she was collecting her underwear.

Right.

The sweat from the dance floor and their frantic coupling was turning to ice on his back and chest.

"It's cold," he said.

"Yes." She wrapped her arms around her torso. He still couldn't see her face.

"Better get inside."

They turned toward the door. She led the way, dragging the heavy fire door open. The heat and noise of the nightclub hit them like a wall as they stepped inside. Maddy stopped in her tracks, looking lost and overwhelmed.

"Come on," he said, taking her hand.

He pushed through the crowd, towing her behind him. It wasn't until he was holding her coat for her in the cloakroom that he saw the marks on her back.

Red welts, abrasions from where he'd pushed her against the wall.

He swore under his breath as Maddy buttoned her coat to the collar and began to wind her new scarf around her neck.

He'd hurt her. He'd been so wild to get inside her, he hadn't thought of anything else.

They were silent as they stepped into the street. He watched his breath mist in the cool night air. He didn't know where to start.

"Are you okay?" he asked.

She hunched into her coat.

"Can we do this at home? Please?"

He eyed her for a beat. She turned away and started walking. He caught up with her in two strides. The streets were empty and silent as they made their way through the maze of Le Marais to his loft.

Their footsteps sounded loud on the wooden floor as they entered. He stopped in the living area. Maddy hovered nearby, not quite meeting his eye.

"Did I hurt you?" he asked.

"I'm fine."

"At least let me look at your back."

"I told you, I'm fine."

"Then let me see it."

She stared at him, on the verge of protest.

"If I hurt you, I want to know about it," he said roughly.

"You didn't hurt me, Max," she said. But she shrugged out of her coat and offered him her back. "It's nothing, see?"

He stared at the raised, red marks on her pale skin. In good light, he could see they were more irritation than abrasion. He lifted his gaze to the long, slender column of her neck, bowed before him. There were so many things he wanted to say.

"Maddy, what just happened—" He broke off as she pulled away from him.

"I can't do this right now, Max. I'm sorry."

Without looking at him, she strode for the bathroom. He stared at the door as she closed it between them. After a few long seconds, the shower came on.

He closed his eyes.

Great. She was washing him off her skin. Couldn't wait to do so, in fact.

In all the years that he'd fantasized about having sex with Maddy, not once had he imagined what would happen afterward.

Not this, that was for sure.

MADDY SAT on the closed toilet lid, her head in her hands. Steam from the shower filled the room. She'd turned the water on the moment she entered, hoping the sound would convince Max she was taking what had happened between them in her stride.

She'd screwed up. Badly. She'd seen something she'd wanted, and she'd reached out for it like a greedy child. And now she had to face the consequences.

"Idiot, idiot, idiot," she said under her breath.

She'd seen the questions in Max's eyes. He wanted to know why she'd kissed him. Why she'd rubbed herself against him and pushed herself into his hands and led him outside.

He kissed you back. He wasn't exactly resisting.

She groaned, pressing her fingertips against her closed eyelids until she saw stars.

Of course Max had kissed her back. She'd practically ravished him, climbing all over him, grinding herself against him. He would have had to pry her off with a crowbar and a bucket of water she'd been so turned on and desperate for him.

Her stomach was churning. She swallowed, the sound loud in the small space.

She couldn't take back any of it—the kiss, the trip outside to the courtyard, those hot, hard, fast minutes when nothing else had mattered. Worse, even at the height of her regret and shame and remorse, she wasn't sure she would, even if she could. Those few breathless moments with Max would stay with her forever. She'd never been so wild for a man before.

And yet Max was her friend. She loved him with all her heart for his generosity of spirit and his easy sense of humor and his strength and cleverness. She didn't want to mess up what she had with him. She absolutely did not want to hurt him or make him angry or disappoint him. And in her experience, sex came hand in hand with all of the above.

So why had she risked everything by crossing the line with him?

The bathroom was so thick with steam her dress was damp and her hair heavy with moisture. She stood and used her hand to clean condensation from the mirror. The face staring back at her was tight with confusion and guilt.

She pulled off her dress, letting it drop to the floor. She stepped under the shower and thrust her head beneath it, lifting her face into the flow. For long seconds she let the water sluice over her. Then she reached for the soap and began to wash her body. Her breasts tightened as she smoothed the bar of soap across them and she remembered Max's touch on her skin. She washed the sticky warmth of their mutual desire from between her thighs and she remembered his fingers gliding inside her. She bit her lip, torn between desire and regret.

She shut off the water and wrapped herself in her towel.

The apartment was dark and silent when she exited the bathroom. Max had gone to bed.

Her shoulders relaxed a notch. She made her way to her bed and found Max's old T-shirt beneath her pillow. She tugged it on, then crawled beneath the covers and closed her eyes.

Her body was as stiff as a board, and her back had begun to sting.

The scent of Max rose from his T-shirt to envelop her, just as it had last night and the night before. She pressed her face into the pillow. Tomorrow she would buy a pair of pajamas and stop surrounding herself with Max.

God, tomorrow.

She tried to imagine what might happen, what Max might say in the cold light of day, what she could say to make everything right between them, but she knew there was no easy solution.

They'd crossed the line. More correctly, she'd crossed the line and dragged Max with her. And tomorrow, she was going to have to pay the piper.

She thought of all the lovers she'd lost over the years.

I don't want to lose you, too, Max.

But it was possible she already had.

MAX WOKE EARLY. For a second he stared blankly at the wall beside his bed. Then memory returned in a hot, sticky rush.

Maddy against the wall, thrusting her hips toward his. Maddy's breasts pouting in his hands. Maddy whispering her pleasure in his ear.

Then the aftermath: her injured back; the walk home; the way she'd disappeared into the shower.

He had a flash of the stunned, bewildered look she'd had on her face when they stepped back into the nightclub. At least he'd had ten years of knowing he desired her. What had happened last night seemed to have taken Maddy completely off guard.

And yet…

It had happened. She'd wanted him. She'd invited him to dance with her, and she'd teased him with every move she made. Then she'd kissed him. And led him outside.

She'd wanted him. That much was a reality, even if he'd taken over from there, slamming her against the wall and losing it a little as he pounded himself into her.

He ran his hands over and over the short bristle of his hair, staring at the ceiling. Then he rolled out of bed. He descended the stairs quietly, reluctant to wake Maddy before he was ready to face her.

Given what had happened, there was something he needed to take care of this morning. Something he should have done yesterday, perhaps even the day before.

After a quick shower, he dressed and slipped outside to make a few phone calls without disturbing her. He paused near her bed when he reentered the apartment, his cheeks tingling from the cold outside. Her back was to him, her hair tangled on the pillow.

He could still feel the silk of it sliding through his fingers last night.

He forced himself to keep walking. In the kitchen, he quietly prepared breakfast for one.

He was standing at the table reading the newspaper when he heard her stir. He looked over as she sat up, pushing her hair off her face. She looked flushed and soft. Very sexy and kissable. He quickly returned his attention to the newspaper.

He flicked the page over and concentrated on a story about student protests at the Sorbonne and didn't allow himself to look up again until he heard the scuff of her footsteps. She stopped a few feet away and eyed him uncertainly.

Her face was pale, tense. They stared at each other for a long, drawn-out beat. Then Maddy made an inarticulate sound and crossed the distance between them. He froze as her arms slid around him and her body pressed against his. She held him tightly, her cheek resting on his chest. After a fraction of a second's hesitation he returned her embrace.

"I'm so sorry," she said. "I should never have kissed you like that last night."

Her words were muffled, she was holding him so tightly.

"I don't even know why it happened. You mean too much for me to screw up our relationship with sex. We've been friends for so long, and I value you so much. You're one of the few people I can rely on the in the world and I don't want it to change things between us."

He could hear the tears in her voice. Her body was trembling with emotion. He hated seeing her so upset.

"It's okay, Maddy." He lifted a hand to smooth her hair.

She lifted her face to look at him. Her eyes were shiny with unshed tears.

"I don't want to lose you, Max."

"You haven't. It was one night."

"I don't even know why it happened," she said again.

He squeezed the nape of her neck, then eased out of her embrace.

"You're freaking out over your career, under pressure. And

I've got some shit going on, too. We were just letting off steam," he said.

It was the rational, sensible take on what had happened. A version of events that gave them both a get-out-of-jail-free card.

She studied his face, her brow furrowed. Whatever she saw there seemed to reassure her, because her frown slowly faded.

"Thank you," she said. The tears were back then, and she blinked rapidly.

"We were both there, Maddy. Last time I looked, it still took two to do what we did," he said. "Stop blaming yourself."

"When you've ruined as many relationships as I have, it's hard not to. I mean, I'm kind of the common factor."

She offered him a self-aware half smile.

He needed something to do with his hands, something to distract him from how vulnerable and sexy and appealing she looked, standing there wearing his T-shirt, apologizing for having had sex with him last night.

"You want a coffee?"

"No, thanks."

She sat at the table while he remained standing. He poured himself a coffee and added milk. She reached for the sugar bowl and began fiddling with it, twisting it around and around on the table. When she spoke, he saw there was color in her cheeks.

"There's something else I wanted you to know, too," she said in a rush. "I'm on the pill. And I always use condoms, so you don't need to worry about anything. Just in case you were worried, I mean."

He stared at her. Protection had been about the furthest thing from his mind last night. Score another point for Team Stupid.

"Same goes," he said, his voice coming out a little gruff. "I'm always careful."

She nodded, twisting the sugar bowl around a few more

times. "Good. That's that settled. Now we never have to talk about it again." She smiled to show she was joking, then stood. "I'd better get dressed, I guess."

He watched her walk away, noting the straight column of her spine, the elegant arch of her neck, the grace of her movements.

The bathroom door closed between them and he let out the breath he'd been holding. Then he put down his coffee cup, braced his hands on the table in front of him and let his head drop.

He swore under his breath in French and English. For good measure, he threw in a couple of Spanish curses he'd picked up over the years.

He was an idiot, ten times over. All the bullshit he'd fed himself about only being physically attracted to Maddy. All the justifications for his need for her, his desire to protect her and make her happy and ease her pain.

He loved her. Had probably never stopped loving her.

And she only saw him as a friend. Same old, same old.

Shit.

IT'S GOING TO BE ALL RIGHT.

Her eyes felt gritty, and her head ached, but it was going to be all right. Max had let her off the hook. Or maybe he'd let them both off the hook. Whatever. They'd survived the morning after, their friendship intact.

She wasn't stupid—she knew it would be weird between them for a day or two. But they'd get over it. If it killed her, they'd get over it. She'd made a stupid, impulsive, indulgent mistake, and she was determined to put things back the way they should be.

She brushed her hair and dressed in the slim-fit jeans and grass-green turtleneck sweater she'd bought the previous day. She brushed her teeth, took one last look at her pale reflection, then reached for the door.

"Max, you've officially ruined me. I can't stop thinking about bread," she said.

She stopped in her tracks. Max had a visitor. She was tall and slim with wavy shoulder-length auburn hair and very fair skin, and she was standing in the kitchen having coffee with Max. Maddy guessed she was about twenty-two, maybe a little younger. Her gaze dropped to the other woman's feet, noting the distinctive, giveaway turnout of her toes.

A dancer. Maddy's stomach dipped. She could think of only one reason why another dancer would be standing in Max's kitchen.

"Maddy, come and meet Yvette. She's a friend of Gabriella's. She's agreed to model for me," Max said.

For a moment she couldn't breathe. Max had replaced her. And not in the last ten minutes, either—he wouldn't have been able to conjure another dancer out of thin air just like that. While she'd been fretting and agonizing over what last night meant to their friendship, Max had been quietly, coolly working to replace her.

The other woman was wide-eyed as she stared at Maddy.

"Ms. Green, I am very excited to be meeting you. I could not believe it when Max said you were staying with him. I saw you dance in Berlin two years ago. Your Juliet was so wonderful… I'm sorry, I do not have the words," Yvette said in heavily accented English.

"Thank you. That's very kind," Maddy said. She even managed a smile.

"Not kind at all. Simply the truth," Yvette said.

Maddy could feel Max watching her.

"This way you'll have more time to do your strength training and work on your recovery," he said.

Yvette looked concerned, her gaze darting between the two of them.

"You have an injury, Ms. Green? Not a serious one, I am hoping?" she asked.

"Nothing to worry about," Maddy said. She wasn't about to discuss her knee with the other woman. She already felt exposed enough as it was.

"That is a relief. The world of ballet cannot afford to lose you yet," Yvette said earnestly.

Maddy smiled again, even though her face felt tense.

Max turned to Yvette. "The only thing we have left to discuss is your start date," he said.

Maddy crossed to her bed, sitting on the edge to pull on her socks and boots. Her hands were shaking. She took a deep breath to steady herself.

"I am not working, so it is up to you," Yvette said.

"Well, the sooner the better for me."

Maddy grit her teeth. She wanted to pick up her boot and throw it across the room at him.

"I could come tomorrow. Or I have my dance bag in the car right now if you want to start this morning…?" Yvette offered.

"Yeah? That'd be great. Means I won't be off my schedule," Max said.

Maddy allowed herself one glance toward the kitchen. Yvette was leaning against the table, hands braced behind her, long legs stretched out in front of her. Unable to help herself, Maddy eyed the other woman's chest. She was a good cup size larger than Maddy. A lot younger, too. And she had the kind of legs men dreamed of getting tangled in.

Because she was a glutton for punishment, Maddy switched her attention to Max.

He had his hip cocked against the kitchen counter, one hand tucked into the front pocket of his jeans. His jaw was shadowed with stubble and his shoulders looked ridiculously wide in a black fine-knit sweater. There were no prizes for guessing why

Yvette was so keen to be accommodating. Max was sex personified standing there in his bare feet and faded jeans.

"I shall go get my things from my car," Yvette said brightly.

She headed for the door. She was very tall, Maddy decided as she watched the other woman walk away. Too tall for classical ballet. Maddy felt a small dart of satisfaction. On one front, at least, she had the other woman beat.

Can you hear yourself? Yvette is not *your competition. She will never be the competition because Max is your friend—and that's all he is.*

Still, jealousy burned in her belly, hot and fierce. *She* was supposed to be the one modeling for Max, not some redheaded goddess. Even though continuing to do so would have been strange and awkward and probably very, very unwise after what had happened last night, Maddy hated the thought that he would now be spending hours staring at Yvette's no doubt nubile body.

She stared blindly at her feet, her whole body knotted with tension.

She was officially nuts. One minute she was almost crying with relief that she and Max had managed to recover from last night's transgression, the next she was seething with resentment over another woman.

"Maddy."

She looked up to find Max standing in front of her, his gray eyes watchful.

"I was going to tell you when you got out of the shower, but Yvette arrived earlier than I expected," he said.

"Sure," she said. She even managed a casual shrug. "I understand."

"I know how important your career is to you. The last thing I want is to hold you back by using up all your spare time," he said.

The clatter of Yvette reentering the apartment claimed his attention.

"You can change in the bathroom. There's a robe you can use, if you'd like," he offered, moving away.

Maddy's hands clenched around the bed frame. Now he was offering Yvette his robe—the same robe Maddy had been wearing only yesterday.

She had a sudden vision of how the next few hours would play out—Max and Yvette locked in intense artistic communion as he sketched her naked body, with Maddy lurking on the fringes of the apartment like a female Quasimodo minus a bell tower.

She shot to her feet.

"I'm going out," she said.

Both Yvette and Max looked a little nonplussed by her sudden announcement.

"I need pajamas," she explained. She started winding her scarf around her neck.

"Okay. Don't forget to take the spare key. I might not be around later," Max said.

She nodded, but he was already turning away to organize his supplies. Probably eager to get to the part where he got to stare at Yvette's naked body for hours on end.

She knew she was being unfair, even irrational, but right at this minute her rational self seemed to have checked out of Hotel Maddy.

She had to get out of here before she did or said something stupid—such as going over and kissing Max right in front of the other woman, so Yvette knew to keep her distance.

Nuts. Absolutely crackers.

She grabbed her coat and purse and strode for the door.

"It was lovely meeting you, Ms. Green. An honor," Yvette called after her.

Maddy glanced over her shoulder. Yvette was holding Max's

robe, the deep red silk flowing from her hands, her beautiful face smiling and hopeful.

"You, too," Maddy said, even though it nearly killed her. After all, it wasn't Yvette's fault she was beautiful and limber and sexy. Well, mostly.

Maddy stood in the street and stuffed her hands deep into her pockets, tucking her chin into the folds of her scarf. She had a powerful urge to kick something. Preferably herself.

What was she doing? Sleeping with Max, getting jealous over other women, obsessing over him. He. Was. Her. Friend. When was her thick subconscious going to get the message?

She started up the street, but she hadn't walked more than ten paces before Max called out her name.

Her stomach did an absurd little flip. She swiveled on her heel, her gaze flying to where he stood on the doorstep, the cordless phone in hand.

"My sister wants to know if we'd like to come to dinner tonight," he said.

Maddy stared at him for a long beat, but he didn't say anything else.

"That would be nice," she said.

"Okay. Have fun." He threw her a casual wave before ducking back into the apartment. Maddy stared at the closed door for a long beat.

What had she expected him to say? *Maddy, I'm sorry. The only reason I replaced you is because I can't bear looking at you and not touching you, especially after last night? You're so sexy, I don't know why I never noticed before, you're driving me crazy.*

She made a disgusted sound at her own idiocy. The last thing she wanted was Max making any such declaration because that would mean he cared for her, that he wanted things from her that she didn't have to give. It would be a disaster in the making, the beginning of the end.

Confused, angry, determined, Maddy walked away.

MAX SHIFTED the wine bottle from one hand to the other and wiped his damp palm on the thigh of his jeans. He'd like to blame his clammy hands on condensation on the bottle, but the truth was he was nervous about the night ahead.

He could hear Maddy climbing the stairs to his sister's apartment behind him, the heels of her boots striking the marble steps sharply.

Despite the fact that he and Maddy had lived together for nearly two years, she'd never met his sister. He'd gone to great pains to ensure that was the case—Charlotte was nothing if not perceptive. The last thing he'd wanted or needed was her guessing how he felt about his housemate.

Some things never changed, it seemed.

"I forgot to ask, how did things go with Yvette today?" Maddy asked as she drew alongside him on the landing.

He knocked on his sister's door.

"It was good. Fine. She was a little nervous, but we'll get there."

She wasn't Maddy. She didn't have Maddy's grace or style. But he also didn't feel the stir of arousal every time he looked at her. Yvette was an attractive woman—but she was not the woman he wanted. Consequently, the morning had gone blessedly smoothly. And there had definitely been no need for cold showers afterward.

"Good. I'm glad it worked out."

Maddy smoothed her scarf and tucked a strand of hair behind her ear. She looked nervous, he realized.

"You know, I've always wanted to meet your sister," she said. "Does she look much like you?"

"She has dark hair. But she's a lot prettier."

"I doubt that," she said. Then she bit her lip and looked away.

The door swung open and warm air rich with savory cooking smells swept out to greet them.

"Sorry. I was just taking the soufflés out of the oven. Come in," Charlotte said.

They followed her inside and Charlotte gave Maddy a brief but thorough head to toe as they shrugged out of their coats.

"Charlotte," she said, thrusting out a hand. "Max says you're a dancer, Maddy. From Australia."

"That's right," Maddy said, shaking hands. "Max and I used to live with each other back in the day."

His sister's gaze swiveled around to impale him.

"Max didn't mention that," Charlotte said.

Now Maddy was watching him.

"Didn't you say you just took the soufflés out of the oven?" he asked.

"Merde!" Charlotte said. She took off down the hallway, her high heels skidding on the floorboards.

Max gestured for Maddy to follow his sister into the kitchen.

Half-chopped vegetables were lined up on the kitchen table on a large cutting board, while pots steamed away on the stovetop. Charlotte stood at the counter, frowning at a tray holding three ceramic ramekins.

"The soufflés sank a little," she said critically. "I'm really not happy with this new oven."

He inspected the ramekins. "I'm sure they'll taste exactly the same," he said. His sister prided herself on her cooking and he knew she would give herself a hard time for any small failure.

Charlotte rolled her eyes.

"No, they won't. Being light and fluffy is the whole point of a soufflé. Don't you think, Maddy?"

Charlotte turned to her guest, her interested gaze once again scanning Maddy from head to toe. The first opportunity he got, he was going to tell his sister to cut it out. Maddy was not his girlfriend, and she wasn't there to be cross-examined by his nearest and dearest. Far from it.

"I suppose. Although, to be honest, I'm the last person you should ask about food. As Max will tell you, I can't cook worth a damn," Maddy said.

"Really? Max isn't exactly great, either. Someone will have to learn to cook," Charlotte said meaningfully.

Maddy looked confused for a beat, then her gaze darted to him questioningly.

"Maddy is only staying with me for a week or two," he said.

"Uh-huh." Charlotte looked as though she didn't believe him.

"She has her career to get back to as prima ballerina with the Sydney Dance Company," he clarified.

"Oh." This time Charlotte looked convinced, if disappointed. He could almost see her thoughts and suppositions realigning themselves. God knew what she was going to ask next. He shot Maddy an apologetic look and she smiled faintly.

"So, how are you finding Max's new apartment, Maddy?"

"Um, good. I mean, I didn't see his old one, so I can't compare, obviously. But it's very nice. Lots of space," Maddy said.

"I wouldn't know," Charlotte said, nudging Max in the ribs with her elbow. "My brother hasn't invited me yet. How long has it been now, Max?"

"A few weeks," he said repressively.

Charlotte raised an eyebrow and moved to the cutting board.

"Hmmm. Did you look at those course brochures I gave you the other night?" she asked as she started slicing an onion.

Max frowned for a moment, trying to work out what she was referring to. Then he remembered her thrusting them into his hands as he was on his way out the door with the camp bed.

Brochures for degrees in psychology, teaching and occupational therapy, if he remembered correctly. He'd left them all behind in the taxi.

"Haven't had a chance," he said.

Charlotte had been trying to push him into a new career for a while now. He would have to tell her about his artistic ambitions soon, even if only to get her off his back.

"Maybe you can convince him to start thinking about the future, Maddy. I know he deserves a break after all those years of caring for *Père,* but he can't float around forever, wasting his life."

He felt Maddy bristle beside him and had a sudden premonition that things were about to go horribly wrong.

"I'd hardly call Max's art floating around or wasting his life," Maddy said stiffly. "He's incredibly talented and the art world is going to fall on its ass in surprise when he has his first show."

Charlotte's knife froze above an onion.

"Max's art? Sorry?"

Charlotte's gaze shifted between him and Maddy then back again.

Damn. He should have seen this coming the moment his sister issued her invitation. Maddy had been modeling for him, after all. It was only natural that she'd mention it.

"I'm working on some pieces. Sculpture," he explained. "Larger scale, like that figure I did last year."

"And you're going to have a show?" Charlotte asked. The knife still hovered, the point wavering a little in her hand.

"Yes. Hopefully. If I can get some interest," he said.

"I see." Charlotte sent the knife down into the onion with a thunk.

She was hurt. She had every right to be. They were close, she shared all aspects of her life with him. And he'd deliberately shut her out of his because he'd been cautious about openly acknowledging his ambitions.

"I was going to tell you. I just wanted to have more to show you before I did," he said.

Maddy was looking distinctly uncomfortable. "I'm really sorry," she said. "I didn't realize…"

"It's not your fault," Charlotte said, her voice brittle.

"I'm sorry," he said. "I just… I guess I wasn't sure if I could pull it off."

It was the truth, but he could see honesty wasn't going to get him anywhere with Charlotte tonight.

She crossed to the stove and began shoveling chopped vegetables into a pot.

"I understand," she said coolly.

But she didn't, and he knew he had some heavy spadework ahead to soothe her ruffled feathers.

Dinner was tense. Charlotte apologized too many times for the soufflés, then made stiff, overly polite conversation with Maddy throughout the main course.

She resented Maddy for knowing more about his life than she did, he guessed. The age-old instinct to shoot the messenger. He was doing his best to ease the tension when a high-pitched scream echoed through the apartment.

"Eloise," Charlotte said, standing abruptly. "She's been having nightmares lately."

She'd barely taken two steps before Eloise hurtled into the room, her mouth open in another earsplitting scream. Her dark hair, cut in a shorter version of Charlotte's bob, was tangled and matted around her sweaty, tear-streaked face. Her nightgown was damp around her middle, clinging to her small frame. He guessed she'd wet the bed.

"It's okay, sweetie. Mama is here," Charlotte soothed in French, getting down on her knees to scoop Eloise into her arms.

Eloise was so distressed she fought against her mother's embrace, her body bowing backward, her arms and legs thrashing around.

His three-year-old niece had been diagnosed with autism eighteen months ago, and Charlotte fought a constant battle to connect with her youngest child. Early intervention, expensive private therapies and the best nutrition money could buy were all strategies she and Richard were employing in an attempt to improve Eloise's condition, but they could only achieve so much.

"Let her go, Charlotte," he urged his sister quietly. It was clear Eloise could not accept comfort right now, and she would only hurt herself and Charlotte in her distress.

Charlotte reluctantly released her grip and Eloise pushed herself away so violently she staggered. Off balance, she fell onto her back and began to pound the carpet with her heels and fists, screaming all the while at a heartbreaking, stomach-clenching pitch.

He'd seen Eloise like this before, a victim to the overwhelming fear and anxiety that dogged her world, but it never failed to make him feel powerless and pointless.

"Do you have anything you can give her? Something to help calm her down?" he asked.

"She won't keep it down in this condition," Charlotte said wearily.

He put his hand on her shoulder. Watching a loved one in pain was tough enough, but knowing you couldn't even convey your sympathy, love and comfort to them made the burden doubly heavy.

He caught sight of movement out of the corners of his eyes and turned to see that Maddy was quietly clearing the table.

He hadn't told her about Eloise. He'd known the children would be in bed by the time they arrived for dinner, and his sister could be intensely private and prickly about discussing her daughter's condition. More than anything, she hated for Eloise to be an object of pity.

"Don't bother with that," Charlotte said.

Maddy hesitated, then put the plates down.

"Eloise is autistic," he explained quietly.

Maddy nodded. "Is she… Is there anything I can do?" she asked.

"No. She'll have to wear herself out. Fortunately, her body can't sustain such a high level of anxiety for long," he said.

As he spoke, Eloise's screaming dropped in pitch and became a low, despairing moan. She started to rock from side to side, her arms wrapped around her torso.

Charlotte pressed a hand to her mouth and blinked furiously.

"I hate it when she's like this. Out of everything it's the thing I hate the most," she said, her voice low and vehement.

Max pulled his house keys from his pocket and handed them to Maddy.

"Why don't you go on home?" he suggested. "I'll call you a taxi."

"No! There must be something I can do to help," she said.

"If there was, I would be doing it," Charlotte snapped.

Max made eye contact with Maddy. She nodded her understanding of his silent message.

"Okay. I'll go, if that's what you think is best," she said quietly. She took the keys from him, but hesitated, clearly uncertain about whether she should thank her hostess before leaving.

Charlotte didn't lift her gaze from Eloise's rocking form and Maddy turned away. He followed her to the door and helped her on with her coat.

"I'm sorry," he said when she faced him. "Charlotte's under a lot of pressure."

Maddy held up a hand. "Don't. I'm fine. I completely understand."

In the other room, Eloise started screaming again.

"Go," she said, urging him back. "I'll see you at the apartment."

She squeezed his arm, then she was heading down the stairs, her footsteps echoing hollowly in the stairwell.

Charlotte was holding Eloise in her lap when he returned to the living room.

"I suppose we shocked Little Miss Prima Donna. Not quite what she's used to."

"Charlotte."

"Don't think I don't know what she was thinking. That I'm a terrible mother or I can't cope or—" Charlotte's voice broke and she tightened her grip on her daughter.

"Will she take some hot milk now?" he asked.

He wasn't about to defend Maddy to his sister. They both knew that Charlotte wasn't angry with Maddy. It was simply much harder to rail at life in quite the same way.

"Maybe. We can try."

By the time he'd returned with warm milk, Eloise had quietened. Half an hour later, Charlotte carried her to her room to tuck her into bed. Eloise was limp with exhaustion by then, her eyes puffy from crying.

Max cleaned up the kitchen while Charlotte sat by Eloise's bedside, waiting for her to fall asleep. He was wiping down the counters when Charlotte spoke from the doorway.

"Do you still love her?"

He stilled.

"You think I didn't notice, all those years ago? The way you talked about her, then carefully tried to make it sound as though you weren't, in case I noticed? You think I didn't understand that you were trying to stop me from meeting her?" Charlotte said.

"Stop it, Charlotte. Maddy is not the one you're mad at, and you know it," he said.

His words came out more firmly than he'd intended and Charlotte shut her jaw with a click and stared at him as though he'd slapped her. He crossed the room to draw her into his arms. Even though she remained stiff and angry, he kissed her forehead.

"I'm sorry for not telling you about my plans," he said quietly, trying to find the right words. "It wasn't because I don't care about what you think. I guess I just wasn't sure if I was doing the right thing."

Some of the fight went out of her.

"You know I love your bronzes. How could you think I would be anything but supportive?"

He shrugged. "It's not exactly a reliable career choice."

"So? I want you to be happy. That's all I've ever wanted for you."

He kissed her forehead again.

"Can I come around to your apartment now that the big secret is out?"

"Of course. I wasn't deliberately keeping you away, Charlotte," he said.

She pulled away from his embrace and gave him a knowing, sisterly look.

He shrugged. "Okay, maybe I was, a little."

"You didn't have any trouble telling Maddy, showing Maddy."

"She turned up on my doorstep. It was kind of hard to avoid it."

"That's not why you told her. You love her."

This time he didn't bother to deny it.

"She's very beautiful," Charlotte said.

He just raised an eyebrow. "We're friends. Nothing more."

"Prove it to me. Go out with one my friends. Luisa has been waiting to meet you for months."

"No." The answer was on his lips before he could even think about it.

There was only one woman he wanted. More fool him.

Charlotte shook her head. "I hope you know what you're doing, Max."

He already knew that he didn't. He'd let Maddy back into his life in every conceivable way—into his home, his art, his bed, his heart. And, as always, she had no idea how profound an impact she'd had on him.

For a brief moment he regretted finding her on his doorstep four nights ago. Then he remembered the sweet, searing heat of being inside her. The soft, needy sounds of her desire. The silk of her hair in his hands.

It made him ten different kinds of idiot, but he wouldn't trade that experience for anything in the world.

Which only proved he really was a glutton for punishment.

6

MADDY PULLED ON her new pajamas when she got home and curled up on the couch to wait for Max. She'd hated leaving before him, but it had quickly become clear that it would be easier for both Charlotte and Max if she were gone.

Max's sister didn't like her.

Maddy had had people not like her before—temperamental choreographers, ambitious dancers keen to usurp her position, angry ex-lovers—so it wasn't as though being the object of someone's enmity was new to her. She was surprised by how much Charlotte's reaction hurt.

She'd wanted so much for Max's family to like her. Over the years, she'd often heard him talk about Charlotte. For some reason, they had never run into each other until now. Still, Maddy had always imagined that if ever they did meet, the connection between them would be as effortless and instant as it had been with Max.

Nice idea, shame about the reality check.

Charlotte had started assessing Maddy the moment she stepped over the threshold, and things had gone downhill rapidly when she stepped in to defend Max's fledgling art career. Maddy winced as she recalled the utter surprise and hurt on Charlotte's face when she'd understood her brother had been holding out on her.

Her thoughts shifted to Eloise, Max's niece. Maddy was the first to admit she had next to no experience where children were concerned. But she knew enough to recognize that she had not witnessed a normal, everyday kind of tantrum and that Eloise had special needs. Maddy wondered why Max hadn't mentioned earlier that his niece was autistic. Did he not trust her with the information?

Maddy's stomach tightened as she recalled the high, distressed pitch of the little girl's cries. That Charlotte had been unable to connect with her or comfort her... Maddy could only imagine how the other woman must have felt. How powerless and angry and sad.

A knock at the door pulled her out of her thoughts. She crossed to let Max in.

"Thanks," he said as he stepped across the threshold.

She wrapped her arms around herself and followed him as he moved into the living area. "Did Eloise settle down okay?" she asked.

"Yeah. She's back in bed, dead to the world. Absolutely exhausted."

He peeled off his coat and rolled his shoulders. He looked tired.

"Can I get you a drink? Some cognac? Hot chocolate?" she asked.

He shook his head. "Look, I wanted to explain about Charlotte."

"Max, you don't need to. As I said back at the apartment, I totally understand."

"She's not normally like that. Her husband, Richard, has to travel a lot with his work, so she's alone with the kids most of the time. Lately, it seems to have really been getting her down, but I'm not sure—" He broke off and smiled ruefully. "Sorry. This is probably the last thing you want to talk about after the night you've had."

"Of course I want to talk about it. You're worried about her, aren't you?"

"She's got a lot on her plate. And she never asks for help until she's pushed to the limit."

Maddy sat on the couch, drew her knees up to her chest and rested her chin on them.

"Tell me about Eloise," she asked quietly.

She wanted to know about Max's world, about the people he cared about. More importantly, she wanted to ease the worried crease that had formed above his eyebrows. She wanted him to feel he could share his burdens with her, the way she'd shared hers with him.

He sat opposite her.

"What do you want to know?"

"How old is she? How long have you known she's autistic?"

"She's three. She had the first tests about eighteen months ago, but Charlotte already suspected something was wrong. Eloise was speech delayed, and she hardly ever made eye contact."

"I don't know much about autism," Maddy admitted.

Max explained that there was still a lot of debate about what caused autism, and that patients were diagnosed on a spectrum. Some children grew up to have close to normal lives, while others remained profoundly isolated.

"Where does Eloise fit in?"

"It's too early to judge. She's responding well to early intervention, but there are no guarantees."

"She was so upset," she said.

"Current theory is that most autistic children are profoundly anxious a lot of the time. That's why they respond well to routine—and badly to any break in it."

"Right. That makes sense, I guess."

Max yawned and stretched.

"I'm keeping you up," she said guiltily.

"I probably should turn in," he said, standing. "Yvette's coming around early tomorrow."

Right. Yvette.

"Good night," she said.

He smiled faintly and headed for the bathroom. She watched him walk away.

She fought a sudden urge to race after him and put her arms around him. It seemed wrong that they would be sleeping in separate beds tonight when he was clearly troubled and in need of support. In the old days, if she'd thought he was upset or worried about something, she'd have come up with an excuse to crawl into bed with him.

Things had been a lot less complicated back then.

That's because we hadn't had sex.

It was true, but it was also less than the truth because what was going on between her and Max was about a lot more than just sex.

It was a scary thought, and not one she cared to examine too closely.

Stomach tied in knots, feeling inexplicably lonely, she went to bed.

MAX WOKE TO THE SOUND of humming filtering up from the kitchen below. He rolled out of bed and pulled on a pair of workout pants then headed downstairs. He was shrugging into a T-shirt when he found Maddy slicing a baguette at the kitchen sink. She was showered and dressed and her eyes glowed with suppressed excitement when she greeted him.

"Guess what? Nadine called—finally—and she's recovering from surgery herself."

"That's too bad. Is she all right?"

"A bunion, nothing major," Maddy said. "Guess who her doctor is?"

"Let me see… Someone good? Who she can get you an appointment with?"

She threw the dish towel at him.

"Not just *someone*. Dr. Kooperman. The best of the best."
Maddy pressed her hands together. "I mean, Dr. Rambeau was
great, but Dr. Kooperman! I'm pinching myself. Nadine has a
follow-up appointment with him today, but she's going to ask him
if he will see me instead. Isn't that amazingly generous of her?"

He'd heard of Kooperman. Most dancers had. He was long
established, an early pioneer in dance medicine.

"Fantastic. Great news," he said.

Even though it meant Maddy was one step closer to leaving.

"I know. I can't believe it. Nadine called about an hour ago,
and I've been jumping out of my skin ever since, dying to tell
you. If I had to wait for an appointment the normal way, it
would be months and months before he could see me."

She was so energized it made him realize how subdued she'd
been ever since she'd arrived. For a moment he was afraid for her.
If she didn't get the news she wanted from these specialists…

"I made you breakfast," she said, sliding toasted slices of
baguette toward him.

"What time is your appointment?" he asked as he sat.

"I'm not sure. Nadine needs to check that it's okay with the
doctor before she hands over her appointment time."

She sat opposite him as he spread jam on his toast. Her right
leg jittered up and down nervously, her foot tapping on the floor
so fast it was practically vibrating.

"This could be it, Max. He'll probably want to run some
tests, but if he gives me good news, I can ring Andrew and force
him to reinstate me."

"You won't need to force him, Maddy. You're their star
attraction."

She shrugged a shoulder. "There's always someone waiting
in the wings. You know that. But they'll have to honor my
contract if I get the all clear."

She'd practically packed her bags and boarded the plane

already. He concentrated on his toast, making sure he spread the jam right to the edges. She'd only been back in his life for a few short days but she'd leave a huge hole when she left.

He gritted his teeth. He'd played the missing Maddy game before. He wasn't looking forward to round two. He had a feeling it was going to be even more brutal the second time around. He'd slept with her, after all. He knew exactly what he was missing.

Aware that Yvette was due to arrive at any moment, he finished eating then crossed to his work area to set up his equipment and turn on the extra heater. Maddy began to clean the kitchen, once again humming beneath her breath.

"I was thinking that maybe I could call Charlotte today to thank her for dinner," she said after a while.

He glanced up from his sketch pad.

"Probably not a great idea," he said.

"Oh."

She straightened the salt and pepper shakers on the table.

"Maybe I could buy Eloise a gift, then?"

"To be honest, I think it's probably best to just let Charlotte find her equilibrium."

"She really doesn't like me, does she?"

He considered lying, but they'd both been there last night.

"She doesn't know you. What happened last night was about me not telling her something she felt she had a right to know and Charlotte being stressed. You happened to be standing nearby when the shit hit the fan."

"Hmmm."

The sound of frantic knocking at the front door had his head snapping around.

"Max!"

It was his sister's voice, strident with emotion, and he reached the door in two strides.

"M-Max!" Charlotte stuttered the moment she saw him, her face crumpling. "Marcel has hurt himself at school. They said he fell down some stairs and hit his head and they rushed him straight to hospital."

She was trembling. Max put an arm around her.

"It's all right. Take a deep breath," he said.

He waited until she'd done so before talking again.

"Which hospital?"

"Hôtel Dieu," she said. "I'm going over now, but I can't take Eloise. She'll get too upset, and I need to be there for Marcel."

"I'll take her," he said instantly, guessing that was what she wanted.

Charlotte's eyes filled with tears.

"Thank you! Oh, thank you. I wish Richard was here. I need him. If something happens to Marcel—"

"Nothing will happen to him. Have you called Richard? Is he coming home?" He knew his brother-in-law was at yet another work conference somewhere in Europe.

"Yes. He was due home tonight anyway, but he's trying to catch an earlier flight."

"Good."

Charlotte was on the verge of tears again. Her car keys were jingling in her hands she was shaking so much.

"After last night… It's too much. I can't keep doing this all on my own," she said in a near whisper.

She sounded exhausted and near the end of her tether. He eyed her with concern, not liking the idea of her driving to the hospital in this condition.

He took her keys and went out to collect Eloise from the car, Charlotte hard on his heels.

"I brought some toys for her, and her favorite DVD," Charlotte explained.

Eloise was playing with a brightly colored prism, oblivious

to the drama around her. Thank heaven for small mercies, he thought as he pulled her into his arms while Charlotte grabbed the bag of toys.

"I don't know how long I'll be. I brought her pajamas, in case I have to stay in the hospital overnight." Charlotte's voice cracked and she started crying in earnest.

Max slid his free arm around her and hustled her back into the apartment.

"I'm going to call you a taxi," he said. "You can't drive like this."

"No! I can't wait for a taxi to come. I have to go now. Marcel needs me," Charlotte said, rising hysteria in her voice.

He hesitated, unsure what to do. He hated the idea of her facing whatever waited at the hospital alone, but someone had to look after Eloise.

"Can I help?"

He swung around to see Maddy standing there, determination writ large on her face. They'd been speaking French, but she clearly understood that something was very wrong.

"I can't be in two places at once," he said, articulating his greatest dilemma.

"No," Maddy said with a frown, and he realized he wasn't making sense.

Quickly he explained the situation to her.

"What if I look after Eloise?" Maddy suggested.

"You've got your doctor's appointment," he reminded her.

Maddy shrugged. "I'll call Nadine. I'm sure Dr. Kooperman can fit me in another time. I want to help, Max."

He looked at Charlotte, saw she was battling to pull herself together, swallowing her tears and straightening her shoulders. She would cope, because she had so many times in the past. But he wanted to be there for her if he could.

"If you don't mind, that would be a help," he told Maddy.

"I'll set you up before we go. Charlotte brought Eloise's favorite DVD. She'll watch it as many times as you play it."

Charlotte blew her nose into a tissue and looked set to wade into the discussion.

"This way I can stay with you," he said, forestalling her.

Charlotte opened her mouth, then closed it again. She nodded.

"That would be nice, I think," she said in a strangled voice.

It took him a couple of minutes to get *Milo and Otis* playing and prop Eloise in front of it.

"If she gets hungry, peanut butter sandwiches are her favorite," he said as he led Charlotte toward the door. "I keep a jar in the kitchen."

Maddy nodded with each instruction. Charlotte dug her heels in on the doorstep and turned to add her own instructions.

"She hates loud music, or any loud noises for that matter. There are spare diapers in the bag. And make sure that you do up all her buttons on her pajamas if we're not home until late. She gets upset if her buttons aren't all done up."

"Okay."

"We'll call from the hospital," Max said as he eased his sister from the house.

Maddy nodded an acknowledgment. She looked small but determined as he shut the door.

He knew exactly how much seeing Dr. Kooperman meant to her, yet she'd given up the opportunity without the bat of an eyelid.

If he hadn't loved her already, that one act of generosity alone would have made him a goner.

If Maddy were his, the life they could build together…

But she wasn't.

Grim, dragging his mind back to Marcel and the task at hand, Max started the car and pulled out into traffic.

As Max and Charlotte disappeared out the door, Maddy turned to study Eloise, bundled on the couch and staring at the television.

Despite what Maddy had said to Max, she was nervous. She knew nothing about children. Nada. Zilch. Zero. As for children with special needs... If something went wrong, she'd be absolutely clueless as to how to respond.

Before her imagination could get carried away drafting potential disasters, she took herself firmly in hand. Eloise was perfectly happy. She was watching her DVD, completely absorbed in the adventures of Milo and Otis. And Max was taking his sister to the hospital, offering Charlotte the support she needed.

Maddy's thoughts shifted to Marcel. He was only six, and he'd fallen down stairs. She felt sick just thinking about it.

One eye on Eloise, she picked up her cell and phoned Nadine. Her friend sounded put out when Maddy told her she wouldn't be able to accept her generous offer of her appointment. Nadine explained that she had already called Dr. Kooperman to ask his permission for the exchange and he had agreed to do so—but not before giving Nadine a hard time. Guilt assailing her from all sides, Maddy outlined the situation as best she could but when she hung up she had the distinct feeling she'd lost her chance at an early appointment with one of France's best dance medicine specialists.

It had been a week since her fateful meeting with Andrew. The longest she'd gone without rehearsing in her life. She felt adrift, totally at sea without the familiar anchors of classes, rehearsals, gym sessions, costume fittings, meetings with choreographers and fellow dancers. She felt like an exile. And she hated it. She wanted her life back.

The familiar panicky dizziness hit her, and she forced herself to take big, deep belly breaths.

Eloise shifted on the couch, pulling at the blanket Max had

wrapped around her. Maddy watched her, taking in her smooth brown hair and intent, serious round face. If Max had children one day, they would look like this, she realized. Dark, with his olive skin.

She shook her head, the moment of panic over. Eloise needed her. Max needed her. And she still had Dr. Rambeau lined up for next week. She would get at least one second opinion, even if it wouldn't carry quite the same ring of authority that Dr. Kooperman's would.

She straightened her shoulders and crossed to the couch to sit beside Eloise. The little girl didn't acknowledge her in any way, not even with the flicker of an eyelid. Maddy sat back to watch the movie.

Milo and Otis were escaping from yet another near-death experience when the doorbell rang half an hour later. It was Yvette. Max had forgotten to call her and cancel their session. Maddy apologized on Max's behalf and arranged for Max to call her to reschedule. To her credit, Yvette was all concern and asked Maddy to pass on her best wishes.

Maddy checked her watch as she crossed back to the couch. Why hadn't Max called? Surely if it was good news, he would have rung by now?

She'd just reset the DVD to play for a second time when her cell phone rang.

"How is Marcel?" she asked.

"He has a bad concussion, and a broken arm. They need to operate to set it, so we're going to be a while," Max said.

"Nothing else?" she asked. She remembered a dancer who had tumbled from the stage a few years ago and fractured his skull. "No pressure or anything from the head injury?"

"They've scanned him, and it all looks normal. He's got one hell of a bruise, though. He was damn lucky."

She sagged with relief. "How is Charlotte?"

"Hanging in there. How are you and Eloise doing?"

"*Milo and Otis* still reign supreme, so I guess we're hanging in there, too."

There was a short pause and she could hear Max take a breath.

"I really appreciate you doing this," he said. "You didn't have to."

"You don't need to thank me, Max," she said. "It was the least I could do."

"But you've lost your chance to see Dr. Kooperman," he said.

"I think your niece and nephew are a little more important than my ability to do a pirouette on stage," she said.

There was a profound silence from Max's end of the line for a few beats.

"Well, both Charlotte and I appreciate it," he said. "We'll have to work out some way to make it up to you."

There was a low, warm note in his voice and her hand tightened around the receiver as a half dozen illicit, wrong, hot ideas for how he could do that flitted across her mind.

"I'd better get back to *Milo and Otis,*" she said.

"I'll call later, give you a progress report."

She ended the call and returned to her position on the couch next to Eloise. Once again the little girl didn't acknowledge her presence in any way.

Maddy stared blindly at the television. Her heart was banging against her rib cage as though she'd just danced a solo. Because Max called? Because he'd said nice things to her and made her think about things it was best she never thought about again?

A grinding, clicking noise drew her attention back to the television. The picture was flashing off and on, the image distorted into pixels. She was reaching for the remote control when the machine gave a final mechanical groan and the picture died altogether, the screen cutting to blue.

"Oh, no."

For the first time in two and a half hours, Eloise stirred. She frowned, plucking at her blanket.

"Okay. Okay," Maddy said as she scrambled toward the DVD player.

Maybe the disk had a scratch on it. She pressed the power button on and off a few times, but nothing happened. She could smell a faint burned electrical odor. Not a good sign.

Behind her on the couch, Eloise began to protest. *"Je veux le chat de chat!"*

Maddy's French was rusty, but she got the drift. Eloise wanted her movie back on, pronto.

"I don't think that's going to be possible, *chérie*," she said. "Milo and Otis are having a *petit* sleep."

Eloise was still staring at the television. Her expression darkened ominously. Maddy scooped up the colored prism Eloise had been so fascinated with earlier and handed it to her. Eloise gave it a single disinterested glance before letting it fall to the floor.

"What about lunch? You must be hungry, no?" Maddy tried next. *"Très affamée, oui?"*

She rushed to the kitchen and quickly slapped together a peanut butter sandwich. Eloise became more vocal with every minute, calling out in French for the movie to start again.

"Why don't we eat lunch, first, sweetie?" Maddy suggested, offering Eloise the sandwich cut into quarters.

But Eloise simply wasn't interested. She ignored the plate, pointing at the television. Her voice rising in pitch, she demanded *Milo and Otis*.

Maddy sat back on her heels. She had no idea what to do. Eloise had not made eye contact with her once, and Maddy didn't know if the little girl could understand a word she was saying. Doubtful, given her autism and the fact that Maddy was speaking mostly English with a tiny smattering of French.

Maddy pounced on the bag of supplies Charlotte had brought with her, hauling out pajamas, diapers, some fruit snacks and a well-loved rag doll. She delivered the doll to Eloise with her heart in her mouth, but once again Eloise was not interested.

Just her luck—a kid who knew her own mind.

Eloise's complaints were increasing in volume. Maddy stiffened with alarm as the little girl began to rock. For a split second she considered calling Max, but she didn't want to add more pressure to what was already a stressful situation.

"Okay. It's going to be okay, Eloise," she said soothingly.

She glanced around the apartment, but nothing leaped out at her. In desperation, she did the one thing she was good at—she started to dance.

"Hey, look, *mon petite,* look at this," she said as she did a pirouette, then an arabesque, followed by a deep plié.

She did another pirouette and realized that Eloise had stopped rocking. And for the first time all day, she was focusing on Maddy and following her every move.

A surge of relief washed through Maddy.

"You like this? You like *le ballet?*" She danced a few more steps and noticed that Eloise was moving her arms and legs in abbreviated imitations of what Maddy was doing.

"You want to dance, too?" she guessed.

She danced a few more steps, and again Eloise wriggled in time with her.

"Yes! You do want to dance. What a wonderful idea," Maddy said.

Quickly she located Max's stereo system and shoved the first disk she found into the tray. As Vivaldi's *Four Seasons* poured into the room, she danced toward Eloise and held out her hands.

Her excitement faltered as Eloise simply sat staring at her. Then, slowly, Eloise lifted her hands toward Maddy's and allowed Maddy to pull her to her feet.

Maddy stepped from side to side, encouraging Eloise to copy her. Her tongue wedged between her lips, Eloise rocked back and forth on her chubby baby legs. Once the little girl was moving confidently, Maddy introduced a simple twirl. Eloise's face lit with delight as she whirled in a circle, arms spread wide for balance.

She giggled, her small face flushed with pleasure. Warmth and an odd humbleness filled Maddy as she took in the pure joy on Eloise's face. There was so much honesty there, no pretense or subterfuge or self-consciousness.

"You can feel the music, too, can't you?" she said, even though she knew Eloise could not understand.

Totally immersed in the moment, Maddy began to string a series of simple steps together in her mind. Then, Eloise's hands held fast in her own, Maddy showed her how to dance.

"SHE'LL BE FINE. When I spoke to Maddy they were still watching the DVD," Max said.

Charlotte fretted beside him, hands fiddling with the seat belt as he wove through traffic. Richard had arrived at the hospital half an hour ago. Keen to collect Eloise and take her home, Charlotte had left him to sit with Marcel while Max drove her home. She claimed it was because she knew Eloise hated having her routine interrupted, but Max was aware it had far more to do with Charlotte having taken an irrational dislike to Maddy.

"You know I hate leaving Eloise with strangers," Charlotte said. "It's bad enough when they're trained sitters."

"Maddy's perfectly capable of handling Eloise," he said as they turned into his street.

Charlotte didn't say anything. The moment the car drew to a halt, she was outside and heading for the door to his apartment.

Her expression became grim as she registered the music leaking from his apartment.

"I told her Eloise doesn't like loud noises," she said. "What does she think she's doing?"

Despite his firm belief in Maddy's capabilities, he felt a twinge of concern. He'd seen Eloise howl a dozen times in reaction to anything overly loud.

He opened the door and they both froze on the threshold, surprised into stillness by the sight of Maddy and Eloise dancing together in the center of his work space.

Maddy was leading, her movements simple but graceful, and Eloise was imitating her, pirouetting, leaping, spinning and gliding in a child's interpretation of the choreography. Both were oblivious to their audience, utterly swept up in the moment.

Max's heart squeezed in his chest as he saw how much pleasure Eloise was taking from the experience. Her gray eyes sparkled with delight, and he could hear her laughing above the music.

Charlotte clutched his forearm, her expression torn between shock and amazement. Then Maddy caught sight of them and stopped in her tracks. Her hair had come loose from its topknot and hung in wispy strands around her face and neck. She was flushed, her violet-brown eyes shiny with laughter and fun.

She had never looked more beautiful to him.

"You're back," Maddy said, reaching for the remote control and silencing the music.

Eloise made a noise of protest as she registered that the dancing was over.

"But she hates music," Charlotte said. "I've tried everything. The Wiggles, Disney songs…"

"She loves to dance," Maddy said with a shrug. "She's a natural."

Charlotte shook her head, bemused.

"The DVD player died," Maddy said. "I couldn't find anything else she was interested in, so…we danced."

"You have good instincts. Most autistic children love music and movement. But for some reason Eloise never has," he said.

"Until now," Charlotte said. The look she sent Maddy was searching. "Perhaps she simply didn't have the right teacher."

Maddy shrugged self-deprecatingly. "I didn't do anything special."

Charlotte approached her daughter and knelt so that they were on the same level. Touching Eloise's arm to gain her attention, she held out her arms.

"*Maman* is here," she said with a small smile.

Eloise's mouth quirked to one side in recognition, and she allowed herself to be embraced. Charlotte closed her eyes, savoring the contact.

"How is Marcel?" Maddy asked.

"Out of surgery. Richard is with him. He will have to stay in overnight but with luck he can come home tomorrow," Max explained. "The doctors are very happy with everything, so it seems the worst is over."

"Oh. That's good news," Maddy said with an earnest nod. She tucked a stray strand of hair behind her ear. She looked self-conscious, he realized. Then he understood that she was worried that she'd done the wrong thing with Eloise. Before he could reassure her, Charlotte spoke up.

"I owe you an apology, Maddy," Charlotte said in her forthright way. "I was rude last night. Inexcusably so. I want to thank you from the bottom of my heart for looking after Eloise today, and for making her smile. We don't see enough of that in our house."

She held out her hand for Maddy to shake, and Maddy blinked with obvious surprise before taking it.

"It was my pleasure. We had a lovely time," she said.

"You will have to show me what to do, so Eloise can have a lovely time again," Charlotte said. "And perhaps I could buy you a coffee sometime and we could start again?"

"Of course," Maddy said with a shy smile. "Anytime."

Charlotte looked relieved as she turned to Max. "Thank you for today. I don't know what I would have done without you. I feel like I have been saying that to you a lot lately."

"You know I'm happy to help," he said.

"Still. You have stepped in for us too many times. And I have been pulling my hair out too often. Richard and I will be having some serious talks tonight," Charlotte said solemnly. "Perhaps it is time for him to change jobs."

Max knew that Richard and Charlotte had been walking a fine line the past few years, trying to balance the demands of Richard's high-paying job with the demands of home. They needed the extra income to fund Eloise's early intervention therapies, but Charlotte was clearly reaching the end of her endurance in her role as single parent in all but name.

"Let me know if there is anything else I can do," he said.

His sister flashed him a grateful smile as she began to collect Eloise's things. Maddy extracted the DVD from the broken player and handed it over, then they were out the door, Eloise pressing her face into her mother's neck as Charlotte carried her to the car.

Silence reigned for a long beat after the door closed behind them. Maddy let out a big sigh and flapped the front of her T-shirt.

"Is it hot in here or is it just me?" she asked. "I can't believe Eloise's stamina. She wouldn't let me rest for a second."

He wondered what she would do if he crossed the room and pulled her into his arms and kissed her the way he wanted to right now. She looked so small and strong and sexy standing there. He was fast running out of self-control where she was concerned.

A knock called him back to the front door. It was Charlotte again. She thrust two tickets into his hand.

"Last interruption for the day, I promise. I nearly forgot these. Richard bought them for me for my birthday, but we will not be going to the ballet tonight," she said drily. "You and Maddy go, please. As a thank-you from us both. They will go to waste otherwise."

She flashed Maddy a last smile then was gone again. He studied the tickets. Dress circle, front and center. Good seats.

"What do you think?" he said, glancing at Maddy. "The Garnier Opera Ballet performing *The Nutcracker*?"

"Anna mentioned it when we spoke about Dr. Rambeau," she said. "She's dancing the role of Clara."

He quirked an eyebrow at her, still waiting for an answer to his original question. She nodded.

"Why not?"

"You can glam up. I remember how you like a big event."

"It's been a while since I've been on the other side of the curtain," she admitted.

"I'll take you for dinner afterward," he said impulsively. The idea of wining and dining her held enormous appeal—sitting across a small table from her, sharing good food and fine wine, savoring the flicker of candlelight on her beautiful face. So what if it didn't mean anything and would never lead anywhere? It was a harmless enough self-indulgence, as self-indulgences went.

"You don't have to do that."

"Maybe I want to," he said before he could edit himself.

Awareness crackled between them for a heated moment as they locked eyes. It was the closest he'd ever come to declaring his interest in her. The memory of those few hot moments in the darkness behind The Gypsy Bar hung heavily between them. Maddy broke eye contact, her gaze sliding over his shoulder.

Reality washed over him, cool and undeniable.

You're her friend, remember, idiot? She doesn't want you

looking at her like that or taking her out for intimate dinners or anything remotely romantic.

He shoved his hands into his jeans pockets.

"Maybe we should just have something at home," he said.

"That's probably a good idea."

He bit down on a grim smile. Yeah, he was full of good ideas lately. Just full of them.

MADDY STRAIGHTENED her spine as she climbed the stairs from the Metro station at Place D'Opera in the fourth arrondissement later that evening. Cool night air rushed at her as they stepped from the warmth of underground. She took a moment to absorb their surroundings—the stately buildings, the brightly lit cafés, the art-nouveau streetlights, the well-dressed Parisians rushing past. She swiveled on her heel and caught her first glance of the soaring white Opera Garnier, home to the Garnier Ballet, with its sweeping colonnaded front and gleaming gold statues ranged along the roofline.

"I always forget how beautiful it is," she said as she craned her neck.

Max smiled indulgently and she gave him a dry look.

"That's the problem with you Europeans. You have so many beautiful buildings you take them for granted," she said as he led her across the street to the entrance.

"The way you Australians take your beaches for granted," he said.

She glanced at the facade again and her heart seemed to shimmy in her chest all of a sudden. A strange tension had been building inside her through the whole of their train ride. It took her a few seconds to recognize it: almost, but not quite, stage fright. She tried to shake it off, but the feeling persisted as they entered the foyer and were dazzled by the huge marble columns and elaborate gilt work.

She flashed back to the first time she'd performed here, five years ago. She'd been twenty-four, touring with the Royal Ballet out of London. It had been one of her first solo roles, and she'd sent Max tickets to see her dance. All night she had imagined him in the audience, imagined that she was dancing especially for him. She'd only found out afterward that his father had been ill and he'd been unable to make it.

She could feel him watching her and she forced a smile.

"Lots of memories," she said.

"Yes. When I was growing up, it was always my dream to dance here," he said.

A dream he'd never achieved, she knew. He started up the first flight of marble steps that would take them to the dress circle. She couldn't help but notice the tide of feminine interest that followed in his wake like a vapor trail.

No wonder.

She'd been hard put not to stare back at the apartment, either, when she'd come out of the bathroom in her rose print dress to find him waiting for her. His crisp white shirt, black velvet jacket and waistcoat and charcoal wool trousers fit him to perfection. His clear gray eyes were set off perfectly by the shadowy stubble on his jaw.

On any other man, the velvet would be a clear signal to lock up the Judy Garland collection, but on Max it looked elegant and refined and just right. Very French. Very sexy.

She stared after him for a long moment, aware that she was stalling. For some reason, she was loath to take her seat and watch this performance. Which was crazy. It was one of her favorite ballets and the production promised to be lavish and spectacular. Anna would be dancing, and the rest of the company were all highly experienced, excellent performers. She and Max were in for a treat.

So why did she feel as though she wanted to turn tail and run?

At the top of the stairs, Max stopped to glance at her. His expression was quizzical. He was wondering what the hell she was hanging around for. She made herself move.

"You okay?" he asked when she joined him.

Again she forced a smile. "Of course."

They ascended to the dress circle level and an usher guided them to their row. Max took her coat from her and folded it carefully over the back of her seat. She smoothed the skirt of her rose print dress and sat, concentrating on their ornate surroundings in the hope that her inappropriate nerves would dissipate.

They were surrounded on all sides by well-heeled Parisians and gawking tourists. The low hum of conversation filled the lush, velvet and gilt theater. She dropped her head back to admire the colorful ceiling painting by Chagall. She'd always liked it, although she knew many considered it sacrilege that a painter had been allowed to decorate such a historical theater with a quintessentially modern piece.

The sharp notes of the violinists readying their instruments made her start in her seat. The performance was about to begin.

Her hands found the arms of her chair. She gripped them hard as the lights dimmed. She could feel Max watching her, puzzled by her stiff posture and obvious tension. She knew she should reassure him, but the words stuck in her throat.

The orchestra launched the prelude, the violins leaping above the deeper notes of the bass and brass. The curtain trembled, then rose. She imagined the dancers poised in the wings, ready to perform.

Then, suddenly, the first dancers exploded onto the stage in a flurry of movement, leaping across the space in gravity-defying *grand jetés*. Two men and two women, dancing in perfect time, dressed in lavish, traditional costumes.

It was beautiful, compelling, stirring.

Maddy slid to the edge of her seat, eyes glued to the stage

as she followed their every move. She saw the precision of their turns, the power of their leaps, the practiced skill in their lifts and pirouettes. She held her breath for them, tensed her muscles for them.

Then the soloists came on, one man, one woman.

Her eyes filled with tears as she tracked the graceful power of their dancing. The female lead spun and her partner caught her; she fled and he pursued; he jumped, she soared after him.

The audience watched, rapt, held in thrall by their skill.

And suddenly, in a rush of blinding clarity, she knew.

She couldn't do this anymore.

Andrew and Dr. Hanson had been right. Her body was old, not up to the sort of effort she saw on the stage before her. In her heart of hearts, she'd known it for some time.

She just hadn't been ready to face it.

She would never dance professionally again.

7

MAX STIFFENED with shock as Maddy suddenly shot to her feet. He could see tears in her eyes. She pressed a hand to her mouth. Then she began pushing her way past the people seated beside her until she gained the aisle.

"Maddy!" he called after her, but she broke into a run as she raced for the exit.

The people sitting around them stirred, annoyed by the interruption. Max scooped up Maddy's coat and handbag and excused his way to the aisle. By the time he'd gained the dress circle landing, Maddy was halfway down the stairs to the foyer. He took off after her, barreling out into the Paris night.

He stood panting on the steps, scanning the crowds of tourists. He had no idea what was wrong, but he'd felt the tension vibrating through her the moment they stepped out of the Metro station. That she was profoundly distressed he had no doubt.

He caught sight of her at last, standing to the left of the entrance. Her arms were wrapped around her torso, her head was bowed. As he moved closer he saw that she was sobbing, her body racked with emotion.

"Maddy," he said, pulling her into his arms. He found the back of her head with his hand and pressed her close to his chest.

"I can't…I can't," she sobbed. She was quivering, her whole body shaking. "Not anymore. It's over. It's all gone."

He ran a soothing hand down her back.

"Maddy, what happened in there?" he asked.

She leaned back from him so she could look into his face.

"They're so good. And I could see how hard it was, how unforgiving and demanding. And I realized I can't do that anymore, Max. I don't have it in me. I want it so badly, I need it, but my body has let me down. They were right. It's over for me." Her words were rushed, almost garbled. But he understood.

Her cheeks were smudged with mascara, her mouth twisted with misery. He'd never seen a sadder, more tragic sight in his life.

"You don't know that, Maddy," he said, desperate to reassure her.

She closed her eyes. "No, Max. It's over," she said with heavy finality.

Her shoulders started to shudder, and he embraced her again.

She was inconsolable, devastated. He saw a cab dropping off some late theatergoers and raised an urgent hand. A moment later he was bundling Maddy inside and holding her in his arms as she cried all the way home. It was only ten minutes, but it felt like a lifetime.

Once they hit his apartment he led her to the couch and sat with her in his lap. She curled up against him and wept out her grief.

By the time she began to calm down, his jacket was soaked through. Slowly her tears turned to sniffs, and finally to hiccups. He leaned forward to pluck a handful of tissues from the box on the coffee table, pressing them into her hand.

"Thank you," she whispered.

"Maddy. It's going to be okay."

She was silent, and he tightened his embrace.

"I mean it. We'll work something out. We'll find you some other way to get in to see Dr. Kooperman, whatever it takes. And you've still got Dr. Rambeau to see this coming week."

She shook her head.

"No, Max. There's no point. I think I've known it for a long

time. Ever since I was so slow to recover after my knee reconstruction. My body isn't up to dancing professionally anymore.
I'm not up to being a prima. It's over."

"You don't know that until you've had more tests, seen more
specialists," he said, refusing to let her give up on her dream.
He knew what it was like to stop being a dancer. He wouldn't
wish the pain of separation and the loss of passion on anyone.
Especially not Maddy.

"Everyone has to retire sometime," she said quietly.

He frowned, wanting to argue, to convince her not to give
up. But what she'd said was true. She was twenty-nine. The
average retirement age for ballet dancers was thirty, thirty-one,
tops. A few innovative ballet companies were taking on older
dancers, women who'd had children then come back. But the
reality was that ballet demanded an enormous amount from its
practitioners. It consumed their bodies then abandoned them
when they still had the bulk of their lives left to live.

He realized suddenly that he had never seriously considered
the idea that Maddy might not succeed in her battle to be rein-
stated to her former role with the Sydney Dance Company. He'd
been worried for her, certainly, but he'd been unable to conceive
of a time when Maddy would not dance. It was so much an es-
sential part of her—Maddy was a ballet dancer. She was only
ever fully alive when she was *en pointe,* on stage, performing
for an audience.

He knew exactly how much she had sacrificed to her
vocation. Her distant, detached relationship with her mother,
the result of Maddy having left home when she was fourteen
to travel interstate to train at the Australian Ballet Academy. The
trail of ruined relationships. The lack of any life outside her
career. Maddy had given dance everything. Her life, in fact. And
now she was about to discover what was left over for herself.

They were both silent a long time. Finally, Maddy began to talk.

"I can still remember my first ballet class. I bugged my mom for months before she took me. I was a year younger than anyone else, younger than they normally accepted into the class, but I'd seen Anna Pavlova dancing on television and I wanted to be her so badly that I harangued my mom night and day. That first class, Madame took us through the positions. The other girls had trouble with their turnout, with pointing their toes, with their arms. But it all seemed so natural to me. It felt like home."

He smiled, circling his hand on her back.

"I used to pretend to my friends that I was going to soccer practice and then sneak off to my dance classes," he said. "My *maman* was embarrassed, I think. I'm sure she thought it was the first sign I was gay. But *Père* told me that he had danced a little when he was young, and he always regretted letting his friends' opinions matter more than what he wanted."

"Thank God he did, because you were a beautiful dancer, Max."

He pressed a kiss into her hair.

"And you were a star, Maddy. You dazzled. You lived the dream."

"Yes."

He could hear the grief in her voice again.

"Do you know what's crazy?" she asked after a while. "People are always advising dancers to plan for the future, to save their money or study part-time or something. I never did any of those things because I could never bear to think beyond the end of my career. I mean, I've got some money saved, but I have no idea what comes next. No idea."

"Something will come," he said. "You're smart, disciplined, hardworking. Whatever you put your hand to you'll succeed in."

He could feel her smile against his chest.

"My own personal cheer squad."

"Simply telling it like it is. Just because you can't dance anymore doesn't mean your life is over, Maddy."

"I know that's true. I do. But right now, when I try to project into the future, all I get is…nothing. Emptiness."

He could hear the fear and uncertainty in her voice. At least when he had walked away from his career, he'd walked away for a reason—caring for his father. Even in his darkest moments of self-pity and regret he'd known that he was doing something worthwhile.

"You don't have to make any decisions straightaway. Take some time out. Let yourself get used to the idea before you start making any plans," he said.

"Yes."

She lifted her head and met his gaze.

"I'm sorry about *The Nutcracker*," she said.

He shrugged to show how irrelevant it was.

"I could have at least saved freaking out till the end of the performance instead of the beginning," she said.

"Maddy. Forget it, okay?"

Her gaze dropped from his eyes to his mouth then flicked back to his eyes again.

"Have I ever told what a good man you are?" she asked. "You've never let me down. I bet you've never let your sister down or your father, either."

She pressed a kiss to his mouth.

"Thank you. Thank you for always being there," she said.

She hesitated a second, then leaned close to kiss him again. This time her lips lingered a fraction longer.

He could feel himself growing hard and he willed his body to calmness. The last thing Maddy needed right now was the knowledge that while she was seeking comfort, he was getting horny.

Then Maddy kissed him a third time and he felt the distinct wet roughness of her tongue sliding across his upper lip. Desire thumped low in his belly and his fingers curled into her back instinctively.

He pulled away.

"I don't think that's such a great idea, do you?"

Her eyes were heavy-lidded and smoky with need as she tried to kiss him a fourth time. He held back, refusing the temptation.

"Just for tonight, Max. I don't want to be alone. I don't want to think or feel," she pleaded.

He hesitated. She closed the distance between them and he felt the tip of her tongue trace his lower lip.

She tasted of tears and need, and he was only human. He opened his mouth and her tongue swept inside, sliding along his own sensuously. As soon as he had one taste he wanted a whole lot more and he clamped his hand to the back of her neck and angled his mouth over hers.

She murmured her approval, her body straining toward his. His free hand slid down her shoulder and onto her breast. Her nipples were already hard and she arched into his hand.

His erection pulsed against her backside, eager to get in on the action. He flicked his thumb over her nipple again and again. She sucked hard on his tongue and dug her hands into his back, pulling him close. Then suddenly she was pushing him away and shifting in his lap so that she was straddling him as she reached for his fly.

Her hands were shaking, her breath coming fast. He tugged the straps of her dress down as she slid his zipper open. Her small, pert breasts fell free of her dress as he pushed it down and cupped her in his hands. Her hand snaked into his boxer-briefs and he closed his eyes as she gripped him.

He needed to taste her skin. With one hand behind her back, he urged her close and ducked his head to take a nipple in his mouth. She gasped, her body shuddering. He bit her gently then sucked hard. She groaned and started to pant.

"I need you, Max," she breathed.

Her body arched forward as she rose up on her knees, and then her hands were guiding him into wet heat. The realization that she must have simply pushed her underwear to one side hit him even as she slid down onto his length, taking all of him at once.

"Maddy," he groaned as she gripped him tight.

She started to ride him, her hips sinuous, one hand locked on his shoulder as she drove herself down to the hilt of him then slid up again. Her eyes were closed, her teeth sunk into her bottom lip, her face straining with need as she sought oblivion.

He felt himself starting to lose it. She was so wet and hot, so greedy for it. He'd never been with a woman who was so honest about her own needs. It was the biggest damned turn-on in the world.

He ducked his head to her breasts again, laving them with the flat of his tongue. His hands gripped her hips and he pumped into her, grinding himself against her.

He felt her tighten around him. His own body tensed as his climax thundered toward him. She threw back her head. He felt her begin to pulse around him, her body milking his. And then he lost it, his orgasm hitting him like a wall. He thrust into her one last time, his fingers tightening on her hips, his teeth bared in a grimace of pleasurable pain.

As desire faded, reality crept in. Once again things had gotten out of control between them.

He should have stopped her. Should have been strong enough to resist temptation. But it was hard to feel sincere regret when he was still inside her and his hands still on her warm skin.

She opened her eyes and stared at him. She surprised him for the second time that night by pressing a kiss to his chin.

"No regrets. Not yet," she said firmly.

He wasn't sure if she was issuing an order or giving him an emotional weather report.

His gaze swept over her body, taking in the rosy color across her breasts, her still-aroused nipples, the rapid rise and fall of her chest. Her skirt was bunched around her thighs and he badly want to lift it to see where they were joined.

Before he could act on the impulse, Maddy shifted, rising off him. Sliding free of her tight heat felt like too great a loss and he grabbed her hips before she could move farther.

"Where are you going?" he asked.

She frowned, confused.

"I'm not done with you yet," he said.

He'd surprised her. About time.

He watched as her pupils expanded to fill her irises.

"What did you have in mind?" she asked. He could see a pulse beating in her neck.

"Stuff," he said with a slow smile.

She blinked. Then her gaze dropped to his groin where he was already growing hard again.

"Oh."

"You wanted to forget," he reminded her.

She licked her lips. "Yes."

He stood on a surge of strength, taking her with him. In two strides he was at the stairs to the sleeping platform. She wrapped an arm around his neck as he ascended to the bedroom.

"Take your dress off," he said as he set her on her feet.

She hesitated for a moment, then her hands reached for her zipper. He watched as her dress fell to the ground in a rustle of silk, leaving her standing in nothing but a pair of lacy white panties.

"Get rid of these," he said, sliding his thumb inside the side elastic and letting it snap back against her skin.

She swallowed. The look she flashed him was full of anticipation and desire. She pushed her panties down her legs and stepped out of them.

"Why aren't you undressing?" she asked.

"Lie down, and lift your hips," he said, ignoring her question.

Again she hesitated for a few seconds before doing as he'd said. He slid a pillow beneath her hips.

"Now spread your legs for me, Maddy," he said, his voice low with need.

She sucked in a breath, her gaze meeting his across her prone body. Slowly, she let her thighs drop open. He let his gaze trail over her body—the straining peaks of her breasts, the taut plane of her flat, muscled belly, then finally to where she was wet with need for him.

She was pretty and pink and plump and so much more desirable than he'd ever imagined.

"Get comfortable," he said.

And then he went down.

MADDY CLOSED HER EYES as Max's dark head neared the heart of her. Suddenly she realized that she wanted to see him do this, wanted to watch him savor her.

It should have been a shocking thought: Max, her friend, about to go down on her. Instead, a deep, primitive thrill rippled through her and she grew even wetter and hotter with need.

Her eyes snapped open as she felt his breath warm on her inner thighs, then she felt the first wet, rough rasp of his tongue against her. Her whole body shuddered and her hips jerked involuntarily. He gave a murmur of approval and used his hands to explore her intimate folds while he teased her with his tongue.

Her head fell to the pillow. She was liquid with desire, her blood as thick and sticky as toffee. She groaned deep in the back of her throat as Max opened his mouth over her and kissed her passionately, his tongue firm and fast.

His hands caressed the tender skin of her inner thighs,

soothing, kneading. She slid her hands into his hair and hung on for dear life.

He began to circle her inner lips with one deft finger, gliding through her slick desire, driving her crazy. She had to grab at the sheets then, her hands fisting in the fabric, desperate for something to anchor her in a sea of sensation.

He slid a finger inside her at last and she clenched around him hungrily.

"Yes," she murmured. "Please."

He used his free hand to spread her wide, exposing her utterly as he feasted on her. Her body bowed with desire as he slid his finger in and out of her, his tongue teasing her all the while.

It was too much. He was too much. Her climax hit her, vibrating through her body in shuddering waves. The last tremor had barely left her body before Max slid inside her, his thick heat stretching her in the best possible way.

She sighed as he began to pump into her.

He supported his weight on one arm as his free hand roamed her body, caressing her neck and her shoulders before finally claiming her breasts. His eyes were dilated with desire, his face hard with tension as he drove himself into her. She stared at him, amazed at his beauty, amazed that she had spent so many years not wanting him. How was that possible when her whole body was on fire for him?

He squeezed her nipples, then soothed them in the palm of his hand. She felt the tension growing in his body as he slid both hands beneath her, cupping her backside as he thrust into her again and again.

He felt so good, so hard, so right inside her. For the third time that night, desire coiled in her belly. She gripped his hips with one hand and slid the other onto his hard butt, glorying in the flexing of his muscles as he rode her.

"Maddy," he groaned.

She tilted her hips and gave him everything she had. He shifted higher, his hard shaft pressing where she needed him most.

She lost it, hands clutching at him, gasping for air, her world reduced to the warm, throbbing place where their two bodies became one.

He shuddered, his body hard with tension, his hands clenching her backside almost painfully. He pumped into her one last time, then pressed his face into her neck as he came in a hot rush.

He collapsed on top of her, his breathing harsh. She stared at the ceiling, stunned by the intensity of what had just taken place.

After a while he withdrew and rolled onto his back. They lay side by side, sweat cooling on their bodies, the smell of sex surrounding them as their heart rates gradually slowed.

She hadn't meant to kiss him. She'd meant to thank him, to somehow express the enormous gratitude she felt for his comfort, patience and understanding. Then she'd pressed her lips to his and smelled his skin, tasted him and instantly wanted more. And, like always, he hadn't denied her.

She turned her head so she could look at him. God, he was so beautiful. She'd seen plenty of naked men in her time, but Max's body was something special. Those big, strong thighs. That hard ass. His powerful shoulders and ripped belly.

She closed her eyes, unsure what to say or do. Unsure where this left them now that they'd once again crossed the line.

A warm knee nudged her.

"Hey. Wake up, sleepyhead."

She opened her eyes. He was watching her, his eyes hooded.

"You're not allowed to sleep yet," he said.

She stared at him, unable to believe that he wanted more when they'd just consumed each other. Her gaze dropped to his thighs where he was growing harder by the second.

Unbelievable.

"You *are* T-Rex," she said without thinking. "Insatiable."

"Maybe it depends what's on offer," he said, his French accent very pronounced.

He rolled toward her, his hand finding her breast as he leaned close to kiss her. Warmth cascaded through her body as his tongue stroked hers.

There was no time for regret, she realized. Not tonight. This wasn't over, not by a long shot.

MAX WOKE TO FIND HIMSELF tangled in Maddy's hair. She lay curled away from him on her side.

He couldn't get enough of her. He'd made love to her all night, like a man possessed. He'd brought her to climax again and again, and always she'd met him, matching need for need, passion for passion.

She'd asked him to make her forget. He figured he'd fulfilled his part of the bargain, and then some.

He disentangled himself and slid to the edge of the bed, feeling the full weight of what lay in store for him today. Another speech about regret and friendship from Maddy, no doubt. And, more than likely, her departure. Now that she had faced the reality of her retirement, there was nothing to keep her here. She'd want to go home, back to her apartment and her friends and her life.

He glanced over his shoulder, his eyes tracing the curves of her body. She was so beautiful, so compelling. How was he ever going to forget her?

He closed his eyes and let his shoulders drop. The old, familiar ache tightened his chest. Stupid to fall for the same un-attainable woman twice in one lifetime. But it was done, and only time would undo it.

"Good morning."

Her voice sounded husky, deeper than usual. He glanced across in time to see her pulling the sheet up to cover her breasts.

The contrast to the easy, erotic intimacy of last night was profound. Just in case he had any doubts about where he stood, her instinctive gesture told him everything he needed to know.

"How are you doing?" he asked.

She was still his friend, after all, and last night had been a watershed in her life.

She shrugged a shoulder.

"I'm not sure. I feel like I'm waiting for something else to happen. The other shoe to drop."

"Yeah. But it will get better. You'll work it out." He took a deep breath. "I guess you'll be heading home soon, then?"

There was a short pause before she answered.

"I guess so. There's nothing keeping me here anymore, after all."

Was it his imagination, or was there a slight question in her tone? He studied her, but her expression was unreadable.

Grasping at straws, man. Have a little dignity.

He reached for his boxer-briefs, lying discarded on the floor. He didn't need to look to know she glanced away when he stood and pulled them on.

The joys of the morning after.

"I'm going to grab a shower," he said.

That would give her time to pull herself together, something she clearly wasn't comfortable doing while he was around.

"Sure."

He headed down the stairs, his shoulders rigid with tension. Suddenly the thought of her going, of her not filling his space with the sound of her voice and her flowery perfume seemed like a really great idea.

He shut the bathroom door with too much force. What he really wanted to do was kick it, or punch a hole in something.

She'd offered him a taste of what he wanted, and he was going to have to live off the memory for the rest of his life.

Meanwhile, she would walk away having found comfort or indulged her curiosity or whatever the hell she'd been doing last night and the other night at the Latin club.

"Putain de merde!" he swore harshly, turning away from the mirror so he wouldn't have to look at his own sorry face.

He turned on the shower full force, welcoming the bombardment as he stepped beneath the water. He turned his face into the flow, then reached for the soap to wash her scent from his skin.

The screech of the shower curtain being yanked open filled the bathroom. Startled, he turned to find Maddy standing there wearing nothing but his shirt from the night before, the tails flapping against her bare legs, her hands planted squarely on her hips.

"I just want to know one thing," she said, her chin thrust out. "Did you sleep with me last night because you felt sorry for me and you were playing knight in shining armor again?"

"I could ask you the same thing."

"What's that supposed to mean?"

"We've been friends for years, and suddenly out of nowhere sex has become part of the equation. Why have the rules suddenly changed, Maddy?"

She opened her mouth, then closed it without saying anything.

"I asked you first," she said.

He stared at her.

"You kissed me," he reminded her. "Both times."

Her gaze slid over his shoulder and she shuffled from one foot to the other. The silence stretched between them.

She didn't want to say it, he realized. Didn't want to tell him she'd had an itch and he'd scratched it, that any handy man would have done.

"Fine," he said, reaching for the shower curtain, ready to shut her out.

"I saw you," she said in a rush.

He froze.

"That day when Charlotte called having problems with the babysitter. I knocked on the bathroom door to let you know she needed to speak to you, but you didn't answer. So I opened the door to tell you. And you were…you had your hands full. Really full," she said meaningfully.

Shit.

He closed his eyes as a wave of fiery heat rushed up the back of his neck and into his face. Even as a teenager he'd never been busted taking care of business. That Maddy had caught him red-handed—while he'd been fantasizing about her—was as bad as it could get.

"It was the sexiest, hottest damn thing I've ever seen in my life, Max."

For a second he thought he'd imagined her words. He opened his eyes and stared at her. She was the one blushing now, but her gaze was unwavering.

"I never let myself think about you like that. Ever. I valued you as my friend too much. But seeing you naked and hard…I couldn't get it out of my head," she said.

He blinked. Maddy was hot for him. Finally, after all these years, she was hot for him.

Her hands were twisting in the fabric of his shirt, and one foot rubbed the other self-consciously as the silence stretched.

It had cost her to confess what she'd seen. He felt he owed her the same honesty.

"I've always been attracted to you," he said boldly.

Her gaze flicked up, locked with his.

"What?"

"I've always wanted you. From the moment I first met you."

Her eyes widened.

"That day in the shower I was thinking about you. Imagining you were in here with me. Imagining I was inside you, touching you."

For a moment they stared at each other.

"This changes everything," she said. She sounded dazed.

"Yes," he agreed. "Come here."

She took a step closer and he hauled her the rest of the way into the stall, shirt and all. In seconds the fabric was plastered to her body, her nipples showing darkly through.

He backed her against the wall and pressed his body to hers. Then he lowered his head and kissed her, tracing her lips with his tongue before dipping inside her mouth to taste her properly. She slid her arms around his neck and wound a leg around his thigh. Her hips moved against his in a sinuous demand.

"Stay," he said when he broke their kiss.

"For how long?" she asked, a frown forming.

"A week, two weeks. A month. Does it matter?"

He wanted to say a lot more, but he wasn't a fool. Well, not a complete fool, anyway.

She searched his face. He slid a hand down her belly and between her thighs. It was cheating, and he knew it, but—

She quivered in his arms as his fingers slid into her slick heat.

"Yes," she breathed. "Yes."

It wasn't a promise. It certainly wasn't a commitment but it would do. For the time being, anyway.

8

THREE WEEKS LATER, Maddy frowned at the front page of *Le Monde* as she stood at the kitchen table, trying to translate the main story.

"What does *méchant* mean again?" she asked.

Max was at his workbench, adding some shading to his latest sketch.

"A big cigar. Or, depending on the context, a cruel man."

"So helpful. Not," she muttered under her breath.

"You'll get the hang of it," he said confidently.

Maddy was not so sure. She'd learned all the ballet technique phrases in French because she'd been passionate about her craft, and she'd picked up enough menu and incidental French to get by over the years. But actually remembering and understanding the grammar and syntax of another language seemed like a Herculean task, especially when she had no idea how to conjugate a verb in her own language, let alone a new one.

"I learned English when I was a kid," Max reminded her as he crossed to the kitchen table. "A new language is not so hard."

Warmth washed through her as he stood behind her, sliding his arms around her. For a delicious moment she savored the heat of his strong body, letting her weight rest back against him.

Three weeks of him, of this, and she still couldn't get enough. Three weeks, and she couldn't remember what it was like to not want Max, to not crave his touch. How had she ever looked at him as only a friend?

"That's different. Your mind was young and nimble. Mine is nearly thirty and stiff and arthritic," she said, only half joking.

Max laughed, the sound vibrating through her body. She felt the brush of his fingers as he pushed her hair out of the way to bare her neck. Then he kissed her, his tongue moving in lazy circles against the tender skin behind her ear.

"Mmmm." She'd been modeling for him and was wearing one of his old T-shirts and nothing else. She felt his erection pressing against her backside through the thin fabric.

"It's a wonder you ever get any work done," she said, rubbing herself against him shamelessly.

"I know. I consider it a miracle. Maybe I should give Yvette a call again."

He'd chosen to use Maddy instead of Yvette for the rest of his sketch studies. Every day Maddy modeled, and every day their sessions inevitably turned into lovemaking. Sometimes Max took her when she first disrobed, his eyes hard with desire as he walked toward her. Other days, like today, he waited until he'd captured the poses he wanted before giving in to the need they both felt.

She smiled with anticipation as one of his hands slid inside the baggy neckline of the T-shirt seeking her breasts. The other moved down her body to cup her backside.

His hands massaged her and she closed her eyes.

He knew exactly what to do to make her wild.

She moaned as he dipped his fingers between her thighs, widening her stance to invite him in. Delicate, teasing, he delved into her intimate folds.

She held her breath as he slid a finger inside her, then another.

Instantly she was on fire, her heart racing, her body clamoring for him.

"Max." She reached behind her, finding the stud on his jeans and popping it open.

In seconds he was free of his underwear, his erection rubbing against the lower curve of her backside. She leaned forward, hands stretched before her on the table, back arched, butt high, offering herself to him. He didn't need to be asked twice. He slid home in one smooth thrust.

"Maddy," he groaned.

She tilted her hips, encouraging him to move. He obliged and within seconds they were both gasping, their bodies tense with approaching orgasm.

He curled his hands into her hips and pumped into her hard and fast. She quivered, her head dropping forward bonelessly as she came, her inner muscles trembling around him. His own orgasm followed hard on the heels of hers and she felt him shudder as it gripped him.

She collapsed flat onto the table, the smell of fresh newsprint strong in her nostrils. Opening an eye, she saw she was sprawled across *Le Monde*.

"What's so funny?" Max asked.

"Maybe I've been going about learning French the wrong way," she said.

He laughed. "I can think of worse ways to learn a language. Maybe I will whisper it to you while we make love. Perhaps that will help your recall."

The thought of Max speaking soft French words in her ear while he rode her sent a shiver up her spine.

"You like that idea, do you?" he asked.

She could feel him growing hard inside her again.

She'd never had a lover like him. Insatiable. Knowing. Tender and passionate. Earthy and imaginative. It was possible he'd ruined her for any other man.

The thought made her stomach dip. One day—probably

soon if her track record was anything to go by—this fling with Max would be over and she would be forced to stop basking in the here and now and think about the future. About a life without dancing, and a life without Max.

"*J'aime te faire l'amour,* Maddy," Max murmured as he flexed his hips.

She felt the slow, delicious slide as he stroked into her. She closed her eyes and concentrated fiercely on how good it was, how good they were. As always, everything else slipped away. The future could wait another day.

"*Tu te sentez si serrée at chaude.*"

She grasped the edge of the table as one of Max's hands slid around her rib cage to find her breasts.

"*Quand je suis a l'interieur de toi—*"

They both tensed as a knock sounded at the door.

Max swore. "Perfect timing," he said with heavy irony.

"It's Charlotte," she said, suddenly remembering. "She mentioned she was going to drop by this morning."

"Of course it's Charlotte. It's been a whole day since we saw her last," he said.

She laughed, then gave a little gasp of loss as he withdrew from her.

"Blame my sister. I plan to," he said.

His obvious frustration was flattering and funny.

Charlotte knocked again, longer and louder this time.

"For Pete's sake, stop jumping each other and answer the door," she called.

Maddy reached out to tag Max's arm. "You're it," she said, taking off at speed for the bathroom.

"Hey!"

"Tell her I won't be a moment," she called over her shoulder as she shut the bathroom door.

She could hear Max laughing ruefully behind her. She had

a smile on her face, too, as she hastily pulled on underwear, a black turtleneck and jeans. She secured her hair in a low bun on the back of her neck and decided she was presentable.

"Let me guess. You were busy 'working,'" Charlotte was saying as Maddy joined them.

"Something like that."

Max was making coffee and Charlotte stabbed a sisterly finger into his chest.

"I don't know what's worse—worrying about you being single or worrying about you and Maddy wearing each other out."

Max laughed. "You'll be the first person I call from the hospital."

"How delightful for me," Charlotte said.

She caught sight of Maddy and her face lit up.

"Maddy!" She drew Maddy into a hug, kissing both her cheeks warmly.

After a rocky start, she and Charlotte had decided they liked each other. Maddy had had several more dancing sessions with Eloise, and Charlotte was warmly grateful for the pleasure her daughter found in the experience. Underneath all the stress and tiredness of managing two children on her own, Max's sister was as charming as Max himself, and Maddy had quickly discovered she liked having a female friend who discussed more than the freshest gossip from the ballet world or the effectiveness of the latest diuretic tablet or corn pads.

As Charlotte began to regale them with an update on Richard's search for a new job, Maddy felt the weight of Max's stare. She glanced over, and sure enough he was watching her, one hip propped against the kitchen counter, arms crossed over his chest. He looked very serious—brooding, almost. As soon as she made eye contact with him he smiled and the moment of intensity was gone, leaving her wondering if she'd imagined it.

"I can't believe I'm going to voluntarily subject myself to

this, but tell me what you two are up to this afternoon," Charlotte said, crossing her legs and raising an eyebrow in inquiry.

Over the past weeks, Maddy and Max had developed a routine of sorts. Most mornings she sat for him, then he worked on his sketches and other projects until midafternoon. After that he took her out into the city, showing her his Paris. So far they had toured Père Lachaise, explored the tangled streets of Montmartre, visited the Picasso museum and wound their way through the city via the secret covered corridors that made it possible for a pedestrian to walk under cover from Montmartre all the way across the city to the Palais Royal.

She didn't kid herself that their excursions were for any other reason than to entertain and distract her from her ever-circling thoughts. Max shared a bed with her—he knew she woke in the night sometimes, grief welling up inside her for the life she used to live. She never let herself cry, because it never made her feel any better. Still she couldn't stop herself from remembering and regretting and mourning.

Pointless. A huge waste of time. But she couldn't stop it. She'd spent almost her whole life wanting to be a ballerina, striving, enduring—and now it was all over. It was going to take some time to adjust. She kept thinking that if only she had known, consciously, that this was going to happen, she could have savored her last season, stored up memories, made each moment on stage count. But she hadn't. And she couldn't go back and change anything. It was what it was.

Maddy looked to Max. "We haven't decided yet."

"I was thinking the Rodin museum," he said.

"I find it hard to believe that there won't be a picnic associated with this expedition," Charlotte said archly. "Or at least a visit to a bonbon shop or a patisserie."

Maddy laughed. "Max, you see how predictable we are?"

"I can live with it," he said.

"You're going to make me fat."

He loved feeding her all the things she'd denied herself for so many years. Chocolates. Éclairs. Macaroons. She'd nearly cried when she tasted her first passion fruit and chocolate macaroon from Pierre Hermé in St. Germain last week. Max had bought one for her every day since.

Charlotte stood and collected her handbag.

"Before I forget—Richard wants to go back to Côte d'Azur again this summer, and it looks as though we can get the same house," she said to Max. "What about you? Do you have plans to go away?"

"Not yet," Max said.

Maddy knew that the city basically shut down for the month of August as Parisians headed for the coast for their summer holidays. Charlotte had already told her that good holiday houses were as scarce as hens' teeth, so it didn't surprise Maddy that she was planning ahead.

"You and Maddy should come with us. There's a private apartment attached to the back of the house—it would be perfect for you two," Charlotte said.

Maddy looked at Max, not sure how to handle the question. August was months away. She didn't even know if she would be here next week. More importantly, she didn't know if Max wanted her to be here, either. It was one thing to have great sex, as often as possible, but it was another thing entirely to start making plans together.

"I don't think so," he said. "But thanks for thinking of us."

Charlotte started to say more then shrugged. "Fine. But if you change your mind, the offer is still there."

She kissed them both goodbye then left, letting in a blast of chilly air before the door closed behind her.

Maddy found herself focusing on the hem of her sweater, fiddling with a stray thread there rather than risking eye contact with Max. She was hurt by Max's easy rejection of his sister's offer. Was he so certain she would be gone from his life by summer?

Even as the thought circled her mind, Maddy kicked herself. She couldn't hang around Max's apartment, existing on the fringes of his life for six months, even if he wanted her to. She had her own life to live—whatever that might turn out to be.

"If you keep picking at that, it's going to fall apart."

She glanced up to find Max standing close to her, his gray eyes unreadable.

"I know." She released her grip on her sweater.

Something of what she'd been thinking must have shown on her face, because he cocked his head to one side as he studied her.

"You didn't want to go to Côte d'Azur, did you?" he asked lightly.

"Of course not. It's ages away. I'll probably be teaching Pilates at Bondi Beach by then," she said.

There was a small pause before he smiled. "I thought you were going to be a personal trainer."

Over the weeks, they'd made a game out of cycling through the various professions most dancers wound up in once they'd retired. So far, they'd toyed with Maddy becoming a ballet mistress, an arts administrator and a personal trainer.

"That's so last week," she said with mock disdain.

The moment of odd tension was gone as they bantered back and forth. Max helped her into her coat and she wound his scarf around his neck, ensuring he'd be well protected from the wind.

Hats and gloves on, they walked to Rue de Rivoli, stopping along the way to buy a bottle of wine, a baguette, some cheese and a bag of grapes. Max led her to what had become her favorite picnic place, the small park at the very tip of the Isle de la Cité, the home of Notre Dame. Despite the fact that the garden had been reduced to a bunch of twigs sticking out of gravel at this time of year, Maddy loved it and dragged Max to it as often as possible.

"It's a terrible cliché, coming here, you know," he told her as they sat on a bench and tore their bread into chunks. "Perhaps the most clichéd picnic venue in Paris."

"I don't care. It's close to the river. I don't know what it is about the Seine, but it makes me feel good whenever I see it," she said. She raised her face to the sun and closed her eyes, savoring the weak warmth.

"Are you homesick?" he asked quietly. "Winter in Sydney's nothing like this."

Maddy considered the question as she smeared Camembert on her bread.

"I miss the light from home, if that makes sense. It's so bright and clear in Australia. I can see why the Impressionists went crazy with all that hazy, dazy light in their paintings over here in Europe. Everything is much softer, gentler."

"I know what you mean," he said. "I have photographs from when I was living in Sydney. They're so bright they almost hurt my eyes."

She smiled, then saw he had bread crumbs caught in his scarf. For some reason, seeing him sitting there wearing his sophisticated scarf and superbly tailored coat and Italian shoes with crumbs down his front made her heart squeeze in her chest. How could a man be so devastatingly attractive yet so boyishly appealing at the same time? Suddenly she remembered something one of Max's girlfriends from long ago had once said to her. "It's not his good looks or his body or how smart he is that really gets me. It's those gray eyes of his. They always look as though they're about to laugh at me."

Maddy realized she was staring and forced herself to look away.

This is a fling, Maddy. Don't go getting ideas. Remember your track record with men.

But Max wasn't like any of the other men she'd slept with. He understood her. He knew her. They knew each other. And she no longer had to share her time between dance and the man in her life. Max could have her night and day, week in, week out. If he wanted her.

Maddy gazed out at the river. She knew what a psychologist would say she was doing—using this thing with Max to divert herself from the hole dancing had left in her life. Max distracted her with sightseeing and gastronomic indulgences, and she rounded the job off by fixating on what was happening between them, building it up into something it probably wasn't, and probably never should be.

It wasn't fair to Max that she latch onto him to stop herself from going under. He deserved a hell of a lot more than that.

Beside her, Max crumpled the empty bread wrapper into a ball.

"Come on. Art awaits," he said, standing and holding out a hand.

She let him pull her to her feet. He was an amazing man. The best. And she had to be careful not to abuse his generosity and kindness by overstaying her welcome. She had to make sure she left before the sex palled and she became a burden instead of a friend in need.

Max tucked her arm through his and led her off the island and onto the left bank. As they walked, he pointed out his favorite buildings and told her a little about their histories. Being Paris, the stories were all colorful and drenched in blood and revolution.

She let herself be wrapped in his warm charm. It was wrong to lean on him so much, but right now she wasn't quite sure how to stand on her own two feet. Soon, she would find a way to be strong again.

The Musée Rodin was in a stately old mansion with spacious, highly manicured grounds. Like so much of Paris, it was beautiful and elegant and Maddy looked around admiringly as Max bought their tickets.

He grew quiet as they walked into the first room. He stopped in front of each sculpture, no matter how small, his eyes caressing the curves and planes Rodin had created.

"This is like a church for you, isn't it?" she said quietly after they'd toured the ground floor and were climbing the stairs to the second level.

"He changed the world," he said simply. "Breathed life into sculpture again."

Finally they wound up out in the gardens, standing in front of two enormous cast bronze doors; the entire surface of them was writhing with figures, animal and beast, bursting from the surface into three dimensions. Torsos twisted, arms lifted beseechingly, legs flailed in torment. Appropriate, given the piece was titled *The Gates of Hell*.

Maddy's eyes were wide with awe as she cataloged the detail, the sheer breadth and scope of the work.

"This is…amazing," she said.

"Yes."

He turned on his heel and started up the gravel path leading deeper into the garden. She knew from consulting the map that there were no more sculptures in that direction, but she followed him anyway. At the far end was a fountain, dry at present, and he sat on its rim and stared at his loosely clasped hands.

She sat beside him, tucking her own hands into her pockets for warmth. After a few minutes, Max started talking.

"The first time I came here was with my grandfather. I bitched and moaned all the way because I wanted to ride my bike with my friends instead. But my grandfather was determined to introduce me to a bit of culture. Then I walked in the door and saw the first sculpture and I stopped dead in my tracks." He shook his head, smiling at the memory. "My heart was pounding. I wanted to close my eyes. The sculptures seemed so dynamic and powerful they scared me. My grandfather didn't say a word. He took one look at my face, then led me from room to room. I think we were here for over three hours, that first visit."

Maddy watched Max's face as he went on to talk about the art they'd seen, smiling now and then at his passion, the way he gesticulated so energetically as he tried to evoke an image or underscore his meaning.

"I'm probably boring you into a coma," he said after a while. "Blink for me. Prove to me that you're not catatonic."

She laughed. "You're not boring me. I'm learning a lot. I'm basically ignorant about almost everything in the world except for dance, you know. I didn't even know how a bronze was made until you explained it to me. I love listening to you talk about art."

He rolled his eyes and she nudged him with her elbow.

"I do! You get all French and you get this light in your eyes."

"Like a crazy man."

"Like a man who's found his passion," she said.

He shrugged self-consciously.

"I'd give anything to be like you. To have something else I loved as much as dancing," she said.

The words were out before she could edit them, and she bit her lip.

"That sounds so greedy, doesn't it? I've had all these years of dancing at the top of my game, and you didn't even get to really explore your dancing career. Now you've got a second chance to do something you love and I'm sitting here grouching about how jealous I am."

"Stop giving yourself such a hard time for being a human being, Maddy," he said.

"I just wish there was something—anything—that I wanted to do," she said.

The despair that crept up on her in the dead of the night threatened, and she curled her hands into fists inside her pockets. All her life she'd lived through her body, but now her most evocative, finely honed tool of self-expression, therapy, exercise and solace had been taken away from her.

"Come here," Max said.

He tugged on her arm until she allowed him to pull her into his lap so that she sat straddling him.

"Something will come up," he said, as he had said so many times over the past few weeks. That, and variations of *give it time, don't rush yourself*. She knew he was right. She only wished whatever it was would get a wriggle on. She needed something to hold on to, stat.

In the interim, she clung to Max as he kissed her.

Their bodies quickly grew heated beneath their coats. Max tugged off his gloves and slid his hands under her top and onto her breasts. She sighed into his mouth as he squeezed her nipples gently. Under the guise of ensuring she was warm, he opened his jacket so that she nestled inside the flaps. She swallowed with excitement when his fingers found the stud on her jeans.

"Max. We're at a museum," she whispered, even though she was slick with need.

"I can't think of a better place for it. Think of it as performance art."

She bit her lip as he pulled down her fly and slid his hand inside her panties. She felt him brush through her hair, then he was gliding into her heat.

"So wet, Maddy," he murmured, kissing her neck.

"I wonder whose fault that is?"

His clever middle finger found her and began to stroke her firmly. She clenched her thighs around his hips and gripped his shoulders. At the far end of the walkway she could see a tour group turning onto the gravel path.

"Someone's coming," she said, trying to pull his hand away.

"I know," he said.

She couldn't help but laugh.

"Not me. Real people. Tourists," she said.

She bit her lip again as he upped the pace.

"We'd better be quick then, yes?" he said.

Useless to pretend that the danger, the illicit nature of what they were doing wasn't a turn-on. Desire built inside her and she gasped as her climax hit her. Max kissed her, swallowing her small cry.

By the time the tourists arrived at the fountain, he'd buttoned her jeans again and she had her flushed face pressed against his neck.

"Don't think there won't be payback," she said when the tourists had gone. "Sleep with one eye open, because you are going down, mister."

"And that is supposed to be a punishment, Maddy?" he said, sounding very French as he laughed at her.

She tapped him on the nose with her finger.

"Mark my words—you'll get yours."

"Oooh," he said.

They stood and slowly walked back to the museum.

Max slid his arm around her shoulder and kissed the top of her head. A warm glow spread through her—and it had nothing to do with the orgasm he'd just given her. She loved that she could make him laugh, and that he'd talked to her about his art and that even after three weeks, he still seemed to desire her. She loved his tender touch and his endless patience and kindness and optimism.

As they walked past a window, Maddy caught sight of their reflection, saw the small, private smiles on their faces, the way they were twined around each other as though they couldn't bear to not be touching.

They looked like a couple. Lovers, in the full meaning of the word.

Don't turn this into something it isn't, she warned herself. *Don't mix great sex with your grief and gratitude and his kindness and come up with something that doesn't exist.*

She forced herself to release Max on the pretext of adjusting her scarf. Then she forced herself to shove her hands into her pockets to resist the lure of putting her arm around him again.

It seemed like an awfully long walk home.

A WEEK LATER, Max lay in bed, his arms behind his head. He could hear Maddy puttering around in the kitchen below, and he smiled to himself.

"How are you doing?" he called out.

"Fine. Stay there," she warned.

She'd promised him pancakes for breakfast when she'd rolled out of bed twenty minutes earlier.

"And not those thin, ungenerous French excuses for pancakes, either," she'd said on her way down the stairs.

Charlotte had made a valiant attempt to interest Maddy in haute cuisine, but finally they had both agreed that simpler fare was more Maddy's thing. So far, she had mastered scrambled eggs, pancakes and a chicken and vegetable soup.

He made a bet with himself over what would go wrong this time. Something always did. Maddy had a knack for creating drama in the kitchen.

He was about to head downstairs to ensure he had a ringside seat when the phone rang.

"I'll get it," he called, reaching across the bed to take the call.

"Bonjour," he said into the phone.

There was a slight pause before someone spoke.

"Ah, *bonjour.* Ah, *non parle français, pardon moi.* My name is Perry Galbraith. I'm looking for Madeline Green." Perry's accent was broad and flat, as Australian as they came.

"Sure. I'll get her," Max said.

He frowned as he levered himself up off the bed.

Who the hell was Perry? And why was he calling Maddy in France?

"Maddy. It's for you. Some guy from home called Perry Galbraith," he said.

There was a surprised silence.

"Perry? I hope everything's all right."

She climbed the stairs to take the call. He resisted the urge to demand more information. Because he desperately wanted to eavesdrop on their conversation, he pulled on some clothes and forced himself to walk away and give her privacy.

He'd started work on his first sculpture five days ago and progress was slow but sure. He was opening a new slab of clay in preparation for the day's work when Maddy joined him ten minutes later.

"Everything okay?" he asked.

"I think so. Perry's my neighbor. I e-mailed him and asked him to collect my mail for me. He was worried about a letter that he thought might be an overdue bill."

"Was it?"

"Yeah. I'll jump online later and take care of it. I told Perry to forward the rest of my mail onto me here. I hope that's okay?"

The tension banding his shoulders relaxed.

She wasn't going home. Not yet.

"Of course. My home is your home, Maddy, you know that," he said.

"I should have thought about my bills. I've been so disorganized. Just letting the days drift away."

Her face was very serious. He'd woken in the night to find

her lying beside him more times than he could count, stiff with anxiety as she stared into the darkness. She was worried about what to do with the rest of her life—and he didn't have any answers for her. He'd busted his ass over the past four weeks, doing his best to keep her busy and entertained and distracted. He hated seeing her sad, couldn't bear the broken, deserted look she got in her eyes sometimes.

He wiped his hands on a rag and approached her.

"It's only been four weeks," he said, putting his arms around her. "You deserve some time to get used to your new reality. You've earned it."

She pressed her cheek against his shirt.

Even as he spoke, he wondered how self-serving his advice was. How much of what he was saying was for Maddy, and how much was about keeping her close, extending their time together, building the connection between them so that she might begin to see him as more than a friend and a warm body to bump against?

Hope springs eternal.

Whoever had coined that phrase had known what he or she was talking about. Max had already had more of Maddy than he'd ever imagined he'd get. To crave more, to allow himself to imagine her as part of his life, a permanent fixture in his bed and his apartment…

It was asking for trouble, being greedy. Setting himself up for a mighty, mighty fall.

And yet he couldn't stop himself from hoping. The past four weeks had been the best of his life. Sexually, emotionally, professionally—it was all coming together. If only there wasn't the growing sense that the clock was ticking, that one day soon Maddy was going to make a decision about her future—and it wouldn't include him.

He had no idea how she felt about him. He knew she desired

him. Her body told him that every time he looked at her or touched her. One kiss, one stroke of his hand on her skin was enough to make her heavy-lidded and hungry for him.

He knew she enjoyed his company and appreciated his sense of humor. She liked his family, despite the rocky start with his sister. But she'd never said a word or done anything to give him reason to believe that what was happening between them was anything more than a new aspect to their already established relationship. They were friends—and now they were friends who slept with each other.

She pressed a kiss to his jaw and stepped away from him.

"I'm a coward," she said, pushing her hair over her shoulder. "I know I should stop treading water, but I can't quite make myself do it just yet."

Treading water.

Right.

While he was building castles in the air, Maddy was keeping her head above water.

His jaw was tight as he reached for his clay cutter and began slicing thin, uniform slabs from the block.

"I'd better get back to those pancakes," she said.

She turned away, then turned back again.

"I meant to mention—I saw in the paper that more tickets have been released for Madonna's concert next month. I saw her a long time ago in Sydney. She was so fantastic. You should definitely go if you get the chance."

He looked at her.

"Come with me," he said, sick of all the uncertainty. He'd played it safe when his sister mentioned the August holidays but the concert was mere weeks away. If Maddy couldn't commit to that, then he was kidding himself well and truly.

She looked arrested, then thoughtful. Then she frowned.

"It's more than a month away, Max."

"So?"

"That's a long time for me to hang around your neck."

He couldn't tell if she was serious or joking. Whether she was looking for an easy out or if she was genuinely concerned.

"Maybe I like having you around my neck," he said, striving to keep things light. "Maybe I think you're better than a winter scarf for keeping out the cold."

She studied him before she smiled.

"Okay, let's go. But you have to tell me the moment I start getting on your nerves," she said.

"Scout's honor," he said, holding up a random number of fingers.

Another month to look forward to. Four weeks more of Maddy.

Anything could happen.

"Very convincing. Remind me not to ever get lost in the bush with you," she said, laughing.

Her eyes were bright with amusement, and soft color warmed her cheeks. All of a sudden words were crowding his throat, demanding to be said.

Words like *I love you* and *Don't ever leave.*

Words that filled his head, swelled his chest.

He dragged his gaze away from her, forced himself to concentrate on the cool, smooth, slippery texture of the clay beneath his hands.

It's too soon, he repeated to himself for the tenth time that day. *Too soon.*

But maybe, one day, he would reach the tipping point where he risked more by staying silent than by speaking out.

9

THE NEXT MORNING, Maddy rolled over in bed and felt the coolness of empty sheets beside her. Already half-awake, she sat up with a frown and stared at the indentation Max's head had left in the pillow.

She hadn't heard him get up. She felt ridiculously cheated. Lingering between the sheets in the morning with her head on his chest, his hands moving in slow circles on her back was one of the highlights of the day. Inevitably they wound up making love—long, slow sex that seemed to last for hours.

She couldn't think of a better way to start the day.

"Max? Come back to bed and warm my feet," she hollered.

The profound silence that greeted her confirmed she was alone. She pulled on one of his T-shirts and made her way downstairs.

She found his note propped against the toaster. Her love of all bread-based products after years of self-imposed deprivation had become a running joke between them—the toaster was the one appliance he knew she'd make a beeline for on waking.

Maddy, am helping Richard shift furniture. Back after lunch.
Max.

She remembered now that Charlotte had asked Max to help

move the furniture from their spare bedroom into storage so Richard could set up his new home office, an idea his employer had agreed to try in order to avoid losing Richard's expertise.

The question was, why hadn't Max woken her? She could have helped.

She had a sudden mental image of the big bed and the even bigger chest of drawers and bookcase that furnished the guest room. Okay, probably she wouldn't have been an enormous help. But still. She could at least have stood on the sidelines and cheered and made coffee.

"Pathetic," she said, shaking her head.

Surely she could survive a few hours without Max.

She straightened her shoulders and reached for the fruit loaf that Max had left for her. After she'd munched her way through three slices, she cleaned up, washing last night's dinner dishes while she was at it, then straightened the rest of the kitchen. From there she went on to sweep and mop the floors, then put in a load of washing.

It felt good to work. To have a purpose and a goal, even a short-term one. She missed the certainty and order and purpose of her old life.

All the sightseeing and fun with Max, all the indulgences and distractions—she could tap-dance around and paper over the cracks all she liked, but the truth was there was a huge void in her life where her vocation used to be and nothing was going to fill it or make it go away.

Hard on the heels of the acknowledgment came a rush of emotion, the ache of loss rising up inside her like a flash flood, all the feelings she'd banked for the past few weeks swamping her.

Suddenly she was gasping, tears flooding her eyes, her chest aching with grief and anger and a strange kind of resentment.

She was twenty-nine. Most people her age were just starting

to hit milestones in their chosen professions, moving up the food chain, getting pay raises, buying bigger cars, bigger houses. She was washed-up. She'd peaked and crashed, and now she was going to be playing catch-up for the rest of her life, trying to make do with a career that paid the rent but didn't feed her soul.

A great wave of despair hit her and she fought back a childish desire to throw back her head and wail, "Why me?"

She pressed a hand to her chest where it hurt the most, gulping back her sadness.

The worst thing was, she didn't feel like herself anymore. She'd always been inseparable from her career. Now, she was an empty shell, a doll with her insides all scooped out. Only when she was with Max was it possible for her to feel normal and forget, because he made her laugh and aroused her and challenged her.

She was hyperventilating, in the grip of a panic attack. She snatched up her phone and pressed the first digits of Max's number.

He would come to her. Or she would go to him. It didn't matter. Once she was with him, she would be okay.

She was about to press the send button when she realized what she was doing: using Max as a security blanket.

She threw her phone onto the couch and sat beside it, her head in her hands.

She was such a mess. Her career was over, she had no idea what she wanted to do with the rest of her life, and she'd embarked on a hot, breathless love affair with one of her best friends as a bizarre form of coping mechanism.

You can't keep running. It's all going to catch up with you eventually.

Maddy sucked in big mouthfuls of air, trying to slow her frantically beating heart. Her body was filled with adrenaline, responding to ancient fight-or-flight instincts triggered by her bone-deep fear of the future and the vast sorrow inside her.

"Get a grip, Maddy. For God's sake," she muttered into her hands.

Tears had squeezed out of her eyes but she wiped them from her face and stood, shaking her hands to try to relieve the tension banding her body. She needed to do something, to get out of the apartment, out of her own head. She needed to—

She closed her eyes then as she understood what her body and soul wanted, needed, demanded. She crossed to her dance bag and pulled out her pointe slippers. She found an old leotard in the bottom of the bag.

Calm washed over her as she dressed and tied her slippers and walked to the center of Max's work space. It was still essentially empty, since he'd begun work on his first piece beside his workbench near the wall. She had room to move. Room to dance.

She didn't need any music. It was all in her head. Head bowed low, she struck a position and slowly unfurled, arms rising even as she came up *en pointe*. Eyes closed, she let the music in her head and the memories in her body guide her.

She danced. She spun. She soared. She sweated. She ached. She burned.

It was heaven and hell—the thing she was born to do, but was no longer free to pursue.

MAX ROLLED his aching shoulders as he walked into the kitchen of his sister's apartment. She was busy making sandwiches, but glanced up.

"You owe me. Big-time," she said.

He raised his eyebrows.

"Excuse me? I thought I was the one who just shifted around fifty tons of antique furniture," he said.

"I had to stand in line for half an hour for those macaroons you wanted for Maddy," Charlotte said, indicating a white-paper-wrapped parcel on the bench. "In the cold. With a bunch of desperate macaroon lovers who would have killed me to take my place if they could have got away with it."

"Maddy will be eternally grateful. I will make sure she knows that sacrifices were made to secure these macaroons," he said.

Charlotte rolled her eyes. "Don't try to charm me. It doesn't work, I'm your sister."

Still, she was smiling.

Max checked his phone messages as Charlotte slid a plate his way.

"Thank you for helping out today," she said as Richard entered the kitchen.

Thin and wiry, Richard stood a full foot and a half taller than his wife. He stopped to drop a kiss onto the crown of her head before leaning over her to snare a sandwich.

Max put his phone away. No messages from Maddy. He felt a ridiculous sense of disappointment. They'd been apart a whole three hours. Unless the apartment had caught fire, there was no reason for her to call.

Unless she missed him the way he missed her.

When he looked up, Charlotte was watching him knowingly.

"What?" he said.

"Have you told her how you feel yet?"

"Charlotte…"

"You might as well answer her," Richard said around a mouthful of sandwich. "You know what she's like. She won't let up until you've given her name, rank and serial number and the keys to Fort Knox."

He slid his arm around his wife as he spoke, and she leaned into his embrace.

"Maddy and I are fine, thanks," Max said.

"Perhaps," Charlotte said.

Max narrowed his eyes. What the hell did that mean? Had Maddy said something to her about him, about them? The two women had gone shopping together the other day. He could only imagine the interrogation his sister would have subjected Maddy to.

He forced himself to take a bite of his sandwich and chew slowly. He'd regressed to high school for a full twenty seconds there as he teetered on the brink of pumping his sister for information. It was vaguely disturbing, but so much of his thinking where Maddy was concerned was off the charts. He loved her more every day, the warmth and size and scope of it expanding never-endingly. He adored her. Worshipped her. Craved her. And his fear of losing her grew exponentially at the same time.

"I've been worried about Maddy," Charlotte said.

He frowned, all his good intentions flying out the window. "What do you mean? Has she said something?"

"No. It's just that when I'm with her, I always get the sense that she's covering. She's smiling and laughing, but I can feel the sadness inside her."

Max put down his sandwich and pushed the plate away.

"She misses dancing," he said. "But she's getting over it. Transition is a hugely difficult time for dancers. That's why there are counseling services in the U.S. and the U.K. to help dancers come to terms with life after dance, to retrain and find a different path. You've got to understand, it's not just a job Maddy has lost. She's lost her identity, her community, her routine. It's going to take time."

"You sound like a brochure," Charlotte said.

"I've been reading up on it," he admitted.

"Have you ever thought that this is probably the very worst time that you two could get together?" his sister asked.

Max frowned.

"It's true, you know it is. She's a mess. She needs you. You love her. Not exactly the best basis for a relationship."

"It's not a relationship," he forced himself to say.

"You want it to be. Don't pretend you don't."

He reached for the parcel of macaroons. "Thanks for these. I'd better get home."

Charlotte reached out a hand to stop him leaving.

"Max. I know you think I'm being an interfering cow, but I love you. I want you to be happy more than anything. I think Maddy is great, you know I do. I would love for things to work out between you."

"But?"

"But she might not be ready. She's in crisis. In mourning. Confused, anxious about the future."

"You don't think she's with me for the right reasons?" Max asked.

"I don't think she knows up from down right now. She's surviving from day to day. So just… I don't know. Take it easy."

He laughed humorlessly. "Right. Thanks. I'll try to remember that."

He decided to walk home rather than take the Metro. Buds were starting to appear on the trees lining the Seine, and there was a definite hint of warmth in the air. Winter was drawing to a close, and soon it would be spring. The tourists would flood back into the city, and the streets would be full of bikes and pedestrians.

Would Maddy be here to see it?

He wanted to pin her down so badly it hurt. He wanted to declare himself and commit himself and have her do the same, to end the doubt and uncertainty forever. Ten years he'd been waiting for Maddy. Now he had her in his bed, in his life, and he wanted to keep her there.

He stopped on the small pedestrian bridge that joined the Isle de la Cité to the Isle Saint Louis. A busker on a piano accordion played an Edith Piaf tune for the tourists as Max stared down at the rushing gray waters of the Seine.

After long moments his head came up and he turned toward home with renewed purpose.

He would tell her. He would let her know how he felt, how he'd always felt. Then it would be up to her.

A strange mix of anticipation and relief washed over him. Finally, he would know. No more doubt.

He stepped up his pace. Past the Metro stop at St. Paul, into the Jewish quarter. Past the Place des Vosges. Then he was on his street, the peeling red paint of his front door calling him like a beacon.

He balanced the parcel of macaroons on one knee as he fished for his house keys and slid them into the lock.

"Maddy, I'm back," he called as he walked into the warmth of the apartment. He glanced toward the loft, then the kitchen, then the couch, but Maddy wasn't anywhere.

"Max."

His head shot around and he saw Maddy sitting on the floor against the wall, her knees pulled up to her chest, arms wrapped around them. She was wearing her pointe slippers and a leotard, and her eyes were so filled with sadness and grief that he felt as though someone had punched him in the gut.

"Maddy," he said.

He dropped the macaroons onto the nearest table and crossed to her, falling to his knees.

Her skin was covered in gooseflesh and she was shivering. Sweat darkened the fabric of her leotard and her hair was damp. She'd been dancing, he realized. Dancing until she was dripping with sweat and exhausted.

Wordless, he wrapped her in his arms. She clung to him, buried her face in his shoulder.

"I'm sorry," she said. "I thought I was doing okay but once you were gone and I was on my own, I just…fell apart."

"You don't need to apologize to me for feeling sad, Maddy," he said, one hand stroking her hair.

"It's so big," she said quietly. "This feeling inside me, this horrible emptiness. I don't know what to do with it."

"Maybe you don't have to do anything with it. Maybe it just is."

She shivered then, pressed herself closer to him.

"What if it never goes away? What if I feel this sad for the rest of my life? Max, I'm so scared. I don't know what to do next. I know I need to pull myself together, make some decisions, but there's nothing I want to do except dance. Nothing."

She sounded utterly bereft and exhausted. Max closed his eyes and held her tight, wishing he could take away the pain for her.

"Come on, let's get you into the shower."

He helped her to her feet and led her into the bathroom, turning on the hot water and kneeling to untie her ribbons. She rested a hand on his head for balance, her fingers in his hair.

"You're so good to me, Max," she said.

She peeled off her leotard and stepped into the shower. When he started to draw the curtain across behind her, she caught his hand.

"Aren't you coming in with me?"

There was a plea in her eyes and he knew what she wanted, needed from him.

Silently he stripped and joined her. Silently he kissed her, his hands sliding onto her breasts. He kissed and caressed and teased her until she was trembling in his arms then he turned off the water and carried her to the loft where he dried her gently and made love to her until she was liquid and lax in his arms.

She fell asleep with a small smile on her lips and a hand curled around his bicep. He lay awake beside her for a long time. Then he slid out from beneath her hand, rolled out of bed and made his way quietly downstairs to his desk.

His address book was there and he picked it up and thumbed through it, thinking of his friends, of past colleagues and contacts. Picking up the phone, he called the first number.

Over the next hour he spoke to half a dozen of his old dancing friends. One was in the Netherlands, two in New York, one in Australia, one in London. He told them what he was looking for and why and for whom. Then he rejoined Maddy. She stirred in her sleep, burrowing into him. He put his arms around her and lay with her hair spread across his chest and his shoulder, the scent of her filling his senses. Closing his eyes, he inhaled deeply and savored the feel and the smell and the sound of Maddy in his arms.

MADDY WOKE LATER that afternoon to find Max standing beside the bed, a tray in hand.

"Hungry?" he asked.

She blinked and pushed the hair from her eyes. Her body felt sore, tired, and her eyes were gritty. She remembered, then, in a rush of self-consciousness.

"God. I'm so sorry. You must think I'm a fruitcake," she said.

"I've got croissants, quiche and a green salad, and a nice glass of pinot noir for you," he said, ignoring her apology.

She sat up and he lowered the tray onto her lap. Then he sat on the edge of the bed and helped himself to one of the plates he'd prepared.

She watched him, feeling acutely foolish.

She'd arrived on his doorstep out of nowhere after eight years of sporadic contact, thrown herself on his chest, cried on his shoulder, jumped his body and fallen at his feet in despair. She was like an over-the-top ballet, all high notes and melodrama.

"Maddy. Stop thinking, start eating. I swear I don't think you're a fruitcake."

"Maybe I am." She picked up her fork. "Penelope Karovska had a nervous breakdown when they retired her. Joulet became an alcoholic."

"If she wasn't one already. And you're not like either of them."

She sliced off a chunk of quiche with the edge of her fork.

"You're heartbroken," he said simply. "Something you love has been taken away from you."

She stared at the food on the end of her fork, then forced herself to put it in her mouth. Max had bought this for her. While she slept off her crazed dancing bout, he'd prepared food and come up here ready to listen and offer yet more advice and patience and wisdom.

She looked at him, her gaze taking in the charming unevenness of his dark hair, growing out from the harsh cropped style now, the elegant blades of his cheekbones, the full sensuousness of his mouth. He hadn't shaved today and his jaw was shaded with bristle. His clear gray eyes stared back at her, slightly crinkled at the corners, a question in them.

"What did I do to deserve you?" she asked quietly.

For a moment there was a flare of something in Max's eyes. Then he blinked and shrugged.

"Something really decadent," he said. "I'm hoping you'll give me a live action replay of it later."

He leered so comically that she had to laugh. She ate another piece of quiche and took a sip of her wine. He told her about his morning moving furniture with Richard, showing off his scraped shin and bruised knuckles. They laughed over Charlotte's bossiness, then he produced a white parcel with an all-too-familiar name on it.

"How did you get these?" she asked, sitting up straighter. "I thought you were working all morning."

"I have my ways."

Reverently she peeled the paper from the box. The scent of

sugar and vanilla and almonds rose up to greet her and she inhaled deeply.

"Your country truly has a great gift for doing wonderful things with flour and sugar," she said.

"Don't forget butter. We're no slouches there, either."

He picked up a macaroon and brought it to her lips.

"One bite. Tell me what it is," he said.

Her teeth crunched through crisp meringue and into a creamy fondant center. She savored the flavors on her tongue for a few seconds before swallowing.

"Easy. Vanilla and pistachio," she said smugly.

"Humph. What about this one?"

They worked their way through the box and she only got one wrong. As a reward, Max ate the last macaroon off her belly then slid lower for dessert.

As she fisted her hands in the sheets and arched beneath the teasing, enticing ministrations of his hands and mouth, she felt the last of the sadness and grief she'd experienced drift away. Not gone for good, she knew that, but gone for today. Thanks to Max. Beautiful, sexy, strong, kind, patient, funny Max.

"I want you inside me," she said as she felt her climax rising. "Now, Max, please."

She felt as though a new understanding was building inside her, keeping pace with her desire, and she welcomed him into her body with greedy need.

The familiar weight of him, the rasp of his hairy, strong chest against her breasts, the slide of his body inside hers. She wrapped her legs around his waist and held on for dear life, held on to Max, as her orgasm hit her.

He came at the same time and she bit her lip as the fierce thrust and shudder of his body in hers pushed her higher and higher.

Afterward, he rolled onto his back, taking her with him so that she sprawled across his chest. His hands stroked her hair and her back and she listened to the thundering of his heart as it slowly returned to normal.

A fierce, warm awareness spread through her, a sense of well-being and belonging. This man…she'd thought she'd known him, top to bottom, inside out when she lived with him years ago. But she had never really looked at him or understood him.

He was… She didn't have the words for it.

No, that was a lie. She had the words. She simply didn't know how to say them to him yet.

She frowned, smoothing a hand over his arm, tracing the curve of his muscles. It wasn't what she'd come to Paris to find. But it had happened anyway.

She'd fallen in love with Max.

It was both a terrifying and an exhilarating thought. All her life, she'd held off from intimacy with men because experience had taught her that intimacy always came hand in hand with demands, because she'd never found a man she'd been prepared to compromise her love of dancing for.

But dancing was no longer part of her life. Briefly she wondered if being forced into retirement had allowed her to see Max differently, allowed her to make room in her heart for something other than ballet. Then she remembered the powerful need to see Max she'd felt the day she'd been given the news her career was over. Was it possible that deep down inside she'd always known that Max was the one?

The phone rang and Max stirred beneath her.

"I'd better get that," he said.

She murmured her protest and he smiled.

"It might be important. I'm expecting a call."

She let him edge away from her then shifted onto her belly and inhaled his scent from the sheets, a foolish smile on her face.

She was in love. Possibly for the first time in her life, if the feeling in her chest was anything to go by. It literally ached with fullness, with the need to wrap her arms around him and invite him into her body and protect him and adore him and love him. She squeezed her eyes tightly shut, feeling as though she was riding a roller coaster of realization and emotion.

Max. After all these years.

She heard his feet on the stairs as he returned from taking the call. She wondered if her love was in her eyes, blazing there for him to see. She felt as though it was radiating from her body, a physical energy pouring from her like light from a lamp.

She wanted to tell him, to declare herself. And yet she was scared, because he had never said anything to her about his feelings. He had been kind. He desired her. He loved her, she had no doubt, as a friend. But was he *in love* with her? Could she really be that lucky?

She turned and propped herself up on her elbows as Max stopped at the end of the bed. He still had the phone in one hand, and she saw that he'd pulled on a pair of jeans.

"Maddy, I have some great news for you," he said.

She frowned, because her mind was totally elsewhere. "Sorry?"

"I called around, spoke to a few old dancing buddies. Remember how you told me Liza was with the Nederlands Dans Theatre?"

Her frown deepened. "Yes."

She had a sudden horrible thought. Max hadn't bought them tickets to a performance, had he? Because she wasn't up to watching other people dance yet. Certainly not someone she had once shared a stage with. One day, she would enjoy being in the audience at a ballet again. But not yet.

"She phoned to let me know that the company is forming a new offshoot, a sort of collaborative partnership, I guess, headed by some of their senior dancers. People like you, Maddy, who've been pushed into retirement before they're ready. Liza wasn't sure on the details, but she gave me a number and I called. They're looking for experienced, skilled dancers, people other companies won't consider because of their age or injuries. The plan is to choreograph to their strengths, to perform ballets that rely more on the advanced skill and technique of the dancers instead of athleticism and flexibility. I just spoke to Gregers Roby. They'd love to meet you and talk to you about dancing with them, Maddy."

She stared at him, his words ringing in her ears.

"Dance? But I can't, Max, my knee…" she said, shaking her head.

"They would play to your strengths, Maddy. Shorter sequences, shared responsibility for leads. Whatever it takes to keep someone with your skill and talent onstage for as long as they can."

She dropped flat onto her back, staring blindly. She felt dizzy, overwhelmed. She could dance again?

She could dance again?

Hard on the heels of a burgeoning, tentative hope came the realization that Max had done this. He'd contacted his friends, asked around, found something for her. Found a way to give her what she most wanted.

Found a way to send her back into her life, her old life. Her life without him.

"Why?" she asked.

She felt the bed dip as Max sat.

"Because you're an exquisite dancer. Because they'd kill to have you," Max said.

"No. Why did you call your friends? I don't understand."

There was a short pause, as if he considered his response.

"I knew you were unhappy. I thought if maybe there was a teaching role, choreography, even dance notation available, that maybe… I know you didn't think you wanted to do any of those things, but I thought that at least you would still be a part of the dance world. You wouldn't have to give it up entirely. But Liza had heard about this new company being formed, and she made some inquiries for me."

She closed her eyes. She wasn't sure what she was feeling, whether she could dare to believe in this potential reprieve.

"They know about my knee?" she asked, in case he hadn't made it clear enough to them and they thought they'd be talking to a whole dancer. "They know about my injury?"

"Yes, of course. And they still want to talk to you."

She pressed her hands to her face, overwhelmed.

"Are you okay?" Max asked.

"I can't believe it," she said.

She sat up then and faced him.

"I don't know what to say to you. You've given me so much already. Max…you've saved my life these past few weeks. And now this…"

His expression remained serious before he smiled.

"You were born to dance, Maddy," he said.

"Yes."

She flung herself at him and held him so tightly her joints ached with the effort of it.

"Max. Thank you. Thank you," she said.

"Maddy." His arms tightened around her just as firmly.

They sat that way for a long moment, holding each other fiercely. Then a horrible thought hit her.

I'll have to leave him. I'll have to leave Max to dance.

No.

The single word resounded like a shout in her mind. No. She couldn't leave Max. She couldn't possibly walk away from these feelings.

Max's grip slackened and she sensed he was about to break their embrace. She couldn't let him go. She *wouldn't* let him go, she decided. As he tried to ease away from her, she maintained the embrace. After a few seconds, he relaxed into it again, intuiting her desire—her need—for the contact.

Quickly she made plans in her mind. The company would be based in the Netherlands somewhere, probably Amsterdam, just a short flight from Paris. She could visit Max between tours, and when she had a break from rehearsals. And he could come visit her. They could take turns. She could watch his sculptures come alive. She could still have him in her life.

Only when she'd organized her thoughts and decided she could have it all did she bring herself to release him.

"They want to see you the day after tomorrow," Max said. "I know it's late notice, but they're in the last stages of planning and your availability was a bit of a wild card for them."

She widened her eyes in shock, a thousand practical considerations hitting her like an avalanche.

"My God. I'll need to book a flight. Shit, I don't even have a suitcase. What am I talking about? I came here with barely anything. I've got nothing to put in a suitcase." She laughed, feeling a little dizzy with the newness of it all.

He watched her, his gaze intent.

"Happy, Maddy?" he asked. "This is what you wanted, isn't it?"

She thought of what lay ahead—the opportunity to dance, and the chance to have Max by her side while she did it. Her two great loves, hand in hand.

"Yes, Max. This is what I wanted."

It just about killed him, but he got through the evening and the next day, and he drove Maddy to the airport for her flight to Amsterdam that night.

He thought about flying with her, holding her hand through

the interview, but Maddy didn't need him for any of that. She knew how to dance without him.

He lay awake for a long time that night, aware of the space in the bed beside him.

Better get used to that, he told himself. *The sooner the better.*

She called from her hotel room the minute she got in from her interview the next day. He wiped the clay off his hands with a towel and held the phone to his ear with his shoulder as she raved about how nice everyone was and how much she loved the ethos of the new company and how excited she was about their ideas for shows and tours.

"They offered you a place, then?" he asked drily when he could get a word in edgeways.

"Yes! Yes! Didn't I mention that? God, I'm so excited I don't know whether to sit or do a handstand. Oh, Max, I wish you were here. We could go out and celebrate."

He dropped the towel and gripped the receiver.

"You'll have lots of things to sort out. Your apartment in Australia. You'll need to find a place in Amsterdam," he said.

"I know. They want to start rehearsals within the month. There's so much to sort out. Thank God for the Internet."

He took a deep breath. "I can get your gear together here, send it on. That will save you one trip and a bit of time, anyway," he said.

"Oh, no, I'll come back to Paris. I need to say goodbye to Eloise and Charlotte and talk to you. We need to plan your first visit to Amsterdam, Max," she said.

His grip tightened on the phone. "It's a nice idea, Maddy, but probably not a good one."

There was a short pause.

"Me coming back to Paris? Or you coming to Amsterdam?"

He could hear the hurt in her voice. He steeled himself. "Both, I guess."

"What about— What about us, Max?" she asked. Her voice was quiet and low. He imagined her sitting in her hotel room, her face crumpled with confusion.

But any hurt she was feeling would soon pass. She had a second chance at her career. The few weeks they'd had together would soon fade into insignificance as she lost herself in her craft again. If they'd ever had any significance in the first place. As Charlotte had so eloquently pointed out, Maddy needing him while he loved her was not a recipe for success. One of these things was definitely not like the other.

"I'll never forget it, Maddy. But we both know it only happened between us because of what was going on in your life. Let's quit while we're ahead," he said.

There was a long silence. He could hear her breathing on the other end of the phone.

"What about your sculptures? I mean, I'd like to know how you do with everything."

"Of course. I'll let you know if I ever get a show, send you pictures. You're my friend, Maddy. We'll always be friends."

Except it would kill him to see her, to talk to her, to hear about her life and how she was getting on without him. He'd do it, because he didn't want to hurt her and she would be hurt if he cut all contact. But he needed some time between now and whenever he next saw her to get his shit together. To find a way of surviving the next little while with this ache in his chest.

"I'll get your stuff together tomorrow and send it to you at the hotel," he said.

"Okay. Thanks."

She sounded as though she was crying. He closed his eyes and swore silently.

"I'll miss you, Max," she said.

"I'll miss you, too, Maddy."

There was nothing much else to say. He'd found a way for

Maddy to continue living her dream. Now he had to work out how to live his life without her in it.

He ended the call and stood staring at the phone for a long time. Then he walked to the kitchen and dug out the last bottle of cognac from his father's collection.

He poured himself a drink and took the bottle and the glass with him to the couch. Then he sat down and proceeded to get ball-tearingly wasted.

MADDY DIDN'T KNOW what to do with herself. She sat listening to the dial tone in her hotel room for a full five minutes before it occurred to her to hang up.

Max didn't want to see her again. He didn't even want her to come back to Paris to say goodbye properly. He'd just neatly excised her out of his life and waved *au revoir* without a backward glance.

She stood, then realized she had nowhere to go and sat again.

She simply hadn't expected it. She'd thought—she'd *assumed* that what she'd been feeling had been mutual. How could it not be, when her own feelings had been so all-encompassing and compelling?

But apparently not. Apparently Max had decided that their little fling had run its course. He'd found her this opportunity, and now he was going to pack her bags and send her off into the world, their liaison a thing of the past.

Was that all it had been, all it had meant? A liaison? A few weeks of sex between friends, no strings, no emotions, no consequences?

She put her head in her hands and pressed her fingertips to her forehead. How was it possible to feel so happy and so sad all at the same time? Max had found a way for her to dance again, but he'd also gently nudged her out of his apartment and out of his life. Time to move on, Maddy, he'd said in all but words.

I'll never forget it, Maddy. But we both know it only happened between us because of what was going on in your life.

What did that mean? That he'd been sleeping with her because she needed him? Because she'd been upset? Because she'd turned to him for comfort and, ever her friend, he'd given it?

Nausea swirled in her stomach as her memories of the past month were viewed through this new prism.

Max as her lover out of compassion. Max as her lover out of consideration and concern for a friend.

A sour taste filled her mouth. Surely not? Surely she hadn't fallen for him while he'd been *comforting* her?

Then she remembered the look in his eyes when he'd walked toward her sometimes, all hard body and harder erection, ready to claim what he wanted. And the times he'd thrown her onto the bed and made love to her with a greedy passion that had made her knees tremble and her insides melt.

Not a man acting out of friendship or concern. Max had wanted her. He'd said it himself, hadn't he? He'd always found her attractive. Always wanted to sleep with her.

Now he had. And, for him, their attraction had run its course. While for her, it had burgeoned into something far more profound and life-changing than mere sexual attraction.

She'd fallen in love with him, after ten years.

And he considered her nothing more than a friend.

She huffed out a humorless laugh. It figured that the only time she'd ever really, truly fallen in love she'd fallen for the one man who didn't want to make demands on her or wrest her away from her career. Far from it. Max didn't even care enough to make demands.

Like a child releasing a balloon, she let go of the idea, the hope that had been forming in her heart: a life with Max, good times shared with his family, standing proudly by Max's side as he sent his art out into the world, dancing knowing he was in the audience, watching her.

None of it would happen. She would never again have a chance to hold Eloise's warm, sweaty hands and look down into her joy-filled face as they danced together. She'd never again exasperate Charlotte with her failure to grasp the intricacies of handmade pastry. And she'd never wake up in Max's arms again, his body warm and hard against hers.

Dry-eyed, she crawled beneath the covers and pulled the blankets tight around herself.

Thank God she had her dancing, because she honestly did not know what she would do without it.

MAX FROWNED in irritation as he registered the knocking at his front door. He sighed heavily and abandoned the chisel and file he'd been working with to answer the summons.

Charlotte glowered at him when he flung it open.

"I've been knocking for ten minutes."

"I didn't hear you."

It was true. He'd been so absorbed in his work that he'd only registered the noise when he'd stepped back to check his progress.

Charlotte trailed after him as he returned to the five-foot-two-inch bronze figure poised beside his workbench. He was removing the marks from the sprues, the channels where the bronze had been poured into the mold made from his original clay sculpture. Two more bronze figures waited beside the first in various stages of completion.

He picked up his file, eyeing the shoulder he'd been working on. It still wasn't quite right….

Charlotte was huffing and puffing beside him as she surveyed his apartment. He didn't need to look to know what she was seeing: clothes piled on chairs, dishes overflowing the sink, newspapers in stacks near the door, take-out food containers and empty bottles of wine stacked beside the couch.

"You have to stop living like this. You're like a caveman. You only come out to get enough food to survive then you hole up back here in your apartment. When was the last time you shaved or did a load of laundry or changed your sheets?"

"Don't know. Don't care," he said, moving in to work on a molding mark.

"Will you stop that damned noise for five seconds and talk to me? I'm worried about you," Charlotte said.

He glanced across at her and saw how pale and tense she was.

"There's nothing to worry about. I'm fine. I'm working. I have a show in two weeks' time, in case you'd forgotten."

He still couldn't believe his luck. He'd been at the foundry supervising the casting of his second figure when Celeste Renou had seen his work. She owned a gallery in the exclusive Place des Vosges and had offered him a show on the spot.

He smiled grimly as he reflected that only Maddy's absence from his life had made it possible for him to come even close to making her deadline. He'd worked like a madman since the day Maddy left—morning, noon and night—channeling all his energy and regret and anger and frustration and lust and hurt and resentment into his art.

Three months. She'd been gone three months and he still woke to thoughts of her. He still smelled her perfume in his apartment, on his sheets and towels and shirts. He still found long strands of brown hair on his coat, his scarf.

He still loved her.

He was starting to wonder if that would ever change. Perhaps the best he could hope for was that his feelings would become dormant, as they had before. Lie down and play dead—until the next contact with Maddy, the next time he saw her or heard her voice.

"Max, this isn't about your show or your art or anything except for you. Have you looked in the mirror lately? You look like shit. You've lost weight. The homeless man on the corner has better personal hygiene. Talk to me."

"I'm fine."

"No, you're not. You're not over Maddy. You're not even close to being over Maddy, and I'm worried about what it's doing to you."

"I'll survive. The show will be over soon. I promise I'll shower before then."

She didn't smile. She looked as though she was struggling to contain herself.

"Okay, I'm going to say this because I think it needs to be said. You know I loved Maddy. I adored her. But the fact remains that she took off the moment she had a whiff of her career being resuscitated, and she didn't even bother to say goodbye to any of us. Including you. I'm sure she's had to learn to be so self-centered to survive in her profession, but it's not so great for everyone else in her life. Is she worth it, Max? I guess that's what I'm trying to ask you. Is Maddy worth all this angst and isolation?"

"Leave it, Charlotte."

"No. I think you need to hear this. While you're turning into a smelly crazy man, she's off dancing the light fantastic somewhere. Can't you see the imbalance? Can't you see—"

"It wasn't Maddy's fault, okay?" he snapped, unable to listen to his sister rail at Maddy when he knew the truth. He'd held his tongue through Charlotte's shock at Maddy's abrupt departure and Eloise's disappointment at losing her dancing teacher. He hadn't said a word. But for some reason, the closer the date for the opening of his show came, the more it chafed on him that he'd let his sister assume the worst about Maddy.

"Maddy didn't get a job offer and just take off. I found the opportunity for her through an old friend, set up an interview for her, encouraged her to go. And she wanted to come back to Paris to say goodbye, but I told her not to. So don't blame her if you're upset. Blame me."

Charlotte was openmouthed with shock.

"You *sent Maddy away?*" she said, her voice rising on a high note of incredulity.

"I found a way for her to dance again."

"In another country. And then you told her not to come back?" Charlotte's face was creased with confusion. "Why would you do that to yourself when you love her so much?"

He threw the file onto his workbench.

"You saw what she was like. She was brokenhearted about having to retire. I found her a second chance to do something she loved."

Charlotte sank into a chair. "My God. I always knew you had a Sir Galahad complex, but this takes the cake."

"I wanted her to be happy," he said defensively.

"I got that, you noble idiot. Did you at least tell her how you felt before she left?"

He looked at her but said nothing.

Charlotte swore loud and long. "Max! Are you telling me you packed Maddy off and you never said a word to her about how you feel?"

His continued silence was answer enough. Charlotte shot to her feet, throwing her hands in the air in exasperation.

"All this time I've been angry with Maddy for abandoning you, and she was the one I should have felt sorry for. Why didn't you say something to her before she left, Max?"

"There was no point."

"Why?"

"Because I know how she feels. I've always known how she feels."

Charlotte closed her eyes and made a sound like a kettle boiling. "You are such a…man!"

"What's that supposed to mean?"

"You have no idea how Maddy feels."

"I've known her for ten years. I know exactly how she feels."

"No, you don't. You think you know, but you don't, because you never asked her. You never told her how you feel, and you never asked her how she feels."

"It wouldn't have made any difference," he said stubbornly.

Charlotte stepped close and grabbed his arm, her eyes intense as they bored into him. "You don't know that."

He stared at her, and she shook his arm.

"You sent her to Amsterdam without telling her you didn't want her to go. How do you think she must have felt, Max? First you find her a job thousands of miles away, then you drive her to the airport and tell her not to bother coming back. My God. Even if she didn't love you she must have felt as though she'd overstayed her welcome."

For the first time he considered what had happened from Maddy's point of view. She'd been thrilled about the new role with the Nederlands Dans Theatre. He knew he was right about that. But she'd spoken about him visiting her in Amsterdam. And she'd wanted to come back to Paris to sort things out with him.

What if his sister was right? What if he'd pushed Maddy away when he should have been pulling her close? What if he'd been so busy giving her what he thought she wanted and protecting himself that he'd destroyed his one chance at happiness?

"I've spent so long believing it would never happen between us I couldn't see any other way forward," he finally admitted.

"Call her."

He shook his head. There were things he needed to say that couldn't be said over a phone. He needed to see her in person, to look into her eyes.

"She's coming for the show at the end of the month," he said.

"You could fly over and see her before then. After you spend about a week in the shower detoxing and de-fleaing yourself."

"No."

An idea was forming. He reached for his diary, flicking through the pages. There was almost enough time. Hell, he'd make the time if he had to.

"Max…"

"No. There's something I want to do first. Something I need to do," he said.

It was an idea he'd had for a while, something that had been tickling at the back of his mind ever since he finished the last model for his full-size bronzes. A smaller piece. An intensely personal, private piece to complete the series.

He crossed to his workbench, started assembling the materials he'd need.

"Here we go. The mad genius at work," Charlotte said.

He barely heard her. He was too gripped by what he needed to do. Somehow, he needed to show Maddy how he felt, to make her understand. If he was going to declare himself, he was going to do it right.

MADDY CHECKED her lipstick for the fourth time as the taxi turned into the narrow streets leading to Place de Vosges. She was nervous. No point kidding herself. She had no idea how she was going to handle seeing Max again.

She'd spoken to him exactly three times since the night he'd told her not to return to Paris. He'd called to let her know when her things would be arriving, then she'd called him to ask about Eloise, concerned the little girl was missing her dancing lessons. She needn't have bothered—Max had already stepped in to take her place and he'd reported Eloise was thriving.

The last time they'd spoken he'd invited her to his show. It had been awkward between them. She hadn't known what to ask, where to start. The same question kept bubbling up inside her, begging for release.

Did it mean so little to you? Do I mean so little to you?

She tightened her grip on her purse as the cab rolled to a stop. She'd already pulled a twenty-euro note from her wallet and she handed it over then slid from the car.

Warm spring air danced around her calves as she slowly walked along the elegant, covered walkway of Place des Vosges. More than any other part of Paris it reminded her of the Hollywood ideal of a European setting—a huge square bordered on four sides by identical brick buildings, all uniformly five stories high, all in red brick. The square in the middle had been nothing but gravel and stark, bare trees when she left. Tonight, it was filled with Parisians enjoying the warm weather, picnicking on the grass, studying, kissing, laughing beneath arching green trees.

She hadn't realized how much she'd missed Paris until the taxi had hit the old center and she'd caught her first glimpse of cobblestones. Max lived here. That was why she loved it. Paris was the city where she'd fallen in love.

There were several galleries facing the Place des Vosges, but only one was filled with elegantly dressed people sipping champagne.

Max's opening. She was full of so many different emotions she felt she might overflow. Pride, love, hurt—she didn't know where one ended and the other began.

Her high heels tapped on the stone walkway as she made her way to the gallery entrance. She couldn't see anyone she knew—Charlotte, Richard, Max—and she tried to calm herself. The gallery interior was stark white with high arched ceilings, all the better to show off the art, she guessed. There were so many people present she couldn't see Max's work, and she started to move into the crowd, determined to see at last the fruits of their time together.

She'd sat for him for hours in the end. When he told her he'd been offered a show, she'd wondered what his work would be like. If he had used her as his model, or if he'd found someone else. Yvette, or another dancer.

"Maddy. There you are!"

She turned to see Charlotte bearing down on her, arms wide, a glass of champagne in one hand.

"You look gorgeous, as always," Charlotte said, holding Maddy's hands out to the side so she could inspect her deep red velvet sheath.

"That can only be French," she said with a knowing eye.

Maddy smiled. "Actually, it's Italian," she said.

Charlotte pulled a face. "We'll keep it quiet, no one will know."

Maddy's eyes slid over her shoulder, searching the crowd.

"He's toward the back. We both saw you arrive but he's stuck with some boring arts patron who keeps fondling Max's arm like a pet dog or something," Charlotte said.

"Oh."

"Ah. Here he is now."

Maddy swiveled on her heel, her heart in her throat, her palms suddenly sweaty.

Her eyes ate him up, taking in his elegantly messy hair, the sharp lines of his face, the crispness of his white shirt and midnight-navy suit. Cuff links glinted at his wrists and his shoulders looked impossibly wide.

"Maddy," he said.

His gaze scanned her face intently before finally his eyes locked with hers and they were staring at each other for the first time in three months.

A deluge of memories hit her: Max looking into her eyes as he made love to her in the shower, Max laughing at her disastrous attempts at cooking, the solemn watchfulness on his face as he'd told her about the opportunity in Amsterdam.

"You look beautiful," he said.

Heat raced up her spine as his gaze skimmed over her breasts and down her waist. She still found him enormously attractive, even though they were only supposed to be friends now.

Not for the first time, she wondered how she would survive tonight with her pride intact. How was she going to stop herself from telling him how she felt, what she wanted?

"This is a wonderful turnout," she said because she couldn't think of anything else to say. "You must be pleased."

He shrugged. "I've been waiting for you to get here."

Another wave of heat raced up her spine.

Don't get carried away, Maddy. He's just being friendly.

But there was something in his manner, the way he reached for her hand, the way he hesitated before threading his fingers through hers.

"There's something I want to show you," he said.

He led her deeper into the gallery, towing her behind him. She studied the strong column of his neck, the white collar of his shirt. Her gaze dipped to his backside, remembering the flex and contract of his hard muscles as he pumped into her. Her breath caught in her throat and her hand twitched in his.

Suddenly she was filled with an intense longing. She wanted things to be the way they had been during those magical few weeks in Max's apartment. Even in the midst of her grief over losing her career, she'd never been happier. And now she had her career but no Max. She knew which state she preferred, which grief was surmountable and which was not.

The crowd parted before Max, people smiling and watching him avidly as he passed. Without even seeing his work Maddy understood that he was a hit. People watched him as if he was a star, a somebody.

Then a man stepped to one side and she saw the first sculpture—a ballerina arching forward in a perfect arabesque, the muscles of her slim frame straining. Her face was lifted, her expression serene, as though she was exactly where she needed to be.

The detail in the piece was extraordinary—the curve of the dancer's naked breasts, the texture of curls between her thighs, the hollow beneath her armpit, the lines around her mouth and eyes. For a second Maddy fell victim to a wave of acute self-consciousness. This was her naked body, her face, depicted so faithfully, in such detail. This was so much more than what she'd imagined when she'd agreed to model for Max. He'd captured her forever. And then the self-consciousness was washed away as awe at his skill, at his power, swept over her.

"She's beautiful," she said, overwhelmed by Max's talent. "I almost feel as though she's about to move."

"She's you, Maddy," he said quietly. He tugged on her hand. "There's more."

He led her to the next dancer, caught forever in the middle of a pirouette. Maddy looked into her own face, cast in bronze, the expression there a mixture of pain and joy.

"Do I really look like that when I dance?" she asked him.

"Yes. When you danced for me."

The next figure was a dying swan, the dancer languishing at their feet in despair. Then there was a dancer executing a grand plié, and finally a seated posture, the ballerina contemplating her sore feet as she slipped off her shoes in a quiet moment.

"Well, those are definitely my bent toes," she said drily. "When did you do this sketch?"

"When you weren't looking. I wanted a quiet, private moment."

He'd found it. She was blown away by the beauty and energy and fineness of his work. Blown away, also, by the fact that all the dancers were her. He hadn't used Yvette or anyone else.

Max was watching her expectantly and she realized that there was one last sculpture remaining, a smaller figure placed beyond the adult dancers.

She took a step forward. Then her hand went to her mouth as she understood what she was looking at.

A little girl stood there, one hand on the barre, her feet turned out, the other hand raised over her head in a graceful arc. The little girl's head was tilted so she could follow the line of her raised hand with her eyes, and the look on her face was pure joy, the expression of a little soul who had found her calling in life.

Maddy's eyes filled with tears.

"I thought I was finished when I'd cast the first six. But then I realized that I wasn't," he said.

"How did you…?" The resemblance to her four-year-old self was uncanny.

"You had a picture in your room a long time ago," he said.

"And you remembered?"

He nodded. She studied the figure and a slow understanding dawned on her.

She saw the deep, abiding love that was evident in every line of the figure and the hollowness that she'd carried inside her for three months evaporated as she turned to look at Max. He couldn't have made this sculpture and not feel something more than friendship for her. It simply wasn't possible. Surely…?

He was holding something in his hands, and she frowned as she recognized it.

"My scarf," she said stupidly.

"Maddy, I've been wanting to say this to you for a long time. Ten years, in fact. I love you. I've loved you from the moment I met you. I've loved you every minute since. This scarf…well, frankly, I stole it so I could have something to remember you by. But I'm giving it back tonight because I'd rather have you."

For a moment all she could do was stare at him. What he

was saying changed her world. Changed everything. Their shared history. Her present. Her future. She blinked, trying to come to terms with what she'd just heard.

Max had always loved her. Always. When they were living together. When they were dancing together. When he was offering her comfort and solace.

All that time he'd loved her.

Suddenly she noticed how tight his jaw was, how square his shoulders were. Tension emanated from every muscle. He was waiting for her, waiting for her reaction. She didn't know whether to laugh or cry she was so touched by how uncertain he was.

"Max," she said. She had no words for the feeling expanding in her chest. Shaking her head at her inability to articulate her emotions, she settled for reaching up and holding his face as she stood on her tiptoes and kissed him. His hands found her face, and they pressed their mouths together in an intense, fierce meeting of souls.

Finally she broke the kiss and looked up into his face, just inches from hers.

"Max, I love you, too. I've spent the past three months living without you and I never want to be that unhappy again in my life."

For a heartbeat Max stared into her face. She saw how deep the doubt went in him, and it almost broke her heart as she understood how hard it must have been for him to love her for so long without any acknowledgment from her.

Then his eyes cleared and a smile tugged at the corners of his mouth.

"Maddy," he said. He kissed her, his tongue sliding into her mouth, his body pressing against hers, his hands sliding into her hair to hold her steady so he could drink his fill of her.

They broke the kiss to stare at each other again. Maddy found herself smiling the same goofy, slightly bemused smile that Max was smiling.

"I thought you sent me away because you were sick of me," she said.

"I sent you away because I wanted you to be happy, to have what you wanted," he said.

"I wanted you. Only you. The chance to dance again was a nice surprise, a lovely chance for me to say goodbye to a part of my life. But you're my future, Max."

His smile broadened into a grin as he absorbed her words and he pulled her into his arms, lifted her and spun her in a circle. He was about to kiss her again when the sound of a clearing throat alerted them to the fact that they had an audience.

They glanced up, registering for the first time the circle of interested art lovers surrounding them. Charlotte stepped forward, one eyebrow raised.

"I think the Americans have a phrase for this, yes?" she said. "Get a room? Is that it?"

Max threw back his head and laughed. It was the best sound Maddy had ever heard in her life, but suddenly tears were squeezing from beneath her eyelids and running down her face. Max's smile faded and he reached out to cup her cheek.

"Maddy, don't cry," he said, his face a picture of dismay.

"I'm so sorry," she said. "I'm so sorry for not understanding sooner. For not seeing. All those times I climbed into your bed. All those times I bitched to you about my boyfriends…"

He shook his head and pressed his fingers to her lips.

"No. No looking back."

"But—"

"No. From this moment on there is only now, and tomorrow. Nothing else matters."

He started pulling her toward the front of the gallery. A tall white-haired woman intercepted them.

"Max! Where are you going?" she asked, eyebrows disappearing into her white hair.

"I need to consult with my muse," he said.

The woman looked outraged. "Now? You need to consult with your muse now?"

Max shot Maddy a dirty, dirty look.

"Definitely. And at great length."

He pulled Maddy out into the street.

"Who was that?" she asked.

He shrugged. "Gallery owner."

"Oh my God."

She pulled her hand free and raced back to the gallery entrance. "We'll be back. Half an hour." She thought again, remembering what it was like when she and Max were skin to skin, how crazy they got. "An hour, tops."

Max slid his arms around her and kissed her soundly when she rejoined him. She could feel how hard he was, his erection pressing against her belly. She was so ready for him she wanted to pull him into a doorway and have her wicked way with him on the spot.

"An hour?" he said. "I'm going to need more than an hour to show you how much I love you, Maddy."

"I know. But we've got the rest of our lives, right?"

He stared into her face, his fingers curling possessively into her hips.

"Yes. We have forever."

Then he took her home.

SIX MONTHS LATER, Maddy stood in the wings and waited for her musical cue. Through a gap in the curtain she could see a sliver of the audience in the stalls and the dim shadow of the dress circle in the background. She lifted her gaze to Chagall's roof, savoring the sight, the moment.

It felt absolutely right that her last performance as a prima ballerina should be here at the Opera Garnier. Paris was her home now. And this was a special place, a fitting place to draw the line under her career.

She would miss performances like this one. A part of her would always grieve the end of her career. But she had new things to look forward to in life. Dancing wasn't her earth, moon and stars anymore.

She smiled as she thought of Max, her husband now for all of a month. His would be one of the first faces she saw when she took to the stage, sitting front row center.

She took a deep breath. She loved him so much. More every day.

He'd sold every piece from his debut exhibition and was working on a second show. They'd moved to a new apartment two months ago, hanging on to his old one so he could convert it into his atelier. It was going to be tough for the next few years, financially speaking, but she had every confidence that Max was going to have a great art career.

She was looking forward to modeling for him again, in between her new studies at the Sorbonne. She was training to become a dance therapist. Her work with Eloise had shown her that there were many different ways to weave dancing into her life and she planned to specialize in working with autistic children if she could. The idea of going back to school after so many years away was frankly terrifying, but she was determined to rise to the occasion. She knew how to work hard, after all. Hopefully the rest would follow.

She stepped back from the curtain as the music swelled. It was time to say goodbye.

She found her starting point, took a deep belly breath…

And then she was on the stage, defying gravity, doing the thing she loved, had always loved. She savored each pirouette, every arabesque. Her last performance. Her swan song, her goodbye to her first love.

In the audience, she caught sight of Max's face. She could see his pride, see the tears shimmering in his eyes.

Her heart lifting, she gave herself over to the music and danced.

* * * * *

NAKED AMBITION

BY
JULE McBRIDE

Jule McBride is a native West Virginian. Her dream to write romances came true in the nineties with the publication of her debut novel, *Wild Card Wedding*. It received a *Romantic Times BOOKreviews* Reviewer's Choice Award for Best First Series Romance. Since then, the author has been nominated for multiple awards, including two lifetime achievement awards. She has written for several series and currently makes her happy home at Blaze®. A prolific writer, she has almost fifty titles to her credit.

1

EVERY TIME SHE SO MUCH AS LOOKED at J. D. Johnson, Susannah Banner could swear she felt his big, hot hands removing all her clothes, never even bothering to leave behind the panties. Even worse, the undeserving man had had this bothersome effect on her since she was only five years old, knee-high to a grasshopper her daddy had called her.

Yes, J.D. had started ruining her life as early as grade school, where she'd had the misfortune of first meeting him, Susannah fumed as she drove her compact car along Palmer Road, past Hodges' Motor Lodge. She then cornered off the main drag and into the back parking lot of Delia's Diner to hide the car so J.D. wouldn't see it if he followed her. She'd been young when she'd met J.D., and well, what little girl—especially one so innocent as Susannah—could have seen through a male as duplicitous as J. D. Johnson?

Years later, when Susannah was old enough, she'd fantasized about him for hours, a mistake that had led to hot-heavy sex and feelings of sincere regret. Not even in a proper bed, she reminded herself, her fury rising, but in the bed of his daddy's pickup truck.

Just minutes ago, J.D. had drawn his last straw, and she was still reeling. Oh, Susannah knew he hadn't been born with the sense God gave a gnat, but then what man had? J.D. possessed the devil's double-edged tongue when it came to sweet-talking his way out of bad tasting situations, too. And he'd been gifted with a singing voice that could charm the skin off a rattlesnake, and worse, the pants off any female country-western fan in America.

Susannah wasn't like those women, though, she thought as she headed toward the door to Delia's. Why should Susannah be impressed by J.D.'s good fortune, after all? Like everybody else in Bayou Banner, she'd known him before he was rich and famous. In fact, she was one of the chosen few who knew what the initials J.D. stood for.

"I just wish I hadn't married you, Jeremiah Dashiell," she muttered. It had been her biggest mistake. Tears shimmering in her soft blue eyes, she tossed one of her trademark oversize handbags into the corner that she and her best friend, Ellie Lee, occupied every Saturday morning for breakfast.

As Susannah scooted in after the bag, Ellie set aside a tented white reserved card written in Delia's calligraphy.

"Please forgive me!" Susannah began, scarcely registering that Ellie was still wearing sunglasses, although the day was overcast. "J.D. made me late." Susannah shook her head, making the ends of her long, wavy sun-streaked blond hair swirl around her face. "God, I hate him! I just wish I'd had sex with somebody besides him just once. But no," she continued, "I've always been faithful." She'd doubted that was the case with J.D., and now her worst fears had been realized. She blinked back tears. "Do you realize he's the only man I've ever slept with, Ellie?"

"Sure, I was born the day after you in the hospital in Bayou Blair," Ellie reminded. "So I've known you even longer than you've known J.D. And I agree. I think you should have slept with that banjo player, at least. Remember the hottie who played in J.D.'s band in high school? The one who looked like Justin Timberlake?"

"The one who called every time me and J.D. hit the skids?"

Susannah muttered, wondering how she was going to tell Ellie what had just happened. Thinking about the banjo player was a welcome diversion. She'd kissed him and let him feel her breasts, but that was all. "How could I forget him? Of course, three weeks after I saw him, I married J.D." She glared down at the gold band on her ring finger.

"You should have insisted on an engagement," Ellie mused, eyeing the band. "That would have given you time to consider the consequences."

"True." After his career had taken off, J.D. had offered to buy her a diamond, so it would look as if they'd been engaged, but Susannah had refused, since that would have ruined the spontaneity of their wedding night. Now, of course, their whole marriage was a lie. "You think I would have stayed single if I'd talked to somebody with a crystal ball?"

"Honey, not even Mama Ambrosia could have seen your and J.D.'s future."

The local fortune teller had a cabin on a meandering tributary near Bayou Banner. As angry as she was, Susannah could admit Ellie was right. Not even a professional such as Mama Ambrosia could explain the magic that still happened sometimes between Susannah and J.D. They'd even made up their own private language for it, with code phrases for lovemaking such as *scarves and cards* or *hats and rabbits*.

J.D.'s slow drawl rumbled in Susannah's ear, and she could almost feel his warm breath tickling the lobe. "What about a game of scarves and cards, Susannah?"

He'd proposed on one of those liquid-velvet nights the Mississippi Delta had made famous, when the moon was just right, and shadows on the surface of the bayou rippled like fairy wings, making everything seem like an illusion, including scents of forsythia that stirred in the midnight air as gently as the cream in Madame Ambrosia's darkest love potions.

Their prom clothes—his tux and her butter-yellow dress beside them—they'd been lying naked on their backs on pine needles, stargazing through the waving fronds of willow branches. With a voice as smooth as the inky sky, J.D. had sung the traditional song, "Oh, Susannah"—something he always did, since his family had come from Alabama—then he'd whispered, "I want to marry you right now, oh, Susannah Banner."

She'd smiled into blue eyes, threading her fingers in the dark hair of his chest, then she'd kissed him, his light goatee tickling her nose and chin. "You want to marry me right now?" she'd teased, just to hear him say it again. She'd never heard anything as sexy as his drawl, and everybody else felt the same way. His voice was smoky and mysterious, a low bass rumble that came from his chest and shot into a listener's bloodstream like a Cupid's arrow tinged with sex. "I want to marry you this very second."

"Why should I say yes?" she'd kindly inquired.

"Because when we're legal, we can lie in bed all day."

"Now there's a typical J.D. answer." She'd laughed. "Sex is never far from your mind, is it?"

"Does that bother you, oh, Susannah?"

"Your sex drive is the only thing I like about you, J.D.," she'd assured, although secretly she'd hadn't much minded his sense of humor, either.

She had been eighteen then, and since her parents had died the year before when their car crashed on the road between

Bayou Blair and Bayou Banner during a flash flood, there had been nobody left to stop Susannah from marrying bad-boy J.D., except her big sister, June, who was ten years older. And of course, Susannah had never once listened to June.

"Well, J.D.," she'd said reasonably. "All we have to do is drive into Bayou Blair and find ourselves a preacher and a place to get a blood test."

And so, by the next morning, they were husband and wife.

Back then, J.D. had been playing music in clubs around the tristate, and he and his band could haul equipment in nothing larger than a cargo van. Now he came with an entourage, and she was lucky if his publicist, Maureen, would even share his most current cell phone number. Susannah had never been interested in gadgets, but her traditionally decorated house was full of them at the moment—everything from new phones to fancy laptop computers and an intricate home alarm system she couldn't even operate.

"Susannah? You gonna have the usual?"

Delia's voice cut through her reverie. Thankfully Delia was the polar opposite of J.D. Nothing had ever changed the diner owner—not two divorces, or losing her mama to cancer, or having her last boyfriend run off with the librarian from Bayou Blair. Come hell or high water, Delia remained as steady as a rock. She was a little plump, with a pretty face that never aged, and she'd always worn the same tan uniform and white apron. As always she was unsheathing a pencil from a mussed bun of tawny hair as if it were a tiny sword. She pointed it at an order pad, ready to do battle.

"What are you girls having?" she drawled.

Susannah shrugged undecidedly, thinking that Delia had even looked this way years ago when Susannah and June had come here with their folks every Saturday morning. Memories made Susannah's heart squeeze. After her folks had passed, Ellie had begun meeting Susannah here every Saturday, keeping up the Banner family tradition. When nothing else in the world helped, smelling sausage frying on Delia's grill could usually soothe Susannah.

"I'm not sure, Delia..." Susannah forced herself to stare at the menu, only to notice her wedding ring and feel a wave of depression. "I'm not very hungry. Maybe toast—"

Groaning, Delia dropped the order pad into her apron pocket and planted her hands on her hips. "I should have known something was wrong by the crazy way you pulled into my parking lot. What did your devil in blue jeans do now?"

"Not a thing," Susannah lied, knowing if she opened her mouth—at least to anybody except Ellie—her dirty laundry would be hanging out for all of Bayou Banner to see. Of course, before J.D., Susannah's own mama had caused a few eyebrows to rise around town, too.

Still, the Banners had been the town's most prominent family, and Susannah had hoped to uphold tradition. However, instead of decorating the town square's Christmas tree or spearheading the Easter egg drive, she'd spent most of her time apologizing for her rowdy husband and his big-city friends, all of whom made her mama look tame.

Suddenly, something inside Susannah's chest wrenched, and she almost uttered a soft cry; she could swear her heart had done three somersaults and now, it was aching to beat the band. How could she get the old J.D. back? The sweet, gentle man she'd married?

If only her mama was alive! Barbara Banner would have known how to handle J.D. She'd been a delicate woman who read too much, painted in her spare time and was overly emotional and prone to indulge too many fantasies, the type to take to her bed in winters, and to get involved in dramas of her own making. Still, her advice about men was always on target. Realizing Delia and Ellie were staring at her, Susannah blinked.

"You sure you're okay, honey?" asked Delia.

"Fine," Susannah lied. Knowing only a hearty appetite would appease Delia, she added, "I changed my mind. I'll have the usual. In fact, you'd better add extra grits." As she said the words, her stomach rumbled. Like most Southern women, Susannah included, Delia had inherited enough mouthwatering recipes to open a restaurant. For years, Susannah had been begging Delia to share her recipe for strawberry-rhubarb pie, but Delia kept refusing, saying the ingredients were top secret. "I'll have my favorite pie for dessert," Susannah added.

For Delia, having dessert after breakfast showed proof of mental stability—it was as good as formal papers signed by the board of health—so she sighed in relief, then took Ellie's order and headed for the counter, saying over her shoulder, "I'm puttin' cornbread on top of them grits, too, honey-bun. That'll keep that miserable excuse for a man from scrambling your noggin. Yes ma'am, the only thing I allow to be scrambled in Delia's Diner is my own damn eggs."

Lifting a hand so as to display her airbrushed nails, Delia held her thumb and forefinger an inch apart to indicate the minuscule length of J.D.'s penis. "Johnson's johnson," she called loudly, just in case Susannah hadn't caught the allusion.

Susannah wished it were true, but unfortunately J.D. was hung like a racehorse, and he knew how to use every inch of his equipment. Otherwise Susannah would have divorced him by now, or at least that's what she told herself.

"You look like you've seen a ghost," Ellie drawled as Delia put in their order.

"I have. Of my own husband. Oh, he was always kind of wild. Everybody knows that, Ellie. I hate to admit it, but that's why I fell in love with him. I think J.D.'s shenanigans remind me of Mama. Remember how dramatic she could be? So full of life? How she'd race around town in that little pink convertible Daddy bought her? But this…" She shook her head. "He threw another wild party."

"That's nothing new."

"True." But the house they shared, Banner Manor, meant the world to Susannah, and one of her dreams had been to restore its former glory. She and June had grown up there, and despite its sizable acreage and isolated location, nestled in a grove of mature oaks, Susannah had kept living there after her folks were gone. By then, June had moved into town with her husband, Clive, and they'd had two kids.

So naturally J.D. had moved in after he'd married Susannah. They hadn't even discussed it, no more than they'd talked about having kids or sharing finances. At eighteen and twenty-two, respectively, passion had been their focus.

"What?" prompted Ellie, drawing Susannah from her reverie once more. "Did some cigarette-smoking guitar player burn another hole in the upholstery?"

Susannah visualized a nicotine stain left on her mama's favorite love seat, wishing it were that simple. She swallowed around the lump in her throat. "Do you remember how I was going to that two-day seminar you turned me onto, in Bayou Blair? The one about how to start your own business?" Because she figured J.D.'s new friends would only destroy any improvements she made at Banner Manor, and she wasn't going to have kids while J.D. was acting like a kid himself, Susannah was considering opening a shop, although she didn't yet know what kind.

"You went, right?"

"Yeah. I got back this morning, so I figured I'd stop by the house before I met you, drop off my bags and say hi to J.D. I mean, I've been gone for two days." It was her longest trip away from home since high school, and the sad truth was, she'd enjoyed it, except that the seminar had been in the town where she and J.D. had eloped.

"You found a house full of people?"

"You knew?"

"You just missed Sheriff Kemp. He told everybody in Delia's that he got complaints last night about noise."

"Sheriff Kemp? Was he in here flirting with Delia again?"

"Yeah, but he didn't ask her out yet."

Ever since Delia's boyfriend left her, the sheriff had been sniffing around. "How could he get a complaint about our house? You know how isolated it is!"

"Gladys Walsh drove up to the door out of sheer nosiness."

The woman was a known town biddy. "Next thing you know, Mama Ambrosia will see parties in her crystal ball and start communicating with busybodies telepathically." Susannah sighed. "I'm at my wit's end," she added, her throat closing with unshed tears. "J.D.'s a grown man. He ought to be thinking about settling down." At first, she'd enjoyed the parties, been excited to share J.D.'s new success, but things had spun out of control, and lately she missed the normal life they'd once shared. But now the stuff had really hit the fan….

"He's under pressure," Ellie ventured.

"I know," Susannah said. In the past six years, he'd become Bayou Banner's most celebrated native son, the only home-grown talent, and she and Ellie had discussed the issues related to his good fortune many times. Nevertheless, even Ellie's lover, Robby Robriquet, wouldn't hang around J.D. anymore, and those two had been as thick as thieves since birth.

"When I married him, we had sex every five minutes, and I was ready to start a family. Everybody said I was too young, but Mama and Daddy were gone, and June was married, and I wanted that life for J.D. and me. I figured he'd keep playing music on weekends and take over the bait-and-tackle shop when his folks retired to Florida, since he worked there all his life."

Instead, two years into the six-year marriage, J.D. had hired someone else to handle the shop, and Susannah had been trying to get pregnant. She and J.D. had even seen a fertility specialist, but he'd just said their timing wasn't right.

Susannah squeezed her eyes shut, recalling the day J.D. and his band had auditioned to be on a nationally televised talent show. They'd gotten on, then won, but only J.D. had been pursued by a record company; they'd insisted he work with a new band. Not that his buddies held a grudge about that. Everybody agreed that J.D.'s talent was special. Still, one thing had led to another, and there were rumors that J.D.'s third record might be nominated in the coming year for a prestigious music award.

"He's so full of himself," Susannah continued. "Like a stranger. And not a stranger I'd want to know." Sometimes after dark, she would sit in her car, in the driveway of Banner Manor, dreading going inside her own home. It was as if the world's worst forces were in there, fighting to claim J.D.'s soul and he was losing.

"When I got home this morning, the door to Mama and Daddy's old room was open. And you remember how I asked J.D. to keep that room off limits to his buddies?" Musicians, groupies, a cameraman and publicist were staying in the house, and more than once, Susannah had run into people in her own kitchen whom she'd never met before. "It's the one thing I made J.D. swear he'd do for me."

"I witnessed that conversation." Ellie frowned. "And that woman was there, too. You know, the tall, gorgeous one who looks like a model?" Pausing, Ellie added, "I think she'd be more attractive if she lost the military look. She's always wearing those heavy boots and flak-inspired jackets?"

Boy did she. "That's her. Sandy Smithers." She was with a group who'd come, supposedly, to help J.D. arrange music for his new lyrics. "Until this morning, I thought she was with that lanky blond bass player," Susannah said.

"Joel Murray?"

"Yeah. He's a studio musician." Susannah nodded, feeling sick. She'd never changed anything in her folks' room, and since their passing, that had comforted her. But… "When I went in this morning, Laurie—"

"Laurie?"

"Was in Mama and Daddy's bed with Joel."

"Laurie? June's daughter? Your niece?"

Susannah nodded.

"She's fifteen! That's statutory rape!"

"She hadn't slept with him yet. They were just… Well…she was wearing panties, but he was naked."

"The guy must be at least thirty. What did you do?"

"Shrieked like a banshee, tossed him into the hallway, then told Laurie to get dressed and wait in the car. After that, I headed for my and J.D.'s room—"

"And?"

"Oh, Ellie," she said in a rush. "J.D. was in bed with that woman Sandy Smithers."

"No!"

Invisible bands tightened around Susannah's chest and

she couldn't breathe. "Well, I must have screamed. I don't really know. I was in such shock. She jumped up, grabbed the sheet and ran—"

"She was naked?"

"Totally. By then, J.D. was up, and I said…" Shaking her head, she decided she'd never repeat what she'd said. Already the words were haunting her, and she had to fight the impulse to run home, find J.D. and take everything back. Just as in the past, a tender touch would make everything all right. Surely there was a reason he'd been in bed with Sandy. But what kind of excuse would explain that.

"Susannah?"

She barely heard her friend. "I told him I'm leaving him," she managed. "Among a few other choice words. I love him, but I shouldn't have stayed this long, Ellie."

"Well, you never had a choice."

"True." Susannah was his. And J.D. was hers. Even as kids, they'd recognized they belonged together. He'd been mean at first—tweaking her braids at school and trying to get a glimpse of her panties every time she climbed trees, tomboy that she was. Later, he'd played the big brother she'd never had, defending her honor. Then, he'd started touching her in a way no other man ever would, proving there was more to sex than the mere merging of bodies. Call it chemistry. Or magic. But a thousand men could walk past and Susannah's pulse wouldn't race, and her knees wouldn't weaken, and she wouldn't feel breathless and painfully aware of every sweet place she wanted J. D. Johnson—and only J. D. Johnson—to touch.

Just thinking about loving him sent a rush of adrenaline through her system. Tingles skated down her spine, her nipples peaked and suddenly, she was aware of her upper thighs, not to mention the ache between them. A slow, enticing longing made her shudder. The truth was, she could almost orgasm just thinking about J.D. Dammit, she fumed, he was supposed to be her everything—her lover forever. A father to the kids they were meant to make together.

"Falling out of love is the worst thing that can happen to a person," she whispered miserably. Could she get through a night without cuddling his hard, muscular body, or listening to his steady breathing lull her to sleep? Even now, when they were fighting, she spent hours craving the lovemaking they used to share, before they'd started growing apart. Her hands wanted to cup his broad shoulders, then trace over his pectorals and his washboard-flat belly.

Worse, with her mother gone and June married, there was nobody to give advice except Ellie—and Ellie had never been married before, either. Still, Susannah's marriage had ended before this morning. Sometimes the spark would ignite unexpectedly, of course. Flames would devour Susannah and J.D., and for a moment, she'd believe their estrangement to be over, only to experience heartbreak once more.

"Mama used to say the secret to love is learning to forget," she murmured. But now Susannah had no choice but to acknowledge all the things J.D. was doing wrong. An image of him and Sandy flashed in her mind, both naked as jaybirds.

"Where's Laurie now?" Ellie finally asked.

"I dropped her off," Susannah said. "June thought she'd spent the night with a girlfriend. Laurie was wearing an inch-long skirt, ripped fishnets, knee-high boots, and she had a fake tattoo on her thigh, of a skull and crossbones."

"J.D.'s a lousy influence. Did she realize you found him in bed…"

Susannah quickly shook her head, her heart aching. All these years, she'd suspected him, but now…

"Here you go, ladies!" Delia arrived, setting down two oversize platters. "Eat hearty. Those plates better get so clean that I won't have to wash them."

"Ellie!" Susannah exclaimed when Delia was gone and Ellie removed sunglasses and lifted her fork, only to use the tines to toy with her eggs. Where Susannah was tall and willowy with honey hair and brown eyes, Ellie had a square-shouldered, almost boyish build. Her jaw-length, jet-black, wavy hair was pressed right up against her peaches-and-cream skin, making her look like a forties film star. "Your eyes are more red, white and blue than an American flag," Susannah said. "You've been crying."

"All morning."

"I'm sorry! I'm so fixated on J.D. that I didn't notice. What's wrong?"

"Everything."

"I thought things were great. Your daddy's about to announce you'll be running your family's company after he retires next week, right?" Ellie was a shoe-in, mostly because she'd come from a family of n'er-do-well brothers—the sort of man Bayou Banner bred like fire ants. Ellie's brothers weren't reliable enough to run such an accurate polling service.

"Robby promised me that when Daddy made his announcement, we'd tell him about us. Then we made love all night."

Susannah slid the charm along the chain around her neck as she did when she felt worried. Ellie had an identical necklace, and both charms had been engraved with the words, *Remember the Time*. Years ago, on a rainy Saturday in Bayou Blair, they'd asked a jeweler to make them.

"Then what?" Susannah prodded. After Robby had finished graduate school, he'd begun working for Ellie's father, a man known around town as Daddy Eddie.

"When I woke up, I could tell he'd been staring at me while I slept."

"And?"

"He said Daddy's giving him the job."

Susannah gasped. "Lees have run the company since it started. And that was back in the eighteen-hundreds."

"Right. So I called Daddy. But he said it's true. Robby could have told me last night, but before we made love, he sat there listening to me talk about how we'd work it out, once I got promoted and he was reporting to me."

"Robby accepted the job?"

"This morning he said we should get married, and I should quit work and raise our family."

"That snake in the grass!" Susannah exploded. She'd set out to be a homemaker, but Ellie had gone to college and graduate school. "You got honors in economics and statistics, and all the while, you were running Lee Polls. Your brothers were in school up North for years, flunking out of their classes, too." Every single one of Ellie's life decisions had been made with an eye to running the company, but Robby had just started working for Daddy Eddie this year. "What are you going to do?"

Ellie's blue eyes turned steely. "Go to New York and start another polling business to compete with Daddy and Robby."

Ellie was leaving Robby *and* Lee Polls? It would work out fine, of course. Ellie had traveled more than Susannah, especially since Susannah had come to hate accompanying J.D. when he'd started playing to larger crowds. People had treated her like arm candy, and that had been a blow to her ego, invalidating her many years with J.D.

"Come with me, Susannah."

"To New York? To do what?" Her résumé consisted of a

high-school diploma and the two-day seminar she'd just attended at a hotel near the airport in Bayou Blair. She'd always planned to stay in Bayou Banner and raise a family.

"You could find a man," said Ellie. "At least you could say you slept with somebody besides J.D."

"Other guys never got Robby out of your system," Susannah reminded, still reeling. "But not seeing J.D. on the street would help," she suddenly added. "I can't divorce him if he's nearby."

"He'd change your mind for sure."

Yes, he'd start kissing Susannah, delivering those little nibbles which were almost as famous as his music, then he'd take off her clothes, undoing buttons with his teeth, murmuring sweet nothings all the while. He'd trail hopelessly hot, wet butterfly kisses down her neck, the ones he knew drove her crazy, and by the time her panties hit the floor, she'd do whatever J.D. wanted. It had happened every time she'd tried to leave him, which lately, was about once a week. "I hate him," she whispered.

"Divorce is too good for him."

"The only thing I want from my marriage is what I brought to it," Susannah said bravely. "Just Banner Manor. And it would do me good to have sex with somebody else. Anybody, really. Maybe even a few people," Susannah added, the idea taking hold.

"I'm going to sleep with everybody I can," Ellie assured her.

Imagining all the hypothetical studs, Susannah said, "They wouldn't even have to be very cute, would they?"

"No. The whole point would be to get our minds off J.D. and Robby."

"I can't watch J.D. pack his bags," Susannah admitted. "I'd feel too sorry for him and maybe have pity sex. He's the one who should move into Hodges' Motor Lodge." It was where all husbands in Bayou Banner went during separations.

"You have money. You're still handling J.D.'s finances."

She could write herself a check for the trouble he'd caused her, but Susannah never would. "I don't want J.D.'s money." She'd settle for the ghost of the man she married. She'd been so sure she was marrying a guy who would run a tackle shop his whole life, and who'd be a good daddy to his kids.

"We can share a place until he leaves Banner Manor," Ellie urged. "I'll lend you cash until he's out of the house."

It would only be for a week or so. "I hate leaving him in Banner Manor, even for ten minutes." Especially with Sandy there. Fighting tears, she told herself that the other woman was no longer her concern since she was leaving J.D.

"It won't be for long," Ellie said. "Your folks left the house to you. J.D. doesn't need it. Between a lawyer and Sheriff Kemp, all those people will be gone soon."

By then, Susannah should have racked up some flings and J.D. would be just a memory.

"I just wish he wasn't such a…" Pausing, she searched for the right words and settled on, "Alpha man."

"Him and Robby both. Alphas of the Delta."

Susannah almost smiled at the play on words, but her heart was hurting. Suddenly tires screeched outside. She and Ellie craned their necks to peer through Delia's window just as a late-model black truck swerved on Palmer and turned down Vine.

"J.D.," Susannah muttered. "He's going to kill somebody driving like that. And with my luck, it won't even be himself."

"At least he's not in that new boat," Ellie muttered.

Named the *Alabama*, the cabin cruiser was docked at a marina on the river. Given the wild company J.D. was keeping, Susannah had blown a gasket when she'd seen it, knowing that somebody would eventually was going to get hurt. "You're too cautious," J.D. had said. "You've got to loosen up, Susannah. Have a good time."

Like he did last night, Susannah thought once more, an image of Sandy's nude body flashing in her mind. "He's probably headed to June's. I told him I was going there, and that you were on a business trip, so he wouldn't follow me here." Her voice broke. "Oh, Ellie, what happened to him?"

"Fame. He changed, Susannah. He wasn't always like this. He used to be one of the best people I know."

Susannah's eyes narrowed. Suitcases were piled in the backseat of Ellie's car. "You packed already?"

"My flight's in an hour. I came to say goodbye."

Goodbye? Susannah stared at the corner of Palmer and Vine, from which her husband had just vanished. The intersection had been a landmark as far back as she could remember, but now J.D. was out of sight and Ellie was saying goodbye. Susannah was at the crossroad, too. She loved J.D. Still, she deserved a more stable life with a man who wouldn't betray her.

"J.D.'s obviously not home now," she found herself saying. "So…I'll run in and grab a few things."

"Really?"

Susannah nodded. "I'll come with you, Ellie."

A heartbeat passed, then the two women said in unison what they always had when making a new memory together. It was the phrase that had prompted them to have the charms on their necklaces engraved, one that had started so many sentences of their conversations. "Remember the time."

Already, both could hear the other saying, "Remember the time we were sitting in Delia's Diner? You know, the day we left J.D. and Robby?"

In years to come, it might well prove to be their most pivotal decision. "Remember the time," they whispered, eyes locking. Then they hooked pinkie fingers, shut their eyes and made silent wishes. A moment later, after leaving bills on the table, they headed toward the door.

"Ladies!" Delia called. "You didn't clean my plates, and now I'm going to have to wash them! You didn't even eat your dessert. Where are you going in such a hurry?"

"On an adventure," Susannah called as she opened the door.

And then she and Ellie linked arms and stepped across the threshold, toward their future.

2

Eight months later

"SUSANNAH, YOU'RE MORE FAMOUS than J.D.," Ellie teased, smoothing a hand over her black cocktail dress and looking around Susannah's restaurant. "And any minute now, you're going to get the call saying J.D. finally agreed to your terms in the divorce!"

"Don't forget your polling company has been just as successful. Besides, none of this would have happened without you and Joe," Susannah said breathlessly, her heart full to bursting as she glanced around the cozy eatery she'd opened six months before, then at Joe O'Grady the man who'd unexpectedly walked into her life. "When the foxhole shuts, the rabbit hutch opens," her mama had always said. Still, Susannah was nervous about getting the call she expected from her lawyer tonight.

At noon, when she'd spoken to J.D. for the first time in eight months, he'd said, "Susannah, come home. Come tonight. Now. We have to talk."

"Not after what you did."

"I didn't sleep with her."

"Liar."

"Listen to me, sweetheart."

Against her will, she'd felt his voice pulling her heart-strings. "Are your friends still in our house?"

Our house. She'd said the words, knowing Banner Manor would remain hers and J.D.'s even after he was no longer allowed inside. "They're not my friends."

"At least you finally realized that."

"I'll get everybody out."

That meant he hadn't yet. "Promises," Susannah managed to say. "I can't see you," she'd added, then kicked herself for even having considered it.

"Just do it. We're worth it. What about all the years we've spent together? Come to town. Don't meet me at the house. That way you won't see any other people. Go to the *Alabama*," he'd coaxed, picking up on her vulnerability. "Just you and me. No lawyers. No music people. There's a direct flight in two hours. I checked. You'll be at the airport in Bayou Blair by seven this evening, on the *Alabama* by eight. Just go outside right now and catch a cab to the airport. Don't pass go. You know we can't get a divorce."

It was just like him, spontaneous to a fault, showing he'd never change, but she'd begin to weaken, anyway. "I can't."

"You have to, Susannah."

"Why?"

"Because you're my wife."

For a second, it seemed the best argument she'd ever heard.

"Say yes."

The one word—so simple but so complex when it came to J.D.—came out before she could stop it. "Yes."

"Eight o'clock on the *Alabama*," he'd repeated quickly. Before she could change her mind, she heard a soft click, then the dial tone.

For the next few hours, she'd watched the clock, her eyes

fixed on the minute hand until the time of the flight came and went. Then she'd phoned her attorney, Garrison Bedford, and explained that she was being pressured. When Garrison called back moments later he reported that J.D. now understood she wasn't coming, and had to agree to the terms of the divorce. He'd promised to sign all necessary papers and vacate the house by eight, which was when she'd agreed to meet him. Now Susannah was waiting for Garrison's final call.

Just a few moments ago, she'd thought it had come. She'd been called to the phone, but then the caller had hung up. Maybe it was J.D. again. Each step in the separation had been messy. For months, J.D. had tried to keep Banner Manor, if only to antagonize Susannah. "He's saying possession's nine-tenths of the law," Garrison first reported.

So Susannah had settled into the two-bedroom apartment she and Ellie had rented on the Lower East Side. She'd started scanning personal ads, just like Ellie, looking for hot dates, but then Garrison told her to stop, since it would jeopardize her divorce. She's also taken the first waitress job she'd been offered.

By the end of her first day at Joe O'Grady's, she'd realized that sipping sodas while J.D. played music at various venues had taught her reams about the restaurant business and booking acts. Within a week, she'd devised an innovative plan to rearrange Joe's restaurant, expanding seating capacity and revenue, then she'd doctored the pecan pie on his dessert menu by adding ingredients from her mama's recipe, which in Bayou Banner, had been as famous as Delia's strawberry-rhubarb confection.

"She's amazing," Joe had bragged to Ellie, not bothering to hide his attraction when both women dined in his restaurant. "Susannah's got a knack for this industry. She talked to our chef about the menu, and he's desperate to try all her recipes. She ought to open her own place."

"That's a great idea," Ellie had enthused.

"As soon as J.D. agrees to the terms of the divorce, I'm going home to Banner Manor," Susannah had reminded.

"You only have to supervise when you first open," Joe had assured her, having heard about her situation during their interview. "Somebody else can manage the business later."

"J.D. hired somebody to run his daddy's tackle shop," Susannah had admitted, wishing she wasn't still so fixated on J.D. Unlike Ellie, she'd found something wrong with every potential lover in the personals. They were too tall, too short, too smart or not smart enough, and as much as she'd hated to admit it, their only true flaw was that they weren't J.D. Not that it mattered, since she couldn't have a fling till the divorce was finalized.

"Lee Polls is being run by an outsider," Ellie had reminded, as she and Joe had continued talking.

"I'm a financial partner in other eateries around town," Joe had continued. "I backed an ex-chef when he opened his own place and hired a manager here, so I can spend more time downtown booking acts in my jazz club, Blue Skies."

Ellie had shown Susannah an article about the club. "You own Blue Skies, too," Ellie had murmured, admiring Joe's entrepreneurial skills.

"Because my favorite part of the job is booking acts, I'm there in the afternoons when people audition," Joe had explained. "Susannah, if you've got more recipes as good as the one for pecan pie, and if you want to open a place, I might agree to be a partner, and even bring in music acts."

Susannah had started to feel as if she was stepping into a fairy tale. "You're offering to back me financially?"

"I'd have to sample your menu first," Joe had said, his tone suggesting he wanted to try more than just food.

"If we can make money, I'm in, too," Ellie had said.

"Tons," Joe assured.

Ellie and Joe had continued talking about restaurant leases, health codes and liquor licenses, but Susannah had barely heard. She'd begun mentally riffling through recipes handed down by women in her family for generations. The idea of opening a Southern-style eatery like Delia's Diner was so exciting that whole minutes passed during which Susannah didn't even think about J.D. It was the first relief she'd felt, and more than anything else, that had spurred her on.

"I can use Mama's recipes!" she'd exclaimed. "Why, Ellie, you know how everybody always loved her vinaigrette-mustard coleslaw and barbequed lima beans."

"Her hot pepper cheese grits were the best," Ellie had answered. "And nothing beats her cardamom-sassafras tea and home-churned ice cream with fresh-crushed mint."

And so, Oh Susannah's was born in a hole-in-the-wall near the famous Katz deli on New York's Lower East Side, on Attorney Street, close to the apartment they were renting. Even the street's name had seemed fitting, given Susannah's ongoing long-distance legal battle with J.D. Putting her energy into the restaurant had helped her escape negative emotions, and she'd wound up using the butter-yellow and cherry-red color scheme she'd spent so much time devising for the kitchen at Banner Manor. The white eyelet curtains she'd dreamed about covered the windows, and mismatched rugs adorned hardwood floors. Short-stemmed flowers were bunched on rustic tables in mason jars.

A month after the opening, *The New York Times* had run a picture of Susannah, Joe and Ellie, their arms slung around one another's shoulders. The dining experience had been called "down-home elegance," and ever since, there had been a line outside the door. Delia's recipe for strawberry-rhubarb pie had arrived with a note that read,

The article's pinned to the bulletin board at the diner. You and Ellie have done Bayou Banner proud, and your folks would be tickled pink. Seeing as my competition (you) has moved out of state, I'm hoping you won't hurt me with my own recipe. Just promise not to franchise anytime soon!

P.S., J.D. got even crazier after you left town, if that can be imagined. Of course, since Sheriff Kemp finally asked me out on a date (and I'm going), I'll do whatever I can to keep your soon-to-be-ex-husband from getting arrested. But you must know: Mama Ambrosia came in for coffee, and she says trouble is brewing in J.D.'s future.

Later that day, Susannah's emotions had tangled into knots. Since the *New York Times* article was on Delia's bulletin board, J.D. must have seen it, which would serve him right. He wasn't the only one who make a name for themselves. She didn't want to rub his nose in her success, she told herself now, glancing around Oh Susannah's, but the man deserved some comeuppance. Yes…revenge was a dish best served cold, she decided with satisfaction, studying a slice of Delia's pie as a waiter passed.

Still, what had Delia meant when she'd said J.D. was worse than before? Was the gorgeous Sandy Smithers gone? And was there more trouble on the horizon, as Mama Ambrosia claimed.

Kicking herself for caring, Susannah reminded herself of all the holidays, birthdays and anniversaries J.D. had missed. Before he'd gotten famous, holidays had been fun. On Valentine's Day, J.D. had licked chocolate syrup from all her erogenous zones, and now, as she recalled the event, an unwanted shiver of longing sizzled along her veins, then ka-boomed at her nerve endings in a grand finale.

No matter how much she fought it, desire for him felt like a rope uncoiling inside her. Her hands were burning to grab that rope and climb, but it wound around and around her making her dizzy as it spun.

Now she was coming undone, imagining J.D.'s hands grabbing the backs of her thighs, pulling her close. His hips connected, rocking with hers, and his erection was hot and hard, searing her belly. Sensation suddenly somersaulted into her limbs, racing to all her choicest places, and tiny jolts of electricity shot to her toes like lightning.

She could almost taste J.D.'s mouth, too, which was always as sweet as cotton candy. Realizing she'd been swept away again by her own imagination, she thanked God she hadn't gone to meet him on the *Alabama* and groaned inwardly, reminding herself to think of her soon-to-be-ex-husband as poison. And as soon as Garrison called tonight to say her divorce was final, she was going to take an antidote called "sex with Joe O'Grady."

"I can't wait to hear Tara Jones sing," Ellie was saying, nodding toward the stage.

This was the first time live music was being offered. "Me, neither," Susannah managed, but in reality, she just wished she could shake off the aftershocks of her fantasy about J.D. The backs of her knees felt weak and her pulse uneven.

Clearing her throat, Susannah added, "She wants a low-key place to play on weekends, but I'm not sure I can stand to hear country-western," The last thing she needed was to hear Willie Nelson singing "Angel Flying Too Close To the Ground," or Johnny Cash and June Carter's snappy version of "Walk The Line," or Patsy Cline belting out "Crazy."

New York wasn't agreeing with her, either. Even without Sandy Smithers in the picture, Susannah might have run away with Ellie just to escape J.D.'s big-city friends. All their hustle, bustle and hype had been worrying her every last nerve. Now that she'd traded places and was living in their world, she missed Banner Manor even more. A new part-time manager at the restaurant was working out well, so technically Susannah could have toured the city some, but she just wasn't interested.

Ellie was taking to the place like a fish to water, but Susannah was still pretending she was sleeping in her big brass bed in Banner Manor. Oh, it was fanciful, but she'd strain her ears until she could hear willow branches brushing against the windows in tandem with J.D.'s breathing. A chime made out of sterling silver spoons that she'd hung outside would sound, then she'd hear a gurgle from a dam he'd built in the creek to create a nearby waterfall.

Sometimes, if she imagined extra hard, she could almost hear the familiar creaks of the old house settling down for the night, then the whir of crickets and splashes of gators and fish in the wetlands. Music of the swamp, her daddy used to call it. New York's sirens and blaring horns would fade away, drowned out by her own hoot-owls. More than once, she'd cried herself to sleep.

Realizing she'd been staring across the room at Joe, she blinked just as he glanced up from Tara, seemingly oblivious to the charms of the singer's enhanced curves and flaming red hair. After saying goodbye, he strode toward Susannah and Ellie.

"Don't forget," Ellie sang. "Tonight, you and Joe are going to celebrate the call. Cha-cha-cha."

"So much for my plan to have sex with tall, dark, handsome strangers," Susannah said nervously. Joe's hair was blond, and he was no taller than J.D.'s five-ten.

"The longer you put off sleeping with him," Ellie said, "the more attracted he gets. He's practically salivating! I wish somebody was that hot for me! Even Tara Jones isn't fazing him, and she's stunning."

"If it wasn't for Garrison making me wait, I'd have slept with Joe already," Susannah assured, not feeling nearly as confident as she sounded. Of course, Joe had insisted on doing everything but sleep together. He was kinky and inventive and made up silly love games, so Susannah figured it would be easy to turn herself into a real hellcat for him. It just hadn't happened yet.

"As soon as J.D. says he's out of Banner Manor," Susannah vowed, "I'm going to wrap myself around Joe O'Grady like corn kernels around a cob, so he can nibble all night."

"Make a corncob pipe and you two can really smoke."

Susannah chuckled. Joe had kissed her and fondled her thighs under her skirt while they'd been eating hot fudge sundaes at a soda shop. He'd role played too, pretending to be a cop arresting her, and a fireman checking for intruders, which had made her laugh. She felt something, too, just not the sparks she'd experienced with J.D. But that was just because Garrison hadn't given her the go-ahead, she reminded herself.

"Oh, don't look so anxious," Ellie chided. "All men come with the same basic equipment, right? How hard can it be to have sex with a stud like Joe?"

It would be easier if J.D. hadn't been her only lover so far, Susannah thought. "Sex is pure mechanics," she agreed, determined to be her own best cheerleader. "It's just a matter of knowing what to touch, for how long, and when." Still…what if J.D. had ruined her for somebody else? Maybe she could forgive him for being a lousy husband, but for ruining her sex life, she'd have to kill him.

Ellie suddenly murmured, "Joe sort of looks like J.D., doesn't he?"

"No! Joe's got blond hair and brown eyes, Ellie! And he always wears suits! J.D. never bothers with a shirt, much less a tie. He goes around bare-chested in worn-out jeans and cowboy boots. He's dark, too, from staying out in the sun too much."

"I'm talking about Joe's body type," Ellie persisted. "He's medium height and angular, with slightly bowed legs and the same bony cowboy butt. He's even got a goatee."

"That's what's in style now," Susannah scoffed.

"I just noticed," Ellie continued as if Susannah hadn't even spoken. "Maybe you're not going to be able to get over J.D., after all. Are you sure you want this divorce, Susannah?"

Susannah gaped. "You're supposed to be my best friend, the person I can turn to in a crisis. I started using my maiden name again," she added. "If there's any resemblance between Joe and J.D., it's completely coincidental."

"A lot of guys have flirted with you, but you picked Joe," Ellie countered. "His voice is like J.D.'s, too. I mean, not *exactly*. J.D.'s a famous singer, of course. Still, Joe's voice is gravelly and low."

"He's a man, Ellie! All men have gravelly, low voices!"

The argument ended because Joe slipped behind Susannah. As he wrapped both arms around her waist and pulled her against him, Ellie said, "I'll leave you two alone."

"Fine by me," Joe murmured huskily. His muscular thighs strained against the backs of Susannah's and she could feel the nudge of what promised to be an erection soon. "I can't wait for Garrison to call. Excited?"

Susannah's knees threatened to buckle. Ellie was right! His voice was like J.D.'s! Oh, his voice was pitched higher, and she'd never mistake it for her husband's, but there was a resemblance. Why hadn't she noticed before? "Uh...yeah," she managed.

Then she noticed Ellie motioning her to the phone.

Garrison.

"The call," she whispered, panicking. As soon as she spoke to Garrison, she was supposed to sleep with Joe!

He was pulling her toward the phone, but as they reached it, Susannah slowed her steps. Something was wrong, she realized. Ellie had turned chalk-white. Extending the phone, she whispered, "It's Robby."

"Robby Robriquet?" Ellie hadn't spoken to her ex-lover in eight months; no wonder she looked as if she'd seen a ghost.

Taking the receiver, Susannah brought it to her ear. "Robby?"

"I have bad news, Susannah. I just talked to Sheriff Kemp, and we decided it might be better if I was the one to call. Uh...we can't find June."

"My sister?" As Susannah's fingers curled more tightly around the receiver, she visualized Sheriff Kemp on the doorstep of Banner Manor years ago. Clad in a tan uniform, he'd kept his hands in front of him, stiffly holding his hat. "We need to go inside and sit down, honey," he'd said. "It's about your mama and daddy." Susannah's whole body froze. "What's happened to June?"

"No...not June."

Relief was short-lived. Was the call about June's husband, Clive? Or one of her nieces, Laurie or Billie-Jean?

Before Susannah could ask, Robby continued. "June's fine, but we were hoping to track her down before we called you."

"J.D.?" The truth hit her with the power of a freight train. They'd been looking for June, so she could provide Susannah comfort. A cry tore from Susannah's throat, and vaguely she wondered if this was how Mama Ambrosia saw things in her crystal ball not really seeing them at all, but only feeling them deep down in her bones. A hand shot to her neck, and her fingers closed around the engraved charm that lay against her skin.

"I'm sorry, Susannah," Robby was saying. Had he continued talking all this time?

"There was an explosion on the *Alabama* around eight o'clock. An attendant at the marina saw him onboard. The coast guard's bringing what's left of the boat up, but it'll take a few days. Until then, we won't know whether it was mechanical failure, a fire in the galley or the generator. The boat blew sky high, then sank just as fast.

"Because of all the legal goings, on between you and J.D., Garrison's here. J.D. left everything to you. Earlier today, he refused to sign any divorce papers, saying you were his beneficiary. You need to catch the first plane you can. Ellie, too. It would be good if she traveled with you."

"He wanted me to meet him on the boat at eight," she said.

"Oh, no," Robby whispered.

The thought hung in the air. Had J.D. caused the explosion because she hadn't shown up? But no...he may be wild, but he wasn't suicidal. Maybe he was okay. Maybe...

"He's gone, Susannah."

Her consciousness seemed to leave her body. She was floating away, high above the room, staring down at herself as if she were having an out-of-body experience. "I'm on my way," she managed, but the words sounded foreign, as if a stranger had spoken them. It felt as if she were inside a vacuum. From somewhere far off, Tara Jones had started singing one of the last songs Susannah needed to hear, "Precious Memories."

"That publicist, Maureen, keeps asking me about arrangements," Robby was saying. "I guess she's bringing camera crews here. Would it help you if I talked to folks at the funeral home before you get home? Or do you want—"

Camera crews? This was a private matter. "Please," she murmured. She couldn't face this without help. Even then, she wasn't sure she could handle this. "Get those people out of my house," she whispered. "Especially that woman Sandy Smithers. Get her out."

"I will," Robby promised.

Somehow she said goodbye and hung up. The color was still gone from Ellie's face. "J.D.?" She asked hoarsely.

Woodenly, Susannah repeated what Robby had said.

"I'll come with you," Joe said, pushing hair from Susannah's eyes when she looked at him.

Had she really considered sleeping with this man? Joe O'Grady was comparable, but she'd known J.D. since she was five years old. Now J.D. was gone and Joe was all she had, and yet, she only wanted J.D. It was wrong, but suddenly she didn't even care about all the mistakes J.D. had made, including sleeping with Sandy Smithers. "I wish I'd never left Bayou Banner," she tried to say, but no words came out.

"The manager can watch the restaurant," Joe said. "I'll help you pack."

But her dresses were still hanging where they belonged, sandwiched between the cowboy shirts she'd always starched for J.D. although he'd never bothered to wear them. No doubt, her shoes were still in the over-the-door rack. The lefts and rights had probably been switched by J.D., something that always made him laugh because if she was sleepy enough, she'd put her shoes on the wrong feet.

"I have to go alone."

"You need somebody with you," Joe persisted.

She'd have Ellie, Robby and people in her community

who'd known her all her life. Otherwise, she wanted to be alone with anything J.D. had left behind, his effects and memories. Didn't Joe understand? Could anyone? J.D.'s death felt even more private than all the things they'd shared in bed.

Would she really never feel his lips crushing down on hers again? Or the damp, hot spear of his tongue as it plunged into her mouth? Or his huge hands as they glided down her belly, then arrowed between her thighs, stroking and building fiery heat? A whimper came from her throat as she imagined his biceps—bulging with corded muscles, shot through with visible veins—wrapping around her and squeezing.

Due to the exertions of performing on stage, J.D. always worked out, even when he was partying too hard, so he was ribbed top to bottom. She could smell the strangely sweet, musky scent of his sweat, and she wanted to shut her eyes and revel in the feeling of its dampness against her own skin. Right now, she needed J.D. more than ever. Only he could comfort her, but that was impossible. He was gone!

She'd been in denial. She'd never get over him, no matter what horrible things he'd done, but now she had no choice. "Maybe in a few days," she forced herself to say. "Let me go down first, Joe…see what's going on. After the funeral, maybe then…"

"I should come now." His eyes were probing hers. All along, he'd thought she was ready to become his lover. She'd thought so, too. But it was a lie. She searched her mind, hoping she hadn't led him on, but how could she be expected to explain emotions to Joe that she hadn't yet admitted to herself? And besides, she wasn't sure how she felt. She couldn't gauge the compass of her heart tomorrow. Although she hadn't seen him for months, J.D. was her husband.

Joe seemed to respect that. "We'll talk every day?"

"Yes," she agreed numbly, confused but unable to cope with pressures. Would she have called off the divorce? Refused to sign legal papers? A whimper escaped her throat. If she'd stayed home, maybe J.D. would be alive.

J.D. had still wanted her, too! Of course he did! As Joe leaned closer, brushing his lips to her cheek, only one thought raced through her mind—he wasn't J.D. And then, suddenly, J.D. seemed impossibly close. She sensed his presence. Was it his ghost? His spirit?

She was far too practical to believe in apparitions, but she whirled around, anyway, glancing toward the white curtains covering the window. But no…it was only her imagination. She could swear he'd been right outside, though, on the other side of the glass. Shaking her head, she realized she was experiencing shades of her mama, who'd had a reputation for possessing a fanciful mind. Susannah's eyes searched the street, then settled on the name of her restaurant, emblazoned across the glass of the door. Fingers of twilight touched golden letters that spelled, *Oh Susannah's*, but she saw nothing more.

Silently she cursed herself for naming the business after a song J.D. had sung to her so often. More than life, she wanted to hear his husky voice again.

And she could, but only on the CDs he'd left behind.

3

In the living room of Banner Manor, Susannah quit sorting J.D.'s unanswered fan mail, losing herself to his music, feeling unable to pick up the phone when it rang. *Oh, Susannah, don't you cry for me. I've come from Alabama with a banjo on my knee…*

She rarely drank. J.D. always jokingly said she stayed as dry as burned toast in the Sahara, but now she took another sip of brandy, wishing it would blunt the pain. Maybe she should have chosen one of J.D.'s stronger spirits, the whisky or gin. Either way, the most lethal spirit remained J.D. himself, since memories of him were everywhere.

She finally lifted the phone and pressed Talk, figuring it was either Ellie, June or Joe, they'd called daily since the funeral two weeks ago. Of course, Ellie mostly wanted to talk about whether Susannah had run into Robby. Seeing him had made her best friend start obsessing about her relationship again. "You don't have to treat me like an invalid," Susannah said before the caller could speak. "I'm fine."

"Not according to my crystal ball. So, honey, if you care about your future, you'd better not hang up on me."

It was Mama Ambrosia, the only other person who'd been calling. "You again!" Susannah looked beyond the open living room windows, glancing past French doors that led to a patio beyond, then she took in J.D.'s guitar picks, which were strewn across the fireplace mantle. "Didn't I ask you not to call again?"

"Now, darlin', you've never come to see me, and I know you distrust my craft," Mama Ambrosia began. A large powerhouse of a woman, she prattled in a voice made deeper by the hand-rolled cigarettes she chain-smoked. "But your mama trusted me. J.D., too. He and I go back quite aways, which must be why his vibrations are so strong. All night long, I've been getting big ol' shivers."

"Pardon me for saying so, but you're crazy, do you know that? I don't believe in ghosts—I already told you that—so I hope you don't intend to restart the conversation we had the last time you called, which was only—" Susannah looked at the clock on the mantle "—twenty minutes ago."

"Crazy?" countered Mama Ambrosia. "So some say. But I'll remind you, missy, they said the same about your mama at times. Just like J.D., she was a handful, prone to daydreaming. And it's high time you admit you inherited her genes."

"Only the good ones," Susannah assured her.

Previously, Mama Ambrosia had claimed J.D. had been a regular customer, visiting often to hear his fortune, and since she'd divulged facts only J.D. could know, Susannah believed her. Try as she might, Susannah couldn't squelch the surge of hope she felt, either, when Mama Ambrosia called as if she might connect with J.D.'s spirit and say goodbye. Not that she and J.D. could resolve their differences, but still, she'd feel better. Despite being characteristically pragmatic, she found herself prompting, "You said you felt a shiver. What exactly does that mean?"

"That he's in trouble, Susannah."

"He's in far worse than that," Susannah pointed out, taking

another big swig of brandy. She'd scattered her almost-ex's ashes to the four winds. Determined to feel no more pain, she squared her jaw and drank some more, but the hot taste of alcohol only reminded her of J.D.'s kisses. Her throat was scratchy from crying, and the booze soothed it as the syrupy warmth slid slowly downward, burning all the way to her belly. It curled like a ball of fire and felt so good that she knocked back yet another drink, sighing when the scalding heat slid through her veins.

"He's in trouble on the other side," Mama Ambrosia clarified ominously, bringing Susannah back to reality. *The reality of non reality,* she thought, since Mama was clearly as crazy as a loon.

"If he'd caused as much trouble there as he caused in life, I don't doubt it," conceded Susannah, as if this were the most normal conversation in the world. "Maybe he and the head honcho of the underworld are fighting over who gets to hold the scepter or sit on the throne." She realized she must be feeling the effects of the alcohol when she found herself imagining J.D. gripping a pitchfork and wearing a skin-tight red suit that showed off his cowboy butt. Already he possessed the right style of goatee and mustache, not to mention a devilish glint in his eyes.

"Now, now," Mama Ambrosia chided. "You still love him, and that's why I'm calling. Even if you won't admit it, my crystal ball told me so. Besides, I'm morally bound as a fortune-teller to alert you to your dismal cosmic situation."

Yes, Mama was definitely certifiable. "My cosmic situation?"

"Expect a visitation."

Susannah was starting to feel like a parrot. "A what?"

"Visitation. As in when somebody visits."

Susannah could only shake her head. "I know what a visitation is."

"Then why did you ask?"

Not bothering to answer, Susannah said, "A visitation from whom?"

"The dearly departed who was your dearly beloved."

"Very doubtful." Thankfully, her call waiting beeped just then. "Sorry, I really should get the other line," Susannah said, trying to muster an apologetic tone. She was almost as mad at J.D. for dying as she was at all his other transgressions combined, so Mama Ambrosia's wild claims weren't helping her mood. "The last thing I need is a visitation from J.D.," she said. "And if I got one, I might just kill him all over again." God only knew J.D. deserved a fate worse than death for the mess he'd made of their lives.

"Whatever. And the other man on the other line," Mama Ambrosia said, "is the one you dated in New York. I saw him in my crystal ball, too, so I'll let you go."

Susannah couldn't help but ask, "Do you really have a crystal ball?"

"I used to, but it broke," Mama Ambrosia returned sadly. "This new one's plastic, but don't worry, it works just as well. Now answer Joe's call, darlin'."

Susannah was startled to hear his name, but probably, Ellie had mentioned Joe to someone at Delia's Diner when she was in for the funeral, and that's how Mama had heard it. Sighing, Susannah clicked the other line. "Hello?"

"Are you thinking about me?"

"Joe. It really is you."

"Who were you expecting?"

J.D. Determined not to let Mama Ambrosia fill her mind with otherworldly impossibilities, Susannah pushed away the thought. "You," she said. He wasn't even close to ghostly. He was solid and real, and his persistence kept reminding her that life was meant for the living. Suddenly she added, "*Where are you?*" It sounded as if he were right next door.

"Home. I just came from your restaurant. Tara's packing in people, and a guy from Chicago came by to see if she wanted to do a gig there tomorrow, which she is."

"Good." She paused, the idea that Joe was actually in Bayou Banner flitting through her mind. "We really do have a strong connection. Are you sure you're not next door?"

"I wish. But what if I come tomorrow? Ellie gave me her key in case you say yes and are out when I get there. She said there's a direct flight to Bayou Blair in about two hours."

So, Ellie was still playing matchmaker. "Please let me stay and help," she'd begged right after the funeral.

"You don't need to be around Daddy Eddie and Robby," Susannah had argued. "June and my nieces are going to help me, and besides, your business needs you."

"Then promise you'll let Joe come stay with you," Ellie had urged. "You need to try, at least. Let him comfort you."

"I'll think about it," Susannah had promised.

In the meantime, Susannah's new manager was using her boss's absence to shine, so Susannah had been able to remain in Bayou Banner roaming the grounds and sorting through J.D.'s belongings. She'd been listening to his CDs, too, although they made her ache, body and soul.

The soft, melodic songs on his first collection, *Delta Dreams*, had been composed with guitars, harps and flutes. *Welcome to My Town* contained humorous songs about Bayou Banner—"Dining with Delia," "When I left my Wife For Hodges' Motor Lodge," and "Sheriff Kemp's Blues." *Songs for Susannah* was the most recent album, and Susannah still couldn't listen to it without crying. Coordinators for the award ceremony had called; J.D. had been nominated, and they wondered if she'd accept the award if he won. Susannah had said yes, so she had to return to New York in a few days.

Thankfully, Robby had arranged the funeral, then held photographers and reporters at bay, as well as the publicist, Maureen, who'd arrived clad in black, crying louder than the bereaved, including Susannah's in-laws who'd come from Florida. J.D.'s parents and Susannah's real friends had wrapped around her like a security blanket, and the music had been perfect. The church organist played "Amazing Grace" and "Will the Circle Be Unbroken," songs that comforted Susannah even now.

At the river, near where the *Alabama* had sunk, she'd cast J.D.'s ashes to the wind. Cremation wasn't what anyone would have chosen, but the explosion made burial an impossibility. After the funeral, Sheriff Kemp had handed Susannah the only items the coast guard found—a Saint Christopher's medal she didn't recognize. The only saving grace was that Susannah's niece, Laurie, had straightened up overnight. She'd foregone her temporary tattoos, trashy clothes and blue hair coloring, and she was now dressing like a model citizen.

Due to the illogical nature of grief, Susannah had wound up stuffing J.D.'s silly old lumberjack hat into her pocketbook the day of the funeral, and she'd held it in both hands during the service. She'd always hated the hat, which was made of red-and-black-plaid flannel with oversized ear flaps. And because she thought it looked ridiculous on J.D., he'd always worn it to provoke her.

Now she'd taken to wearing it and dressing in his shirts since she could still detect his scent. She'd then wander aimlessly in her own house, sometimes plucking J.D.'s guitars, although she could play only the few songs he'd taught her.

Realizing she'd drifted, her fingers tightened around the

phone receiver. "I'm sorry," she murmured, putting Joe on speaker phone, so she could put down the receiver and drink her brandy. "What did you say?"

"I said I'm worried." His voice floated into the air, husky with concern. "Uh…how much are you drinking, if you don't mind my asking?"

She leaned toward the phone. "Just some brandy. Why?"

"You sound…a little funny."

"You're on speaker. Maybe that's why."

He offered a noncommittal grunt.

Thankfully the brandy was starting to blunt the pain, so she took another sip. "Sorry," she apologized again. "It's hard to be here…"

"Then don't wait for the awards ceremony to come back. Or let me come there. I want to hold you, Susannah."

He sounded so close. "I know," she managed. But she needed to be alone. She'd lost her folks as suddenly as J.D., and now Banner Manor seemed full of ghosts. More so, since storms were rocking the bayou.

Banner Manor lacked central air, and although there were window units, Susannah kept opening the windows. Outside, shadowy trees came alive at night, and alone in the dark, in the bed she'd shared with J.D. for years, she'd awaken in a cold sweat, hearing spooky sounds, then jumping from bed and heading for the window. She'd stare at the lightning, letting rain splash her cheeks like tears. And sometimes, she could swear she saw intruders on the lawn, but no one was there.

Back in bed, she'd shut her eyes and let scents from summer foliage transport her to recollections of physical pleasure she and J.D. could never share again. She'd cup her own breasts, imagining J.D. was touching her, then glide a hand down her belly and between her legs. Slowly she'd stroke, twining her fingers into her own soft curls until, in a haze of half sleep, she'd believe J.D. was touching her. Dampness would flood her and she'd arch, lifting her hips from the mattress just as she felt his tongue circle the shell of her ear. As she climbed higher, squeezing her eyes shut, she'd press her fingers inside, pretending they were J.D.'s hard cock, and then she'd hear his seductive whisper. "Oh, Susannah, how about a little magic? Do you want to play a game of scarves and cards? Hats and rabbits?"

Suddenly, she blinked, realizing Joe was still talking. "Uh…what?"

"I asked if your sister, June, had been there today."

"Not today." Susannah leaned toward the phone once more as she took another sip of brandy. "Her husband's folks came in for the funeral and wound up staying, so she's busy. And anyway, I've got things under control."

"Do you?"

"Sure," she said, but grief had overwhelmed her. Hours passed, during which she was lost to memories and couldn't fully account for time. Everything felt unreal, like she was watching a movie, or reading a book. She kept expecting J.D. to jump out from behind a curtain and tell her this was a big joke.

"If you really don't want me to keep you company, Tara asked me to go to Chicago with her. Just as friends, of course," Joe clarified. "She thinks I can help her negotiate a better deal with the club owner if her audition works out."

"That's sweet of you…"

"But?"

"Oh, I do miss you, Joe," she admitted. Dammit, Ellie was right. Susannah needed to let go of what was no longer possible. J.D. was never coming back, no matter what Mama Ambrosia said. "If you go, will you be back for the awards ceremony?"

"Sure. But right now, my bags are packed and by the door, and I wish you'd let me come see you. Wondering when I'll see you again is torture. When I shut my eyes, I have a vision of you that just won't quit, Susannah. Right now, I can picture every inch of you. I love your body, how soft your eyes look. I can feel your arms around my neck, your long legs gliding against mine…."

She swallowed guiltily. "I know, Joe—"

"No you don't," he interjected, sounding frustrated. "Give us a try. That's all I'm asking. I know you want me. And I want you. Your mouth's so hot." Words were coming in a flood now. "I can't wait to cover it with mine again. I want to crush your lips, feel my tongue inside."

His voice caught and his breath turned shallow. "I…think about your breasts. How they move under your top, Susannah…just like your hips when you walk on those mile-long legs. Sometimes, when you're in the walk-in cooler at your restaurant, I notice your nipples get tight under your shirt." Sucking in an audible breath, he said, "Susannah, I get hard just thinking about you, about the things we've already shared…."

"I know. I—"

"No you don't," he repeated. "He's gone, Susannah. And I don't want to hurt you or sound mean, but you were breaking up with J.D., anyway. You and your husband had been separated the better part of the year. I know you're grieving, but it's not right for you to be alone. Not when so many people care about you. Let me come there now. Or…"

"Or what?"

"I can't keep waiting, Susannah."

"I'm not trying to hurt you," she said. But she was, wasn't she? He wasn't trying to pressure her, but he wanted her, and she was so lonely. Definitely, she wasn't used to not having a man. It had been so long…

"Okay," she murmured, the brandy thickening her speech. "Come to Bayou Banner now, and we can fly back to New York together in a few days for to the awards ceremony."

"I'll be there before you know it," he said quickly.

Suddenly all her deepest recesses ached. God, how she craved to feel strong arms wrapping tightly around her back, and a man's rock-hard, hairy chest pressing against her breasts. She yearned to feel the heat of his searing, blistering mouth when it covered her lips. Already she could feel his thighs straining against hers. She deserved relief from all this sadness and grief. She deserved release.

"I'm on my way," he said. And then, as if afraid she might change her mind, he whispered a quick goodbye and the line went dead.

As the dial tone filled the air, she recradled the receiver and started. Something sounded by the window! Her feet moving of their own accord, she crossed swiftly to the French doors and stared into the darkness. "Nothing," she whispered. Closing the doors, then the windows, she stared outside and gasped.

There! A white flash between trees. As it vanished, her heart hammered, making the pulse at her neck throb.

"Probably a stray dog," she murmured. Or all the brandy. "Yes, it's just my imagination." Shaking off the uneasy feeling by reminding herself that she'd felt jumpy since the funeral, she glanced at the pile of J.D.'s fan mail and the sympathy cards that had flooded the post office. Some of the letters had been written before J.D. died, and she wasn't surprised that so many woman claimed to be in love with him. Some offered to leave their husbands, or included risque pictures.

She lifted a sympathy card, addressed to her.

Dear Susannah,

If it wasn't for your husband's music, I never could have forgiven my man for his two-timing last year. But your husband's new record, *Songs for Susannah*, is so touching. And I knew my husband loved me the way your husband loved you. Now, ever since I let my man come back home, wearing that hangdog expression, he's stayed as straight as an arrow. Your man sang like an angel, and so many of his songs were about getting a second chance. Because of that, he helped a lot of people, and I just wanted you to know how he saved our marriage. He will be missed by the whole world.

Susannah wasn't going to get another chance. An unexpected tear splashed down her cheek. "Is this any way to get in the mood for Joe?" she muttered. She had to quit reading these letters and let go of the past.

The second most-sexy man she'd ever met had plans for her...all of which included sex. She needed to forget self-recriminations, as well as past anger that could never be resolved. "For once, enjoy yourself," she said. It had been a long time since she'd let herself feel good.

"I'll take a long bath, then make the bed with the silk sheets. I'll slip into a negligee, too," she decided. "Then hunt down candles and oils."

Joe had been wanting her for months, and two weeks ago she'd known it was high time she slept with him. Now, she tried to tell herself, nothing had changed. J.D. was gone, but her sex life wasn't over.

Knowing Joe, he'd make that plane, too. Which left her just enough time to spruce up. By the time he let himself in with his key, she'd be in bed waiting.

4

"WHAT SAY WE MAKE some magic, oh, Susannah?" J.D. whispered. "Maybe a little of our own bayou voodoo?" It was too dark to see him, but in the dream, his voice came from the foot of the bed as he curled his big hands around her feet. Playing musical instruments had strengthened his fingers, and the pads of his thumbs massaged deeply, rubbing dazzling circles. Long fingers dipped between each toe, stroking sensitive skin. Susannah tilted her chin up, her head, into the freshly laundered silk pillows.

Lifting both hands, she gripped the headboard of the brass bed where she and J.D. had made love so many times, then released a heartfelt sigh. "That feels good," she moaned.

Yes, only J.D.'s touch possessed the uncanny ability to always transport her to faraway places. With just a flick of a finger, he'd made the night vanish—the hooting owls and rustling leaves, and the gurgling creek and tree branches that traced the windowpanes.

The incredible feelings of her beloved touching her, made her crazy for his kisses. Nothing mattered, not when he was shifting his huge, warm, hands to the tops of her ankles, then casually kneading his way upward, palming her calves, smoothing her bare skin, penetrating the muscles.

"Concentrate very hard on what I'm doing, Susannah."

His voice—a slow, sugary drawl that had thrilled millions of women around the world—lowered, becoming barely audible, his tone teasingly seductive. "Are you concentrating?"

Was she awake or sleeping? Did it matter? Jitters of excitement leaped in her belly, feeling like drunken fireflies taking flight; their brilliant wings swept around her, making everything light up. Her senses sharpened and she felt a hitch inside her chest, then weightlessness since she couldn't quite catch her breath. Her nipples peaked, straining, and a bolt of heat as shattering as lightning shot to her lower belly and exploded. A moment passed, then the fire fizzled, curling up like a purring cat in front of a hearth. "I'm trying to concentrate," she managed throatily, "but you make it hard."

"I *am* hard."

Her heart stuttered, missing a beat, since she was imagining the thick bulge pressing against the fly of his jeans; she'd witnessed her husband's growing arousal thousands of times, but every time, she remained amazed by how fast he got turned on. "Well, that's not my doing," she said.

"I'm not so sure about that."

His voice was as sexy as the ministrations of his fingers—all dripping molasses and swirling sugar canes—and she yearned to hear it, right next to her ear. Maybe he'd play songs for her later and sing her to sleep, the way he had so many times before, or maybe he'd murmur sweet nothings until she shivered and she melted like ice on a hot day.

She wanted to feel his mouth ghosting across her lips, her neck, her cheeks. Then she wanted to experience what she'd been so sure she never would again—the cooler dampness of his tongue. She was imagining everything she wanted to feel…the tickle of his soft hair on her face, the burn of his whiskers on her belly, with the tiny, suckling love-bites he would pepper across her breasts. Yes…in a moment, he'd be a stallion champing the bit. Need would take the reins and pent-up passion would be unharnessed so it could run wild.

Moaning, she squeezed her eyes shut. All was sensation because he knew exactly how to touch her. Where and for how long. He liked to take his time, torturing her with enticing circular movements of strong hands.

Now the stress of the past months was slipping away. Like smoke caught in a strong wind, it stirred higher, whirling skyward, then it tumbled into clouds, vanishing. Could this be real, or was she crazy? Had Mama Ambrosia really foreseen this visitation, or had the strength of Susannah's memories conjured him…?

Yes, the strength of her love had burst through her anger, allowing them to share a final moment….

He had to be an angel. His touch was heavenly. Otherworldly. Ethereal. Surreal. Her mind went blank, hazing as he continued unlocking months of tension that had knotted up inside her. Yes…he was setting her free to love again, setting them both free.

Could they recapture passion, though? Could life return to the way it was before? She swallowed hard around a lump forming in her throat, fighting the urge to cry. Maybe. Oh, she hoped so!

She couldn't live without the old J.D., could she? Hadn't she told Ellie that? Hadn't she tried—and failed—in New York? And how could Ellie live without Robby, too? Life seemed so unfair! Fate would never force Susannah and her best friend to live without love that was meant to be!

Only J.D. knew how to negotiate the tangled maze of her forbidden zones, how to drive his hands deep down into the luscious corridors of her body, around the intricate map of her flesh, just as he was doing now. Only he knew how to correctly interpret her signs and signals. No one else knew that toying with her feet made her wild. Or that massaging the back of her neck could actually make her come. Or that lightly trailing fingers over her breasts could push her to the brink, but never take her all the way, only make her hover, at least until he kissed her.

"Yes," she whispered simply. He was tracing her inner thighs now, and she moaned, her hips arching, begging. He kept his nails trimmed, but long enough to pick guitar strings, and soon, he would rake those nails through her hair, the way he always did, when he wanted to make her super-hot. Licking her lips as she anticipated how he'd soon make her explode with lust, she was reminded that she, too, possessed keys to unlock his secret hot zones.

She opened her eyes, desperate to drink in his body, but could see nothing. She recalled every inch, though, like the back of her own hand. She knew his taut nipples, tender earlobes and inner thighs, then even more intimate places— the smooth skin rimming the head of his penis, the sensitive underside, the taut, steely ridge. Even without seeing, she knew he was hard and dusky with promise. She moaned once more, the sound a shudder, as his thumbs pressured the muscles of her calves deeply.

"Wider," he demanded parting her legs, speaking so softly she could barely hear him. "Open up, Susannah. Let me see everything."

A rustle sounded—he was leaning toward her now—then she felt the heated spear of his tongue. It trailed warm, wet loops upward, from her knees toward the apex of her thighs. Another onslaught of heat blanketed her, wrapping her in steamy bliss, and her hips lifted, urging his mouth toward where she most wanted it. His breath teased her core. Gently his tongue lapped the space above her pubic curls, dampening her silk panties until she shuddered with longing. "You won't see me tonight. Just feel me…feel everything, Susannah."

She parted her legs, further and as she did so, her nightie rose. She couldn't help but wish the light was on, since the delicate thong she wore would drive J.D. to distraction. But then, the darkness was freeing and seductive. Pitch-black, it formed a comforting cocoon in which she could play the brazen temptress, or coy girl, or scorned wife. It created the palette upon which they could paint their wildest, hottest, most wicked fantasies….

She couldn't see J.D., but she could imagine him, as surely as if the bedroom were bathed in light. Arousal had turned his blue eyes violet, the way it did sometimes, so they were the color of the sky in the darkest hours before the dawn. Usually sparkling with good humor, those eyes had gained a predatory glint, as if to say foreplay, however mild, had already reached the point of no return.

She sensed his broad shoulders were breaking a sweat, making his golden tan glisten and the sprawling crop of black hair on his chest gleam. Her eyes followed the trail of curls, and she studied where it tapered between pectorals, then raced down his flat tummy. Resting his hands on her knees, his fingers tightened, and she heard a pant of breath. "Oh, Susannah," he sang. "Now don't you cry for me…"

And then the room was silent again. So silent, that she could have been alone after all. Suddenly she wished she'd put on another CD. "Are you there?" she whispered.

He was there all right. His tongue, anyway. Slow, torturous pinwheels teased one thigh, then the other. Then he crooked one of her legs, lifting it higher, his kisses deepening until he was suckling hard, drawing skin between his lips, surely leaving marks, and she plunged, spiraling downward into oblivion.

Just as whiskers roughened her skin, his tongue soothed, then love bites wounded her once more. Everything seemed to be underwater, as if they were making love on the bottom of a pool. Silk was swimming over silk, and she had no idea where his saliva ended and her juices began.

Dangerously, she arched, insisting on feeling more of his mouth, and as he delivered, her heart swelled. Fate had returned him to her. Maybe this was their last chance. Releasing her grip on the headboard, she brought her hands to the mattress and rested them at her sides, ready to grab his shoulders, wanting to drag him on top of her, but also wanting to draw out the pleasure.

He seemed to vanish once more, and she gasped, wondering where he'd gone, but then a fingernail traced her panties. A whine tore from her throat.

His mouth disappeared. Then she heard him shrug off one of the shirts he so rarely bothered to wear. A swoosh followed as he stepped from boots and socks. Brass clanked—his belt buckle. Then a snap popped, followed by the sound of metallic teeth as he slowly dragged down a zipper.

"Take them off," she whispered.

His scarcely audible chuckle hung in the silence, then from somewhere outside, cicadas whirred and an owl hooted. He climbed onto the bed, his knee landing between her legs, his weight depressing the mattress. Hairy legs, not denim, brushed her inner thighs. She shivered in anticipation, tracing a hand over his bare back.

She was waking up, realizing it wasn't a dream. "Now we're getting somewhere," she whispered. Vaguely, from somewhere far off, she thought she heard something…a phone ringing? A dead bolt turning? A door opening?

And then, for a second, everything seemed jumbled. Had she drifted back to sleep? Was the downstairs mantle clock chiming the hour? Was it midnight? But no…hadn't it just been two in the morning? How long ago?

She'd tumbled into some netherworld, a fantasy land between waking and sleeping, where rationality ceased. Here, in the darkness of dreams, nothing bad had come between her and J.D., and emotion surged, making her heart feel full to bursting. All at once, she felt as overwhelmed with joy as she had on her wedding day.

Was she going to treat him like a ghost in his own house forever? And how could she have felt so possessive about Banner Manor, anyway? When she thought of her selfishness, tears stung her eyes. She felt J.D. brush his lips against the strands of her hair. "My home is wherever you are, sweetheart. It could be a shack in a swamp, for all I care."

"Love me," she sighed.

I always have, Susannah, and I always will.

Had he really said the words, or had she only thought them? "Now."

Not tomorrow?

"I needed you yesterday."

A burning finger fluttered over her panties again; this time, he parted her folds through the silk. Softly grunting with pure male hunger, he seemingly registered how ready she was, right before his mouth settled on hers for a claiming kiss.

Against her belly, she felt his hand curl over the waistband, and he ripped down the silk, slowly dragging it over the lengths of her legs. Heat flushed her face. She was drenched and aching, her breasts chaffing the negligee. Instead of feeling nice and soft, it felt rougher now and much more bothersome. She had to get rid of it! Gripping the hem, she pulled the nightie over her head, tossing it away just as his fingers threaded into her pubic curls, toying. When he tugged lightly, she disintegrated, into bundles of knotted nerves, and her hips twisted from the mattress, moving involuntarily, urging him on.

"I missed this," she whispered.

What? Making love?

He hadn't actually spoken, had he?

Her hands cupped the bunched muscles of his shoulders, pulling him close. Gliding upward, he lay on top of her, skin to skin. His rigid flesh was burning, pressed where she was hot, moist and open, and she felt as skittish as a colt. He delivered a series of butterfly kisses.

"Never leave me again," she murmured, her lips barely moving.

She heard his voice in her mind. *You left me.*

But she hadn't…not really. Not in her heart. How could he have hurt her so much? *Only because you made me.*

I'd never make you do anything, Susannah.

Liar. He was supposed to be her one true love, her whole life, her family. Sliding a hand between them, he reached between her legs, cupping her pubis, and she rocked against his damp palm, melting and gasping when he squeezed. In response, he pressed the heel of his hand harder, and his mouth found hers, his firm lips nuzzling hers apart. His tongue followed. Hers met it with fire as it moved, languid and thick, pushing deeper, testing her teeth, exploring her inner cheeks. Lower, the love-slick tip of a finger circled her clitoris, gathering moisture as his tongue began thrusting.

"Oh…oh," she whispered against his lips as two thick fingers entered her. Her hips slammed upward, her backside tightening as her nails dug into his shoulders, encouraging each maddening touch. His free hand tilted her chin farther back, and he changed the angle of his mouth on hers, slanting across her lips one way, then another, while he loved her with his fingers, strumming her until need consumed her....

In this netherworld, their love was protected and no harm could come to it, she thought. There was only hopeless desperation filling her as she climbed, nothing more. She was drowning in his kisses, lost. A surge of heat swept her away, and she felt desperate to come—she had to come!—

"Please," she begged, reeling as his fingers quickened. "You're good...so good..." There was no other man for her. No other who could solicit such explosive responses.

His mouth crushed down on hers and his free hand found a breast. Squeezing and pinching the nipple, he made her scream with pleasure. The night seemed so strange and dark and silent. Starless and moonless. Curtains of foliage beyond the windows further blocked any light, and the rain had ceased. She could see nothing at all....

Only feel.

He dragged his mouth from to her chin, then to her breasts. Ragged and labored, his breaths came in hoarse, raspy tufts as he twisted his magical fingers inside her. *Sleight of hand.* Her belly somersaulted as his tongue simultaneously swirled a nipple, licking circles, but not lingering, trailing farther down to her solar plexus...and down to her ribs...and down to her navel....

Heat exploded in her tummy. Yearning claimed her. Fever took her, her whole body boiling. Chest hair brushed her thighs. She gasped as his mouth dropped. His fingers were still inside her, but he was catching her curls between his teeth now, too. And suddenly, he burrowed, nuzzling his face, muttering senseless nothings.

She whimpered mindlessly as his tongue parted her, cold

where she was burning. The whole pad of his tongue sponged her, and she bucked, threading fingers into his hair. Thick and wavy, they rushed over her hands. Fisting the strands, she dragged his mouth closer, until his tongue went wild, the side of it laving her clitoris. Like a flame guttering in a dark, windy room, the tip flicked the bud.

Her quivering thighs wrapped around his neck. Spurred on, he hugged her close and she rode him shamelessly, wild for the kisses, her knees bracketing his head. His scent, so strong and arousing and male, mixed with her musk. She wanted to touch him everywhere, to do everything with him….

But she was powerless; he was feasting as if he'd never taste her again. As she shattered, her cry rent the silence of the room and her hands grasped blindly. Once more, she clawed at the air. He was gone!

But no! She'd lost control, the orgasm was so strong. A hard, hot, heavy chest was sliding upward now, before she could catch her breath, crushing down on her, his rock-hard muscles a salve for her aching breasts. Her insides were mush, but she realized he was only getting started when he uttered a strangled sigh and roughly, without apology, used his knee to push hers aside, creating access.

He covered her mouth once more, his lips possessive. The taste was tinged with her flavor, and when he thrust his tongue, tears of joy mixed with the kiss, and she reached between them, her fingers hungrily wrapping around his familiar length, fisting him, urging him inside. Relief seemed to fill him as a stroke parted her, and tension left his shoulders as the sensation burned away the last veil of civility.

They'd crashed through another dimension. Reality was a dream now. And dreams, the reality. As he filled her, his body straining, desire overwhelmed her once more. Her hands busily remembered each nip and tuck as they roved around the column of his neck, then the sharp bones between his shoulders. She traced the ridge of his spine and the curves of his taut backside, and she climbed once more, flying toward more pleasure.

Any second could be their last, she thought vaguely, her mind clouded by desire. She'd lost J.D. once. Now she had to be careful. She could never let him go. As she came again, she felt his body tighten into a wall of hard rocks and ridges— then he gushed. Although she could never bring this man close enough, she tried, gripping him like a vise. Her arms felt like ropes circling him a hundred times, and silently, she vowed that she'd never let go.

Holding him, she listened to his breathing become even. Slowly, as sleep overtook her, her hands relaxed. Probably, against her will, she dozed....

"What?" she suddenly muttered, batting her eyes, blinking against the darkness, trying to get her bearings. She remembered hugging J.D., and telling herself not to let go, but then she had. He was no longer on top of her, but it was still night. Wishing there was a clock in the room, she whispered, "J.D.?"

Her heart suddenly stuttered, her mind racing. "Oh no..." Her hand flew to her mouth, covering it. She'd been dreaming....

Yes...Joe must have entered the house after she'd fallen asleep and used the key Ellie had given him

"Joe?" she managed.

She could swear she'd just seen a shadow at the door. Had he been standing there? Had he realized she'd been lost in a fantasy? Quickly, she reached across the bed, but it was empty. Tears stung her eyes. Her love for J.D. hadn't conjured his spirit, after all. He was really gone. Forever.

"Joe?"

No answer. Her mind must have latched onto Mama Ambrosia's ridiculous claims. Well…in the cold light of day, it would take more than a little brandy to make her forgive J.D. He'd tortured her with his shenanigans while alive, and apparently, he was going to continue to do so by haunting her dreams.

Realizing she really was naked, she slipped a hand down and checked. Obviously the lovemaking hadn't been the work of a phantom.

Maybe Joe hadn't heard her say J.D.'s name. Maybe he'd just gone downstairs or to the bathroom. She felt the heat of a blush warm her cheeks in the darkness. He might not be J.D., but the lovemaking had been amazing.

She groaned, her head pounding when she started to get up. "Forget it," she murmured sleepily. No doubt, he'd come back to bed soon.

And she'd be right here waiting.

5

"WHAT HAPPENED LAST NIGHT?" Susannah croaked, vaguely wondering what was pulling her from sleep. Oh! J.D. had been here....

But no, everything was coming back. "Joe?" Her mind racing, she squinted, needles of sunlight piercing her eyes, then she glanced beside her. "Not a man in sight," she whispered.

She tingled all over. Transported, she could feel the lap of her lover's tongue, the depth of his kisses, the grip of his hug. For a moment, all was darkness. She and her lover's bodies were joined again, damp with perspiration and completely inseparable. They were riding into oblivion under the canopy of a full moon and bright stars. She needed more....

Shivers danced down her back. Then more recollections intruded, and she gasped. Had Joe gotten mad? Had he realized she'd fantasized he was J.D.? Yes, that's what she'd been thinking as she'd fallen asleep, wasn't it? Had he left last night?

She hoped not. Remembering Joe's hot, husky whispers, a delicious chill swept over her. And to think she'd believed making love to Joe wouldn't be good. Ellie was right—Joe's voice, body type and hair were enough like J.D.'s that Susannah must have suspended disbelief.

Finally Susannah had slept with a man other than J.D.

Johnson. Definitely a red-letter day. As a surge of hope and renewed possibility sang inside her, she realized a phone was ringing, the sound muffled. Rummaging through a mound of J. D.'s clothes, which she'd been sorting the other day. "Hello?"

No answer.

"Who's calling please?" Straining, she heard breathing. Something, she wasn't sure what, made her believe the caller was a woman.

"Who is this?" she demanded more insistently.

A click sounded, then there was the dial tone. Swallowing hard, she recalled the hang-up call she'd received the night the *Alabama* had exploded. The second she put down the phone, it rang again. This time, she answered sharply. "Who's there?"

"Are you okay?"

Relief flooded her. "Joe!"

He sounded concerned. "Who did you think it was?"

"I got a crank call just now," she explained in a rush, her lips broadening into a smile. Ten to one he'd found her car keys and run into town, letting her sleep. "Where did you go?"

"Uh…that's why I called. I wanted to apologize for last night."

Was he crazy? "What for?"

"For pushing you to get more involved."

"No, that's okay," she murmured, wishing she'd given in sooner. "I needed a good kick in the butt. Otherwise I couldn't have made the leap." Her gaze settling on the window, she realized it was later than she'd thought, maybe noon, and she stretched once more.

"Did you go to the store or something?" she asked, coming more fully awake. "Did you take my keys or rent a car when you got in? If you're near the main drag, there's a place called

Delia's Diner. I'd love some of her strawberry-rhubarb pie."
Thank goodness! It seemed that Joe hadn't guessed she'd
been dreaming about J.D. or he would have said something.

"Uh…I'm not in town, Susannah. That's what I wanted to
talk to you about."

So he *had* realized she'd been fantasizing about J.D.! Her
mental gears did a three-sixty. "Oh, Joe, I'm so sorry…."

"Don't be. It's my fault. Last night, after we spoke, I
realized you're not ready. I never should have pursued you."

"How could you say that after last night?"

"Because, like I said, I could hear your real feelings. You'll
be ready for somebody else someday, but not now. I know
you're grieving." Pausing, he exhaled a soft curse. "And I can't
take advantage of that. If you want the truth, someday I hope
I find half of what you two had. J.D. was your life, and I had
no right to involve myself. You weren't even divorced. Last
night I knew we shouldn't keep trying. Fate wasn't on our
side, Susannah. It was just bad timing."

Her head was starting to spin again. Nothing he said made
sense. "You still feel that way? Even after last night?"

"I know you were sincere on the phone, that you wanted
me to come, but…"

A female giggle interrupted. "Joe, the shower's ready!"

Susannah recognized her voice. Tara Jones. "Uh…where
are you?"

"Chicago. That's what I've been trying to tell you. Oh
God, Susannah, I'm sorry. Tara asked me to help her, and one
thing led to another, and we wound up—"

In bed. Susannah's heart hammered. "This can't be happening," she whispered.

"I didn't think you'd take it so hard. To be honest, I figured
you'd be relieved."

Had he really not been here last night? And if not, who had been in her bed? "You weren't here?"

"No." Now he sounded confused. "Why would you think so?"

"Because…" She swallowed hard. She'd shared a bed with someone, and if it wasn't Joe— Abruptly, and without explanation, she ended the call and dialed star-six-nine. The phone was answered on the first ring.

"Hilton Hotel, Chicago."

Breath whooshed from her lungs. Her pulse started pounding so hard that her heart seemed to be beating in her throat. She tried to push questions from her mind, desperate not to ponder the impossible. The ghost of J. D. Johnson couldn't have made love to her. She could barely find her voice. "Joe O'Grady's room please."

"I'll connect you."

He answered on the second ring. "Susannah?"

"It's me," she said, hearing faint rustling on the other end of the line, which meant Tara was still in there. "Uh…I think we were disconnected."

"Aren't we past that, Susannah?" he asked. "Haven't we been as honest as possible? Let's not stop now. I know you hung up on me, but like I said, I didn't think you'd take this so hard."

"I didn't hang up because I was angry," she argued. "Oh, never mind," she added, knowing he wouldn't believe her. "I'm fine. Really. I'm happy for you. It's just that…"

"What?"

Her lips parted, but what could she say? That she had reason to believe they'd shared a night of passion? That those reasons were still evident—in the purplish bruises left by some man's possessive mouth on her thighs, and the burn left by his whiskers. She'd awakened feeling guilty, for pretending Joe was J.D., but now… "You really weren't here?"

she whispered, needing to clarify it once more, panic overwhelming her.

"What did you say? Sorry, but you're mumbling."

"Nothing," she managed. "I didn't say anything important." In fact, she could think of absolutely nothing to say now, so she simply added, "Thanks for calling, Joe."

"I'll call Ellie and have her ask June to come so June can come to Banner Manor," he said. "I'm worried about you."

"Don't call June." If Susannah couldn't explain last night to Joe, she wouldn't be able to explain it to her sister, either. "Uh...in fact," she lied, "I was just headed over to her house. I was just about to go out the door when you called."

"Good." His voice softened. "No hard feelings?"

"None."

"Can we see each other when you come for the awards ceremony tomorrow? We're flying back today."

"I'll try."

"And if, uh…"

"If you're with Tara when she sings, it won't be awkward," she assured him, still wondering who had been in her bed. Even now, she could feel his magical fingers so like J.D.'s, touching her. Still, her lover couldn't have been a ghost. His touch had been too real, as visceral as anything she'd ever felt.

"You're great," Joe was saying. "So understanding."

She barely heard him. As she hung up, her mind was doing cartwheels. She gasped. What if the man been some member of J.D.'s entourage? How many men had keys to the house?

"It was J.D.," she whispered. "I know it."

But how could that be? The man had smelled like him, felt like him, touched her in all the familiar ways. Her throat constricting with worry, she glanced once more at the marks on her thighs. Oh yes, they were real enough, just as real as the love bites on her shoulders. Real, too, was the craving she still felt this morning. She wanted to feel the viselike grip of his arms encircling her again, the hard, muscular heat of his wall-like body pressing insistently against hers. Warmth flushed through her, and she was aware of her melting feminine core.

Rising and pulling the sheet with her, she headed toward the bathroom, then stopped in her tracks. "What?" she murmured, wishing her renegade heart wasn't beating so dangerously out of control.

After the funeral, Susannah had hung J.D.'s favorite hat, the red-and-black hunting cap with the oversize ear flaps, over the bedpost, but now, it was snagged on the neck of a guitar in the corner of the room. "Exactly where he used to leave it," she managed to whisper.

Worse, in the shoe rack hanging on the open closet door, all her shoes had been switched so the rights and lefts were in the wrong slots.

That, too, was a sign J. D. Johnson had come calling.

"ANSWER YOUR PHONE," Susannah whispered twenty minutes later. She knew better than to drive while using her cell, but her circumstances required desperate measures. She'd thrown on the first outfit she'd found—one of J.D.'s favorite dresses, a strapless yellow number printed with blue flowers—and now she was speeding toward Mama Ambrosia's.

"Please," she whispered as she passed Delia's Diner, her free hand gripping the wheel so tightly that her knuckles turned bright pink, then white. "Dammit." Sweat beaded on her forehead as she spun the dial on the AC. The bayou heat was particularly unbearable today. Leaves from the towering moss-covered oaks created a canopy over an otherwise shimmering roadway, but none of the shade was helping. She just hoped she could find the fortune-teller's cabin. It was tucked in the woods and reputedly difficult to locate.

"Robrique here."

Finally. "Robby?"

"Susannah." He sounded surprised, maybe even hopeful, and now she felt bad. Probably, he thought she was calling with news about Ellie. "What's up?"

She could hear the sounds of Lee Polls—the whir of fax and copy machines and shrill ring of phones were as familiar to her as J.D.'s reflection in a mirror, because she'd called to talk to Ellie so many times. Now she pictured Ellie's ex-lover sitting at the desk that should have been Ellie's, his lanky, muscular body sprawled in a chair. She hesitated, then cut to the chase. "Robby, I think I saw J.D."

During the long, ensuing pause, she inadvertently tapped her foot on the gas pedal, making the car lurch. "Robby? Are you still there?"

"Uh…yeah. What do you mean you *saw* J.D.?"

"I know it sounds crazy, but last night he was in our house. I mean, I didn't actually see him," she amended. "It was too dark."

His tone was dubious. "Where are you?"

"In the car, on my way to Mama Ambrosia's. You're not going to believe this, but she's been calling, saying I should expect a visitation from J.D.—"

"Whoa," Robby said, concern in his voice. "I don't want you going over there, filling your head with that crazy lady's mumbo-jumbo." He lowered his voice. "J.D.'s gone, Susannah, and she's trying to take advantage of your vulnerability for a few dollars. I don't want to see you get hurt any more than you already have been. I'm saying this as your friend and J.D.'s. He'd want me to look after you. Come to Lee Polls and we'll call June. She told me you haven't been picking up the phone, and after work, I intended to come to Banner Manor and check on you, but it looks like I might have to pull an all-nighter. Ever since Ellie left, things have been a mess around here."

"I'm fine," Susannah protested.

"We're worried about you. You're not acting like yourself. June says you're still playing J.D.'s records twenty-four-seven and wearing his old shirts. You're wandering around the house in a daze, and now you're saying he was actually *in* the house. What do you mean? Did you see him?"

"No, not really. I told you it was dark."

"You either did or you didn't."

She wasn't about to offer the details of what happened, at least not to Robby. Just thinking about the encounter made heat flood her body once more, and this time it sure had nothing to do with the sweltering bayou. Her eyes stung, burning with unshed tears. "I'm not crazy. He was my husband, Robby."

"I know that, honey. But he's gone. Sometimes people get real distraught in grief, the way you are now, and—"

"I'm not lying," she managed, as she pulled off the main road onto a narrow one lane byway. She scanned the road for signs of the cabin. Hunching over the wheel, she wondered if she was going in the right direction, not that she'd ask Robby. "Something strange happened last night. That's all I know."

"Strange how?"

She thought of the smooth, huge hands massaging her feet, exploring her ankles and gliding all the way up her body. "Just strange. And this morning, I got a hang-up call. I thought it might be J.D."

"It couldn't have been."

"Next thing you know, you'll be saying I'm as fanciful as my mama. But I'm not. Last night—"

"Your mama *was* delicate, Susannah," Robby interjected. "You're a lot more grounded, true, but you're more like her than you want to admit. It's nothing to be ashamed of. You've been under so much stress—"

"Don't patronize me," she warned.

"I'm not. I just—"

"Oh, forget it," she muttered, angry at herself for expecting support when she couldn't figure out if it was real, either. "June will say exactly the same thing. Ellie, too. You'll all think I'm crazy, and maybe I am."

"That's not what I meant."

"No, you're right," she forced herself to say, hoping she sounded more reasonable.

"What did you actually see?"

"Nothing. That's just it. I think I just had a dream."

Squinting against the sun dappling the hood of the car, she finally saw her destination wink through the trees, an abysmal little log cabin with a sagging wraparound porch and bright pink curtains. She turned down a red dirt trail, overgrown with weeds, and inched the car forward. "Robby, I'm glad I called. What would I do without you? You're so reasonable. The dream I had just seemed so real."

"Do me a favor," Robby said as she pulled beneath an outcropping of trees and behind an old, wheel-less car perched on cinder-blocks. "Just don't go to Mama Ambrosia's."

"Okay," she said. But what other choice did she have? she wondered, staring at the fortune teller's house.

"I mean it," Robby continued. "I know J.D. always let her read his cards and look into her crystal ball, but I think you should go to your sister's house instead. Promise me?"

"Scout's honor," Susannah lied as she eyed the front door. No light seemed to be on inside. "I'd better not keep talking while I'm driving."

"Well, don't get mad at me for saying you can be a little like your mama."

"When?" she couldn't help but ask.

"You were always thinking J.D. was having affairs."

She thought of Sandy Smithers. "He did."

"Never happened."

"Whatever, Robby," she muttered.

"Now, don't let your mind run wild."

Susannah sighed. "I'll drive over to June's right now."

"Great. I'll try to check on you later tonight."

Susannah tried to shake off another bout of sadness, but she couldn't. Robby was a decent man, just as J.D. had been, so it was no wonder Ellie had once cared for him. He'd gotten fed up with J.D.'s antics, but seemed to have forgiven him now that he'd passed. "I'll be fine," she said contritely before hanging up.

Then she got out of the car. As she did, a black cat darted from the front porch and into the underbrush. Not a good sign. Nor was how deafening the car door sounded in the silence when she closed it. Leaves rustled in the surrounding woods, and suddenly, as she headed down the walkway, everything felt strangely desolate.

Although the day was sunny and the mercury was shooting into the stratosphere, a shudder meandered down her spine, moving as slow as a gator in a swamp, worrying each vertebrae. "At least Mama Ambrosia will believe me," she muttered, just to hear her own voice.

When she reached the front door, a weathered wooden affair, she noticed a message board hanging over the doorknob. Written on it, in capital letters, were the words: *On Vacation*.

Her lips parted in astonishment. "On vacation?"

"Well, I was just about to go," a voice boomed behind her. She whirled. "Mama Ambrosia!" The woman was only a few paces away. Startled, Susannah brought her hand up to her chest. "How did you creep up on me like that?"

"I have my ways."

The woman looked as mysterious as she always did. Brightly colored rags were twirled in her braided hair and a huge tent of a housedress covered her bulky frame. Beaded sandals adorned her feet, and she wore countless ankle bracelets.

She came forward, her steps heavy, her great weight shifting from side to side, and she squinted against the sun. "Why, I can't believe how you just yelled out my name, as if you were surprised to see me! Who were you expecting?"

"Nobody. I just—"

"Nobody? Now, how could nobody be here? And why would you visit nobody? Only a somebody can be in a house, missy."

She wanted to know the identity of the man in her house the previous night. Was he a somebody? A nobody? Whatever the case, Mama Ambrosia's manner was already making Susannah a little testy. "You're not really in a house," she said, since the woman was always so contrary. "You're outside."

"I won't be if I go in."

Finding the woman impossible, Susannah said, "Look, I just wanted to talk to you for a minute."

"I warn you, if you want advice, I'm on vacation." As if expecting an argument, she continued. "Everybody has to go on vacation. Even fortune-tellers."

"I never said otherwise," Susannah agreed. "But, well...I hope you won't leave just yet. I need to ask you about our conversation on the phone last night."

Mama Ambrosia shot her an innocent glance. "Did we speak?"

Since the woman had called a number of times, Susannah found the comment completely exasperating, but she forced herself to stay calm. For whatever reason, Mama Ambrosia strived to be difficult, but there wasn't much Susannah could do about that. "You said J.D. would visit me."

"Was I right or was I right?"

Little choice there, Susannah thought, so she said, "I think you were right."

"Well, glory be," murmured Mama Ambrosia.

"Can you tell me anything more?" Susannah asked in a rush, now that she'd gotten the woman's attention.

Mama Ambrosia glanced behind her, toward a clearing, and Susannah noticed a late-model SUV with luggage strapped to the rack.

"I don't want to hold you up," she assured her. "It'll only take a moment. Where is J.D.? Is he all right? Is he…" Susannah didn't know how to ask. "A ghost? Can he come back?"

Mama Ambrosia nodded gravely. "This is an emergency."

Without another word, she reached into a pocket, withdrew a key, stepped past Susannah and unlocked the door. Susannah followed. The interior was dim, lit only by whatever sunlight pierced the curtains, and it was pungent with scents of incense, herbs and spices that lined shelves in the front room.

Mama indicated a table near a window. "Sit."

As Susannah took a seat, goose bumps rose on her arms. "It was so real," she found herself saying. "He was in our room…"

Mama Ambrosia chuckled softly as she seated herself opposite Susannah, placed a black velvet swatch on the table, then a transparent ball on top of that. "In your room?"

"Yes."

Placing her hands on the globe, Mama peered into its depths.

"You don't take the ball with you?" Susannah asked, mostly out of sheer nervousness.

"On vacation?" Mama Ambrosia shook her head in consternation. "Clients," she grumbled. "They never allow you a moment's rest. Ask me, your husband had the right idea."

"Right idea?" Susannah echoed.

"In shuffling off the mortal coil."

Once more, Mama Ambrosia seemed to be speaking gibberish. "Do you see anything?"

"Not yet," Mama returned testily. "This isn't like a TV, missy. You can't just turn it on."

Susannah winced. "Sorry."

Long moments passed. "You're not a believer, are you?" Mama suddenly said.

Susannah wasn't sure. "In what?"

"Magic."

She started to say no, but then she heard J.D.'s liquid-velvet voice sound in her ear, as surely as if he were in the room. "Want to play scarves and cards, Susannah? Hats and rabbits?" His slow drawl moved like the bayou's tributaries, lazily winding around her until her knees melted. "Some magic."

"Which kind?"

She could barely find her voice. "J.D.'s and my magic, I guess. I mean, I never believed in the supernatural. I believe in God, of course, but beyond that, I believe in…in human magic I guess." Emotion made her voice husky. "Love." She paused. "That's magic, isn't it?"

"The best kind, child." The woman's hands were floating above the ball now. "You say he came to you…how?"

A blush made her cheeks burn. It was none of the woman's

business, but she might be the only person who she could help. "He made love to me."

"Hmm. He seems very real. Very close. As if he's not a ghost at all."

Susannah's heart leaped. "Will I see him again?"

"Soon."

"When?"

Mama Ambrosia shook her head. "Maybe tonight. Or tomorrow. I see…a golden key in your future. I see an auditorium filled with people. The men are wearing tuxedos, and the women are dressed in beautiful gowns."

"The awards ceremony!" Susannah exclaimed. Apparently Mama Ambrosia really did see the future. "I'm going to New York tomorrow morning. J.D. was nominated for an award, and if he wins, I'm accepting it for him."

The woman's inky eyebrows knitted with concentration, then she abruptly lifted her hand from the ball.

"What?" Susannah asked.

"Nothing."

"What did you see? Something bad?"

"Nothing, child."

Susannah grasped her arm, and was surprised by the muscular firmness. Mama Ambrosia was a heavy woman, but strong, too. "You have to tell me." Why was the woman hedging? Just a moment ago, she'd been more forthcoming. What was wrong?

"There is danger in your future," the woman whispered.

Susannah's heart thudded hard against her ribs. "What do you mean?"

"I don't know. That's all I see."

"Danger from J.D.?"

"No. He will save you."

"From what? How?"

The woman shook her head. "Sometimes I see the future, but other times, the future is something my clients have to live." Standing, she said, "You have to go now."

Just like that? With even more uncertainty than before? Feeling stunned and not knowing what to believe, Susannah rose to her feet. "Thank you for what you were able to tell me."

"Don't worry, you'll be fine in the end."

In the end? Was Mama Ambrosia a charlatan, as many claimed, or did she really see the future? And if so, what danger lurked around the corner?

Whatever the case, a plan was forming in Susannah's mind. Tomorrow, she would fly to New York for the awards ceremony, but tonight, she would battle all her inner demons, and wait for whoever—or whatever—came calling. In truth, fear would be a small price to pay if she could re-experience the hot sex she'd had last night.

Yes. She'd stay awake. And if the ghost of her late husband appeared she would catch him.

6

FINGERS WERE TRAINING SLOWLY up her ribs with a teasing tickle, and Susannah sucked in a quick breath of anticipation as warm hands molded over her breasts, deeply massaging, making her melt. Finding both nipples, her mysterious lover toyed until they ached, playing with the stiffening tips until she offered a shuddering sigh.

"Miss me, Susannah?"

Sexual frustration was building inside her, and J.D.'s seductive drawl didn't help, since it acted on her like a drug. "No, I don't. Why, everybody knows I'm better off without you, J. D. Johnson. Any woman would be. Any man, too. In fact, you can add kids and pets to that list."

"But you love me, anyway?"

"Not anymore," she returned, but she snaked her arms around his neck and tugged him closer.

He felt so good and hard, a lean, rangy male with sculpted, taut thighs that fell between hers, not to mention knees that pressed insistently, wordlessly telling her what he wanted. Angling his head, he swiped his mouth sideways across hers. The friction wasn't much, just a delightful graze of warm, smooth lips, but the kiss burned.

"C'mon, say you still love me."

But she didn't. She never could again. It was over between

them. Against his mouth, she whispered, "Didn't I tell you never to darken our doorstep again?"

"Is that why your arms are wrapped around me?"

He would point out the discrepancy. He was breaking her resistance, and each time his lips brushed hers, she felt more languid and insubstantial; when he feathered butterfly kisses down the length of her neck, she felt as if she were floating, as if she might blow away like a flower in the wind. Twisting her head so his lips couldn't land on hers again, she muttered, "I hate you, J.D."

"I can tell."

She forced herself to let go of him, feeling strangely bereft as she did so, then she planted her hands on his shoulders and pushed. Not hard enough to make him back away, she realized, but at least she wasn't twining around him like a vine, which was what she most wanted to do. She was weak. At least when it came to him. She'd become attuned to him, learning the idiosyncrasies of his body as well as those of her own, committing them to memory, just so she could drive him crazy with lust....

Suddenly, she startled awake. Abruptly her eyes blinked open. She lay perfectly still, realizing that she'd been dreaming. Just as before, her sensual fantasies seemed impossibly real. Perspiration coated her skin. Her heart was racing, too. Her hand was still curled around a baseball bat that lay next to her, in case she needed protection. Beyond that, she'd stuffed pillows under the covers, to make it look as if she was sleeping.

She bit back a gasp. Yes, something had awakened her. Downstairs. Tightening her grip on the bat, she listened, barely able to hear over the blood rushing in her ears. What time was it? Was someone really in the house? How long had she slept?

So much for keeping guard. Clamping her upper teeth down

on her lower lip, she listened. Yes, she strained to hear. A door hinge, squeaking floorboards, soft steps. *Breathe in, breathe out,* she thought. *Stay calm. Don't alert him. If it is a him…*

She had to get out of bed. But would he hear her? Silently, she damned herself for lying down. But she'd waited so long, and she'd gotten tired. Too bad it was such a moonless, starless night. Whatever light might have illuminated the room was obscured by the curtains, and as her eyes adjusted, she could make out vague shapes, the outline of a dresser and night table, a lamp and chair. She wasn't about to turn on the bedside lamp, not yet. Leaving it off had been part of her plan.

Soundlessly she scooted back in bed, resting against the headboard before swinging her feet to the floor. She'd slept in a T-shirt and sweatpants. When her toes touched the floor, the boards creaked and she froze.

Someone was in the house and she was sure that he'd heard her. Her senses heightened, her muscles grew painfully rigid. Who—or what—was downstairs? A ghost? An intruder? A friend or family member with the key? Maybe her sister, June?

Stealthily, someone was creeping upstairs. She definitely heard steps now…slow, deliberate, cautious. Or was her mind playing tricks? She hoped so. That seemed better than most alternatives. Maybe the separation from J.D., then his death, had simply been too much for her.

Icy panic threaded through her veins. Any sensible woman would have gone to June's this morning, she thought. Or to Lee Polls. Or back to the New York apartment she shared with Ellie. Anywhere but here.

And yet how could Susannah leave this bedroom, when she could still smell the scent of the man's aroused, naked, sweating flesh and feel his heat as he crushed down on top of her, his passion as his tongue thrust against hers with senseless abandon? How, when her hands were still molding over his rock-hard muscles, squeezing what felt like sculpted bronze.

Was a phantom about to make love to her again?

Only the heat of last night could cause her to act as foolishly as she was now. Her craving was visceral, inarguable, complete. She'd do anything to feel that passion again....

The hands she'd felt were like a substance to which she'd become addicted—his touch on her bare skin, the only possible fix. Feeling him inside her, pushing deep, dragging her over the top with him was a pleasure she anticipated like a slow, enticing burn. He'd reignited a spark she'd believed gone forever, then left embers glowing, ready to flare into a torch of fire. She wanted to unbridle the lust, give it full rein, let it run wild. A thousand nights would never be enough....

Suddenly her eyes darted toward the window, seeking escape, but she was on the second floor, too far to jump, not that she would. She had to risk whatever was about to happen, to know the truth....

Something made a noise near the upstairs landing.

Get up, she thought. *Right now. Hurry. Don't make a sound.* Gritting her teeth, fearing he'd hear her, she shifted her weight, praying the mattress springs wouldn't creak as she rose, clutching the bat. Her hands were slick with sweat, and she felt she could lose her grip any second.

As soon as she was on her feet, she swayed, whoozy. She'd awakened too abruptly, stood too soon, and anxiety was flooding her body. Using the bat as a crutch, she steadied herself, the back of her throat going bone dry. There was definitely someone in the hallway. Could it be Robby? she wondered. He'd said he was going to check on her, and he'd always had a key. On impulse, she almost called his name, then thought the better of it. What if it wasn't him?

Besides, he'd knock, wouldn't he? She swung the bat to her shoulder. Was this the danger about which Mama Ambrosia had warned? If so, how could J.D. save her, as the woman had claimed?

She sensed someone near the doorway. Slowly, Susannah exhaled, her breath shallow. Would the intruder believe she was sleeping? Could that buy her time to see his face?

She crept soundlessly backward, melting further into shadows, then she inched her free hand to the bedside lamp, pinching the chain between a thumb and forefinger.

As soon as the person came near, she'd snap on the light, and then, if she didn't like what she saw, she was going to use the bat, no questions asked.

Then she'd run like hell.

A shadow filled the doorway. She almost gasped. Scents of pine and nuts, along with peppermints infused the air, and the second after that, the whole room seemed to fill with J.D.'s presence. Her reaction wasn't something she could qualify or quantify. As surely as she was standing there, though, he was here. In the room. With her.

She parted her lips to speak, but she was in too much shock to utter a sound. She tried not to breathe, but his scent was traveling across the room and into her lungs, anyway. She damned her body's traitorous response, knowing the prickles of awareness dancing through her system had less to do with fear than desire. Despite the strange circumstances, or perhaps because of them, breathless anticipation swept over her.

He'd brought the night with him…a thick darkness, a sense of mystery, a promise that hidden secrets would be revealed. Something impenetrable existed here, something she suspected the room's light could never pierce, should she turn it on. Suddenly, every molecule smelled and felt different, charged with unexpected electricity.

He seemed to be emitting sparks in the inky darkness, so they flew every which way, including in her direction. In reality, he was hazy, a mere outline as motionless as a statue. Judging from what she sensed was the tilt of his head, he hadn't yet realized she was awake and watching him....

She tried to stay silent as he started approaching the bed, the movement so fluid he could have been floating. He was still a mere shadow, a phantom. Her eyes were adjusting, but she wasn't sure she could trust them. And if she was able to make out his shadow, why couldn't he see her?

Because he's not looking at you, she thought, answering herself. He was assuming she was in bed, evident when he leaned and touched the duvet. But after a moment, the fabric ceased to rustle. She heard rather than saw his hand make a fist, gathering the material. Abruptly, he turned, glancing toward the door as if expecting to see her there, watching him.

Which she was. One hand gripped the bat, the fingers of the other pinched the lamp's chain. It felt flimsy between her damp fingers, as if it could snake from her tenuous grasp at any second.

She tugged.

The light snapped on.

Blinking hard against the sudden illumination, terrified because she couldn't see clearly, she used both hands to swing the bat backward, ready to strike the second she could locate her target. A hand had flown to his eyes to shield them—whether from the light, or from the bat's possible blow, she wasn't sure. Not that she cared what he was feeling at the moment, especially not when the hand lowered, her eyes adjusted, and she got a better look at his face.

"J.D.," she whispered, tightening her grip on the bat.

He said nothing. He sure didn't look like a ghost. So much for Mama Ambrosia's supposed connection to the supernatural world. As her eyes roved over each inch of him, she wanted to kill him, and yet, she wanted to kiss him, too, because no man had any right to be so damned sexy. His hair was as black as the night, wild with loose curls that licked around his forehead, dipping down into bushy black eyebrows that nearly met whenever he squinted, the way he was now. Fringed by a thick spray of inky lashes, his eyes were slashes of bright blue. Somehow they seemed to arc across his face like traces left by a streaking blue flame.

He wasn't quite beautiful. His nose had always kept him from being too pretty. It was long and craggy, with the kind of crook that had led plenty of people to assume he'd broken it repeatedly in bar fights, probably over a woman.

Intense was the word that best described her husband. His face was marred with premature character lines, lending him a world-weary expression, as if he was wise beyond his years, which of course he wasn't. Still, those eyes said his heart had been broken too many times already, but that he'd never quit loving—especially sexual loving—because it was as necessary to him as breathing.

Of course, in reality, J. D. Johnson was the real heartbreaker, a two-timing liar who excelled at hurting everyone he touched, especially Susannah.

Even now, coiled in his body, was the power that commanded crowds, an unnerving certainty, maybe even arrogance, as if to say he knew his questions would be answered and his desires satisfied. He still hadn't said a word, and she hadn't relinquished her hold on the bat. Her eyes settled on his mouth, which had remained as kissable as ever. It was smaller than one might have expected, especially given his singing voice and the wide, sculpted bones of his cheeks and jaw. His lips were usually pursed and cautious, just as they were right now, giving nothing away, and they were bracketed by a trim outcropping of mustache and artfully contrived stubble that served as a beard, dusting his chin…the same stubble that, no doubt, had left the red marks on her thighs last night.

Suddenly, she was glad she was wearing long pants, which at least hid the damage he'd done. If he saw the beard burns on her skin, she suspected he'd feel a certain sense of power, or worse, pride at the recollection of how she'd turned to putty under the ministrations of his mouth.

She swallowed hard, remembering how good that mouth could feel, and silently she cursed herself for it. He was gorgeous. The kind of man who'd look famous, even if a woman didn't know he was. And yet to her, he'd always be the guy she'd known since she was five…the guy who teased her in school, and whose folks owned the tackle shop in town.

He must have left his boots downstairs because he was barefoot. Otherwise, he was wearing a tight black T-shirt and ancient jeans that had faded to white. As she gazed at his lower body, she could swear she felt heat seeping through the fabric, although that was impossible.

She trailed her eyes upward again, praying that the surprise wasn't evident on her face, not wanting to give him that satisfaction. She fixed her gaze on his chest. For a long moment, she watched the rise and fall of enticing pectorals under the skin-hugging shirt. Finally she managed to say, "Well one thing's for certain, J. D. Johnson."

At the precise second she finished the words, her eyes raised another fraction and landed dead-center on his, her

timing perfect. As if equally determined to feign noncha-
lance, he raised a black eyebrow in such a way that it arched
and curled, as if trying to form a question mark. "What's that,
Susannah Banner?" he drawled conversationally.

"You're still breathing," she said, her gaze flitting to his
rising-falling chest once more.

"And?"

"Do you know what that means?" she asked sweetly.

"What?"

"That you're not dead," she said.

And then she swung the bat.

7

THWACK.

The bat smacked J.D.'s open palm, and he winced, cursing softly. The next few seconds seemed to last hours, maybe because so many impressions assaulted him at once. She'd broken his hand—that was his first thought, and that meant he couldn't play. Automatically he tallied the lost revenues he'd owe the professional musicians he performed with nowadays, and as he did, an image of his old band flashed into his mind. A pang of regret claimed his heart for not having seen them for ages.

Then J.D. remembered he was supposed to be dead, so his play dates had been canceled, anyway. Damn. How could he even think about music right now, or his old buddy when Susannah was standing in front of him? Why did he keep twisting his priorities? And how had he wound up losing his wife, the only thing he cared about?

When she'd swung the bat, she'd accidentally caught the lamp shade, and light from the bare bulb was shining directly into his eyes. Instinctively he flexed his fingers around the bat to protect himself from further assault, and when he did, he realized nothing was broken after all. He was just hurt, like his heart and hers.

He could see well enough to tell how she was glaring at

him, bracing her luscious legs, ready to fight. Not that he was going to let go of his end of her makeshift weapon. Still, it was the wrong time to think about how good those legs had felt wrapped tightly around his back last night.

She didn't look particularly surprised to see him, and *that* threw him for a loop. Maybe it shouldn't have. Susannah might not share his belief in the spirit world, but she'd often exhibited a sixth sense when it came to him, although she'd never admit it. Her flashing eyes said she'd suspected he was alive all along, and now that he'd confirmed her suspicions, her worst fears were being realized.

"I know you hate me," he managed to say, thinking that if he really loved her, he'd pivot on his heel and stride from the room without a backward glance. Surprised that his voice had sounded as raspy and sexy as a blues singer's, he wondered where the seduction came from—his longing to get out of the doghouse, or simply seeing Susannah up close for the first time in months. Last night he'd only teased and touched her in the dark, reveling in the feel of her smooth skin, the fluidity of curves that were as familiar to him as his own name. No matter how many songs he'd written, he'd never capture the rapture.

Capture the rapture. Now there was a rhyme worthy of another song about her. He'd written hundreds, maybe thousands. Recalling that, he gritted his teeth once more. Even when he should be using all his skills, searching for the right thing to say to her, he was creating lyrics about her instead....

Well no word or phrase could repair the damage now. Worse, he was still seeing spots and shadows. It was as if he were on stage. Night after night, far from home and lonely, he'd find himself staring into blinding white lights, the audiences beyond reduced to faceless shadows, which was just as well. He'd always been singing to Susannah, although she was never really there....

Even though he couldn't see her clearly, his blood thrummed, tunneling through his veins, ever faster, until it was whirring in his ears and pooling in his belly. He felt himself getting hard, his jeans tightening across his hips. No, he hadn't seen her up close for a while—it had been too long in fact— but he had watched her from afar. More than once, like a lovesick puppy, he'd lurked outside her restaurant in New York, praying he'd see her.

That's why he'd seen Joe, the man he'd overheard on the speaker phone last night. Sudden, unexpected anger coursed through him. Joe had brought a light to her eyes that J.D. had been sure he'd snuffed out, and in the restaurant, he'd watched her and Joe dance until helplessness and fury coiled in the pit of his stomach.

As he took in Susannah's wary expression, pain clawed inside him, and his lips pursed in frustrated, mute fury. He'd returned from his supposed grave to make peace, but all he wanted to do was hurt her for kissing the other man. Had she slept with him? He wouldn't blame her....

But Susannah was his! No other man's hands should touch her, certainly no other man's hard, hungry mouth. Abruptly, J.D. leaned, electricity skating along his arm when her skin grazed his. With a flick of his wrist, he righted the lamp shade, dimming the bulb so he could see, then he gripped his end of the bat harder and tugged. Clearly unwilling to relinquish her hold, she staggered forward a few steps, halting when she was close enough to share his body heat. His skin warmed, and his nostrils flared. The strong scent of her—all soft soap and hot musk—raced to his lungs.

His gut somersaulting, his heart hammering, he fought the

urge to drag her forcibly nearer, knowing he wouldn't rest until he did so. Already he could feel the soft cushioning of her full breasts, the hot catch of panting breath against his ear, the tendrils of silken hair teasing his cheeks, then the rush of heavenly contact when her pelvic bone ground between his legs. Just thinking about her intimate touch made something unexpected hit the back of his throat. His mouth went dry.

When his eyes settled on her moist mouth, he imagined the damp salve of her kiss as his tongue plundered, and when he looked into her blazing blue eyes, he imagined her gaze turning hotter on his naked body. She was so beautiful. Too damn beautiful. The kind of knocked-out, dragged-down, weak-in-the-knees, beautiful that could turn any reasonable man into a wild animal. One glance at her soft, pliable mouth and he wanted to hoot like an owl or howl like a wild beast at the moon.

He became restless, as if he'd never know another moment's peace until he was buried deep inside her, thrusting hard, moaning and groaning and sweating until his passion was spent. She hadn't said a word, and yet just one whisper of her sultry voice could bring him to his knees.

She knew it, too. No doubt, from where she stood, she could hear his heart pounding like a tribal drum. In the back of his mind, he was considering how much she weighed, how easy it would be to simply wrench the bat from her hand and haul her into his embrace. He saw himself turning, trapping her beneath him as he fell onto the bed they'd shared so many times. She'd like it, too. Oh, she'd make a show of fighting, maybe even hit him again, but he would win. He always did. Trouble was, J. D. Johnson was tired of winning, tired of wearing his wife down with sensual manipulations and calculated touches.

Now he wanted the impossible—for her to love him again. Or worse, for her to fall *in love* with him again. He wanted her to be head over heels, surrendering to him like some damsel in an old-fashioned swoon. And more, he wanted to deserve it. Wishful thinking, to be sure, because that was a closed chapter. Ancient history. Water under the bridge. Or at least a flowing river of the good scotch whiskey he used to drink. In truth, if he was lucky, maybe the love of his life would let him deliver his apology before she tried to hit him with the bat again.

Then he'd vanish.

He had it all planned out. He'd melt into the night like a phantom, into the darkness he deserved for making such a wretched mess of their lives.

But now that he'd touched her, he couldn't move. He told himself to forget the apology and leave before he hurt her more, but he was anchored to the spot.

He could still identify remnants of the little girl she'd once been. He could remember each of the countless freckles that had once sprinkled her nose, then faded in bygone days, and how her chubby cheeks had hollowed, creating the angular planes and high cheekbones over which his gaze now roved. Her mama and daddy were gone, and once, she'd told him she loved him because he was one of the few who would always remember her childhood. "In that way, you're like Mama and Daddy rolled into one, J.D.," she'd said.

She was thinner now, which wasn't good—probably from working too hard at her restaurant. But her eyes were steady, her chin rigid, her shoulders squared. Everything about her said, "nobody's doormat." Her nose was long and straight, lending her a patrician air suitable to the Banner name of which she'd always been so proud. It was a name she'd sought to protect, but he'd only run roughshod over it, ruining her heritage with all his drinking and carrying on. She even thought he'd slept with another woman.

Which was why she'd never forgive him. Shadows had begun to dance over her cheeks, making her eyelashes look impossibly long, just like the shadow of her figure that nearly touched the ceiling behind her. Usually lively, her blue eyes were watchful now, more steely than the usual blazing blue of fire.

Her face was chalk-white, as if she'd seen a ghost. Her mouth was a very tempting pink, inviting the sort of relentless kiss that would lead to more. "You don't look surprised to see me," he finally murmured.

"Would it be better if I was?"

Maybe not. He could barely find his voice, and once more he damned himself for putting people through what he had. Everything had happened so quickly and he'd had no time to think. "No," he finally said in a near whisper.

"I had a gut feeling something was fishy," she burst out. "I didn't tell anybody what I secretly suspected—they'd think I was crazy. They'd think I'd gotten fanciful, the way Mama did sometimes. What's going on, J.D.?"

"I can explain."

"Why would I want to hear your explanations?"

"You just asked."

"I guess I did, so you'd better talk fast."

Twisting the bat quickly, he tried to wrench it from her grasp, but she only reclaimed it, swinging it to her side. He felt strangely bereft, with the small connection between them severed. A second ago, he could have sworn he'd felt her pulse traveling along the wood, could have sworn his own heart was beating in tandem with it. "C'mon, Susannah, you don't want to hit me," he said quietly.

"Wrong, J.D. I already tried. And it would feel really good to do it again."

"Well, if you're still mad, maybe you care."

"You wish." He sensed, rather than saw her grip tighten on the bat again. "You bastard," she suddenly added, her eyes flashing. "You've pulled plenty of self-centered stunts in your lifetime, Jeremiah Dashiell, but this takes the cake. What brought on the sick urge to attend your own funeral?"

Her lips clamped together, and he figured she'd just remembered how she'd wept during the service, holding his fool hunting cap. Before he thought it through, he lifted his hand, brought it to her face and trailed a finger down her cheek, but she veered back, as if his touch stung. In the second before she broke contact, he could swear he saw her chin quiver, but now it looked as hard as granite.

Somehow that hurt the most. He knew she still had feelings for him. For two weeks, he'd been spying on her, so he'd watched her cry, wandering Banner Manor like some mourning Victorian maiden while she sorted through his stuff. "It's a long story," he finally forced himself to say.

"Let me guess. You wanted to see who cried the most?" Her voice lowered. "Did I win? Are you happy now?"

Memories flooded him, and for a moment he couldn't breathe. "Maybe," he said. "I guess I didn't figure anyone would cry at all."

"Satisfied?"

"Not really."

It wasn't what he'd meant to say. Somehow, the conversation was going all wrong. Outside, standing under the windows, watching her from the trees, he'd been practicing a heartfelt speech. But now it seemed useless. Probably because, for the first time in his life, J.D. had no clue what he wanted. The night the boat had blown up, he'd had only one thought: to escape everything in his old life and to try to get Susannah back. But that was impossible....

He tried to focus on what he'd come to say. "The explosion," he began simply, his thoughts jumbled because he was looking at he prettiest face he'd ever seen. Shaking his head, he vaguely wondered how he could write lyrics that made other women swoon and yet become tongue-tied the second he tried to talk to his own wife.

"I was driving to meet you," he began. She glanced away, and he watched her gaze flit from place to place, as if to say anything in the room was more interesting than him. "I thought...hoped...you might meet me on the *Alabama*, the way you said."

Pausing, he shrugged, hoping to find words that would explain the confusion of that night. His friends had still been at the house, but they'd been packing and clearing out. Even Maureen was gone. When Susannah had found Sandy in bed with him, he'd asked *her* to leave, and she had, but she'd come back that day, saying she'd left a bag she had to find.

Trying to concentrate on what was most important, he continued, "I was on the way to meet you, but my truck ran out of gas."

"Out of gas," Susannah repeated, shaking her head, her hair looking as soft and golden as an angel's halo. "I know. They found your truck by the road. And these are just the kind of rambling excuses I should have expected. You pretend to be dead, then come in here, talking about how you ran out of gas. Damn you, J.D.," she huffed. "You're just not normal."

She was right. He wasn't. He'd been a lousy husband, too, forgetting anniversaries and birthdays and family dinners. He hadn't protected their niece, Laurie, either, although she had been his responsibility. "I'm a bastard, Susannah," he said, dragging a hand through his hair, not that the gesture relieved any frustration. "A nasty, selfish SOB who's driven everything I've loved into the ground. I admit it."

"And you rose from your grave just to tell me that? I don't need a ghost to explain it. I could have asked anybody in Bayou Banner."

Once more, he could barely find his voice. "Seemed like you were worth coming back for."

"Maybe some things are better left buried."

"Like me? Our marriage?" Tears weren't even shimmering in her eyes. She'd hardened her heart to him. Since she remained silent, he continued, "So you can cry for me if I'm dead, but not alive?"

"If you vanish for good, we can find out."

As he watched her, he no longer knew why he was here. He told himself to turn and leave, but he simply couldn't. "My truck ran out of gas, like I said, but I was sure I filled the tank. Nobody else could have driven my truck, either." Shaking his head, he thought back to the long, dark stretch of road near the river. "When it died—"

"That's not the only thing that died," she interjected.

He ignored the comment. "Just listen for once. I got out of the truck and started running, Susannah. I was almost there, about a half mile from the marina and the dock, when I realized somebody had taken out the *Alabama*. I thought maybe you—"

"An attendant said he saw you onboard."

"Wasn't me."

"You thought I'd really come to meet you? You're so arrogant! While you're on the road, do groupie girls fall for your pack of lies—"

"There are no girls!"

"You always think you'll get your way!" she shouted. "It's always whatever J.D. wants, whenever he wants it."

"Yeah, it was wishful thinking that you'd come meet me," he managed. "But you never give me an inch, either, Susannah."

"An inch? You take miles!"

His eyes willed her to understand. "I was staring at the boat when it blew. Everything went sky-high. Sparks shot into the air, then flames. Debris was flying. I…think I must have gone into shock or something. Just for a second. I'm not sure what happened after that. At some point, I realized I'd just kept running." His voice broke. "I was sure that you were…"

"Dead?"

"Yeah."

"The way you pretended to be?"

Pain knifed into him. Dammit, how could he have put people through the past two weeks after what he'd felt in that moment? "I was going to call you. Garrison had called before to say you weren't coming, but I didn't believe him. I knew you loved me…believed in us…would change your mind. But then I called, and you picked up the phone and I knew…"

"I wasn't coming?"

"And that it was over…*we* were over." Even now, he could see the flames shooting out of the boat like arrows, illuminating the trees. Leaves were blowing wildly from the surge of the blast. "I hung up on you and ran. The boat was sinking fast—it went down before I could get to the river."

One second, the *Alabama* was coasting in the water— sleek and clean and beautiful, skimming a barely rippling surface that looked as smooth as glass—and the next, the boat was gone. What was left of the craft upended and slipped beneath the wake. A strong swimmer, he'd run to the water's edge, and could still feel his boot heels pushing off the sandy bank as he barreled toward the water.

He'd dived repeatedly, holding his breath as long as he could, then coming up for air, trying to find anyone, thinking maybe whoever had been aboard had been thrown clear of the wreckage. All along he'd feared maybe someone had been injured or sunk to the bottom. The river was deep and dark, home to snakes and gators, the bed strewn with sharp rocks and tendrils of vines that had wound around his legs, clinging.

"After a while—I don't know how long—I heard voices on shore."

"You don't know how long? Just how much had you been drinking, J.D.?"

"Some, Susannah."

"And driving?"

"I wasn't drunk," he defended. But the truth was, he wasn't really sure. There was nothing like whiskey to make the world go away, which was why he'd been hitting the bottle pretty regularly, but he was done with all that. She had to believe him. The booze had just been the dress rehearsal for the main event, which was when he'd walked out of his own life. Now *that* had been the greatest escape.

"I recognized Sheriff Kemp's voice," he said, "and I realized he'd shown up with guys in diving gear. They were already going in."

"And you…"

"Slipped onto the opposite bank and left." He shook his head, once more wondering what to tell her. He'd share anything, of course. She'd always been his confessor, privy to his deepest, darkest secrets, but now his own actions and motivations were a mystery to him, so he didn't know what to say. "C'mon, Susannah," he finally whispered, stepping forward a pace to close the gap between them.

She leaned back, and he instinctively reached, gripping her upper arm. As his fingers possessively circled her flesh, he drew her near, her scent shooting to his lungs again. His body moving of its own unconscious volition, he leaned and pressed his face to her hair, inhaling deeply, and for the briefest moment, the world stopped spinning.

Everything was utterly still. No breath, no heartbeat. Just him and her, alone in the world, with no one to bother them. Surprisingly, she let him nuzzle, and his arms ached to wrap around her so tightly that she could never escape. He wanted to take her away with him, where they could be alone....

He tried to steady himself, but he still felt dizzy. He needed more of her...needed to thrust his hands into her hair and spiral his fingers into the waving curls that were the color of hand-spun golden sunlight mixed with honey. How many times had he awakened with that hair fanning his bare chest? How many times had he finger-combed the silken strands while she breathed softly, her mind lost to dreams?

His leg was pressed hard against the mattress and suddenly he was aware of the bed, and of how Susannah's breasts swayed under her T-shirt. He could make out the sloping flesh, the contours of the nipples, and he visualized them—soft, pink, relaxed, full, ready for his mouth. His groin ached, the sensation of longing undeniable. It was like a craving for a drug, something that just kept coming at him, demanding action.

He thought about last night—the sweet, salty taste of her— and how she'd responded. And he remembered how she'd called him Joe.

But *he'd* been her lover. He wanted her to know it, too. He wanted to strip off her clothes and remind her of why they'd kept loving each other all these years, through thick and thin. He could remember her soft voice uttering their wedding vows, *for richer, for poorer, in sickness and in health.*

"I just took off that night," he found himself saying, his voice husky. "I knew Sheriff Kemp's men were better equipped to keep diving. I just started walking, cut through the woods." He'd been drenched and shivering. "I wound up at Mama Ambrosia's. She put me up for the night. Plied me with some herbal concoction, too." Ever since, he'd wondered what kind of spell she'd cast on him, not that he figured even her most potent charms could reverse all the lousy luck he kept bringing on himself.

"That charlatan! She's been calling here, saying I should expect a visit from your ghost. She knew all along...."

"Oh no," he muttered.

"And where are you staying now?"

"For a while, I went to an abandoned cabin down the bayou, and then I..." His voice trailed off. "Oh, forget it. Does it matter?"

"No."

His grip on her arm loosened, because he knew better than to do what he wanted, which was to rub slow, sensual circles on her skin. If she came an inch nearer, he couldn't vouch for what he'd do. He'd missed her so much. "I wasn't thinking—"

"You never do, J.D.! That's my point!"

"I had to get away. To think."

"Your parents!"

"I called them. Then I went to see them. They know I'm all right."

"When?"

"A few days ago."

Now she did hit him again. She raised a hand, hauled it

back and punched him. What bothered him most was the in-effectual way the blow connected with his chest, not really hurting at all. He wished it had. He could have taken another whack of the bat, too. Or a slap in the face. But the sissy's smack wasn't Susannah's style. He'd wounded her, weakened her. He could see that now. And it was the last thing he'd ever wanted to do. Susannah was born strong and tough, more than she knew.

"You told your parents you were alive, but not me?"

"I wanted to tell you myself."

"They didn't call me?"

"They wanted to."

"You stopped them."

How could he explain? "I…watched you for days," he said, his voice sounding faraway and gravelly, like something made from scrap metal or rusted tin. "I saw you wandering through the house in agony, and I just couldn't decide which was worse—telling you that I was still around, or just doing you a favor and disappearing forever."

From the expression on at her face, he wished he'd done the latter. That's what she'd have wanted. He understood that now. Later, he figured she'd learn to love some other man. She seemed to like Joe. "I thought…you'd be better off without me. Maybe if I just vanished…"

"You wanted off the hook. Out of our marriage!"

"That's a lie!"

"You wanted to sleep with all those groupies!"

"Not so. That's your own baggage, Susannah. Your fears and your jealousy."

"Oh please! Fess up to it, J.D.!"

"I won't, because it's a lie." Steel was in his voice, thread-ing through his words. "There was a time I wanted success," he continued, biting out the words. "I've never not admitted that. The lure of fame was strong. What man wouldn't want it?" Girls had been all over him. Producers telling him he was far more talented than he really was. Men fawning, hanging onto his every word because he had the power to help them in their own careers. His family had never had much money, but suddenly he could buy anything he wanted.

"I was weak," he managed. "But I didn't know how—"

"How what?" she interjected, scoffing. "To live your own life? And so you took the first opportunity to walk out of it? Once more, J. D. Johnson chooses the easy way! Why am I not surprised? But this time you had the nerve to pretend you were dead!"

Reeling back, she broke free of his grasp. "June," she suddenly said with horror. "Clive. The girls." She shook her head as if memories of the funeral were flooding back to her. "Laurie was heartbroken. Ellie and Robby. Everybody in town. That publicist tried to make a circus out of the funeral. Robby could barely fight her off."

"I'm sorry," he said softly.

"You drive around in that truck, half-drunk, running traffic lights in town," she said, speaking as if she were verbalizing a rant she'd often had in her own head. "It's amazing you haven't done more damage than this!" She gasped. "And *who* was on the boat?" Her eyes widened. "Somebody else was on it! It wasn't me, the way you thought. Or you. But there was a body. They said it was…"

"Unrecognizable?"

She nodded.

"I don't know who it was. But I'll find out. I swear I will, Susannah." He reached for her once more, settling a hand on her shoulder, the touch so possessive that he dared her to pull away. "I haven't had a drink since that night. I want you to know that. I'm going to make everything right, I swear."

She merely shook her head again. "You break everybody's heart and now you want brownie points for apologies?"

"No."

"Then what?" Her voice cracked. "Why did you come back?"

"Are you going to deny that we belong together?" Stepping closer, he wedged a thigh between hers. "I can handle your anger, Susannah," he murmured softly, his breath catching as he drew in her scent. "Even your hate. In fact, I can handle anything you throw at me."

"Why did you come back?"

"For this, damn you." Abruptly his mouth swept hers. "And this." His lips settled, firm and moist, raw and searing. They molded to hers, just long enough to experience the sweet pressure and escalating heat. He whispered, "And because I've been watching you."

Her head veered back, but he grabbed her, holding her close. Inches away, her eyes lit into his like lasers. Blue on blue, fire to fire. "You were spying? I bet you loved doing that, J.D."

"Of course I didn't."

"Oh, yes, you did," she accused. "Your ego has loved every minute of the past two weeks. The eulogies. The music. The flowers. Everybody's tears."

"Screw you, Susannah," he bit out, a sudden surge of anger barely restrained. "You act like I'm the only one who plays games with emotions."

"Aren't you?"

"No. And sometimes, I never want to try to share mine with you again. Maybe I won't. Not tonight. Not ever. It killed me to watch my own funeral."

He'd been so sure nobody cared about him anymore. He'd

been surrounded by false friends. Susannah had walked out on him. His best buddy, Robby, wasn't exactly hanging around anymore. Ellie had always sided with Susannah, which meant she'd been treating him like a two-timing pariah, which he wasn't, then she'd left town, his wife in tow.

"You know me well enough to know I didn't mean to upset you."

"No, I don't think I know you at all, J.D."

It was the meanest thing she could have said, but he barely heard her. He was still thinking about his funeral. He could see the whole scene: His folks crying. Little Laurie, his niece, looking contrite as a nun and all straightened out, wearing a trim navy suit as if she were going to a tryout for the Junior League. He'd been so happy to see her in a decent outfit that he was truly glad he'd passed to the next life.

For months, he'd only seen Laurie wear ripped black dresses and trashy fishnet stockings. Susannah had been clutching the hunting hat she professed to hate so much and wearing dark sunglasses to hide her eyes. His parents were stoic, which was how they dealt with things. Delia and Sheriff Kemp were side by side, so J.D. figured the man had finally asked her out.

Some of J.D.'s newer friends had tried to come, and although he and Robby weren't speaking much, Robby had run them off, just the way a best buddy would. He hadn't seen the gorgeous chick, Sandy, the one who dated Joel, and who had been in bed with him, but Maureen, the publicist, was there. Hidden by an outcropping, and watching the service through a window, J.D. could only marvel at how much he'd destroyed the great life that had once been his. He'd known the world's best people, truly the salt of the earth, and he'd blown it.

"That day, I realized you might miss me, Susannah." It was the first time he'd been honestly sure she might. "More than you're admitting right now."

"Well, I don't."

"Liar," he managed. She knew which buttons to push, but he was determined not to react. When the boat blew, he'd been half blinded with emotion. Even after he'd been assured that she was okay, he'd remained scared that Susannah had been on board. At that moment, life had seemed fleeting.

So he'd acted on impulse, with no thought of the consequences. He'd just wanted to remove everything Susannah hated from their lives. Vaguely he'd thought he could turn himself around, quit drinking, get rid of his so-called friends, then get her back. And so he'd walked away.

"I didn't even realize people would believe I was on the boat," he explained. "After I left Mama Ambrosia's, I went to an abandoned cabin and I nursed myself off the booze. By the time I figured out I was supposed to be dead, my funeral had already been planned."

"There were remains," Susannah whispered.

"Somebody else's. Like I said, I don't know whose."

"And you?"

"Took off. I've been wandering around like a ghost for weeks. I thought you might be better off if I…"

"Never came back?"

"Yeah."

"But you spied on me?"

"I heard you through the windows last night, talking to Joe. And I saw you with him in New York."

She gasped. "In New York?"

"A couple of times before…uh, before the accident."

"Why?"

"I was thinking about you. That's for sure. I dressed in a

disguise, a hat and glasses. I like what you did in your restaurant...." Pausing, he cursed softly, the word scarcely audible. "That's an understatement! I was proud of you, Susannah. I'm not finding the right words. I never do with you. I can write songs, but when I talk to you, sometimes... Anyway, I always knew you wanted to do great things in life. And when I saw how you decorated the restaurant, I..."

"What?"

"Hated myself even more. You decorated it the way you'd planned to do our house, all the things you used to talk about—the drapes, tablecloths, curtains. I realized the only reason you'd never done it was because of me and the people who were staying here."

"About those people," she said coldly.

She'd accepted the brush of his lips a moment ago. She hadn't responded, but she hadn't pulled away. But he realized that might well be their very last kiss. Ever. Pain seared through him like a knife. How could he live without loving her?

"I never slept with her, Susannah," he suddenly said.

"She was in our bed."

The same bed that was right beside them, the duvet already turned down, the sheets inviting. "She got into bed with me after I fell asleep. She said she'd been partying, thought she was in another room with Joel. Nothing happened."

"Passed out would be a more accurate phrase."

"I won't argue with that."

"Then I guess we're fresh out of things to say."

"How could we be? What other two people can talk like us, Susannah? I know my tongue gets tied sometimes, but think of the songs I've written for you. And how many nights have we lain awake talking until dawn?"

"Don't try to sweet-talk me."

It was his only chance. "The restaurant was incredible," he forced himself to continue. "You've...done so much better without me. You look good." Suddenly his throat was aching again. "And Joe. He seems like a nice guy. He really does. Attentive, unlike me. He was listening to every word you said."

"And what else do you know about him?"

"Just what I saw when you were talking in the restaurant, and last night on the phone."

"Through the window?"

"The French doors were open, too."

"I knew I felt someone watching me!"

"I wanted to come inside, to say something to you. I was thinking about it when the phone rang. I didn't mean to eavesdrop. I know I've ruined everything. You don't have to tell me. Maybe you can't love me anymore. I don't even care what you did with...with him," he managed to say.

It was a lie. The thought of another man helping Susannah orgasm made him feel as if he'd just been sucker-punched. Or mortally wounded. At the though, he wanted to double over in agony. But she needed love. Care. Decency and respect. Someone with whom to share life's ups and downs. All the things he'd been so lousy at providing.

"My life is none of your business, J.D."

Technically it was. They were still married, but he was smart enough to know this it was the wrong time to point that out. "I want you to be happy."

"So you drank like a fish, brought crazy people into my house, left the scene of an explosion, where somebody apparently died, then pretended to be dead yourself—"

She shouldn't have looked so sexy right then. She was sleep-rumpled and every time he looked at her he remembered what happened last night. Once more, he wanted to trail his tongue over every inch of her body until she writhed and moaned. He wanted to kiss her until she swore she hadn't really enjoyed anything Joe O'Grady had done to her.

Abruptly, he tightened his grip on her and dragged her close. Her lips were a mere inch away, the lower one quivering. Her eyes were unblinking and unforgiving, but she wanted him to kiss her again. He'd known her for years, so he knew she was waiting for it. Angling his head, he leaned a fraction nearer so their mouths nearly touched, but then he couldn't bring himself to give her—or himself—the satisfaction. No, he wanted her to admit she still cared, still wanted him, still craved his kiss.

"You've got me twisted in knots again. You always do. One look at you and I lose my head, or act like a fool, or do stupid things like walk away from an explosion."

"Don't blame me for your actions," she warned.

"I'm not. I'm just trying to say there's no escape. For better or worse, Susannah. For richer, for poorer."

"In your fantasies. People divorce all the time, J.D. Fifty percent of the lucky population, in fact. And I signed my papers months ago. Besides, weren't you going to get that post-nuptial?"

"I never agreed to that."

"Maybe you should have!"

"Because we're divorcing?"

"Not anymore. You're dead. Remember?"

"Not so dead I can't feel this," he insisted right before his lips found their mark. Just that flare of heat and spark was enough to make him lose control. Suddenly, his warring emotions surged. He hated her as much as he loved her. Hated her because she was withholding her body. Loved her because he simply did. He always would.

He sank into the kiss. Drowned. His lips parted with hers, and he was at the bottom of the river once more, diving into the black swirling depths, swept away by wild, racing currents. His tongue thrust hard, then harder, the kiss all-consuming because he was sure it might be their last. It thrilled him to realize she was kissing him back, too. The first touch of her tongue was slow, exploratory and tentative, as if against her will.

Dragging her down to the bed, he did what he'd been thinking about since the first moment he'd seen her. Rolling fluidly on top of her, as he'd done a thousand times before, he whispered, "You're right. I'm dead. As far as the world knows, I'm gone, Susannah. So it's just you and me. No one else. No concerts. No publicists. No groupies and musicians. No one to come between us."

She planted her hands on his chest and pushed. "You have to come clean. Your fans wrote sympathy cards. I read them. Apologize."

"I am. To you first. I wish I'd never learned to play," he said, whispering the words against her cheek. "I wish I had just gone to work in Dad's shop, the way we figured I would. I hate everything that's separated us."

"You can't waltz in and take back years."

"I did last night," he reminded.

When she tried to pull away, he held tight, his heart pounding harder with every flicker of his tongue on her skin, because he wanted to devour it, smothering each inch with kisses. "What did you think last night? Did you remember this morning? Did you ever think it was me?" he whispered. "I heard you use Joe's name, but did you really think another man could love your body the way I do?"

"You heard Joe's name and left?"

"Yeah."

"I thought I was dreaming," she admitted, her voice hitching, reminding him of how much he loved it. It was soft and sweet and lilted like an Irish lullaby, making him want to sing.

"You weren't dreaming," he assured her, gently tonguing her ear. "And it wasn't him. It was me…"

"I went to see Mama Ambrosia today," she said as she let him continue kissing her neck, as if she might actually let him make love to her. "She said your ghost was going to haunt me."

He shifted his weight and poised his mouth above hers, hovering. Her body tensed now, as if for she was debating between fight or flight, but she was trapped beneath him. Nibbling, he feathered the gentlest of kisses across her lips. "Let me haunt you," he whispered.

"No, J.D."

"Yes." His mouth covered hers once more. The kiss flared, sparked, sizzled, then burned. Her hungry mouth clung, and to make her respond more fully, he used his knee to part her thighs and let his hips fall between them. Relief filled him, his whole body sighing as he enjoyed the familiarity of their joining. His hands thrust upward, the fingers splayed, rushing into her hair. Fisting the strands, he dragged her mouth closer and moaned.

"Let me shanghai you, Susannah," he muttered as his tongue swept wetly across her lips. "Kidnap you and take you to a forgotten cabin," he whispered, his tongue thrusting now, plunging. "Or maybe to the rocky, windswept shore of some faraway island. Anywhere but here. Let's go where there are no memories of us fighting. Come with me and hide from the world."

"You're good with words, J.D.," she whispered.

It implied his actions never measured up. Still, his breath caught, since she was his again, if only for a moment. She needed him desperately. Memories of her nails digging into his shoulders the previous night caused a visceral thrill as his mouth assaulted hers once more, his tongue pushing ever deeper between her lips. Lightly, he tugged once more on her water-soft hair, stroking her scalp, knowing how it affected her, until she tilted her head and uttered a series of cooing cries.

Yes…she was his now. They were going all the way. As he deepened the kiss, his own cry of need stifled in his throat. He'd never wanted anything as badly as he wanted her now. The kiss turned languid, slow and unbelievably wet.

"This is what I came for," he murmured. Warmth broke over his skin. His erection felt heavy, his jeans impossibly tight. Shifting his weight, he inched upward, climbing higher between her legs, gasping when her pelvis chaffed his zipper, the feeling torturous and intense. He feared he'd come without even being inside her, but he was powerless except to move against her anyway, his mind exploding as he melted into the heavenly heat he could feel through her clothes.

Far gone, he let his tongue stroke down the length of her's, the tip flickering like butterflies' wings, until they were both panting hard. His chest constricted. He was aching, so hot that he couldn't stand it one more minute. Slanting his mouth across hers again and again, he muttered between kisses, "Doesn't it feel good? Don't you want it?"

When she didn't respond, he reached down, catching the hem of her shirt. Pushing it roughly upward, he rustled his fingers beneath. She gasped as he opened his mouth wider, sweeping his tongue against the slick interior of her cheek, then he cupped a breast, squeezed and kneaded. A second later, his fingers rushed to the nipple. Molten fire shooting to his loins, he registered the tautness of the bud. Rapidly he rubbed, his nails playing with the excited tip.

As he toyed, she bucked, her hips suddenly twitching and

wild, wrenching and seeking. Fire touched fire. As fast as lightning, he responded, his hips grinding, his buttocks tightening. Her mouth assaulted his, tussling back, and his tongue thrust blindly, his mind empty. Feeling her chest heave, he felt his heart singing.

She still loved him. And he loved her. He was throbbing, about to explode in his jeans. Momentarily he thought he really might, the way he had years ago when they were teenagers, before they'd had the nerve to sleep together. Back then, she'd tease him. She'd stroke him through his jeans and curl her fingers around the aroused length until he was mad with lust. And then one day, she'd finally unzipped his fly….

He raised himself on an elbow, careful not to break their kiss. Years ago, she'd been tentative and unsure, but so eager to please him. She had, too. Beyond his wildest dreams. And now he was going to return the favor.

Sliding his splayed hand down the silken skin of her ribs, he reached between them and undid the snap of his pants. Her open mouth captured his frustrated sigh as he jerked the zipper downward, over his erection. Glad he hadn't worn a belt, he pushed the denim over his hips just a fraction before he found her waistband and pulled down her pants.

When flesh met flesh, his frustration climbed, since ecstasy was now within reach. He was throbbing against her, burning, and in just a second, he'd be inside. He'd feel release.

"Oh, J.D." she sighed.

Hearing her words, his heart felt as if it were tumbling like a star from the sky. A brick from a tower. He had a dazed feeling, as if a rug had been snatched out from under him. "Susannah," he whispered, panting.

But she was pushing his shoulders again, twisting from under him. He reached too late as she scrambled to her feet. As he rolled over, he caught her leaning to grab the bat once more.

Her voice was shaking. "Get out before I call Sheriff Kemp. You're supposed to be dead, so maybe it's better if you stay that way, J.D. I'm not falling for sweet talk. Do you know how many people you've hurt? Not just me, J.D. And the past still exists. You can't erase it. Not tonight. Not ever."

Her mouth was the color of shiny rubies. Her T-shirt was raised on one side, almost enough to expose her breasts. They were visibly aroused, the nipples pert and straining against the cotton. Just seeing that, another wave of heat poured into his groin. His eyes trailed downward, and for the first time, he realized she was still wearing her wedding ring.

So was he. Not that he cared. His whole focus was how she'd affected him physically.

Somehow, he stood. His heart hammering, he yanked the zipper halfway over his truly bothersome erection, uttering a soft grunt of frustrated protest. Leaving the snap undone, he walked toward her. "Say you love me, Susannah. Say you miss me. That you forgive me. I know we can start over. Say you'll help me make our lives right again."

She smacked his cheek. The blow stung, but not nearly as much as the judgment in her eyes. "You can't play with people's emotions, J.D. I was angry enough to divorce you before, but this? People were devastated!"

"*You* were devastated," he corrected.

"Not anymore."

Once more, anger shot through him. "It hasn't been easy to have so much change in our lives, Susannah. My career and the fame has been a rush. Unexpected. More than we dreamed of. But where have you been? Supporting me?"

"You're a hard man to support."

He was hard. That much was certain. Every last nerve in his body was sizzling, craving her. "Maybe. But I'm not nearly the bad boy you make me out to be," he assured her, reaching for her again. This time, his hand cupped her face, his fingers curling under her chin. "You've been scared, but you'll never admit it."

She gaped at him. "Scared?"

"Yeah. Scared I'd run off with some girl in another town while I'm playing music, or that my fast life would become more interesting than you. That's why you keep accusing me of sleeping around, even though you know I never would. That woman, Sandy, got into bed with me. I was sleeping. And that's all."

"Just leave, J.D. I have to get my beauty rest. First thing tomorrow morning, I'm flying to New York to attend an awards ceremony, since my dead husband can't accept his prize if he wins."

His lips parted in surprise. He'd forgotten all about the awards. "You don't have to do that."

"I wouldn't miss it for the world. The lights. The cameras. The action." She glared at him. "A million reminders of the life I never wanted to live."

"Then go ahead and torture yourself."

"Gladly. But I'd rather do it alone."

"Have it your way. But you're the one who needs to 'fess up. I've supposedly always been the bad boy, which leaves you in the position to be the good girl. But one day, when I'm gone, you're going to have to take a better look at yourself."

He pivoted then, vaguely realizing that nothing had gone as he'd hoped. He walked out of the room and into the hallway, then down the stairs of his home for what might be the last time, but not a thing had been resolved between him and Susannah.

At the front door, he finally managed to snap his jeans closed. Then he flicked on a light, glanced at his guitar rack, some picks on the mantle and posters made from his CDs.

All the objects seemed to have been taken from another man's life. Maybe because without Susannah, none of them mattered. All his accomplishments seemed as if they'd been he'd done a million years ago. Was he really about to walk out the door and away from his life? Again?

He glanced up the stairs for a hopeful second, but she hadn't followed. She knew he was alive, and she didn't care if he lived or died. Oh, he'd seen the spark in her eyes, and felt the raw lust in her kisses, but the real love, whatever could fix the completely unfixable in life…well, that was gone, snuffed out like a candle that had once burned brightly.

As he leaned to pull on boots he'd left near the door, he squinted. *Sandy*, he suddenly thought. There was a small pink duffel near the door, half buried by a pile of his music books. The duffel was barely big enough to hold a couple pairs of jeans, but he was sure it belonged to her.

After Susannah had discovered her in bed with him, he'd asked Sandy to leave. She'd been incredibly apologetic, even offering to explain things to Susannah, claiming she'd been partying and was so tired that she'd wound up in the wrong room, thinking J.D. was her friend, Joel. Not that J.D. had believed her. He sensed something duplicitous, but still wasn't sure why.

Recalling the conversation made J.D. cringe. As he'd talked to her—looking past her beauty to the gaunt figure and vacant gray eyes—he wondered how he'd brought a person such as her into his and Susannah's lives, however accidentally. Why hadn't he noticed how the woman looked before? Not tall and slender, but almost waif-like? Joel, the man she'd come with, was a talented musician, but he was a loser in every other aspect of his life, a man who'd alienated his family and lived for the road. The kind of man J.D. was becoming…

He cursed under his breath. And to think little Laurie almost slept with the man. As it turned out, Joel and Sandy weren't even that close. After she'd gone, Joel was distressed, but Sandy had seemed to leave him without fanfare. It was strange. The last time J.D. had seen her was on the day of the explosion. He'd been alone in the house; she said she'd forgotten some of her things, but if so, why hadn't she taken the duffel? Had she not been able to find it?

What if she returned to ask Susannah for it? Preferring the bag not be found here, he grabbed the strap and lifted it onto his shoulder. As light as it was, it felt heavy, a reminder of how he'd lost Susannah. Still, he had to get going and couldn't leave it.

Opening the front door, he crossed the threshold to the porch and realized he was again straining his ears, hoping to hear Susannah's voice, yelling, "Wait a minute, J.D."

Digging into his pocket, he withdrew the house key he'd used for years. His hand trembled slightly as he placed it on a table beside the door. A moment later, the door shut firmly behind him, locking him out of his home, away from his wife.

And then he did the right thing—freed Susannah—and vanished into the night.

8

As the front door closed, Susannah realized her hand was pressed over her racing heart. Her lips felt swollen from J.D.'s kisses and her breasts were sore from wanting his touch. The delicious crush of his taut body had left her belly jittery, and she reached for the bedside table to steady herself.

Leave it to J.D.! He'd wound her up and made her as breathless as a groupie. Exhaling a shuddering sigh, Susannah tried to get her bearings, but the world seemed to tilt, shifting on its axis. At seeing her husband alive, she'd been more shocked than she'd let on, and thankfully he'd misread her stunned stupor.

"He *would*," she muttered furiously. He was the same old J.D. all right, more concerned about himself than anyone else, especially her. From the second she'd laid eyes on him, though, she'd realized she'd never been convinced he was gone, not deep down. Oh, she'd believed it at the funeral, she supposed. Why wouldn't she trust the sheriff and Robby? She'd been too distraught to ask questions, so she'd trusted everyone else to make the arrangements.

But something had always niggled, like a sixth sense, telling her he wasn't really gone. She'd put one foot in front of the other, anyway—mechanically getting on the plane with Ellie, numbly choosing an outfit for the funeral, cleaning the house. But she'd known the truth. And not just because Mama Ambrosia had started calling, acting as if she possessed inside information about J.D.'s death, which, as things turned out, she had.

"No wonder that charlatan left town," Susannah whispered. "Why, she must have been trying to make me look for J.D., trying to get us back together since she knew the truth." J.D. had probably given Mama a sob story about wanting Susannah back.

Not a believer in the paranormal, Susannah had written off her premonitions, thinking they were due to her being mad at J.D. After all, how could fate let the most annoying man in the world die before Susannah had given him a final piece of her mind?

Of course, now that she'd told him off, she didn't feel quite satisfied. Had he really announced that *she*, not he, had been the problem with their marriage? As if she were insecure! Or afraid scantily clad young women could excite him more than she! It was just like J.D. to pull some mind-blowing, self-centered stunt, then come swaggering in, blaming her!

Now her every last nerve was itching to chase him down and finish the argument! Not that she gave a rat's ass about J.D. In fact, she hated him more than mice hated cats, or cats hated dogs, or dogs hated rain. They'd been stuck together as if glued, true enough, but lately, they'd become fire and water, raw elements that could never mix and survive.

She just wished his lips hadn't felt so good, nibbling her skin, landing on her mouth and tasting as sweet as chocolate. A cry escaped from between her lips. How could her fool husband still be alive? She'd been so sure she'd never feel his heavenly touch again....

Had he really quit drinking, the way he claimed? Had he changed? Wouldn't she be a fool if she believed him one more time? Finally, who had been on the *Alabama* if it hadn't been J.D.?

One thing was certain. Somebody had been on the boat, and the poor soul hadn't escaped the fiery inferno. Was someone—a lover or friend—fretting about that missing person, wondering why he or she hadn't come home? Had their opportunity to grieve been taken away? Would J.D. discover the person's identity as he'd promised?

Telling herself she was motivated by civic duty, not lust for J.D., she shoved her feet into shoes, strode into the hallway, took the stairs downward two at a time and then went outside, bounding onto the long paved driveway.

The night was sultry and quiet, and when she strained her ears, she still didn't hear a car engine. Did that mean J.D. had arrived on foot? From where? He must be nearby, she decided. He would know that he couldn't get away with feigning his own death forever.

Or could he? Fear as well as other equally potent emotions she wasn't about to analyze, shot through her so she speeded her steps, then broke into a run. "J.D.?" she yelled, panting.

No answer.

Her breath quickening, she glanced behind her. The farther away she ran, the darker the house became. Trees surrounded her now, their leaves blocking the moonlight. Why hadn't she turned on the outside lights? Wait! There! To her right! Headlights winked through the trees!

So he'd driven after all! Through the foliage, she could see a car doing a U-turn on a nearby access road. It was heading back to Banner Manor. She watched it turn onto a red dirt path, which was a secondary way to get to the house.

Of course he'd come that way, she realized. If he'd risked approaching on the main driveway and parking in front of the house, somebody might have seen him. Intending to meet him halfway, she veered off the paved driveway, cut through the trees, and landed on the dirt path.

It was darker here thanks to a gauntlet of trees that banked the overgrown path. Overhead, thick, twisted branches stretched like long arms, meeting in the middle, obscuring stars. Leaves rustled in wind, and faraway, water rushed over rocks in the creek. Suddenly, she heard the soft chugging of the car's motor and glimpsed headlights again. Glancing toward the house, she saw a glimmer from the light in her and J.D.'s bedroom.

Then all the lights vanished.

The car was close now. Was he driving with the window down? Could he hear her? "J.D.?" she shouted.

She speeded her steps, her thighs straining, the muscles beginning to ache, her throat raw, burning from the sharp intake of air. There! Lights again! Then the motor cut off, the lights extinguished, and in the silence, she heard a door open and shut.

He was just ahead, standing under a shadowy copse. "It's just like you to run when we're not done talking!" she yelled.

His figure appeared in the road, jogging towards her. Raising her knees higher, she bolted in his direction. What if he'd decided to leave and never come back? What if he vanished, this time forever?

Not that she wanted him back, of course. And so, she had no idea what she'd say once he was in front of her, only that she was powerless but to chase him. If he disappeared again, only she would know he was alive! Only Mama Ambrosia would share the secret, and Mama had left town….

He was close now. Twenty yards…ten…five. Her heart stuttered. It wasn't J.D.! His steps were heavy, spaced too far apart. Too late, she tried to halt her own, but she was barreling toward him now, lunging on her own momentum. Thoughts crowded into her mind. Men were still dredging the river, searching for debris from the *Alabama*, looking for the definitive cause of the explosion. Could the person running toward her be involved in the recovery effort?

As they collided, he wrapped his arms around her. Screaming, she blinked in the pitch darkness, desperate to see as she twisted from his grasp. Then her heart flooded with relief. "Robby?" She gulped fast swallows of air. "Oh God...you scared me!"

"What are you doing out here? It's the middle of the night, Susannah, almost dawn!" Before she could answer, he disengaged himself, keeping a hand on her shoulder. "Like I told you earlier, I was going to check on you. I had to pull a near all-nighter and just got off work. I figured you understood that. When I saw you running toward me, I didn't know what to think. I—"

He must have taken the back road since it was the closest route from Lee Polls. "You scared me," she managed once more, barely able to catch her breath, her eyes darting to the trees. Her heart was beating dangerously hard, her words coming out fast. "I thought you were J.D. He was here, Robby. Right upstairs. In the bedroom. Just now. I swear I saw him. J.D.—he's alive! Someone else was on the boat!"

"No," Robby muttered in disbelief. He turned her toward the house, then grasped her hand. "C'mon," he murmured gently as he twined their fingers together. "We'd better get you inside."

She snatched away her hand. "You don't believe me?"

"Oh, Susannah," he whispered noncommittally.

"You've got to believe me! He was in our room!" Whirling, she bolted toward the main road. "I heard only one car motor," she called over her shoulder. "Yours. That means J.D.'s out here somewhere! Help me find him, Robby!" She raised her voice. "J.D.! Answer me!"

Lowering her voice, she asked, "Why did you tell me the body was J.D.'s, Robby? What proof did you and Sheriff Kemp have?"

Footsteps sounded behind her, then Robby's hand grabbed her shoulder once more. Forcibly turning her, he shook her lightly as if to bring her to her senses, but all she could think was that the arms didn't belong to J.D. Where Ellie might swoon, she felt nothing at this man's touch—no warmth, no passion, no need.

"Susannah," he said, "an attendant at the marina said J.D. was on board the *Alabama*. We found a man's remains. I don't know what just happened, but it looks like you've just had a bad dream. You've got to come inside now. J.D.'s gone. We spread his ashes to the four winds. Remember? You've got to accept this."

"No!" Panic filled her. Not even her best friends were going to believe her! What could she do? "And don't patronize me!"

"C'mon, sweetheart. Everybody's worried about you. When we get inside, I'm calling a doctor."

Robby was the one who was out of his mind! Did he really think she'd had some flight of fancy? Imagined something, the way her mama had sometimes? Just moments ago, J.D. had been in their bed again, lying on top of her, ready to make love. Now she wished they had! Emotions warred within her, tearing her apart. Her husband was gone, and no one would believe he was still alive! She loved him still…and sometimes, she hated him, too.

"He's out here!" she insisted. "In the trees, watching us." She raised her voice. "J.D.! Dammit, you've got to answer me! Make Robby believe me!"

Robby's grip tightened. "He's dead. I hate to be so blunt,

but it's for your own good. You have to get a hold of yourself, Susannah."

"You're wrong!"

"I wish I was."

"You're not listening because you don't care about him anymore."

He shook his head. "Not the way I used to. He changed, and we quit hanging out together, but I still consider him…a past best buddy."

She shook off his grasp once more and simply ran.

"Where are you going?" Robby shouted.

"To find my husband."

"I'M NOT LEAVING YOU later tonight," Ellie whispered the next evening in New York, leaning closer so Susannah could hear. "I promised Robby. I don't care what you say. He told me you were a mess last night, and I'm worried about you."

"Please understand," Susannah insisted, knowing how hard it had been for Ellie to talk at length with her ex. "I'm not up to attending any after-parties, but this is your chance to have a great time. You know, sleep with somebody other than Robby. Screw whatever he said to you about my mental health."

"He's concerned."

"I just…had a bad dream."

Susannah glanced toward her friend, but Ellie was busy taking in the crowded auditorium where the awards ceremony was being held. It was hard to believe that less than twenty hours earlier, Ellie's ex had been chasing Susannah around the grounds of Banner Manor. He'd finally dragged her inside and called a doctor, as he'd promised, who had tried to give her tranquilizers, which she'd just pretended to take. This morning, she'd caught the first flight to New York, only to land in a rainstorm that had continued all day.

As her plane had taken off this morning, she'd peered down at the tributaries and bayous receding below, half expecting J.D. to appear, but he hadn't. She shook her head, recalling how, the previous night, Robby had called Ellie, and for some time, they'd talked about Susannah's supposed near-breakdown.

Ellie squeezed her arm, her eyes narrowing. "Are you sure you're okay?"

"Am I going to crack up on stage if I have to accept the award for J.D., you mean?"

"I didn't say that."

"It's what you meant."

"Don't be mad. You know I can't stand it when we fight. I'm just worried. And I'm definitely going home with you after the ceremony."

"No," Susannah insisted. "I need to be alone." What if J.D. had followed her here? The man had attended his own funeral, so who knew? Maybe he'd have the nerve to attend his awards ceremony, too. "Really," she went on. "Go to all the parties, Ellie. It'll be fun. And while you're at it, convince people to make surprise appearances at my restaurant."

The idea seemed to appeal to Ellie's business sense. After all, she was an investor. "If I'd wanted to know any of these folks—" she glanced around the darkened auditorium once more "—I'd have hung around your house when they came to visit J.D."

"This is a different crowd," Susannah argued. "Mostly, anyway." Maureen, J.D.'s ex-publicist, had found Susannah and offered condolences that hadn't sounded particularly heartfelt. Worse, Susannah could swear she'd glimpsed Sandy, but then she'd vanished. Had J.D. told the truth about not having sex with her?

Would he appear again? He couldn't leave Susannah hanging like this! Someone else might have been killed in the accident on the *Alabama,* and Sheriff Kemp needed to be contacted. Someone had to do something!

But thanks to Robby, Susannah couldn't even tell Ellie what had happened. She was convinced that Susannah had been confused by a bad dream, then run outside, looking for J.D. Sheriff Kemp would be of no help, either, since she couldn't ask him to track a missing person he'd already pronounced dead. So Susannah was on her own.

"It would be a pity to waste that dress," Susannah ventured, coaxing Ellie so she could be alone. She didn't need a mama hen hovering over her tonight. Tomorrow she'd return to Banner Manor. Was J.D. there, maybe enjoying the house in her absence? Waiting for her return?

Susannah found herself surveying the crowd. All day she'd expected him to come around the corner, or walk through the door. Whenever a cell phone rang, she'd startle, sure he was calling. Even now, she felt his eyes on her back.

Realizing her hands were damp, she clasped them in her lap. Any moment, they would announce the award for which J.D. had been nominated. She might have to get up. The stage seemed impossibly far away, and from every direction, cameras were flashing, the bright lights blinding her so she wouldn't see him even if he were here.

In any case, he wouldn't show his face at a gathering of music industry professionals, would he? No...not even in disguise. She glanced at Ellie again, desperate to tell her the truth.

"Really," Susannah whispered again. "You have to go to at least one of the parties tonight. For my sake. I'll feel even worse if you don't." Fortunately, Ellie wanted to go. Who wouldn't? All around them were big names in the music industry, glamorous women wearing couture gowns and dazzling jewels, and rugged men in tuxedos, not all of them with dates.

"Are you sure you won't go with me?"

Relief filled Susannah. "No, but you go ahead. I'll wait for you at the apartment."

"Okay. But how can you think about parties right now? They're going to announce your category next."

"I only have to go up if J.D. wins."

"He will." Ellie paused. "But are you sure about the parties? I thought we might go to the restaurant. Maybe see Joe."

"And Tara?" Susannah shook her head. She'd promised Joe she'd stop by and she knew he was anxious to feel things were smoothed over between them, but not tonight. "I want to be alone. Do me a favor and go enjoy yourself tonight, though."

"It'll be good for you to get out."

"I don't want to."

"But you look amazing."

"Thanks." The dress wasn't as formal as those worn by some of the other women, but then, Susannah wasn't a singer. "J.D. bought the dress for me on one of his trips."

"When I imagined you inside this wrapper," J.D. had drawled, breezing through the door and handing her a box, "I only had one thought."

She'd laughed, opening the gift and tossing aside tissue paper. "Which was?"

"Taking that dress off you."

"I'll bet," she'd murmured, staring at the simple, calf-length garment. Swaths of criss-crossed champagne crepe fabric formed the bodice and a long matching shawl draped her shoulders, trailing to tattered ends that swirled around ballerina slippers studded with rhinestones.

Because his homecoming had degenerated into another fight, J.D. had never seen her in the dress. Tonight, she'd added diamonds—dangling earrings, a delicate bracelet and teardrop necklace. Suddenly, a voice drew her from her reverie, saying, "The nominees for CD of the year are…"

As the names were read, she held her breath, knowing J.D. was destined to win. His supposed passing had weighed in his favor, and while she resented what his craft had done to their marriage, she could admit his work deserved the prize.

Ellie's hand slid over hers as the announcer opened the envelope containing the winner's name. "Remember to smile," she whispered. "Win or lose, but I know he'll win." Ellie's voice caught. "I'm so sorry," she added in a quick whisper. "I wish he could be here for this, Susannah."

"Maybe he is. I mean, in spirit."

"And the winner is…" A drum roll sounded, and the announcer leaned nearer the microphone. "J. D. Johnson. For *Songs for Susannah.*"

Time seemed to stop. A melody from one of J.D.'s songs played. As J.D.'s voice filled the auditorium, her heart squeezed. He was singing about her—for her—the voice wickedly intimate. And yet, she had to be magnanimous and share that love with so many people she barely knew.

She could barely rise. So many people were watching! Tape from television cameras was whirring. The applause was thundering. Ellie gave her arm a final squeeze, and somehow she stood. Thoughts fled her mind. There was only the moment, and she was floating effortlessly toward the faraway stage. As she neared, the stairs looked daunting, her shoes, although flats, seemed dangerously unstable. What if she fell?

Before she knew it, she was traversing the stage, and a man was pressing a bronze statue into her hand. As her fingers curled around the cold metal, the applause died and she could have heard a pin drop. Staring into the sea of faces, she looked for J.D. but she could see only bright light. *This is what he sees when he sings,* she realized. No people, only shadows.

She had to say something! What choice did she have but to accept the award in good faith? It was hardly the right time to announce that J. D. Johnson was alive and well.

Besides, the audience, too, would think she was crazy. She imagined him calling out from the crowd, using this moment to surprise everyone, but he didn't. So she began her prepared speech.

"The work of so many people goes into making a CD that it would be hard to thank them all," she finally said. After a few more such comments, she concluded, "Everyone, from the artists who design the covers, to the technicians who mix the final sound, are completely necessary. My husband always knew that. If he were…"

She paused, barely able to lie. "If he were still alive," she forced herself to continue, feeling another burst of anger at J.D. for involving her in his dishonesty. "He would want me to thank every one of you. And you know who you are."

As J.D.'s music played again to thunderous applause, she silently cursed herself. Was she going to cover for J.D. forever? Furious as she was guided off the stage, she found herself back in her seat, clutching the statue, before realizing her ordeal wasn't over. J.D.'s music continued playing, in tandem with a montage of photographs of him projected onto a big screen. Then came the short interviews with musicians who spoke about the joy of playing with him. Casting a quick glance around the auditorium, she could see the emotion on the people's faces as they watched the tribute.

All at once, she felt overwhelmed—sad, wistful, angry

and yet somehow strangely selfish, too. She'd felt the same way at the funeral, since it was a reminder that J.D. was meant to be shared with the world, not just her. Had he been right last night? she suddenly wondered. Was she jealous? Afraid of his fame?

But no…she didn't feel jealous, exactly, just confused about the boundaries of their public and private lives. And now, seeing how many people had been positively affected by his music, she wished she'd tried harder. But would she, if given another chance? Unshed tears stung her eyes. Yes, she realized. He'd been right about her. Maybe she did fear his love for her wasn't strong enough to withstand fame and fortune….

Leaning toward Ellie, she whispered, "I'm going to cut out early."

Ellie looked concerned. "You have to stay, don't you?"

Promotional pictures had been taken at the beginning of the event, so Susannah shook her head. "No one will miss me. I did my duty. They'll understand." They'd believe her acceptance of the award had made her distraught about her husband's death. "I need to go back to the apartment."

"You're sure they won't miss us?"

She could hear the disappointment in Ellie's voice. "I'm going alone," Susannah said. When Ellie protested, Susannah shook her head. "I mean it. I just want to be by myself for a while, Ellie. It's been a big night."

Looking torn, Ellie frowned. "Are you sure you don't want company, Susannah?"

"Absolutely," she said.

But it was a lie. She wanted company all right—J.D.'s.

She wasn't sure what she'd say if she saw him again, but one thing was certain. He always made her body tingle, and she longed to feel his lips on hers again, if only for a goodbye kiss.

9

"HURRY!" From the back seat of the cab, J.D. peered through the windshield at the rain-streaked New York night as they got off the expressway. He was almost there! Good! The rhythmic thud of the wipers were like water torture as he closed his fingers around Sandy's bag. He'd taken it from Banner Manor days before, but he'd only looked inside a moment ago.

Now his stomach lurched as he visualized the contents—love letters addressed to him, written in a dark scrawl, along with defiled photographs of Susannah and a heart-shaped charm engraved with the words *I love you*. He'd given Susannah the pendant years ago, and presumably Sandy had stolen it. There were diary entries that even threatened Susannah's life…

"Can you try dispatch again?" he said.

"Don't worry. They called the cops. And we're almost there," he explained, his hawklike eyes assessing J.D. in the rearview mirror. "Are you sure your wife's in some kind of danger?"

"She could be."

"Like I said, dispatch called the cops."

Could Sandy be stalking Susannah? Holding Sandy's bag and his own duffel in his lap, he got ready to bolt from the cab. Silently he cursed himself for not rummaging through Sandy's things sooner, but why would he? He'd never given the woman a second thought. Besides, just thinking about her prompted bad memories.

"Damn," he whispered, remembering their arguments about his having so many near strangers in their house.

"You say something back there?"

"Just hurry."

"I'm trying." The man did a double-take. "You know, you look sort of like that guy…what's his name?"

J.D. managed a shrug. His own cheap cell phone wasn't getting a signal, and since it would have confused matters, he'd offered a false name when he'd asked the cabbie to call the police to Susannah and Ellie's Lower East Side address. Now J.D. was focused on getting there himself. He had no idea what he'd say when the cops got a good look at him, realized who he was and that he was alive.

"You know," the cabbie persisted, seemingly unfazed that they were heading toward a place where his passenger half expected trouble. "You look like that country-western singer who died a couple weeks ago. Did anybody ever tell you that?"

J.D. shook his head.

"His picture was in the papers. He got drunk and wrecked his boat or something." He paused. "Well, whatever his name was, you look like him. Not exactly. I think he might have been blond."

Here today, J.D. thought, gone tomorrow. He'd let his beard grow for the past few weeks, and he was wearing glasses and a baseball cap. Not much of a disguise, but he realized it didn't matter. People believed he was history. They certainly didn't expect to see him. Nobody looked too deeply, and nobody looked twice.

Realizing that, he suddenly wanted Susannah back more than ever. Their time together had meant something—it was

real. In the music world, everything was fleeting and imper-
sonal. His career had delivered the glamor it had promised,
but nothing J.D. had really craved.

And now Susannah could be in danger! It was his fault!

They'd just turned, and now the traffic was bumper to
bumper. He tried his cell again, but it still wasn't getting a
signal; the cabbie hadn't had a phone he could use. He'd have
called Robby at Lee Polls, too, and Sheriff Kemp. God only
knew what they'd say when they found out he was alive. Still,
things he'd found in Sandy's bag looked truly threatening....

Worse, J.D.'s gut said Sandy could be here. In New York.
Where Susannah was. If anything happened to her, J.D.'s resurrection from the grave would be the least of his problems.
He'd truly want to die if Susannah met any harm. As it turned
out Susannah had been right all along—while the other
woman had been in their house, she'd had her eyes on J.D.,
not Joel. That was why she'd stripped and slipped into bed
with him. She'd *wanted* Susannah to find them together.

His eyes darted to the sidewalks, scanning corners, looking
for pay phone or a police officer. Having the cab company's
dispatch operator call the police was all he could do. "I can't
believe this," he whispered, his mind conjuring a thousand
worst-case scenarios. Thankfully, they were almost at
Susannah's apartment.

"What?"

"Nothing," he muttered tersely, his fingers closing more
tightly around Sandy's bag, his stomach churning at what
he'd seen. Along with the rambling unsent love letters and
charm, there were some of his favorite pictures of him and
Susannah in bygone happier days. Susannah at the beach
wearing a pink bikini, her body wet, and another taken at a
picnic with her in shorts and a T-shirt. A silly lopsided,

devil-may-care grin had stretched her lips from ear to ear—it had been scratched out with a sharp object. One of Sandy's diary entries had read, "Only when I get rid of her can J.D. and I can be together. I know that's what J.D. secretly wants."

Hardly. After his fight with Susannah the other night, he'd gone to Mama Ambrosia's cabin. She'd said he could use it to, as she put it, "screw his head on straight" while she was on vacation. Then today, he'd decided to follow Susannah to New York. Until now, he'd forgotten about Sandy's bag. He hadn't felt right about tossing it. After all, maybe something valuable was inside….

He suppressed a shudder, replaying his conversation with Susannah the day the boat exploded. He'd been startled as he'd hung up the phone. Sandy had been standing there, silently watching and listening to him. How long had she been there? he'd wondered. When had she returned to Banner Manor? He hadn't seen her since he'd first asked her to leave months ago. As before, she'd apologized profusely, saying she'd wound up in his bed accidentally.

Now he knew it was a lie. Obviously she was crazy. And worse, crazy about him. He hadn't figured it out then. As always, his mind had been fixated on Susannah. Sandy claimed to have returned for some forgotten belongings, and although most of his friends had gone, J.D. had thought little of it. Maybe she'd come for the bag, but been unable to find it.

A chill raced down his spine.

"Oh, God," he whispered with dawning comprehension. The diary, photographs and stolen charm were disturbing, but the woman had known he was supposed to meet Susannah on the *Alabama*.

Had she blown up the boat? To kill Susannah? To get her

out of the way, so J.D. would love her instead? Was that why he'd run out of gas that night?

"I knew I had a full tank," he muttered softly.

For a second, it seemed improbable, but he was sure he was right. Maybe Sandy had siphoned off gas, so he'd be stranded and unharmed when the boat blew. But then who had died in the explosion?

Last night, as he lay on Mama Ambrosia's couch, his true predicament had really sunk in. Everybody thought he was dead, and Susannah, the one person he wanted to know the truth, had rejected him. He couldn't redeem himself in her eyes. He'd slept fitfully, waking only hours ago, knowing he had to see her again.

He'd called a private pilot he'd used in the past, sworn him to secrecy, and headed for New York, figuring he'd talk to Susannah after the awards ceremony. A car was supposed to meet them, and when it hadn't, he'd caught the cab.

But none of that mattered now. On the way downtown, he'd finally opened Sandy's bag. Of course, he'd barely noticed Sandy Smithers. He knew nothing about her—not her favorite color, or birthday, or where she was born—and yet...

"I let her in our house," he whispered. *Susannah's house.*

Once more, he thought of the photographs in the bag, the slashes across his wife's face. His thighs tensed, his fingers itched and he knew he couldn't wait. Maybe the subway would be faster. J.D. was sure Sandy was out there some-where, and Susannah didn't even know she'd long been the object of another woman's hatred.

"Thanks," he suddenly said. "But I've got to get out." Leaning, he offered bills to the driver as he opened the door, stuffing Sandy's bag inside his own again so it would be easier to carry. What had been a small pink duffel only moments ago would soon become police evidence, he was sure of it.

Slinging his own bag over his shoulder, he thanked the cabbie once more, then ran headlong into the rain.

"THE LAST UMBRELLA," Susannah said with relief as she took out money, then heaved her oversize purse onto her shoulder, grunting with the weight, since J.D.'s award was inside. After paying the kiosk owner, she opened the inexpensive black umbrella. It wasn't very sturdy, but with luck, it would hold for a couple blocks until she reached her apartment.

"Or not," she muttered as a gust of wind threatened to turn the umbrella inside out. She pointed the tip downward like a spear so it wouldn't catch the wind again as she started jogging.

"Great," she groaned when the bronze statue started thumping her side. J.D. had already left her with enough bruises, emotional or otherwise, and the last thing she needed was this. The handbag had looked ridiculous with her fancy outfit, of course. Still, she'd have been lost without it, so she'd hidden it at her feet during the awards ceremony.

"What a life," she whispered, her mouth catching drops of rain. Everyone believed J.D. was dead, and now the prize for his work, one of the industry's most coveted honors, was stuffed into her purse like a worthless trinket. The moment defied anything she'd ever imagined. Weren't she and J.D. supposed to share this? Break out champagne? Make love?

Not that she was going to allow that to happen again, she vowed. She just wanted him to come clean so he wouldn't be deceiving so many people, and so that the authorities would start looking for the body of whomever had really been aboard the *Alabama* during the accident. She shook her head, shuddering as Robby's words from weeks ago replayed in her mind. *We think a faulty generator blew*.

"What a shame," she sighed, thinking of what a beautiful boat it had been. At least the explosion hadn't been J.D.'s fault. Still, she wished the real victim could be identified so they could be laid to rest. And where was J.D.

Mud splashed her hose as she landed in a puddle, and she groaned. A limo was to have picked her up after the ceremony, but because she'd cut out early, it hadn't been available, and she'd hailed a cab instead. Then the driver had missed a turn, and since he couldn't take her down her one-way street, she'd decided it was simpler to walk the rest of the way, despite the rain.

Speeding her steps, she felt relieved when Oh Susannah's came into view across the street. At the end of the block, she only had to turn a corner and she'd be able to see her and Ellie's front door. Not exactly home sweet home like Banner Manor, but the first floor, walk-up unit would be warm and dry.

Her teeth chattered in response to the chill that had come with the rain. After the trip down South, it felt as if the mercury was settling nearer to fifty degrees than sixty-five. At least Oh Susannah's was packed since the weather had driven people indoors.

Feeling drawn by the homey atmosphere—the lace curtains, country tablecloths and bright flowers in mason jars—she almost changed her mind about going to the apartment, but it was the wrong night to chat with Joe and Tara, so she kept running, rounding the corner. Besides, she'd visited the restaurant earlier today, to take care of business. And now she felt sure J.D. might materialize. He couldn't vanish....

Or could he? Maybe he was still at Bayou Banner. Here, the street was deserted, the windows dark in neighboring apartments. The Lower East Side had become more popular recently, but it wasn't as well trafficked as other downtown neighborhoods, and right now, it looked downright eerie.

Suddenly, her heart started hammering, and for no reason she could fathom, she stopped in her tracks. Turning to peer over her shoulder, she instinctively grabbed her purse, either to protect J.D.'s award or to use it as a weapon—she wasn't sure which.

But no one was there.

Her eyes scanned the street. Who had she expected to see? J.D.? She tried to push aside the foreboding that had plagued her all night, but she couldn't. She felt as if someone were following her…watching her.

"It's just the rain," she whispered nonsensically, mostly to hear her own voice. Reaching into her purse as she mounted the steps to her building, she dug inside for the key. As she inserted it into the lock, her hand quivered. God, she felt unsettled!

She wrenched around. She'd had the same spooked feeling at Banner Manor. Countless times, late at night, she'd go to the windows, believing people were outside, watching the house.

"And it was J.D.," she reminded herself as she opened the door onto the foyer. She tried to catch her purse, but it slid from her shoulder. Letting it fall to the floor, she used it as a doorstop for the outer door while she shook excess rain from the umbrella. Relief flooded her as she stepped from the stoop into the hallway. Finally she was home. Since the door to the apartment was within reach, she simultaneously opened it as she set the umbrella aside, then reached back for her handbag.

While the apartment door was swinging inward, she realized the answering machine was playing. Drats. She'd never make it to the phone.

Robby's voice filled the apartment. "Sheriff Kemp and I have been trying to track you down for hours, Susannah. We tried the awards ceremony, but they said you couldn't be disturbed. It's about the boat. I don't know if you got my other messages. We found something…and well, you need to call me as soon as possible. The explosion…it wasn't an accident, as it turns out. We thought it was the result of a faulty generator, but now we think there might be foul play."

She started to dart into the apartment to grab the phone, but she didn't want to leave the outer door open for strangers. Tilting her head, she remained quiet to listen to the rest of Bobby's message.

"And, Susannah?" he added. "I think you should get out of there. Ellie, too."

Then the line went dead. She quickly snatched her purse from the floor. She sensed there was more to the story, but he'd said enough. Something was wrong. Did it have to do with J.D.'s reappearance? She'd have to call Robby back right away. Swiftly, she reached to shut the outer door, but as she did, she heard a *pa-ching*.

Something sprayed her stockings! Her eyes darted downward. Splinters? Yes, wood had been gouged from the door frame, inches from her leg.

"What?" She turned to get a better look. Just then, something slammed her hard from behind, knocking the wind from her, sending her sailing toward the open apartment door.

Everything went black.

She heard the outer door slam shut, then she felt herself being half dragged into the apartment.

She tried to scramble away, reaching for the statue to use as a weapon as she made her way behind the sofa. Her mind raced. What was going on?

Blinking against the darkness, her heart pounding, she watched a bulky shadow lunge to the window and lift the curtain's edge, then the shadow ducked. She heard a soft clink before the glass shattered. Something hit the wall behind her. *Pa-ching. Pa-ching. Pa-ching.*

Are those bullets? Oh my God!

The man dove, hauling what looked to be a large bag. With his free hand, he yanked her to her feet. "Is there another way out?"

"J.D.?"

"We have to be quiet. We have to get out of here. Now."

She bolted wordlessly toward a bedroom fire door that led to a back staircase and the basement of the building. Moments later, they'd cut through a laundry room, emerging in a back alley.

Tightly, he grasped her hand, twining his fingers through hers. Even now, under the circumstances, she couldn't help but feel a shiver of longing at the touch. She felt the dry skin and strength of his muscles, the perfect fit of the hand against her palm. Despite the hatred she kept professing to have for him and whatever danger they were in, her heart was soaring, since he'd returned. But just as quickly, annoyance rushed in.

"Robby called just now," she said as they ran. Her shoes were thin, and the pavement was cold, strewn with debris, and it slowed her down.

"What's making that noise?" he whispered, glancing at her bag. His voice was steady although she was starting to feel winded.

"Your award," she whispered.

"Lose it," he urged. "Just toss it."

She couldn't, it was irreplaceable. She held onto it, her breath shallow with exertion, her lungs burning as the apartment receded behind them. One block, two…she counted. Three…

Suddenly, she gasped, doubling and grasping her side. "I can't run in these shoes anymore, J.D."

Tugging her arm, he pulled her behind some trash cans, and she squatted, the hem of the beautiful dress he'd given her soaking up mud. He craned his neck, scanning the alley, and the longer she took in his profile, the harder it was to hate him. His eyes were alert, almost predatory, his body tense and impossibly still. Power coiled inside him and he looked ready to pounce. Just looking at him made her feel safe.

"Were those gunshots?" she gasped, gulping air, already knowing the answer. A girl didn't grow up in Mississippi without knowing how a gunshot sounded.

"I think so."

Something had definitely gouged the door frame and shattered the window. "What on earth's going on?"

"It's a long story."

"You know why somebody just shot at me?" It was just like J.D. to be cryptic. Annoyance flared. "Dammit, J.D., if somebody's shooting at me, and you know why, I have a right to know, too!"

"Not here."

"I'm not going a step farther until I get some answers." Even if it meant she had to crouch behind smelly garbage and what was probably a safe haven for city rodents. She added, "Robby just called saying the explosion on the boat wasn't an accident."

J.D. turned toward her, and as his gaze trailed from the top of her head to the tips of her toes, she felt a rush of unbidden sensual burning heat. As much as she wanted to ignore the sensation, she was being quickly reminded why she'd married the man. He wasn't winded, but his chest expanded and fell with deep breaths, making his pectorals look infinitely touchable.

He exhaled a heartfelt curse when his eyes landed on her feet. "You're practically barefoot."

Once more he was blaming her for something that was really his fault, and she felt another rush of pique. "You're the one who bought me the shoes."

"Yeah," he said simply.

Suddenly, everything was too much. She was in some sort of danger she didn't understand. Drenched. And wearing a see-through dress to boot. Without looking, she knew the eye makeup she'd worn for the ceremony had melted down her cheeks. Her stockings were dirty and shot through with runs, and J.D. was exactly right. She *was* practically barefoot. No longer warm from running, the night air caused her to shiver.

"I didn't exactly anticipate running in this weather?" she huffed. "I mean, it's not like I want to catch my death out here, J.D." Pausing, she acerbically added, "Not everybody is as happy as you to go to their grave, you know."

Wordlessly he rummaged in his pocket and withdrew a handkerchief, swiping it beneath her eyes. Sure enough, her mascara had run. And leave it to J.D., she thought with escalating fury, to remind her that he was the only man she knew who actually still carried handkerchiefs. He might forego underwear with frightening regularity, but he always had a hanky handy for the ladies.

Now he brushed away a damp lock of hair that had fallen into her eyes, and his gaze softened, as if he was relieved to see she was fine. "C'mon," he said, standing.

"Whither thou goest, I will go?" she guessed as she stood, too. "Isn't that a bit demanding for a guy who's supposed to have passed onto a better life?"

They were toe to toe, and rocking back on her bare heels, she surveyed him. Only her fury at J.D. could override her sense of self-protection and worry over what had just happened at her apartment. "And is it really a better life?" she continued, feigning real interest. "I mean, pardon me for asking, but I've never had the opportunity to interview somebody who's just come back from the other side. What do they have there? Pearly gates? Harps for all your musician friends?"

Puffing his cheeks, he stared at her a long moment, his searing blue eyes narrowed and his lips pursed tightly, as if it was costing him not to offer snide retorts. He could, too, she knew—J.D. had a way with words. He gave her a pointed look, as if to ask if she were done with her tirade. Then, silently, he re-shouldered his duffel. Before she could protest, he leaned agilely, hooked an arm under her knees and simply scooped her into his embrace—handbag and all.

The next thing she knew, he was cradling her against his chest. She told herself that she had no choice but to wreathe her arms around his neck, but as she did so, she was assaulted with pine and peppermints, a combination of scents that was pure J. D. Johnson. Or almost. She sniffed. "For once, I don't smell whisky," she commented.

"Told you," he muttered. "I'm on the wagon."

"Better than on your boat, apparently. And what do you think you're doing?" she said with pique, trying to ignore a traitorous beating of her heart against his.

"Carrying you."

"Hmm. Well, if you think we're going to get more physical than this, you're dead wrong."

"Fine by me."

She doubted that. "Am I allowed to know where we're going?"

"To find Ellie." He paused. "And then home to Banner Manor. A plane's waiting at the airport."

"Flown by whom?"

"A pilot I know."

"Aren't you afraid he'll tell the world you're alive, well and having a great time?"

J.D. was actually starting to look rattled. So much so that she was beginning to enjoy herself. "Nope."

"And why's that?"

"Because I'm not having a great time right now, Susannah."

"That makes two of us. Now, what about my place?"

"Before I got there, I called the cops. They're on their way."

Sure enough, she could hear sirens. Of course, in New York, that wasn't unusual. Her heart beat double time as the long strides of J.D.'s jeans-clad legs continued swallowing the pavement. Somehow, she wasn't surprised to find her husband could manage both her weight and his duffels without stumbling, but she still had no idea what was happening.

"Were those really gunshots?" she asked again, realizing the shock of the past few moments was starting to subside. "Why did you suspect something was wrong? How did you know to call the police?"

His face drew her eyes like a magnet, and she couldn't help but stare up at him, registering the heady scent of his breath. She watched as his jaw clenched, making enticing shadows flicker over his cheeks in the darkness. Finally he said, "Remember Sandy Smithers?"

She stiffened in his arms, and everything inside her turned to ice. "The gorgeous naked woman who was in bed with you? How could I forget?"

"I think she got into bed with me on purpose that morning," he said, releasing a worried sigh as they reached a main avenue. He seemed to be looking for a cab.

"No kidding," she returned angrily, wiggling against him. Moments ago, she'd been kept warm by the exertion of running and then from his body heat, but now, she'd rather brave the dirt and mud of the streets than continue to let him held her. "Look," she muttered, squirming. "Why don't you put me down?"

He did so, then watched as she crossed her arms over her chest. Catching his gaze, she realized once more how wet she was, and how the delicate fabric of the dress had become nearly transparent. Her arms had just served to lift her breasts, as if offering them for his perusal.

"I'm not going anywhere with you until you tell me what's going on," she stated firmly, trying to ignore the heat and hunger flaring in his eyes.

"I think she's stalking you, Susannah," he said simply.

She gasped. "Who? Sandy Smithers?"

"Yeah." He nodded. "I think she may have just shot at you." He paused. "And me. And I think she blew up the *Alabama*."

It was the last thing she'd expected him to say. Her lips parted in shock. "Why would she do that?"

For the first time in her recollection, J.D. actually looked scared. "Because she thought you were the person on board, Susannah."

10

BECAUSE SHERIFF KEMP WAS a massive man, his tan uniform nearly burst the shoulder seams as he hunched to scrutinize the contents of Sandy's bag, which were laid out on his desk. He'd been called away from a date with Delia, and at first, when he'd seen J.D., he'd been shocked. Then he'd quickly begun questioning him about the explosion.

Now, when he glanced up, his brown eyes, visible through blond bangs, held less judgment than J.D. knew he deserved. That made him feel guiltier, if it was possible, and as self-loathing filled him, he damned himself for all the trouble he'd caused. He was beginning to wish the earth would open and swallow him, and since that's what so many people thought had happened to him, a bemused smile tugged his lips—only to disappear when he thought of the danger in which he'd put Susannah.

"Well," said the sheriff, "do we tell the media you're alive?"

J.D. shrugged, ready to ignore anything that didn't pertain to Susannah's safety. Not that he could. Robby had shown up to help, and if it weren't for the circumstances, it would seem like old times. Robby was leaning against a wall, an inscrutably furious scowl on his face, almost like the one he'd worn throughout his hardscrabble childhood, during which his mama was gone and his daddy was drinking all the time.

Displaying his usual attitude of defiance, Robby's hands were shoved angrily into the slacks pockets of one of the fancy suits he always wore to work, and he looked gaunt and harried, like the workaholic he'd become. His chestnut hair was shaggy, as if he'd been too busy to visit a barber, and it nearly obscured his glittering eyes, but not enough to hide his emotions. Astonishment was warring with betrayal, then something that might have been pleasure that J.D. wasn't really dead, but Robby was trying to hide the latter.

Susannah had claimed the room's only armchair, and she was wearing white tube socks, compliments of the sheriff, along with her ruined dress. Her shoes were drying in a windowsill. A gray wool army blanket was slung around her shoulders, looking incongruous with a diamond necklace and dangling earrings. Unfortunately, there had been no clothes for them to change into on the plane, so Susannah had just toweled herself dry. Now J.D. felt a surge at his groin as he recalled how good she'd looked, slowly dabbing her bare, shapely, mud-streaked legs after she'd stripped off the ruined panty hose.

The woman he'd feared he'd never hold again had felt great in his arms, too, even if he'd been cuddling her against her will. He pushed his thought aside. This was no time to have sex on the brain; then again, that was a tall order when Susannah was around.

At least for him. His estranged wife was studying everything in Sheriff Kemp's office, from the gunmetal-gray desks to the gleaming white tile floor to the area maps that adorned the walls. *Anything but me,* J.D. realized ruefully.

An unwanted memory assaulted him of the day he'd first seen the dress she was wearing. It was in the window of a dressmaker's shop. Maybe it was the sensual skirt, made of airy, multilayered fabric, or the unusual tattered hem, but whatever the case, the champagne-colored garment had stopped him in his tracks, and he'd known it was tailor-made for Susannah's statuesque figure, nipped waist and full breasts.

"She'd look gorgeous in it," he'd whispered.

And she had. Although he'd never seen her wear it until tonight, and their run through the rain had destroyed it. How was he going to forgive himself if something happened to her? He'd give his life to save Susannah. If Sandy Smithers had really destroyed the *Alabama* and tried to kill Susannah, what would the woman do next?

Thoughtfully, J.D. chewed the inside of his cheek, then stopped when his gaze landed on the sheriff's desk. *Amazing,* he thought. One of the most coveted awards known to the music industry was propped there, next to Susannah's oversize purse. The award meant nothing now. A chintzy hunk of gold not worth the pain it had brought into his and Susannah's lives. J.D. wished he'd never learned to play music. To hell with the hours of pleasure it had brought him.

Shaking his head, he made a silent vow to himself. *If Susannah doesn't get hurt,* he thought, *I swear I'll never play again.*

"Uh…J.D.?"

Glancing up, he realized the sheriff was speaking to him. In fact, everybody was staring at him. He was so preoccupied that he hadn't paid any attention to the conversation. "We do whatever you think is best," he said to the sheriff. "I'll play this any way you want." *Anything, if Susannah is safe. Please.* The closest thing he'd ever felt to humility filled his soul. *Don't let my mistakes hurt my wife.*

"Glad to hear it." Sheriff Kemp nodded abruptly and feathered a splayed hand through his blond curls. Then he used the eraser end of a pencil to prod the items on the desk again. They made J.D. shudder, especially the destroyed pictures of Susannah.

"We'll send these to the lab," Sheriff Kemp said, thoughtfully turning the pages of a diary decorated with childish hearts and cupid's arrows. Words on the pages flew by: *Sandy loves J.D. Sandy and J.D. forever. Sandy wants J.D.'s babies.* Toward the back of the book, the woman's scrawl became less legible; she'd been pressing the pen point harder, causing tiny tears in the paper, and she'd become more obsessed with Susannah. *Why can't J.D. see through her? Doesn't he know she's a big fake? Why doesn't he leave her?*

And later: *Somebody has to save J.D. by showing him the truth. He's too nice to see through that bitch. She doesn't love him. She's just using him for his money and fame. I wish she'd die.*

"We'll look carefully where you kept your truck parked that night," Sheriff Kemp continued, "and where we found it the night of the explosion.

"Gas might have soaked into the ground near the road, but it's rained since then." The sheriff nodded distractedly. "We'll check though."

"When the truck stopped running, I guided it under some trees," J.D. said helpfully.

"There was no need to examine the area before, but if Sandy Smithers is responsible for the events tonight, or if she's the reason you never reached the *Alabama* so you wouldn't be onboard when it blew, then maybe we'll find evidence."

"And the truck itself?" asked Robby, studying the photographs where Susannah's face had been defiled. "Maybe there's a compromised fuel line. We had towed it to the garage," he continued. "It's been there for the past two weeks.

The owner said we could keep it there until the estate gave word about what to do with it."

"Any idea where this woman might have gone?" the sheriff asked.

"None," said J.D, "but my gut says she's the one who shot at us in New York. Maybe she's still there."

"Or maybe she followed you here." Robby's voice was a low rumble akin to a growl. Clearly he was none too happy about Ellie possibly being in danger.

Sheriff Kemp kept on point, addressing J.D. "Did the shooter see you?"

J.D. shrugged as the sheriff started taking notes. "I figure. I headed to the awards ceremony from the airport, but when I saw the contents of the bag, I changed directions. If my hunch was right, and Sandy was in town, I knew I'd be better off going to the apartment to make sure Susannah was safe. I didn't think Sandy wouldn't try to hurt her at the ceremony. There's just too much security."

"Don't talk about me as if I'm not here, J.D.," Susannah said.

He could do nothing right at the moment. Taking a deep breath, he said, "Sorry, Susannah." Then he continued, "Because of the rain, I waited a couple doors down from Ellie and Susannah's, under an awning. Susannah came home from the other direction, so I didn't see her at first. It was dark and an umbrella was covering her face. She was nearly inside before I realized it was her."

Pausing, he shook his head, trying to remember. "I saw a flash from my left from behind a parked car, just as Susannah got the key in the door. It was just a bolt of light, and I heard a gunshot."

Sheriff Kemp was listening hard. "And then?"

"I ran toward Susannah." He hadn't thought, only acted. "I hopped a rail, ran up some stairs and pushed her inside."

"But you didn't see the shooter?"

"No."

"But the shooter probably saw you."

J.D. nodded. "Yeah. I guess. I mean, the porch light was on when I ran inside."

"Was it still raining?"

"Yeah. Hard."

With the pencil, the sheriff nudged a photograph on his desk. It was a five-by-eight of Susannah in the prom dress J.D. had so carefully removed before making love to her the night they'd eloped. The picture had been stabbed repeatedly, maybe as many as thirty times. "A knife or scissors," the sheriff said absent mindedly.

Susannah gasped. "I knew pictures were missing. While I was cleaning the house after…" She paused. "After J.D.'s funeral." She shook her head. "Most of those were in an album near the downstairs TV, but that one was in a frame upstairs."

"Susannah's face has either been scratched or cut out of ten pictures, at least," J.D. said, anxiety gnawing at him. "How dangerous do you think Sandy is?"

Sheriff Kemp shook his head. "We don't even know she's connected to the explosion. All you've got is proof she's obsessive and has a violent imagination." Sheriff Kemp glanced toward the door to the evidence room. "However, we now have proof explosives were onboard the *Alabama*. That's why Robby was trying desperately to reach Susannah. Unfortunately, they didn't speak before you two were shot at. Still, that doesn't mean Sandy Smithers is the perpetrator."

Surprisingly, when she spoke again, Susannah's voice was rock steady, and maybe, J.D. thought, that was the worst thing. It was as if she'd prepared for this long ago. Obviously, she thought such trouble was a natural consequence of loving J. D. Johnson.

"What's going on in New York?" she asked.

Sheriff Kemp shrugged. "When you two arrived, I was just hanging up with the NYPD. They closed shop at your apartment. Some bullets hit the door frame, and they found footprints. Heavy boots, maybe military, small size."

"Sandy usually wore boots," J.D. offered. "She was pretty, but—"

Susannah snorted. "Try gorgeous."

"But she didn't dress in a feminine way," J.D. finished.

"Too bad they didn't find something more personal," Susannah offered dryly. "Panties. A bra, maybe. Then J.D. could really help."

She was testing his patience. While he didn't expect Susannah to support him after all his mistakes, he'd never slept around. "Let's keep it private, Susannah."

"That's rich coming from you."

At the sheriff's heavy sigh, she pursed her lips. He said, "And there's nothing else of hers at Banner Manor?"

Susannah shook her head. "While I was cleaning, I never saw anything I didn't recognize."

"What about the bag?"

"I never noticed it. J.D. said it was half buried under some of his stuff. I'd started cleaning upstairs and in the living room. I was…"

"Distraught?" suggested the sheriff.

"However unnecessarily," Susannah conceded.

They all fell silent.

"Well," the sheriff continued. "Like I said when you first got here, you heard bullets, all right. As it turns out, they're from a twenty-two revolver."

"Not much of a weapon," commented Robby.

Susannah gasped. "What about your gun, J.D.?"

"Oh no," he whispered. Years ago, he and Robby used to target shoot with a twenty-two all the time, knocking soda cans off hay bales. He hadn't used it for years, another reminder of his estrangement from Robby. "I take it out once a year and clean it," he stated. "It was in the back of the bedroom closet, on a top shelf."

"I didn't touch anything there," Susannah said.

"She took your gun," Robby muttered.

"Registered?" asked the sheriff.

"Sure," J.D. said. "It was a gift from my dad."

Sheriff Kemp sighed as if to say it was going to be a long night. "An officer told me Ellie will be staying with a fellow named Joe O'Grady. I don't think she's in any danger, but it's a necessary precaution." Sheriff Kemp glanced at Susannah. "Do you know him?"

"Uh…yeah." And then as if simply to cause J.D. pain, she added, "Pretty well, actually."

"Then he'll take care of her," the sheriff said with a nod.

"That's crazy!" Robby bellowed, looking furious. "I'm going to New York."

"I don't think you should," Susannah put in quickly.

It had been so many years since they'd all gotten along, J.D. thought sadly. He and Robby used to fish the bayous, using bait from his dad's shop, while Susannah and Ellie watched, sunning themselves in bikinis on a blanket. Or they'd jam on drums and a guitar, while Susannah and Ellie danced.

Withdrawing his hands from his pockets, Robby crossed his arms. "Ellie could be in danger, too. She could have been with you tonight."

"She'll be fine with Joe," Susannah assured him. "He's

got a new girlfriend, by the way," she added to smooth his ruffled feathers. "And don't forget, Robby, this woman hates me, not Ellie."

"I'm going," Robby said resolutely.

"I think we ought to do whatever the sheriff thinks best," J.D. offered.

Robby sent him a look that was full of fire but still chilled J.D.'s blood. "You've caused enough trouble," Robby warned. "I came here for Susannah and Ellie, not you."

A long silence fell; it was more than J.D. could take. He wanted to argue, fight back and protest, but Robby was right. He hadn't deserved such good friendships. Not with Robby and Ellie, and least of all, with Susannah.

"What about my restaurant?"

J.D. could almost see Susannah's mind working. Would Sandy Smithers sabotage the eatery? Destroy it the way she had the *Alabama*? At the same time, was Sandy even the culprit? Had J.D. shut his mind to the possibility that someone else was responsible as the sheriff kept implying? Maybe, J.D. admitted. After all, he wanted to know the identity of the enemy immediately. It made what was happening seem more manageable. More contained. And it made fighting back easier.

"I need to keep these items as evidence, of course," the sheriff remarked.

J.D. nodded.

Sheriff Kemp shook his head. "For whatever it's worth, I do figure you're right. This woman may well have let the gas out of your truck so you couldn't meet Susannah. She didn't know Susannah wasn't coming. After the explosion, maybe she thought she'd killed you accidentally. She must have hated herself. Then…"

"She saw him." Susannah inhaled audibly, her eyes widening. J.D. watched as her hand flew to her neck. As she did when she was anxious, she touched the charm she wore around her neck; Ellie had one just like it.

Running the charm up and down on its chain, Susannah said, "Maybe Sandy's been watching the house all along. I felt someone outside the whole time I was there. Later, I thought it was J.D. But maybe, when he came back, she was out there, too, and she saw him."

"She could have felt even more betrayed that he'd survived," the sheriff agreed. "Or that J.D. was more duped by Susannah than ever."

"Then she started to target me again," Susannah posited.

Sheriff Kemp shook his head. "We'll find out. In the meantime, you and Ellie are safe. We'll run a background check to see if this woman had reason to know anything about explosives."

"She never said anything about them," J.D. mentioned, still watching Susannah toy with her necklace, the creamy column of her neck completely captivating. "I would have remembered something like that. She didn't say anything about guns, either."

The sheriff nodded. "Do you mind if I look around the house?"

Susannah shook her head. "I can walk you through."

"Not yet. Tonight you two can't go back to Banner Manor," the sheriff returned. "Better safe than sorry." He looked at J.D. "And there's no need to muddy up the waters by announcing you're alive. Let's hold that card close to the vest, in case we need it."

"Whatever you want," returned J.D. "The only other person who knows is the pilot who brought us here. For a minute, I thought a cabbie in New York recognized me, but he didn't. Oh," he added, "Mama Ambrosia. She knows, but she won't say anything. She offered me her cabin while she's out of town."

"Excellent." The sheriff nodded, looking relieved. "You and Susannah can stay there."

"What!" Susannah exploded. "With him? No offense, but you're as crazy as Sandy Smithers. I'd rather run the risk of being shot at again."

"I don't have the manpower to protect you," the sheriff returned calmly.

"I'd offer," Robby said, giving J.D. a long glance of censure, "but I'm going to New York to make sure Ellie's safe."

"I don't know how she'll react to that," Susannah said gently.

"I'm going anyway," Robby said.

"I'll go to Hodges' Motor Lodge," Susannah vowed.

J.D.'s heart was sinking. "I know how you feel about me, Susannah. Robby, too. That's a given. But the sheriff's right. He doesn't have manpower, and you'll be safer at Mama's. I'll keep to myself. Even if Sandy's heard of Mama Ambrosia, she couldn't know the location. The cabin's tucked in the woods. Half the time, even locals can't find it."

"No way am I going to some fortune-teller's house," Susannah protested, still worrying her charm.

J.D. was about to respond, but his blood quickened, and before he thought it through, he was striding across the room. His hand closed over the chain, and something inside him softened when he felt the warmth of Susannah's hand. "What's this?" he asked, voice strangely hoarse.

"My chain." Susannah suddenly gasped. "The other chain...the one the sheriff gave me after the *Alabama* blew. He said they found it in the wreckage. It's a Saint Christopher's medal, and I'd never seen it before, but I thought you might have gotten it recently. The sheriff thought it was yours, and in a state of shock…"

"Oh, dammit. I'm so sorry," Sheriff Kemp suddenly interjected. "There's no excuse for the shoddy work we did. It was incompetent, but we'll correct that now. I'm not asking you two to forgive me. You know we never get crime like this around here, and the media was pressuring us. Besides which, we all knew J.D. personally, and that public relations lady from New York was harping all the time. If the truth be told, I'd been thinking of nothing but Delia all the time, anyway. Everything happened so fast…

"And we were so sure it was J.D. We'll question the attendant again, but he said he'd left the marina to pick up some for dinner, and when he returned, he saw the boat on the water with J.D. in it."

"I called and told him to have it ready," J.D. said. "He must have just assumed it was me."

"We'll talk to him again." Sheriff Kemp blew out a sigh. "He told us that you've never let anybody else play captain, either."

"No," J.D. said abruptly, "I didn't." He was still staring at the Saint Christopher's medal that rested against his palm. He thought it was supposed to ensure safety, but this time around, it hadn't.

"You did a fine job," she assured the sheriff.

"Given what you knew, it seemed the person onboard had to be me," J.D. agreed. "But I think it was a guy named Joel Murray."

Susannah glanced up at him. "Joel?"

"He was a studio musician without any family," J.D. explained to the sheriff. "He travels to play with different bands. He's not much of a concert musician. Anyway, the record company sent him here to work with me. He brought Sandy, but she wasn't nearly as interested in him as he was in her."

Somehow J.D. pulled his gaze from Susannah's eyes. He glanced over his shoulder at the sheriff who said, "Why do you think Joel Murray was onboard?"

"Because he always wore a Saint Christopher's medal," J.D. said. "And he wore it on a strip of leather, not a chain, just like this."

11

AT MAMA AMBROSIA'S, Susannah rubbed a patch of condensation from the bathroom mirror and peered at her reflection. "Passable," she decided, then mentally berated herself for caring about her appearance at such a time. Still, how could she help but feel vain when J.D. practically salivated every time he looked at her?

Mama's cabin was far more inviting at second glance. The main room Susannah had visited previously wasn't much to look at, mostly due to the utilitarian shelves lined with potions and herbs and an antique potbelly stove, but farther down a hallway, toward a back door that opened onto a porch with a rocking chair, were three cozy bedrooms, all laid with wide-planked floors and paneled with hardwoods. The curtains were clean and white and the beds made with crisp sheets and pastel quilts.

"I'll take this room," J.D. had said, nodding toward the smallest as Susannah headed for the shower. "It's the one I was staying in before."

"Are you sure Mama isn't going to mind?"

"She offered me her cabin while she's gone."

Susannah suspected Mama had been matchmaking, not that the ideas she'd planted were going to bear fruit. "Are you sure you don't want to sleep outside?" Susannah had continued sweetly, as if to say J.D. should seriously consider it. She'd expected some testy retort; maybe she'd even been trying to rile him intentionally, to take the edge off the fact that they weren't exactly in spacious Banner Manor, but alone in a cabin the size of a postage stamp. He merely nodded, not rising to the bait. "You could be out there with your friends, the animals," she'd added.

A beat passed, then he'd simply said, "I'll fix some food, Susannah. I figure you're hungry."

"I'll just take a shower," she'd huffed, turning on her heel and heading inside the bathroom, hardly wanting to examine her pique. Surely she was spoiling for a fight just to make sure she kept J.D. at a distance, not because she wanted to get into a heated discussion with the man.

Still, she was starting to feel sorry for him. Clearly bothered by Sandy and by Robby's cold reception, J.D. had kept silent on the way to the cabin. Sheriff Kemp had followed Robby to Banner Manor to get Susannah's car, then they'd picked up food supplies at a store halfway to Bayou Blair. Robby had brought her a pair of flip-flops and a bag of clothes from the same store, mostly sweatpants with logos from sports teams Susannah didn't recognize. She'd rather have had things from her own house, but Sheriff Kemp didn't want her to return there until he was sure she'd be safe.

After she finished dressing in a white T-shirt and gold drawstring pants and a matching hoodie, she took a deep breath and headed toward the kitchen, her throat suddenly aching when she recalled the disdain with which Robby had treated J.D. It was so sad. Worse, Robby would blame J.D. further if something happened to Ellie.

Pushing aside thoughts of the gunshots that could have taken their lives, Susannah walked toward the scent of seasoned meat. Pausing in the doorway, she waited to see if J.D. would turn around, but he continued lifting lids on pots and stirring the contents. "Is that you?"

"No, it's Sandy Smithers."

"Not funny."

He was right, it wasn't. It was easy to stare at his back, though, especially since he'd taken off his shirt. He had nice broad shoulders and pronounced shoulder blades, a back strong enough to make any woman shiver, with myriad ridges and sloping contours, not to mention invitingly smooth skin. As Susannah's eyes settled on his behind, her fingers itched. Unbidden, her gaze settled hotly just above the thick, hand-tooled belt he wore with his jeans.

"What's cooking?" Despite the fact that the food smelled heavenly, she added, "Did you season with spices from those jars down the hallway?"

"I would have, but I couldn't find any herbs that would make our problems go away."

"Which ones?"

"Any of them." He shot an apologetic glance over a bare shoulder as he transferred steaks to the plates. For the briefest second, when she saw his eyes, thoughts of Sandy Smithers ceased to exist. A man hadn't been killed. The world didn't think J.D. had passed on, and the two of them hadn't run for their lives through the streets of New York. Just looking at J.D. had always made her feel safe. Which was ridiculous, since he was the most dangerous and annoying man she'd ever known.

As she surveyed the steaks, Susannah was suddenly aware of her rumbling stomach and watering mouth. Now it was she, not J.D., who was salivating. She felt a surge of relief, too, since the object of her emotions was a sirloin, not her almost-naked nearly ex-husband.

At least until he turned fully around, a plate in each hand, and her throat turned as dry as dust. Maybe it was the smoothness of the skin, the wealth of wild black tangled chest hair, the muscular pectorals or the nipples that looked just a tad too taut. Whatever it was, her body was responding, her chest filling like a sail on a sudden intake of breath, then growing tight when she inadvertently held it.

Then the moment passed. He'd set napkins and cutlery on the center island, and she sidled closer, seating herself on a tall stool, just as he did. She eyed him as he set her food before her, then she dug in, cutting a healthy bite from the meat. "It looks good," she conceded. "Even worse, it tastes divine."

"You don't want to like it?"

"No more than I want to like you."

"I don't blame you."

Damn, she thought, feeling strangely miffed again. "It's not like you to be so agreeable."

He shot her a look. "I can't even do that right."

Warm and succulent, the meat was as good as a juicy kiss, and her tummy melted as she swallowed. Before she thought it through, she added between her next bites, "You always were a good cook."

He was eating just as fast as she, as if starved. "When I bothered to do it, anyway."

She let that pass, but as she silently devoured the best meal she'd had in awhile, at least outside her own restaurant, she felt further unsettled. Guilty even. Oh, J.D. had gotten too full of himself. In fact, for the past couple years, he'd morphed into the incarnation of every bad male quality known to womankind—rolled into one hunky package. And he never should have let so many strangers crash land into their lives. Definitely, he shouldn't have made a split-second decision to let the world think he was dead.

But he couldn't have known Sandy was crazy. While tonight's events were hardly a blessing in disguise, over the past weeks—from the day Susannah had thought J.D. was gone forever—she'd been reminded of all his good qualities. The power of his voice captured aching hearts and healed wounded emotions after all. And he was perfect in bed.

"Why, J.D. was wild," Delia had said two weeks ago, as she'd offered condolences, "and I know you two always fought like cats and dogs, but it was nice to watch you make up."

Just as J.D. could turn the most humble ingredients into a tasty meal, he could fix any gadget around the house, and draw a bath that was always the right temperature. As Susannah polished off her plate, she recalled the fan letters she'd read after the funeral, especially one by a woman who'd forgiven her two-timing man. Suddenly a dull ache claimed her heart. Her husband's songs had saved marriages on the rocks, mended broken family rifts and soothed lonely people to sleep.

When she finished eating, he said, "Seconds?"

She'd been thinking about how he hadn't really cheated on her. She shook her head and stared down at the empty plate. "I'll do the dishes," she said contritely, and once more, she felt a stabbing little pain of emotion. It had been so long since they'd shared a meal or discussed domestic details like this.

"Don't worry. I'll get them."

She yawned. "What time is it, anyway?"

"Late. About three in the morning."

Fear had kept her alert. "The bewitching hour." Just as she

said the words, she could have kicked herself. She half expected J.D. to say, "Time for some magic, Susannah? Scarves and cards? A touch of my magic wand?"

But he was silent.

Hours ago, she'd been in New York, dressed to the nines and attending an awards ceremony. If she couldn't see the statue on the kitchen counter, she'd scarcely believe it. His eyes followed hers to it, and his jaw clenched. He started to say something, then changed his mind.

After that, it seemed too quiet. The night had settled, just as surely as an old house, and it made her miss Banner Manor. Even insects and owls had simmered down, as if to better hallow the wee hours. Through a window was low, leafy foliage, making her feel hemmed in and surrounded. She knew better, but she shook her head ruefully, and said what was in her mind. "This reminds me of years ago, back when you were playing local gigs."

He seemed to know what she meant and nodded. "Yeah."

By the time the band had walked off stage, loaded their equipment and arrived home, it was usually about this time. Still keyed up, tired but not ready for sleep, she and J.D. would sit at the kitchen table at Banner Manor, either talking or simply staring at the moon. At some point, he'd take her hand, and they'd go to bed and make love, sometimes until the rose fingers of dawn began touching the windows.

Abruptly, she stood. "I'd best turn in. It was an exciting evening, to say the least." She shot a sudden, tense glance outside. "Do you really think we're safe?"

"Sheriff Kemp says so. Definitely safer than at Banner Manor, I figure. I already checked all the locks." He paused. "Nobody knows about my relationship with Mama Ambrosia."

"I didn't know you were close enough to stay in her house."

He shrugged. "I've been letting her read my cards and tell my fortune since I was a kid."

"And what did it say last time she looked into her crystal ball?"

A cloud passed over his eyes, so she didn't believe him when he said, "I have a bright and rosy future."

"Lucky you. 'Cause she said I was in danger."

"I'm sorry, Susannah," he said softly.

Suddenly she wanted to talk about so many things—about how Robby had treated him tonight, and how easily Sheriff Kemp had taken his reappearance in stride. She wanted to discuss Sandy, too, although she didn't quite know what to say, except that she believed J.D. now. He'd definitely never slept with her. And what about Joel Murray? she thought. Was he really the victim?

Rather than voice her thoughts, she silently nodded and began walking toward the hallway, deciding to let J.D. clean up, since he'd offered.

"Susannah."

He'd spoken so quietly that she almost thought it had been her imagination. It seemed a mere phantom, the way it sounded when she listened to his records sometimes. Like it was simultaneously him and yet not him.

Turning, she leaned against the door frame and arched an eyebrow. "Hmm?"

"I didn't sleep with her. That's all. I want you to believe me. Just about that one thing."

She nodded. When she'd found Sandy lying next to him in bed, she'd been shocked and outraged, not thinking clearly. Sometime later, she'd realized that he'd looked surprised. Because he'd gotten caught, she'd thought at the time. Now she knew that his being in the buff meant nothing; he always slept that way. He'd been shocked to see Sandy there. "Obviously," she managed, "Sandy was obsessed with you."

"I didn't know she was in bed with me."

"I know." She paused. "But you brought some pretty strange people into our lives."

"That's an understatement."

"I'm trying to be kind."

"I didn't leave enough space for just the two of us."

And that had been the real issue. "If it helps, you were right about a lot of things, J.D.," she said, wondering if it even mattered to admit it at such a late stage of the game. "I was never really jealous, not the way you said at Banner Manor. I mean, I didn't think you'd run off with some other woman. But I figured it was only a matter of time until this whole new world you'd entered completely swept you away. It got to where, every time you'd leave to go play, I half expected you not to come back home."

Just as she finished speaking, he got to his feet, circled the kitchen island and strode toward her. When he was a foot away, she could feel his breath and the warmth rising from his bare chest. Her hands yearned to reach for him, her fingers longed to touch. Suddenly, her voice broke. "You were always so much bigger than me, J.D."

"Not so," he returned in a husky whisper, made even sexier because of his slow drawl. "I can't believe what you've done without me, Susannah. I knew you could do it, but the restaurant—"

"It's sad, though," she interjected. "Our lives diverging. I used to think of us as one river, flowing together, but it's like we hit a solid rock, J.D. Now I'm going one way, and you're going another." *If we even survive this,* a tiny voice inside her said. "Only danger brought us back together."

"I'll never let anything happen to you, Susannah."

"Sandy Smithers's actions aren't in your control, J.D."

His lips pursed, just slightly, as if in displeasure, then something dark and unreadable crossed his features. She watched the lips part, a fraction, and in the silence, she heard a release of breath that sounded strangely labored. All at once, she was aware of promise, desire and hope. Something quickened inside her, sparking and igniting, flowing through her veins, and beneath her top, she could feel the arousal of her unrestrained breasts. The cotton chaffed against her taut nipples.

Heat surged to her extremities, and she felt a blush rising on her cheeks. Inadvertently, her eyes dropped hungrily over her husband, his hairy chest and the inny belly button of his flat belly.

When he spoke, his voice sounded hoarse, almost strangled, as if he'd reached some sort of breaking point. "You'd better go to bed, Susannah."

Her gaze found his, locking on intense, searing blue eyes. His chest gave away his desire by rising and falling just a little too quickly. She could see the pulse at his throat, the tip of his tongue when it darted out to touch his lips, as if licking away their dryness.

"You'd really better go to bed, Susannah," he repeated.

Although she knew better, she found herself whispering, almost against her will, "Alone, J.D.?"

12

ALONE?

J.D didn't figure she wanted to make love—not tonight, not ever. But her eyes affirmed her feelings, looking hyperalert, narrowing to shining slits the color of lakes under sunlight. He saw hesitation, then frank sexual arousal, which he shared.

"Dammit," he muttered under his breath. "Can't you see how hard this is for me, Susannah?"

"Hard on you?" she echoed.

"You, too," he conceded. Still, had she confronted the fears about his traveling and other woman he'd known she harbored during their marriage? He exhaled heavily, and planted his palm on the door frame beside her head. Without moving, he could feel the still-damp strands of her hair, and he imagined how sensual they'd feel stroking the sensitive spaces between his fingers. He felt breathless, as if some robber, hell-bent on stealing his heart, had just duct-taped his ribs so it couldn't escape.

He could smell her body, too, fresh and musky from a shower, scented with apple-blossom soap. She'd pulled a half-zippered hoodie over a plain white T-shirt. She was braless—obviously so, since the cotton fabric of the shirt stretched taut between her breasts. The relaxed nipples were visible, tempting him, making him sharply aware of the painful, irre-sistible pang bothering his groin. Like the badgering voice of some annoying harpie, the irritation wasn't going to abate, he knew, not unless he got some of the satisfaction only this woman could give.

Which he wasn't. And that meant there was no use driving himself crazy with lust. When he found his voice, it was less steady than before, throatier and carrying a steely undercurrent of raw frustration that he didn't even bother to try to conceal. Why should he when it was evident in the slight forward thrust of his hips, his elevated respiration, the sharpness of his roving gaze. "C'mon—" He didn't enjoy sounding as if he were begging, but maybe he was. "Just go to bed, Susannah."

She didn't move immediately, and he knew she must be as needy as he. Not that she'd give in to temptation. She was merely toying with him right now by offering him sex. Soon enough she'd spurn him, then ask for a divorce again. And he wasn't about to let her do it. "You're not taking me to the edge, then changing your mind," he said softly.

"You think that's what I'm doing?"

"Oh yeah."

When she inhaled sharply, then held her breath as if suppressing a telltale shudder, he felt completely breathless, himself. Instinctually his gaze dropped in time to see her nipples constrict, the nipples beading against the white cotton, forming delicious pert points. He gritted his teeth, trying to brace himself, but it didn't stop the liquid fire that shot between his legs, making him feel heavy and swollen and as if he was losing his mind.

He was like a gun and she was the target, and he was fully loaded and ready to shoot. Every inch of her was begging for his fingers and tongue. As heat continued pouring into his groin, he reflexively clenched his teeth once more against the unwanted sensations.

Her voice was husky. "Do you really want me to go to bed, J.D.?"

"Yes and no." She might as well be teasing him with a strip number, and she knew it. Just looking at those aroused breasts was almost as bad as seeing her in the wet dress earlier.

Truth be told, in the past eight months, he hadn't so much as looked at another woman. And right now, he wanted sex so bad he could taste it. With her. Each nip and tuck had been visible, the fabric clinging like a second skin. Now, she hadn't even touched him, and he had to fight not to shut his eyes and let them roll back in his head in ecstasy just from the memory. He felt—really felt—the delicious tension between his legs, the fiery pulse of the erection increasingly worrying his zipper.

No doubt she was reading his mind, the way she always had. Not that it was all that hard to read. He was a hundred-percent male, so what he was thinking wasn't very complex. "This would hardly be the first time we've felt a little hot but managed to avoid sex," he finally offered, the words gruff.

She didn't say anything.

"Hell, Susannah," he added, really wishing she'd leave him alone, "Sexual avoidance had become the hallmark of our marriage, anyway." He paused raising his eyes to hers. "And there it is again," he accused. "That spark of challenge in your eyes. You'd make love to me just to prove you'll always have that power over me, wouldn't you?"

Her lower lip trembled, either from pique or passion, he wasn't sure which. "Of course not, J.D. I just had a weak moment," she assured him, turning away.

He couldn't control his movements; his hand found her shoulder. For a second, he was sure he'd draw her closer, saw himself grasping her hand and bringing it between his legs, where he wanted to feel it…had to feel it. "Contain it then," he said huskily, his words a soft warning as she turned to face him again. "Don't start this, Susannah."

"Start what?"

As if she didn't know. "You're being intentionally difficult."

The slight smile that touched her lips was too much like a smirk, and he suddenly wanted to kiss it away. "Is that what I am…difficult?"

And so much more. His gaze dropped to her breasts again, then to the curve of her belly, and he suppressed an urge to mold his hands over her hips. Already he could feel his hands tightening against her flesh, the shock of desire when he pressed her pelvis to his. "I thought you wanted a divorce."

"What's that got to do with you and me having sex?"

Nothing maybe. Everything. Despite his determination to start behaving like the gentleman he'd never been before, he muttered, "Start what, you say?" He eyed her. "Be careful how you ask questions like that, Susannah, because I might decide to answer you, and my answer won't be in words."

"You and your idle threats, J.D.," she drawled slowly, shrugging his hand off her shoulder and turning to leave. "Forgive me if I had a lapse in judgment. That should be understandable, given how long we were married. But don't take it personally. I just haven't been with a man for a while."

"Joe?"

"We never…went all the way."

But they'd done other things. Even if he hadn't seen them kissing while he'd spied at her restaurant, he'd have intuited it from her gaze now. The thought of it made him want to leave his mark, remind her of their past. And it he felt doubly frustrated since he'd been as celibate as a monk.

His hand closed over her upper arm now, and he yanked her closer, his heart pounding uncontrollably when her chest brushed his, electrifying his blood, making it dance, even after she leaned away from the contact. Every fiber of his being awakened.

A malicious glint sparked in her eyes, or maybe he just imagined it. "Anyway, I guess Joe is my business."

"Payback?" he guessed. "For Sandy?"

"It didn't have anything to do with her."

His grip tightened, and the tense, whipcord lash of his lean body hardened against hers. Thighs met thighs and he let her feel how hard he was. He tried to take a deep, steadying breath. Somehow things had gotten turned on their head. His supposed affair wasn't the issue, but hers was. He had to ask again. "You didn't sleep with him?"

"Would it matter?"

"How could you even ask?"

The room seemed utterly still. She was pressed against him. His heart was hammering hard. Suddenly, heat exploded inside him, bursting into flames as surely as his boat. One kiss, he thought, and he'd be just as devastated. He'd blow sky high and to smithereens. Nothing would remain except splinters and dust washed up on some sandy shore. Dammit, he'd be a pile of ash. Susannah would sweep him up as if she were Cinderella.

It was funny. The destroyed boat was the perfect symbol for their marriage, wasn't it? Beautiful and sleek, lovingly crafted and nurtured, and now dashed on the rocks. If the music world didn't think he was dead, maybe he'd write a song about it.

"I didn't sleep with him," she said. "He's seeing someone else. Does that make you happy?"

"I tried to tell myself it did," he admitted slowly, drawing out each vowel. "I kept thinking you deserved better than me, better than what I brought into our lives. And now, with Sandy out there somewhere…?" He shook his head. "Dammit," he muttered, interrupting his own train of thought. "I hope she's the one who blew up the *Alabama*, not someone else…"

Susannah sounded surprised. "Why?"

"Because if it's not her, they'll have to start the investigation over from scratch." God only knew the enemies he'd unknowingly fostered. He sighed, wishing the maddening scent of apple blossoms wasn't knifing from Susannah to his lungs again. The scent was cloying, enveloping him as if in a cloud, reminding him he was trapped with a woman who didn't love him anymore.

"I kept telling myself I didn't care," he continued, picking up his earlier thread, "and now I'm starting to remember what our marriage was really like."

"I'd divorce you," she offered in a deceptively light tone, pressing closer, teasing him with her lower body, tilting her chin as if to better peer into his eyes. "But it's hard to get a dead man to sign legal papers."

"I'm sure you'll find a way," he muttered. "Otherwise you've become quite the heiress."

That was a strike to her honor, and the response was quick and hot. "All I ever wanted was Banner Manor!"

And he'd refused to give it, saying possession was nine-tenths of the law. He'd done so, since once Banner Manor was gone, Susannah would be gone, too. "Just go to bed," he said again, although his own hand was what stayed her.

When he finally released his hold, only her eyes moved, drifting down his bare chest as if she'd hadn't dared to hope she'd see it again. Unbidden, images from his funeral assaulted him—her tears, the silly hunting hat she'd carried, which he'd taken from the house later, and put into his bag as a reminder of her love. He recalled her softening expression when he'd handed her his handkerchief tonight, too, and the loosening of her body when she'd given in and let him carry her through the rain.

"We'll talk tomorrow," he said, his chest feeling impossibly constricted, almost as tight as his jeans.

"About?"

Everything. He shrugged. "Sandy. The boat. Whether it was Joel onboard. All the real reasons we're together. The truth is, if you weren't in danger, we'd never have seen each other again."

"Not so. You came to the house, J.D., long before you saw the contents of Sandy's bag."

He settled on saying, "I care about your well-being, Susannah. I can't have you hurt because of something I've done. I'm going to protect you. Then you can go your own way. I'll go mine."

"Where are you going? Back to the grave?"

As always, she was as impertinent as hell. And usually right. "I'll…fix that, somehow."

She stared into his eyes, her gaze unnervingly inscrutable. "Why? Because you're a changed man. Right, J.D.?"

He'd told her so, hadn't he? And yet how many times had he vowed he was turning over a new leaf only to prove himself wrong? He wanted to say yes, but it would be a lie. "I don't know. Only time will tell."

"Well it looks like we've got plenty of that on our hands."

"And what are you suggesting?" he bit out, his gaze lacerating hers because of the cheapness of what she seemed to be implying. "That we spend our time here in bed? Have a little roll in the hay? A tumble for old time's sake?" He paused a fraction closer, his lips registering her breath. "Do you want me to get mad? To feel I have to prove what I can do to you? That I get you so hot you're begging me?"

"It's what you want, isn't it?"

"No, it's what you want." His hands moved of their own accord, and they rested on her shoulders. Suddenly, he felt twisted into knots, utterly confused. "Hell yes, I want it," he admitted, his voice low, the scalding heat flooding his loins forcing him to tell the truth. "I never stopped wanting it. Never stopped wanting you. Maybe I never will, Susannah. But that's not the point."

"Which is?"

That unless they were getting back together, he didn't want to risk loving her physically. It would only lead to emotional pain later. He settled for answering with a sigh.

"If you really care about my safety," she said calmly, "then why not just hire a real bodyguard?"

She was right. Hell, what had he been thinking? He'd hired a pilot, after all. Besides, a bodyguard wouldn't have to see him or know he was alive. But in Sheriff Kemp's office, J.D. hadn't considered that, had he? He'd been too intent on what might happen when he was alone with Susannah in the cabin. "Tomorrow, I'll do just that."

"Glad that's settled," she said firmly.

He could scarcely breathe. "Good night, Susannah."

"Good night, J.D."

When she turned stiffly on her heel, he felt heartsick. Worse when his gaze settled on her backside. A backlash of lust claimed him as the gaze traveled slowly down her long legs. What was wrong with him? Any normal man would have taken her offer. He tried to shake himself loose of the physical sensations rocking his body, but he couldn't.

She disappeared down the hallway into her room and he dragged a hand through his hair and headed toward the sink, lifting the dirty plates. As he washed them, he got his mind off of her by staring through the kitchen window. Slivers of silver moonlight were making their way through the thick trees now. Otherwise, it was silent. If anyone was out there, he figured he'd sense it.

But he hadn't realized Sandy might be dangerous before. He pushed aside the admonishment, his hawklike eyes scanning Mama Ambrosia's yard. It was tempting to rifle through her herbs, but he was fairly certain there was nothing there to quell his current problem—lust. As soft as it was, the sudsy dish water could have been her hair. The room's darkness, when he shut off the kitchen light, could have been the midnight of her eyes.

Then he heard her bedroom door shut. Thankfully, his hard-on was subsiding. Somewhat. Maybe enough that he could sleep. He'd be damned if he was going to give in and pleasure himself, not when his wife was right down the hall. Sighing, he rechecked the locks on the doors and windows, then headed down the hallway, deciding to leave on that light, in case Susannah had to find the bathroom in the night.

He didn't bother with the light in his own room; the hallway was casting a soft yellow glow over it. He'd chosen the most modest room, decorated only with a twin iron bed, a chest at the foot and a nightstand beside it. If he'd picked the smallest room to punish himself for what he'd done to Susannah, it wasn't going to help. Moonlight was slanting through the window, and although it was muted by pines and oaks, it was decidedly romantic. Exhaling another long sigh, he moved toward the bed.

Just as he reached it, he heard a click, then footsteps. Susannah. She was coming down the hallway. Not knowing what to expect, he turned around. Still dressed, she'd slipped on some rubber flip-flops that Robby had brought her.

Thinking of his ex-best friend, he felt a stab of pain, but he pushed it away. "Do you need something, Susannah?"

"Yeah." She was framed in the doorway, her face in shadows. "Sex," she said simply. "I can't be in the same house with you and not have sex, J.D." When he didn't respond immediately, she added, "I hate myself for it."

This conversation was getting ridiculous, he decided. "Well, I'd hate for you to hate yourself."

"Nice of you."

"If it's any consolation," he said, his gaze drifting over her. "You can't hate yourself as much as I hate myself."

"And why do you hate yourself?"

"For putting you in this mess."

Something vaguely resembling a smile curved her lips in the semi-darkness, lifting his spirits, reminding him of how things used to be between them. The moonlight helped, touching her face like fingers, illuminating the partial smile.

"Since we're in mutual hate, we might as well do it," she said reasonably.

That was just like Susannah. Sex first, talk later. It was the kind of behavior of which she always accused him. They were more alike than she knew, he decided, not that he'd tell her. He considered a long moment. "Misery loves company," he finally said.

"That's exactly what I was thinking."

"Well, since strong emotion is always key in the bedroom, whether it's love or hate may be immaterial at the moment," he conceded. He'd let her take the lead. Hell, this was her big idea, right? And every move he made seemed to turn out wrong. "Should we move to the big bed? Your call."

He could see her throat working as she swallowed hard. It

must have been hard for her to come back and proposition him again, he suddenly realized.

"The little bed's fine," she said.

She must be damn aroused, he thought, if she couldn't allow time to move to a more comfortable locale. Or else she wanted to make sure the bed was his, since that way, she could leave when she liked. "Less time to change your mind?"

"Closer proximity."

"I'm taking no responsibility for this," he warned, crossing his arms over his bare chest. "So the first move is yours."

"And after that?"

"After that—" He shook his head. "I can't vouch for a thing."

His heart stuttered as she crossed the room, and he took in all the nuances—the careful steps, the swing of unconfined breasts, the trembling fingers.

She stopped in front of him. "What are you looking at me like that for?"

His hands settled on her shoulders once more, and he simply pulled her close, his lips brushing her hair. Drowning in the scent, he nuzzled, his voice lowering to a hoarse whisper. "I'm gauging how you want it."

"Want what?"

"You know."

"And how do I want it?"

"Maybe slow or fast," he murmured, pressing his mouth deeper against nearly dry strands of silken hair that teased his lips like the most intense kiss. "Or hard and deep...or gentle and playful."

"It's been awhile. You'll have to remind me."

His hands slipped from her shoulders, pushing off the hoodie, and as she started shrugging out of it, he became aware of his groin once more. It ached, his erection straining with this promise of coming satisfaction. Still, she'd taken him near the brink before and walked away, leaving him hot, angry and frustrated. But this time…

Sucking air through clenched teeth, he dragged the hoodie down her long, bare arms, leaving only the T-shirt. "Teasing," he murmured, inching back a fraction to glance down the length of her body. Lust surged when he realized she probably wasn't wearing any underwear. Soon he'd find out.

Lifting both hands, he pinched the nipples through her shirt, watching in fascination as the already constricted buds performed, growing more taut as he toyed, rolling them between his thumb and finger. As he watched her face—how it filled with rapture—he jutted out his lower lip, then bit down on it hard, his buttocks tightening, his hips tilting.

Lightly he brushed his jeans against her pants, reveling in the puzzle-piece fit of his hardness to where she was so soft, and he bit down on his lip even harder, almost hard enough to draw blood. Again and again, he pulled her nipples, plucking them like flowers. Still pinching, he moved them in slow circles, soliciting a soft whine that stirred his blood.

"Hard and hot," she whispered.

"Not gentle like this?" He was still teasing, sweeping his lower body against hers, letting her feel the heat trapped inside his jeans. Suddenly it was too much. His hands rustled the shirt upward and abruptly covered her bare breasts, kneading as he roughly whispered, "So you want to play some scarves and cards, Susannah?"

"I want to get so hot that I vanish," she whispered back as his mouth claimed hers.

A sunburst exploded, undoing whatever thread was holding him together. He plunged and plundered with his tongue, stroked her cheeks and tasted her teeth. As his hands explored the sides of her breasts, the slopes and cleavage, he knew wanted to remain dead to the world forever. He never wanted to return. Susannah and a cabin was all he wanted. By the time he found her nipples again, his wet tongue kiss had driven her to distraction. She was bucking.

And then her tongue lashed wildly to his like a sail in a storm. It flickered quickly like a guttering flame in wind. He thought of the many times he'd felt that tongue elsewhere...on his neck, his belly, between his legs. Now it pushed deeper between his lips, the passion a wave held back by a breaking dam.

"Abracadabra," he whispered huskily, his mouth trailing her jaw, the column of her throat. Then hungrily, he added, "Take your pants off."

"Why don't you take them off me, J.D.?"

"Gladly." Turning, he grabbed her hand, twining it through his as he half dragged her to the bed. "You said you want the little bed," he growled, his jeans bursting at the seams. "Fine by me. But you'd better get on it."

She didn't argue, only scrambled onto the mattress, settling by the headboard. His mind went blank, and he could only stare. She had an angel's face, and her chest was heaving against the see-through T-shirt, which was still pushed above her breasts.

With a grunt, he undid his belt buckle, then with a gasp, he opened the snap and pulled down the zipper, wincing when it raked skin. Pushing the pants over his hips, he stepped out of them just as she grabbed the hem of her shirt. She pulled it over her head, her ravenously hungry blue eyes shining with desire as they fixed on his aroused body, making him doubly aware of his burning erection.

Nearly dry now, her tawny strands of hair, which he'd mussed, cascaded over her bare, glowing shoulders, looking as golden as the pants she wore in the low light. Blindly he moved toward the bed. When he reached her, he threaded a hand into the gorgeous blond strands, dragging her upward to take his mouth. She tilted her head to give him access, her back arching with uncanny suppleness, bending over his arm, and this time, when his lips closed over hers, she seemed to know the kiss wouldn't end.

With his tongue, he built the fire raging inside, his practiced hands grabbing the drawstring of her pants, then urging the fabric over her long legs as smooth as glass. Just as masterfully, her hands nestled between his legs, and when her fingers circled him, his mind blanked once more. Blackness overtook him, leaving him with just a cloud of sensation.

But he kept driving his tongue between her lips, thrusting, although his thoughts were breaking apart. He didn't give a damn that they were divorcing. Didn't care if he never saw her again. All he cared about was right now. This second. His whole energy was focused on the moment.

It was sheer bliss. She was stroking him slowly. Fingers curled in his pubic hair, then fondled the shaft. Fisting, she squeezed until perspiration coated his skin. His wife had lost her girlish fears of appearing too brazen years ago, and she could pleasure a man as boldly as he'd pleasure himself. Now, confidently, she was pushing him to the edge, and his head snapped, veering backward.

His lips found her mouth, slamming down greedily. He was gasping between kisses. Suddenly, his hand stayed hers. But he was powerless, and his palm merely slid over the back of her hand, guiding her movements.

"Stop," he whispered.

She did, knowing he could take no more. A second later, he was on top of her. There were no condoms, but it wouldn't matter. They'd had no other lovers, and they'd never been able to get pregnant, not even after seeing a doctor. That had bothered him more than Susannah ever knew. Surely, if she loved him more, she'd have their baby, he'd thought when they were trying, however illogically.

Now he counted his blessings. She hated him. She craved his body but she hated him. And he didn't blame her. No, he didn't....

But he craved her. He ran a splayed hand from her breasts to her ribs. Releasing a shuddering sigh, he pressed his mouth to her belly. Every inch was so damn silken. Like air or water. As soft as soap. His fingers twined into her damp, springy lower curls. His middle finger, curled and dipped, and what he felt next undid his last shred of resistance.

She was wet...so impossibly wet. The kind of wet that meant she was on the edge. One touch and she might come. And so, abruptly, he thrust harder, breaking the kiss so he could watch her neck tilt in pleasure, her eyes roll back. She arched and squirmed, and he leaned closer, panting on the wet kisses he'd trailed on her skin.

His gaze roved over her. Her lips, drenched from kisses a second before, turned dry, and she licked them senselessly. And licked. And licked...

"Maybe I won't let you come," he teased.

"Damn you, J.D.," she whispered, her breath uneven, her eyes glazed and dreamy, the expression naked.

Curving his finger, he lifted moisture and drizzled it around her clitoris. She was still uttering soft little cries as he moved on top of her again. Looking down into her face, she drove both hands into his chest hair. Grabbing fistfuls of dark curls that glistened with perspiration, she raked nails down his bare flesh.

"You know what that does to me," he whispered.

"Not as much as this," she whispered back, her legs parting.

"Or this," he agreed, penetrating her with ease. Her hands flew upward, and he shuddered as her fingers clutched his shoulders. She was tensing, bracing herself. But he rested. Waited. Let her feel every inch.

Glorious relief claimed him at being enveloped in his wife's encapsulating heat. Maybe she wouldn't be that tomorrow. Or next year. Or whenever she got her way and divorced him. But tonight she was still his wife. Legally. And he would remind her of it.

On her chest, he laid the heel of a palm, settling it between her breasts. Having realized the Saint Christopher's medal wasn't his, she'd removed it, and that touched his heart. She might not love him the way she once had, but she'd meant to wear a reminder of him forever. Now he examined the other necklace she wore. Engraved on it were the words, *Remember the time*.

"That's what I want you to do right now, Susannah," he murmured.

She sounded far away as if the connection of their bodies was taking her to some faraway place. "What?"

"Remember the times," he whispered.

She stared into his eyes in the moonlight. "Which times?"

There were so many. "All of them."

"Help me remember," she whispered.

And so he thrust hard, pushing deeper, opening her completely, making her gasp, pushing her upward on the mattress until her head collided with pillows.

Sheathed inside, buried deep, he lay skin to skin, motionless. And then slowly, torturously, he rolled his hips, grinding, prompting endless whimpers until she convulsed. As he felt fluttering palpitations, his eyes remained fixed on her face, the softening of her jaw, the parting of her lips for another kiss.

He could have let go then. Everything had vanished. Outside, the night was nearly gone. It, too, had peaked, and was sliding towards dawn. Shots of gray were mixing with yellow moonlight. He should have been tired, but he wasn't, only hopelessly aroused. Sandy and Joel were far away, as was the mystery surrounding the *Alabama*. Hell, he was no cop, he thought vaguely. Let the law figure out what had happened. J. D. Johnson had other troubles at the moment…woman troubles.

When Susannah's eyelids batted open, his stomach did a somersault, tumbling into oblivion. And when her gaze found his, she looked as if she couldn't decide what to say. He was still throbbing inside her, hard and burning. He was about to explode, his body blistering and slick with sweat.

"You always did have more control than me, J.D.," she finally whispered.

He couldn't help but smile, just a wry grin that upturned the edges of his lips. Even more amazing, she smiled back. It was dazzling, he decided. From day one, it had stopped him in his tracks, hadn't it? Her white teeth gleamed in the near dark, and the smile turned a little saucy.

Somehow, he found his voice, such as it was. "It's not a contest, Susannah."

"No?"

"Maybe," he conceded, still smiling. He leaned to whisper the next words into her ear, his slow drawl drizzling. "But since I just won the first round, maybe you'll stand a better chance in the future, wife of mine."

"We're getting divorced," she reminded him throatily, but at the moment, her heart wasn't in the fight.

"Not tonight, though. And since we're still married, you have some conjugal duties to fulfill."

Lifting a finger, she pressed it to his lips and murmured, "Then let's not waste time talking, J.D."

"You always were a wise woman," he agreed. It was why he'd married her. Leaning a fraction closer, he nipped her earlobe. Releasing a sudden shudder, he thrust again. "Hard and fast this time," he whispered simply. "Tonight you're mine."

Tomorrow was another day.

13

"OH, SUSANNAH, now don't you cry for me," J.D. sang. Bare-chested, since she was using his plaid shirt for warmth, he was wearing yesterday's jeans and a tawny Stetson hat. He was propped on one elbow in the grass and settled his free hand on her belly.

"I'm not crying, J.D.," she drawled, as he glided a hand beneath the hem of her T-shirt, stroking her ribs as if they were strings of his guitar. At times, since last night, she'd thought she might cry, of course. Now, hearing him sing rekindled her passion. They'd slept most of the day, and when she'd opened her eyes to the afternoon sun and realized his kisses were tickling her awake, she'd felt at peace.

It couldn't last, it never did, but sometime after sunup, they'd switched to the bigger bed, and she'd sprawled in it luxuriously, yawning and stretching. The eight and a half months since she'd left J.D. seemed like a silly dream, as did all the characters who'd peopled their lives temporarily, such as Sandy and Maureen and Joel.

But they weren't mere figments, Susannah reminded herself, fear edging into her consciousness. Joel was probably dead, and even if Sandy wasn't responsible for the explosion aboard the *Alabama*, she'd maliciously destroyed pictures of Susannah, written about how much she hated her and possibly fired the shots in New York. How could such a gorgeous woman have gotten so scrambled? Men were still dredging the river, looking for evidence near the explosion she might have caused.

"Given the magnitude of the blast, it'll take time," Sheriff Kemp had said the previous night. "Now that we know the boat's destruction wasn't accidental, Bayou Blair's offering more manpower."

Not that Susannah blamed Sheriff Kemp. He was a small-town sheriff, unused to crimes of this caliber and dangerously understaffed. "It's not your fault," Susannah had assured him. "Before this, J.D.'s antics were the worst thing you've had to deal with."

Shaking off the memories, Susannah surveyed J.D., smiling at his bad-boy grin. As usual, the man was congratulating himself on how well he'd satisfied her in bed. Not that he didn't deserve to preen. About an hour earlier, they'd finished making love again, this time in the grass under a romantic, lacy canopy of leaves, before they'd dressed again.

"What if somebody's watching," she'd protested as they'd first taken off their clothes.

He'd looked enticing in the buff, sunlight shimmering on a pelt of sleek black chest hair, his skin glowing. "We're safe," he'd assured.

Probably that had been his hormones talking. She glanced around. "I don't feel watched, the way I have sometimes over the past few weeks," she admitted. "But Sandy could show up, don't you think? I mean, if she's responsible for everything that's happened, she's capable of anything. And she *was* in our house."

"Yes, she was," J.D. agreed soberly.

"She could have seen…" Susannah's voice trailed off.

"Something to connect you to Mama Ambrosia. Or overheard you making an appointment to get your cards read."

"Impossible," he assured her. "I would just show up."

She smirked, feeling relieved. "Very like you."

"I'll make appointments in the future," he promised contritely. "Months in advance. First thing in the morning, too, preferably before 7:00 a.m."

"Unlikely."

"Anyway," he added. "Mama Ambrosia's on vacation."

"I wonder where she went." From what little Susannah knew about Mama, it was hard to guess.

"Vegas," he supplied. "She said she was going to drive herself to the airport in Bayou Blair, then fly to a fortune teller's convention. At least that's what she told me. I kid you not."

"A fortune-teller's convention?" Susannah chuckled, the cloud passing. She thought of the bedding strewn in the hallway. "We'd better clean her cabin before she gets back."

"She's not due for a week. And I'm not making the bed yet. What's the point when you're going to mess it up again?"

"Me?"

"I'll help," he promised. "Just to be nice."

"Same old J.D.," she complained, now considering his housekeeping habits. Yet she believed he'd changed. He hadn't touched one drop of whisky, although Mama had plenty.

"Oh, Susannah," he sang again. "Don't you cry for me."

She offered a lopsided grin. "Oh, boo-hoo."

"You might not be crying now," he warned, his gaze searing and lazy as he tapped her nose with the blade of grass, then leaned to kiss her. "But you were last night. And a minute ago."

"After a fashion," she conceded as he delivered a slow, languid kiss, then stood, grabbed her hand and hauled her to her feet, pausing so she could slip into her flip-flops. Just as she shoved her feet into them, she gasped. "You!"

He chuckled.

He'd changed the position of her shoes, the way he always did, and they'd wound up on the wrong feet. "You're juvenile. You know that, J. D. Johnson?" she accused, lifting his shirt from the ground and handing it to him. "Put that on," she added when he merely slung the shirt over his shoulder.

"C'mon," he said. "I haven't got all the sex out of my system yet. But next time, I want to do it in a bed again. Then for supper, I'll make you some pan-fried spiced chili that will really make you weep."

"Hmm. I see you have my whole life planned out."

"Only the good parts."

"You're definitely the same old Jeremiah Dashiell. And it's just like you to lace everything with cayenne."

"I'm a hot guy," he returned, playfully swatting her behind as they walked through the woods, toward the cabin, their bodies moving together perfectly.

"Hmm. Or you have to doctor the taste of your cooking."

"I'm the best cook in Mississippi and you know it." He shot her a saucy grin. "As for doctoring, my lovin' is the best medicine, sweetheart."

"Then why are you not cured yet?" She squinted at him. "Are you sure you didn't use one of Mama's herbs on me last night?"

"I put some love potion in that steak," he admitted. "But don't you call me that."

"What?" she asked innocently as the cabin appeared, winking through the trees. "Jeremiah Dashiell?"

Resettling the Stetson on his head, he shot her a lopsided grin. "Just don't tell anybody."

"And if I do?"

He winked. "I've got special ways of punishing you."

Truth be told, she secretly liked the name, so the words were out before she'd thought them through. "If we'd had a baby, J.D., that's what I would have named it."

Too late, she saw his eyes widen. She could swear she saw a flicker of hope there, but he didn't miss a beat. "Well then, it's a good thing that baby we didn't have wasn't a girl."

She couldn't help but chuckle. "A girl named Jeremiah Dashiell?"

"Well, Johnny Cash did okay with a boy named Sue," he offered with a smile, referring to the title of a famous Johnny Cash song.

Her chest tightened, her heart breaking at the reminder of her husband's music career. He'd always had music on the brain, and she'd wanted children just as desperately. Who knew where things were heading now? In the past twenty-four hours neither of them had said much about their marriage.

This is just about sex, she tried to remind herself. They were never going to share their lives again. In fact, she'd been a fool to succumb to his charms last night and this morning. And yet, she'd come onto him, hadn't she? Could she really let him go?

J.D. tilted his head. "Is that my phone?"

She didn't hear anything.

He patted the pocket of the shirt draped over his shoulder. "I was sure I brought it." Flashing another heart-stopping smile as he speeded his steps, he said, "You distracted me."

"Guilty as charged," she returned.

As they raced for the phone, she thought he looked gorgeous, as carefree as in the past, the wind riffling his thick, dark hair, the sun glistening in the strands, his toned muscles rippling. They entered the cabin, and just as he reached the cell, which was on the bedside table in the smaller bedroom, the ringing stopped. Immediately, another shrill ring sounded from the front room.

"Mama's phone?"

It rang only once. As they reached the answering machine in the front room, it clicked on. Sheriff Kemp's voice was urgent. "I just tried the cell. Pick up if you're there."

Susannah sprang forward, but J.D. reached the phone first and snatched the receiver. "We're here."

Sheriff Kemp was talking loudly, but Susannah leaned closer to hear him anyway, almost just to be nearer to J.D. "You should probably get out of there," the sheriff said. "I'm on my way with Robby and some men from Bayou Blair. I'm calling from my car."

J.D.'s eyebrows raised in alarm. "What's wrong?"

"Early this morning, we used Robby's key to get into Banner Manor. You're right. The pistol that's supposed to be in your closet is gone." Sheriff Kemp continued, "But it gets worse."

"Worse?"

"Your truck's still at the garage, so we went over it, and the fuel line was cut, just as you suspected. Turns out this woman's military trained, J.D. We just found out. She did a tour during the Gulf War, so she knows how to shoot and plenty about explosives.

"Her folks were glad to hear somebody found her. They've been searching for months. Said they felt let down by the army's response to their troubles. They tapped their own resources to hire a private detective to find their daughter."

"Unbelievable," J.D. whispered, then wolf whistled.

Susannah merely shook her head, shocked.

"Her folks told me Sandy just wasn't right after she got back in country," the sheriff continued. "Whatever she saw overseas scrambled her head, and she wound up hospitalized. Doctors said it was post-traumatic stress, but her folks said she'd been better lately. Then suddenly she took off, leaving a note saying she had found a new mission. She was in love and hitchhiking South to see her new boyfriend." The sheriff paused, then added, "I guess she meant you, J.D."

"Oh, no," Susannah whispered as her mind registered the tragedy. All at once, she remembered a different Sandy. Not the extremely pretty, model-thin groupie, but the wan woman with haunted eyes. Sandy had seemed tough, too, well-muscled for being so thin, but Susannah had assumed she'd worked out, not gone to boot camp. Maybe that also explained the fatigue print clothes she wore with combat boots. For many in the music scene, such styles were seen to be trendy, but for Sandy, it was apparently more....

"Whoa," J.D. was saying. "Sandy must have made a point to meet somebody close to me, in the studio or the band..."

"Joel," Susannah supplied.

"Well, everybody says she's a beauty," Sheriff Kemp put in. "A real knockout."

Still could a complete stranger walk into the home of a famous man without anyone protesting? It was a testament to how uncontrolled their lives had become. Susannah considered what she knew about her own husband's hormones, and she supposed it was possible. Sandy was truly beautiful, and J.D. had said Joel was lonely, without family. If a girl as hot as Sandy had shown interest, Joel might not have asked questions. Because he had played music for so long, people naturally accepted his girlfriend.

Susannah sighed. She and Ellie had been confused about whether Joel and Sandy had even been a couple because the relationship had seemed one-sided. Now it made sense. Sandy had seemed distant, but Joel followed her around like a puppy dog. All the while, Sandy had only wanted to get close to J.D.

Gasping, Susannah instinctively reached for J.D. as if to steady herself. His arm slipped around her waist, feeling comfortable and familiar, making her pulse accelerate. "Maybe Joel found Sandy in bed with you, too," she whispered. She thought of her niece, Laurie. "That could be why he came close to having sex with Laurie—he wanted revenge." *Just like J.D. accused me of doing with Joe.* And wasn't there some truth in it? Wasn't that why she'd run to New York? To get back at J.D. for making such a mess of their lives? Foolishly her own mind had been so fixated on J.D. that she'd hardly noticed all the tiny details.

Now they were adding up.

The sheriff was saying, "Sandy was trained in field work, and knew how to ingratiate herself. Her ex-commander said she was being groomed to spy. She's apparently very smart. He'd hoped she'd wind up working overseas in an embassy capacity."

He paused, adding as if in afterthought, "Ellie's still at Joe O'Grady's. She's fine. She told Robby she didn't want to see him and for him to stay put. So he's in the car behind me. We're almost to Mama Ambrosia's. Some guys are going to fan out over the property and check it out.

"Oh. And the body onboard *was* Joel's," he finished. "I was going to tell you when we got there. But we found…" the sheriff's voice trailed off "…more remains. Dental fragments. Since J.D. identified the Saint Christopher's medal, and we have Joel's name now, we were able to make a match."

J.D. squinted. "The case seems to be clearer now, so why are you headed out here?"

Sheriff Kemp's voice was grave. "Because Sandy Smithers landed in Bayou Blair about an hour ago. It might be best for you two to drive into town, stay in my office. There are a couple men there from Bayou Blair. Delia called me from the diner to say hello. She didn't know about the case, but she said a stranger, some woman, just had coffee there. Delia said she was asking about the whereabouts of Mama Ambrosia's."

"Oh, no," Susannah whispered.

"The woman matched Sandy's description," Sheriff Kemp said.

Susannah leaned closer to the phone. "When did she leave Delia's?"

"About ten minutes ago," said the sheriff. "Delia didn't know what was going on, so she gave her directions. Still, you know how hard it is to find Mama's. Even locals get lost."

Small comfort. Sandy had arrived at about the time Susannah and J.D. had been making love. What had they been thinking? Chalk it up to how hot they could still get for each other.

"Didn't anybody check for *credentials*?" Susannah exploded after J.D. hung up. "Didn't somebody know this woman? Didn't you ask, J.D.?"

He was thrusting their few things into his duffel, his expression wan, as if to say he knew his antics had gone too far. He slipped on the Western-style shirt he'd been carrying, re-situated the Stetson on his head, then looked at her, the brim of the hat casting a shadow over his eyes. Raw terror then anger, then steely determination flashed in his gaze. As he slung his bag over his shoulder, he turned to face her, looking positively sick. He shook his head. "I thought Maureen checked everybody out. It was her job."

"But you didn't know!" she burst out. And Banner Manor had become a party haven. A free-for-all. A place where dangerous people could walk in the door. "You're famous, J.D.! You have to protect yourself!" she exclaimed, even as the tragedy of Sandy's situation was sinking in. The woman had fought for the country, only to be harmed herself, maybe for life.

Understanding pierced Susannah's awareness. Maybe that's why Sandy had been so attracted to J.D.! His public career had drawn him into a similar arena where everyone around him had their own agenda. By saving him from users, as she believed Susannah to be, she would be saving herself.

"I thought Maureen—"

"You're so trusting!" Susannah interjected, not letting him finish. "Deep down, you're a decent guy, so you think everyone else is the same. But Maureen only cared about one thing," she said with disgust. "And that's the record company's bottom line. She didn't care about you, J.D. None of them did." Except for Sandy, in her own warped way.

"Oh, Susannah," J.D. muttered, stepping closer. "I'd do anything to change this."

For him, seeing the contents of Sandy's bag had been a wake-up call. For once, J.D. didn't want to be involved in the world he'd created any more than she did. "I know," she managed, but she was shaking with anger.

After all, hindsight didn't change a thing. Life threw curve balls that shifted the game. For J.D., the curves had been re-latively easy—fame and fortune. Poor Sandy had been dealt the card of a war she hadn't started, and it had scrambled her mind as surely as Mama Ambrosia shuffled a deck to tell her client's fortunes. Now a man who'd cared for her was dead. No…Sandy's fate sure hadn't been the best. But then, neither had been Joel's.

Despite the tragedy, operating as a civilian, Sandy had induced fear, destroyed property and most assuredly a human life. Forgiveness was a strange task, Susannah thought. Given her circumstances, had Sandy had clear choices? Had J.D.? Where did responsibility begin and end?

Susannah was no longer sure. As if sensing some deep hesitation inside her, J.D. drew her close. He felt hard and hot, every muscle vibrating. Wrapping his arms tightly around her, he offered a bear hug, and she melted, tilting up her head just as he angled his down. His lips brushed hers in a searing promise.

For a brief moment, she shut her eyes, wishing they were back in the forest again, where they'd been moments before. With a rush of desperation, she wanted to feel the prickly hairs of his rock-hard thighs as she straddled him, the rush of heat as she took him inside her, the greed of his mouth as he devoured her with a kiss. Even now, she could feel him responding, his lower body bending to hers, warming and hardening.

"I love you, Susannah," he whispered against her lips. "More than my own life. You know that. Now, c'mon. I grabbed our essentials. Let's get to town. We'll be better protected at the sheriff's office."

Nodding, she turned, jogged down the hallway, then glanced over her shoulder. "Do we have the keys?"

"Kitchen," he returned simply. "I'll get them, but we'd better leave the door unlocked for the sheriff."

She headed for the front room, the afternoon looking placid through the windows. Silence bathed the yard, and warm sunlight splashed through leaves, creating circular patches of yellow where sunbeams hit the clearings.

She was halfway across the porch when the bang came.

Ducking, she whirled and ran, barreling headfirst into J.D.'s midsection. He doubled over, turning sideways. "Get down!" he commanded.

"I tried to save you," a woman screamed as Susannah

dropped and scrambled on her hands and knees across Mama's front room, crouching behind a sofa.

"I tried to help you, but you killed Joel instead. You put him on the boat. You knew! Just before my bomb went off, I saw him! I saw what you did to Joel, J.D.!"

Sandy. Ice flooded Susannah's veins, and her heart hammered. The woman's head was scrambled, all right.

"That's a lie, Sandy," J.D. shouted, making another wave of terror rip through Susannah as he walked farther out on the porch, the tails of his unbuttoned shirt lifting with a sudden slight breeze. "You've got it all wrong."

There was nothing to shield him from a scorned woman wielding a gun. Desperately Susannah wanted to yell at him, to tell him to get down, but the less Sandy was reminded of her presence, the better.

"I didn't want Joel to get hurt," J.D. called out soothingly, in the same tone that had made so many women swoon. "I swear I'm telling the truth."

The woman's voice wavered, filling Susannah with relief. "You are?"

Susannah peeked over the back of the sofa. Far off, through a window, she saw a shadowy figure emerging from between the trees. It was Sandy, aiming a gun—probably his very own pistol—at J.D. "I know you love me, J.D.," she said, her voice strained with pain.

"You're right, I do," J.D. agreed, making Susannah's heart ache. The woman was coming forward now and lowering the gun. She seemed to be lulled by the soft sincerity in J.D.'s voice. That, and how good he looked in worn jeans, a half-open shirt and a cowboy hat.

No doubt though, his songs were what started Sandy's obsession with him. They could work like a force of nature. Now

J.D. raised his voice calling, "But I don't love you the way you most want, Sandy, the way you most need."

The gun came back up.

"You've got to listen to me, Sandy," he coaxed, remaining calm, his hand steady when he tipped the brim of his hat. "You've got to trust me."

She came almost to the porch, lowering the gun once more.

"We'll have a long talk," he promised, his voice seemingly floating, softly rolling like dust in the air. "Just you and me. 'Cause you're right about a lot of things. There are users out there, and if it wasn't for you, I might not have understood that as well as I do now."

Definitely there was truth in that.

"Now, c'mon, honey," he continued. "Why don't you put down the gun? Enough people have gotten hurt. We don't want to hurt anybody else, do we?"

Slowly the woman shook her head. She was close enough that Susannah could see her better. In faded jeans and without makeup, she looked younger and more vulnerable than Susannah remembered. With relief, she watched her bend, as if to place the revolver on the ground.

Suddenly a siren whooped. Then it fell silent.

"Oh, no," Susannah whispered. Unlike J.D.'s silken voice, the sound of the police car served no real purpose, save to alert Sandy. Susannah watched in horror as the other woman's head jerked toward the cars rolling through the trees. There were three—the sheriff's and Robby's, followed by another from Bayou Blair.

Sandy had mobilized and clutched the weapon now. "You lied to me! You called them!" she shrieked, charging J.D., shooting wildly. Windows shattered. Near Susannah, glass jars of herbs cracked. Liquids splashed to the floor.

J.D. dove through the doorway as Sandy's footsteps pounded after him. Susannah would never be able to piece together what happened next—it happened too fast. J.D. leaped, and she heard the others get out of their cars. Susannah saw a flash of fire as Sandy burst into the cabin, but J.D. leaped over the sofa and flung his body over Susannah's, dislodging his hat, which rolled away.

His voice was thunderous. "Don't hurt my wife."

Maybe Sandy understood the truth then, because she stopped and stared at J.D., who was using his body to shield Susannah. Suddenly she dropped the gun. "You'll never quit loving her," she whispered, sounding lost as men burst through the door. Vaguely, in the periphery of her vision, Susannah registered that Robby and Sheriff Kemp were among them.

"Are you all right, Susannah?" Robby shouted.

Men surrounded Sandy and began subduing her, reading her Miranda rights.

"I'm fine," Susannah managed.

J.D. was hauling her to her feet. "Are you sure?"

She nodded, feeling the strength in his hands as they roved over her, checking each inch. "I'm really fine," she repeated, but she knew she was in shock. She cast a glance toward Sandy who looked just as dazed, as if she wasn't quite sure how she'd gotten to the cabin.

Still, Susannah understood the situation perfectly. She'd almost died. J.D. could have been killed, too. The last few minutes had been surreal. And the last straw. She'd been a fool to think she could make their marriage work.

J.D. was swallowing hard. "I can't believe this."

"Me, neither," she said, shaking all over, her heart pounding violently as the police led Sandy outside. Susannah stared at J.D. She knew him inside and out. She loved him, too. There was no denying it. And maybe he'd even changed.

But she had to stay the course.

Her parents would be heartbroken to see her involved in something such as the scene surrounding her. "Eight months ago," she started, her voice dropping to a near whisper, "when I left…" She paused, her heart lodging in her throat, aching. "I wasn't sure, J.D. But now…"

"Oh, God," he whispered, sensing what was coming. "No, Susannah."

"Yes," she returned simply. "Passion only goes so far, J.D. I love you, but I can't live with you."

He shut his eyes. She watched his chest rise and fall as he breathed deeply, trying to steady himself. When he opened his eyes, they looked startlingly blue, impossibly clear, as if he'd just seen the light. He nodded. "I understand."

She could swear she saw moisture in his eyes, and it almost made her change her mind. In all the years that she'd known him, she'd never seen J.D. cry. "I'm sorry," she said hoarsely.

"Me, too," he returned, sounding shaken.

The end was that simple. Not how she'd imagined it at all. No fireworks now. No fanfare. Somehow she turned away. When she and Ellie had decided to leave Bayou Banner, she'd been at this exact same crossroad. But she hadn't been ready. Now she was. She'd started her own life. She had the restaurant.

Don't turn back, she thought as she walked across the threshold of the cabin's front door. If nearly being killed wasn't the last straw, what would be? How much worse could things get? As sorry as she felt for Sandy's troubles, Susannah had to learn how to be less forgiving. She had to think about herself. Surely, June and Ellie would help her. Yes, they'd tell her she was doing the right thing.…

She headed off the porch, into the warm sunlight. To her left, another car door slammed, and Susannah's lips parted in surprise as Mama Ambrosia emerged from an SUV. Clad in a long patchwork dress, with a strange turbanlike hat on her head, she grunted as she lumbered toward Susannah.

"Lord," she muttered angrily. "A premonition brought me home. I should have known better than to even pack! Mind you, missy, it's not every day that I get to commune with my fellow fortune-tellers, either. And you ruined it. Everybody at the conference saw this coming—in their crystal balls, cards, dice, you name it. Every single attendee said, 'Mama, you'd better get home.'"

She glared at Susannah. "Why couldn't you two kiss and make up, the way I said," she demanded, "instead of destroying my cute little house? Do you know how hard it is to build contacts so I can get some of those herbs? That's why I had to go to my conference!"

Susannah was fighting the urge to turn around and look for J.D., but he wouldn't follow her, not this time. Her throat ached. "Sorry," she murmured numbly. Then she couldn't help but ask, "What about the gold key? You said there was one in my future."

"Oh, you'll see it eventually. And if you keep asking me about it, I might point out that I didn't charge you for your last reading."

"But…what do you see in the future now?"

"Don't worry," Mama huffed. "You'll do all right without him. That restaurant of yours will wind up as a franchise. But believe me, if I could interfere with that fortunate fate, I would, due to all the trouble you've caused me, ruining my vacation and such."

"Sorry," Susannah said again.

"Oh, please! I forgive you," huffed Mama. "Just not happily. Now git!"

Not knowing what else to say, Susannah walked toward Robby's car to wait for a ride back to town. As she got inside, she better understood how J.D. felt. Without love, victories were hollow. Right now, J.D.'s bronze trophy was just sitting on a counter, next to canisters of herbs. Without love, prizes meant little in the end. Even if Oh Susannah's did become a franchise, she wasn't sure she'd care. Not the way she would have in the past.

She scarcely felt the burning heat of the vinyl on her legs when she sat. Now J.D. would sign the divorce papers without a fight, and if he bothered to announce he was still alive, the world would take him back, at least the part of him that belonged to the world. The part that belonged to Susannah…well, who knew what would happen to that.

Her gaze shifted to Mama's cabin. Everyone was inside, except for a couple men and Sandy. They were circling the side yard, presumably heading to another car. They were only a blur, though, and otherwise, Susannah could see nothing at all as her eyes filled with tears.

14

"SUSANNAH! Get in here!"

Susannah swiped her hands down the thighs of her jeans, and used the back of a wrist to push aside locks of hair that had come loose from her topknot. She kept bustling around the kitchen. "What, Ellie?"

"Hurry up!"

As if she didn't have anything better to do than watch TV at the bar with Ellie, Joe and Tara. "Some of us have to work for a living," she called, unable to believe anything might be more important than clearing the remaining lunch dishes so the wait staff could set up for dinner.

She was desperate to keep busy. No matter what she did, though, she still had J.D. on the brain. She'd done the right thing by leaving him, of course, and she wasn't about to change her mind. But all week, there had been stories in the newspapers claiming he was alive. Apparently the pilot he'd hired to take him to New York, the same one who'd flown them both back to Bayou Banner, had sold the story to a national tabloid. And when the cabbie who'd taken J.D. to her apartment had seen the story, he'd come forward, as well.

"I knew it was him the second I saw him," the man had vowed.

J.D. hadn't surfaced, though. No, J.D. wouldn't, Susannah

fumed now. For days, the press had been interviewing his fans, wanting their thoughts on J.D.'s "resurrection." Many had shown up at Banner Manor, holding vigil, at least according to Delia who'd called to gossip and thank Susannah for all the business she was getting. "This place has nothing on the foot traffic Jim Morrison gets on his grave," she'd vowed. And since her new boyfriend, Sheriff Kemp, had shared privileged information, she'd added, "I just hope J.D. stays dead long enough for me to buy that new fryer I've been wanting. I'm making a mint. So's Jack Hodges over at the motor lodge."

"Consider it all payment for the strawberry-rhubarb pie recipe," Susannah had joked.

But it wasn't funny. So many fans loved J.D.'s music. And now the story about Sandy had broken, too. Apparently some journalist had gotten one of the officers from Bayou Blair to talk. On the upside, what had happened to Sandy had called national attention to the plight of many returning war veterans, and the issue of post-traumatic stress, and so Sandy was finally getting the help she needed.

Still, everyone was convinced J.D. was alive, and that he'd gone into hiding because someone was trying to kill him. Or her, since Susannah had been a target. Which meant the media was portraying J.D. as a model husband—totally self-sacrificing and willing to do anything to save his wife's life. It was enough to make Susannah blow a gasket. "A model husband," she huffed out loud, thinking about how close she'd come to being killed.

"Susannah!"

Heaving a sigh, she shoved a dish towel into the pocket of the chef's apron she wore over a white blouse and jeans. Then she scurried out to see the commotion. Joe and Tara were stuck to each other like glue, of course. The only thing unusual was that they weren't kissing. Shoot, they had started a relationship that promised to be almost as sizzling as Susannah and J.D.'s.

Sometimes Susannah would catch her best friend's gaze flickering over the new couple with envy, at least when Ellie wasn't working herself to death to keep her mind off Robby. "Why didn't you let Robby come that night you went to Joe's, Ellie?" Susannah had asked.

"I never want to see him again," Ellie vowed, but it was a lie. Ellie had loved Robby Robriquet, just as Susannah had loved J.D. So at least once a day, the two women would sit down together and share a cry.

"Remember the time we decided to leave J.D. and Robby?" Ellie had asked rhetorically. Susannah nodded, and Ellie continued, saying, "It was the smartest thing we could have done, wasn't it? I mean, what's happened since just proves it, right?"

"Absolutely," Susannah had agreed, wondering how things were going to work out once she started splitting her own time between the restaurant and Banner Manor, which she missed with all her heart.

Sighing, Susannah now followed Ellie's gaze to the TV— and gasped. "J.D." She felt a rush of temper she didn't want to examine. Her eyes dropped over the image of him critically, from the black curls glistening under a tawny Stetson, to the pearl-buttoned Western-style shirt and worn jeans. She'd gotten him the hand-tooled leather belt with a turquoise buckle for Christmas two years before.

"He's at Rockefeller Center," Ellie explained in a whisper. "At NBC."

Just fifty blocks away. Susannah gaped at the screen, warring emotions vying for control. "What's he up to now?" she muttered, watching a brunette in a pinstriped suit lean forward intently to interview him—she was closer than necessary, Susannah thought. "Who's that?"

"Lindy Montgomery," Ellie supplied in a hushed voice. "You know. She does the midday show."

"No clue," Susannah huffed. She didn't watch much TV, and lately, she'd been too preoccupied to care.

"I've been in touch with Sandy Smithers's family," J.D. was saying. "She's getting the help she needs now, and she's in all our prayers."

"And you knew Joel Murray?"

"Yes. I'm grieved by his passing, as are many people in the music industry."

It wasn't strictly true, but still, Susannah thought it was sweet of J.D. to say so.

The interviewer continued. "And this is why you kept out of the public eye?"

J.D. hesitated. "Partly."

"And to protect your wife?"

He looked toward the camera. For a long moment, he stared into the eye of the lens, as if wondering whether Susannah were watching. "Yes." That marvelous voice of his, so rich with texture and the promise of sexuality, wavered however slightly. "I could never risk having anything happen to her."

"But you're not together? Sources say you're divorcing?"

"That's right, Lindy." He turned his attention to the interviewer. "We've been estranged for quite some time."

"What happened?"

He offered the trademark cryptic J. D. Johnson smile, his glance rueful. "She loves me, but she can't live with me."

"And has your fame caused that?"

"Partly," he said again. "So you can see why the heart's

gone from my music. That's why I wanted to come on your show today. I'm changing my path."

"How so?"

"I just need to take time off, and think about how fame and fortune can change a man's life, but not always for the better."

"But you just had a big award win. You remain one of the favorites on the country music circuit and on the charts. Do you want to tell us about your next CD?"

"There's not going to be one."

Susannah's jaw slackened. Her hands flew to her hips and she glared at the screen. "What!"

"There comes a time," J.D. drawled, "when a man knows it's time for him to go. I love singing, but I don't much like the road."

The interviewer looked shocked. "But your fans?"

"I lost my biggest fan," he said. "My wife."

He was blaming her again! Susannah's hands left her hips, and she crossed her arms over her chest. Her head shook swiftly as she stared from Ellie to Joe to Tara. "Can you believe him? It's bad enough he has to break my heart," she muttered. "But now he has to break the hearts of fans."

She realized Ellie was studying her. "Well, you'd better go set him straight, Susannah."

"Somebody should! I mean, if he wants a divorce, that's fine, but he can't blame me for his career choices. That's just not fair," she said.

And a second later, she was charging through the front door of Oh Susannah's.

J.D. STEPPED TO THE SIDEWALK, unsure what he was feeling. Sadness. Heartbreak. Relief. Vertigo. "Freedom," he whispered. That was the main thing. He'd just rid himself of the source of so much of his pain. Music. To hell with it.

Taking a deep breath, he puffed his cheeks and exhaled, not bothering to fight the image of Susannah as she'd walked away that filled his mind.

She'd left his insides hollowed out and empty. Food would never taste the same. Lovemaking would never feel so passionate. His main reason for living was gone. The source of his inspiration. His muse. How could he have explained that during the interview? Without Susannah, there was no music.

And now he wanted rid of anything that had brought pain into Susannah's life, even the music, itself. He'd felt that ever since the night the *Alabama* had exploded.

Susannah had been right about everything. As soon as fame and fortune had come knocking, he'd lost his head. How many birthdays had he forgotten? How many nights had been wasted on the road...nights he and Susannah could have spent together?

But it was too late now.

Every day, he saw Susannah's eyes as she'd said goodbye, and the lost promise would haunt him forever. Love was the only thing on earth worth having. Trouble was, you never knew that until you'd lost it. He dug a pair of sunglasses from his shirt pocket and slipped them on. Tilting down the brim of his hat, he tried to focus no farther away than the dark lenses. Thanks to the interview, some people on the street were starting to recognize him.

As always, his mind had been entirely on Susannah. She was probably at her restaurant downtown, but he wouldn't bother her. She needed to get on with her life. Still, that knowledge didn't stop something gritty from stinging his eyes, and as he blinked back what might have been the beginning of tears, he was doubly glad he had on the glasses.

He start to move, but had no direction. As far back as he could remember, Susannah had been his weathervane and compass. He didn't even have a home. Banner Manor, which he loved, rightfully belonged to her.

Suddenly he turned, sensing commotion. Before he could locate the source, a familiar voice came from nowhere. "Just because we're getting a divorce doesn't mean you can quit your job, J.D.!"

"Susannah?"

She was charging toward him, swiping her hands down a chef's apron, which she wore over jeans, as if she'd run out of her restaurant without thinking. Coming to an abrupt halt in front of him, she stamped her foot, her arms crossing over her chest. "And quit looking at me like that, Jeremiah Dashiell!" she snarled.

He merely stared. Especially since she was so gorgeous. Like an angel who'd just come down from heaven. Every time he looked at her, he felt as if he'd just turned a corner and run into a world-class work of art. But what was she doing here? "Look at you like what?"

"Like you don't even know who I am although you've known me since I was five years old."

His heart was doing wild flip-flops, but he didn't dare to hope. Trying to keep his cool, he crossed his arms over his chest, and surveyed her critically. "I'm beginning to wonder if I do," he drawled slowly. "Because I thought you're the woman I'm divorcing."

Her jaw slackened. "*You're* divorcing *me!* I think you have that sentence turned around, J.D.!"

Lifting his hat by the brim, he held it in his hand and studied the band for a moment. Then he replaced the hat and looked at her again, glad for the glasses since he didn't trust his eyes not to give away his emotions. He tried to sound dumbfounded, which was easy, since he was.

"A divorce is what you want, isn't it?"

"No," she countered, her lips pursed, her chest heaving and her cheeks red, probably from the exertion of getting uptown. "What I want is for you to…to…"

He arched an eyebrow. "To?"

Tears welled in her eyes. "Oh, damn you, Jeremiah Dashiell Johnson," she burst out, stamping her foot once more. "I want you to be happy. And you can't do that without playing music, which both of us know. You're like a lost puppy every time you put down your guitar.

"But now you're trying to torture yourself because you feel guilty about everything that's happened. And as if that's not enough, you're also trying to make me feel guilty so I'll take you back."

She was right, of course. He fought to find his voice, but it stuck in his throat. "I screwed up our lives. Maybe by telling the world, other people can learn from my mistakes."

She was crying now in earnest and he couldn't stand to watch her. But he couldn't touch her, either. That might make her angrier and she'd leave, and well, he didn't want her to leave. So he just stood there, as stiff as a board, watching crocodile tears roll down her cheeks. Finally he said, "Don't you want other people to learn from my mistakes?"

"No!" she exclaimed, as if to say he were the most stupid man in the world. "I want *you* to learn from your own mistakes, J.D."

Vaguely, he was aware that a crowd was starting to form around them, but he wasn't about to let anyone come between him and Susannah ever again. Risking it, he reached and grabbed her hand, then urged her down the street. If memory served, there was a hotel on the corner. He didn't say a word until they reached it, and then he pulled her inside the door.

The doorman seemed to recognize him, and waved, indicating that he'd made sure no one followed. A clerk stepped forward, too, as if sensing the urgency, and he simply slipped J.D. a key.

"We can settle accounts later, Mr. Johnson," he said. "This way. Private elevator to the top floor."

A moment later, he and Susannah were alone heading up to their room. He slid his arms around her waist, holding her tightly.

"See. It looks like you're not really giving up the VIP treatment," she whispered.

"Some things are necessary."

She glanced up into his eyes. "This is necessary?"

Angling his head downward, he tilted his chin and brushed his lips across hers. "Very necessary," he murmured, his heart still pounding, his mind reeling with possibilities. But he didn't dare to hope. He leaned away a fraction, to stare deeply into her eyes, but he was no mind reader. Once more, he could barely find the voice that usually served him so well. "Why are you here, Susannah," he asked gently.

Her eyes were still shimmering with tears. "When I heard you on TV, I knew you were serious about not playing anymore. That's when I knew you were ready."

"Ready?"

"To truly have a life together." She paused, her voice catching. "To put me first. And our family…"

A hand moved to her belly and he gasped. "A baby…"

She shook her head. "Oh, I don't know, J.D. But let's just say I've had my first premonition." She smiled, making his heart thunder at the desire sparking in her eyes.

He was still in shock. "You're coming back to me?"

"On one condition."

"Anything."

"You keep playing music."

His breath caught. Seconds ago, he'd thought he was giving up everything, but now he knew it would all come back to him, tenfold. "Why?"

"Because you love it. And you'll put us first this time."

She was right. "I will," he promised, feathering butterfly kisses across her jaw.

She smiled. "And you need me. You need somebody who cares about all the other parts of you, the man you really are." She paused. "Now where exactly are you taking me?"

He lifted the key.

"Mama Ambrosia said a golden key would figure in my future," she whispered.

He drew her closer, burying his lips in her hair. "Sounds as if you're starting to believe in the supernatural."

"If you can change, J.D.," she murmured, her words landing against his cheek, along with kisses. "Then I guess anything's possible."

"When I...thought I could lose you, I..."

She pressed a finger to his lips. "You've got a way with words, J.D., and you write good songs, but I'm the one woman who always leaves you tongue-tied, so why don't we just wait until we get someplace quiet, where you can tell me how you feel without words?"

As if on cue, the elevator doors opened directly onto a foyer. He opened the door to the penthouse suite and pulled her into the room, heading straight for the master bedroom. "Let's kiss and make up," he agreed. "And then I'll make you as mad as a hornet."

"Why's that?"

"So we can kiss and make up again."

Quickly, they began undressing each other, their hungry

hands undoing ties and opening buttons. "I've changed, Susannah," he said as he stepped from his jeans and pulled her against him. His mouth found hers, and he delivered a slow lazy kiss, then trailed his lips down her neck. After that, he stood back, his gaze smoky as it roved over her, assessing what he was about to claim.

Suddenly, his fingers touched the charm around her neck, the one that was identical to Ellie's, and he thought about Robby's friendship, which he'd lost. But who knew? Maybe Robby would have a change of heart, too.

"Remember the time," he mused, shaking his head, his eyes meeting hers. "I won't forget again, Susannah." They'd shared so much history together, so much chemistry. And he'd almost thrown it all away. He dropped his hands, molding curves he'd feared he'd never touch again. "I feel like I've died and gone to heaven."

"Well, since my husband's decided to reincarnate," she whispered, "what about some magic? A touch of the wand? A little bayou voodoo?"

"Things are going to be different in the future," he said huskily.

"I hope not the magic."

He shook his head. "No, not the magic."

"Then what are we waiting for, J.D.?" she asked, her voice a soft rasp as she pulled him onto the bed. "It looks like high noon to me, cowboy."

"You're right. Time's a'wastin', oh, Susannah," he whispered back, settling on top of her, his body sinking into the delicious flesh he knew as well as his own, his lips silent, but his heart singing since he knew they'd never part again. "Our future starts now."

* * * * *

Turn the page for a sneak preview of

Branded

by Tori Carrington

Jo Aitchison isn't your average cowgirl. She's rough, she's tough and she's sexy as hell. And, regardless of the rules, she wants gorgeous Trace Armstrong. Luckily, Trace wants Jo too! Yet Trace isn't the only one. Can the rough-and-ready rancher win the battle for her heart?

Branded
by
Tori Carrington

WILDEWOOD RANCH LAY an hour and a half outside San Antonio and had been in the Armstrong family for four generations. It boasted over twenty thousand acres of rich southwest Texas land, twenty-six ranch hands and five thousand head of Angus cattle.

And twenty-nine-year-old Trace Armstrong was the successful manager and half owner of the whole operation.

Or, rather, had been for the past six years. But with his older brother, Eric, a marine, coming home for good this weekend...well, Trace expected everything would be thrown into a state of flux.

"Now that's the type of filly stallions will stand in line to service."

Trace tilted his cowboy hat back on his head and stared at the town's sheriff, who stood beside him on the bunkhouse porch. Had the old son of a bitch just said that about one of his ranch hands? Yes, he had. Trace knew this not because he'd followed John Brody's line of vision—even though it had been his own moments before—but because Jo Atchison was the only "filly" currently on the premises.

A couple of cowboys chuckled behind him.

Trace grimaced and rubbed the back of his neck, which the day's drive had coated with dust and grime in the June heat. He was born to this land, so he supposed he should be used to the often explicit nature of the men's exchanges. But for reasons he preferred not to identify, Sheriff Brody's commentary didn't sit well with him.

"Too bad she's already got one," another of the ranch hands said.

Trace squinted into the bright orange ball that was the setting sun, watching Jo talk to her sometimes boy-friend, who had just pulled up on his Harley outside the stables. She was some two hundred yards away, so Trace could make out little more than her silhouette, but oh, what a silhouette it was. Legs that went on forever, full breasts and long, flowing dark hair. Jo was one of the ranch foreman's more recent hires. She'd started six or seven months ago, and had become the guys' favorite topic around this time of day, if only because of the absence of any other female on the ranch, and Jo's lack of response to their interest.

Trace turned away and leaned against the porch railing of the modern bunkhouse, ignoring his own desire to watch her. He told himself he wasn't like the other men, but in the end he was no different. Despite Jo's considerable talents as a wrangler—she bested a lot of the guys on a bad day, and on a good day bested them all—he caught himself staring after her more times than he'd care to admit.

"I don't think you came all the way out here to drool after one of my ranch hands, did you, Sheriff?" he said quietly, taking a couple of beers from the nearby cooler, which had been set out with the barbecue dinner for the two dozen cowboys. He handed the older man a bottle.

"Hell no."

Trace found his gaze wandering back to Jo, his gut tightening at the sight of the biker reaching out for her, and her swatting his arm away. She'd never given Trace cause to think she needed protection from anyone. On the contrary, she went out of her way to prove she was capable of taking care of herself.

He rubbed his chin, hiding his grin as he recalled his exchange with her earlier in the day. They'd been four hours on the range when he'd found his steed steering toward hers. He knew a few details about her. Some were on the form the ranch required all hands to fill out, others the result of an official background check they ran as a matter of course. She was from Beaumont, an only child. She'd had a few run-ins with the law in her teens— assaulting an officer, disturbing the peace and public intoxication—but her record had been clean since.

She had also been a U.S. Marine for six years, honorably discharged the month before she came to work on Wildewood Ranch.

This morning, he'd watched as she took her hat off, piled her black hair on top of her head and put the hat back on, the result making her look not one bit less feminine.

"In the service…where'd you serve?" he'd asked her.

Her blue eyes had registered surprise. But only for a split second, before she recovered her trademark grimace. One of the guys had said she always looked as if she'd just gone for a dump behind a tree and had used poison ivy for cleanup because there was nothing else around.

"He speaks," she'd said, rather than answering his question.

Trace had grinned. "Fair enough."

He hadn't said more than a handful of words to her since she'd hired on, and he remembered all of them—"Welcome" and "See you back at the ranch" the most prominent. His reticence was partly because the other hands had been within earshot, but mostly because he was attracted to her in an awful way.

And it seemed like that wasn't going to change anytime soon. In fact, it was worsening. Just last night he'd woken up with a hard-on the size of Texas…and she had been the dream girl responsible.

Which meant he needed to try another tactic to battle the attraction. It wouldn't stand for him to demonstrate anything but professional courtesy to their only female ranch hand. Forget sexual harassment; it just plain wasn't smart.

"You didn't answer my question."

She'd given him a small smile, her full lips turning up at the corners. "No, I didn't, did I?"

They'd ridden in silence for a couple of minutes, Jo darting out to force a couple of wayward steers back into the herd, then returning to his side.

"My brother, Eric, is in Iraq now," he said. "A member of your family as much as mine."

She'd looked at him from under the rim of her hat. "I met him briefly when I hired on here six months ago. He was home on leave."

Trace had figured she might have. "He's being honorably discharged this week."

She'd nodded. "I heard that."

He hadn't been surprised. There wasn't much else to do on these long drives except gossip and wait for the sun to set. Besides, there was a big welcome-home barbecue planned for Eric. Most of the hands were looking forward to it.

Trace had squinted at Jo, thinking that she wouldn't be one of them. She didn't strike him as a party girl.

"What made you sign up for the military?" he found himself asking.

She didn't say anything for a long moment, then asked quietly, "What made you not?"

He'd shifted his weight in the saddle. Then shifted again as she took off her shirt and tied it around her waist, revealing the snug white cotton tank she wore underneath. It scooped low on her tanned skin and clung to her breasts and narrow waist. Trace leisurely drank his fill of her fine form, then looked up to meet her gaze, finding a knowing look in her eyes even as she pulled her nicely toned shoulders back and readjusted her gloved hands on the reins.

"Look," she said, "I appreciate your effort to be cordial, but if you think you understand anything about me because I was a marine, you're driving your truck down the wrong road."

"I didn't realize I was driving down any road."

She gave him a long look, her eyes raking down his torso and then back up again. She seemed to know exactly where he wanted to put his truck. And for a mome[...] got the feeling she might open the gate for him t[...]

Instead, she dug her spurs into her horse's si[...] galloped ahead.

© Lori and Tony Karayi[...]

2 FREE BOOKS
AND A SURPRISE GIFT

We would like to take this opportunity to thank you for reading this Mills & Boon® book by offering you the chance to take TWO more specially selected titles from the Blaze® series absolutely FREE! We're also making this offer to introduce you to the benefits of the Mills & Boon® Book Club™—

- **FREE home delivery**
- **FREE gifts and competitions**
- **FREE monthly Newsletter**
- **Exclusive Mills & Boon Book Club offers**
- **Books available before they're in the shops**

Accepting these FREE books and gift places you under no obligation to buy, you may cancel at any time, even after receiving your free books. Simply complete your details below and return the entire page to the address below. You don't even need a stamp!

YES Please send me 2 free Blaze books and a surprise gift. I understand that unless you hear from me, I will receive 3 superb new books every month, including a 2-in-1 book priced at £4.99 and two single books priced at £3.19 each, postage and packing free. I am under no obligation to purchase any books and may cancel my subscription at any time. The free books and gift will be mine to keep in any case.

Ms/Mrs/Miss/Mr_____ Initials _____

_____

Surname _____

Address _____

_____

_____ Postcode _____

E-mail _____

Send this whole page to: Mills & Boon Book Club, Free Book Offer, FREEPOST NAT 10298, Richmond, TW9 1BR